Praise for the Christmas novels of Debbie Macomber

"Warm and sweet as Christmas cookies, this new Debbie Macomber romance is sure to be a hit this holiday season."
—*Bookreporter* on *Merry and Bright*

"Heartfelt, cheerful... Readers looking for a light and sweet holiday treat will find it here."
—*Publishers Weekly* on *Merry and Bright*

"Another heartwarming seasonal [Debbie] Macomber tale, which fans will find as bright and cozy as a blazing fire on Christmas Eve."
—*Kirkus Reviews* on *Merry and Bright*

"Picture-perfect...this charmer will please Macomber fans and newcomers alike."
—*Publishers Weekly* on *Alaskan Holiday*

"Tender romance lightly brushed with holiday magic."
—*Library Journal* on *Alaskan Holiday*

"*Twelve Days of Christmas* is a delightful, charming read for anyone looking for an enjoyable Christmas novel.... Settle in with a warm blanket and a cup of hot chocolate, and curl up for some Christmas fun with Debbie Macomber's latest festive read."
—*Bookreporter*

DEBBIE MACOMBER

The Gift of Love

mira

Recycling programs for this product may not exist in your area.

ISBN-13: 978-0-7783-0995-6

The Gift of Love

Copyright © 2020 by Harlequin Books S.A.

The Gift of Christmas
First published in 1984. This edition published in 2020.
Copyright © 1984 by Debbie Macomber

The Matchmakers
First published in 1986. This edition published in 2020.
Copyright © 1986 by Debbie Macomber

This edition published by arrangement with Harlequin Books S.A.

For questions and comments about the quality of this book, please contact us at CustomerService@Harlequin.com.

Mira
22 Adelaide St. West, 40th Floor
Toronto, Ontario M5H 4E3, Canada
www.Harlequin.com

Printed in Lithuania

MIX
Paper from
responsible sources
FSC® C021394

CONTENTS

THE GIFT OF CHRISTMAS

To
Rachel Hauck, Roxanne St. Claire,
Virelle Kidder and Martha Powers,
my Florida sisters

One

Ashley Robbins clenched her hands together as she sat in a plush velvet chair ten stories up in a Seattle high-rise. The cashier's check to Cooper Masters was in her purse. Rather than mail him the money, Ashley had impulsively decided to deliver it herself.

People moved about her, in and out of doors, as she thoughtfully watched their actions. Curious glances darted her way. She had never been one to blend into the background. Over the years she'd wondered if it was the striking ash-blond hair that attracted attention, or her outrageous choice of clothes. Today, however, since she was meeting Cooper, she'd dressed conservatively. Never shy, she was a hit in the classroom, using techniques that had others shaking their heads in wonder. But no one doubted that she was the most popular teacher at John Knox Christian High School. Cooper had made that possible. No one knew he had loaned her the money to complete her studies. Not even Claudia, her best friend and Cooper's niece.

Ashley and Cooper were the godparents to John, Claudia's older boy. Being linked to Cooper had pleased Ashley more than her friend suspected. She'd been secretly in love with him since she was sixteen. It amazed her that no one had guessed during those ten years, least of all Cooper.

"Mr. Masters will see you now," his receptionist informed her.

Ashley smiled her appreciation and followed the attractive woman through the heavy oak door.

"Ashley." Cooper stood and strode to the front of his desk. "What a pleasant surprise."

"Hello, Cooper." He'd changed over the last six months since she'd seen him. Streaks of silver ran through his hair, and tiny lines fanned out from his eyes. But it would take more than years to disguise his strongly marked features. He wasn't a compellingly handsome man, not in the traditional sense, but seeing him again stirred familiar feelings of admiration and appreciation for all he'd done for her.

"Sit down, please." He indicated a chair not unlike the one she'd recently vacated. "What can I do for you? Any problems?"

She responded with a slight shake of her head. He had always been generous with her. Deep down, she doubted that there was anything she couldn't ask of this man, although she didn't expect any more favors, and he was probably aware of that.

"Everything's fine." She didn't meet his eyes as she opened the clasp of her purse and took out the check. "I wanted to personally give you this." Extending her arm, she handed him the check. "I owe you so much, it seemed almost rude to put it in the mail." The satisfaction of paying off the loan was secondary to the opportunity of seeing Cooper again. If she'd been honest with herself, she would have admitted she was hungry for the sight of him. After all these months she'd been looking for an excuse.

He glanced at the check and seemed to notice the amount. Two dark brows arched with surprise. "This satisfies the loan," he said thoughtfully. Half turning, he placed the check in the center of the large wooden desk. "Your mother tells me you've taken a second job?" The intonation in his voice made the statement a question.

"You see her more often than I do," she said in an attempt to evade the question. Her mother had been the Masters' cook and housekeeper from the time Ashley was a child.

He regarded her steadily, and although she could read no emotion in his eyes, she felt his irritation. "Was it necessary to pay this off as quickly as possible?"

"Fast? I've owed you this money for over four years." She laughed lightly. Someone had once told her that her laugh was one of the most appealing things about her. Sweet, gentle, melodic. She chanced a look at Cooper, whose cool dark eyes revealed nothing.

"I didn't care if you ever paid me back. I certainly didn't expect you'd half kill yourself to return it."

The displeasure in his voice surprised her. Taken aback, she watched as he stalked to the far corner of the office, putting as much distance between them as possible. Was it pride that had driven her to pay him back as quickly as possible? Maybe, but she doubted it. The loan to finish her schooling had been the answer to long, difficult prayers. From the time she'd been accepted into the University of Washington, she had attended on faith. Faith that God would supply the money for books and tuition. Faith that if God wanted her to obtain her teaching degree, then He would meet her needs. And He had. In the beginning things had worked well. She roomed with Claudia and managed two part-time jobs. But when Claudia and Seth got married, she was forced to find other accommodations, which quickly drained her funds. Cooper's offer had been completely unexpected. The loan had come at a time when she'd been hopeless and had been preparing to withdraw from classes. They'd never discussed terms, but surely he'd known she intended to repay him.

A tentative smile brushed her lips. She'd thought he would be pleased. His reaction amazed her. She attempted to keep her voice level as she assured him, "It was the honorable thing to do."

"But it wasn't necessary," he answered, turning back to her.

Again she experienced the familiar twinge of awareness that only Cooper Masters was capable of stirring within her.

"It was for me," she countered quickly.

"It wasn't necessary," he repeated in a flat tone.

Ashley released a slow breath. "We could go on like this all day. I didn't mean to offend you, I only came here today because I wanted to show my appreciation."

He stared back at her, then slowly nodded. "I understand."

Silence stretched between them.

"Have you heard from Claudia and Seth?" he asked after a while.

Ashley smiled. They had so little in common that whenever they were together the conversation invariably centered around Claudia and their godson. "The last I heard she said something about coming down for Christmas."

"I hope they do." His intercom buzzed, and he leaned over and pressed a button on the phone. "Yes, Gloria?"

"Mr. Benson is here."

"Thank you."

Taking her cue, Ashley stood. "I won't keep you." Her fingers brushed her wool skirt. She'd been hoping he would notice the new outfit and comment. He hadn't. "Thank you again. I guess you know that I wouldn't have been able to finish school without your help."

"I was wondering..." Cooper moved to her side, his look slightly uneasy, as if he was unsure of himself. "I mean, I can understand if you'd rather not."

"Rather not what?" She couldn't remember him ever acting with anything but supreme confidence. In control of himself and every situation.

"Have dinner with me. A small celebration for paying off the loan."

"I'd like that very much. Anytime." Her heart soared at the suggestion; she wasn't sure how she managed to keep her voice level.

"Tonight at seven?"

"Wonderful. Should I wear something...formal?" It wouldn't hurt to ask, and he hadn't mentioned where he intended they dine.

"Dress comfortably."

"Great."

* * *

An hour later Ashley's heart still refused to beat at a normal pace. This was the first time Cooper had asked her out or given any indication he would like to see her socially. The man was difficult to understand, always had been. Even Claudia didn't fully know him; she saw him as dignified, predictable and overly concerned with respectability. In some ways he was, but through the years Ashley had seen past that facade. He might be refined, and sometimes overly proper, but he was a man who'd been forced to take on heavy responsibility at an early age. There had been little time for fun or frivolity in his life. Ashley wanted to be the one to change that. She loved him. Her mother claimed that opposites attract, and after meeting Cooper, Ashley had never doubted the truth of that statement.

Ashley chose to wear her finest designer jeans, knowing she looked good. At five foot nine, she was all legs. Her pink sweatshirt contained a starburst of sequins that extended to the ends of the full-length sleeves. Her hair was styled in a casual perm, and soft curls reached her shoulders. Her perfume was a fragrance Cooper had given her the previous Christmas. Although not imaginative, the gift had pleased her immeasurably, even though he hadn't given it to her personally, but to her mother, who'd passed it on. When she'd phoned to thank him, his response had been clipped and vaguely ill-at-ease. Politely, he'd assured her that it was his duty, since they were John's godparents. He'd also told her he'd sent the same fragrance to Claudia. Ashley had hung up the phone feeling deflated. The next time she'd seen him had been in June, when her mother had gone to the hospital for surgery. Cooper had come for a visit at the same time Ashley had arrived. Standing on opposite sides of the bed, her sleeping mother between them, Ashley had hungrily drunk in the sight of him. Their short conversation had been carried on in hushed tones, and after a while they hadn't spoken at all. Afterward he'd had coffee out of a machine, and she'd sipped fruit juice as they sat talking in the waiting area at the end of the corridor. She hadn't seen him again until today.

Over the months she had dated several men, and she'd recently been seeing Dennis Webb, another teacher, on a steady basis. But no one had ever attracted her the way Cooper did. Whenever a pensive mood overtook her, she recognized how pointless that attraction was. Whole universes stretched between them, both social and economic. For Ashley, loving Cooper Masters was as impossible as understanding income tax forms.

The doorbell chimed precisely at seven. Claudia had claimed that she could set her watch by Cooper. If he said seven, he would arrive exactly at seven.

A sense of panic filled Ashley as she glanced at her wristwatch. It couldn't possibly be that time already, could it? With one red cowboy boot on and the other lying on the carpet, she looked around frantically. The laundry still hadn't been put away. Quickly she hobbled across the floor and shoved the basket full of folded clean clothes into the entryway closet, then closed the door with her back as she conducted a sweeping inspection of the apartment. Expelling a calming sigh, she forced herself to smile casually as she opened the door.

He greeted her with a warm look, that gradually faded as he handed her a florist's box.

To Cooper, apparently informal meant a three-piece suit and flowers. Glancing down at her jeans and sweatshirt, one cowboy boot on, the other missing, she smiled weakly and felt wretched. "Thank you." She took the small white box. "Sit down, please." Hurrying ahead of him, she fluffed up the pillows at the end of the sofa, then hugged one to her stomach. "I'm running a little late tonight. If you'll give me a few minutes I'll change clothes."

"You look fine just the way you are," he murmured, glancing at his watch.

What he was really saying, she realized, was that they would be late for their reservation if she took the time to change clothes. After glancing down at the hot pink sweatshirt, she raised her gaze to meet his. "You're sure? It'll only take a minute."

His nod seemed determined. Self-conscious, embarrassed and angry with herself, Ashley sat at the opposite end of the sofa and slipped her foot into the other boot. After tucking in her denim pant leg, she sat up and reached for the florist's box. A lovely white orchid was nestled in a bed of sheer green paper. A gasp of pleasure escaped her.

"Oh, Cooper," she murmured, feeling close to tears. No one had ever given her an orchid. "Thank you."

"Since I didn't know the color of your dress…" He paused to correct himself. "…your outfit…this seemed appropriate." He remained standing, studying her. "It's the type women wear on their wrist."

As Ashley lifted the orchid from the box, its gentle fragrance drifted pleasantly to her. "I'm always having to thank you, Cooper. You've been very good to me."

He dismissed her appreciation with a hard shake of his head. "Nonsense."

She knew that further discussion would only embarrass them both. Standing, she glanced at the closet door, knowing nothing would induce her to open it and expose her folded underwear to Cooper. "I'll get my purse and we can go."

"You might want to wear a coat," he suggested. "I heard something about the possibility of snow over the radio this afternoon."

"Yes, of course." If he remained standing exactly as he was, she might be able to open the door just enough to slip her hand in and jerk her faux fur jacket off the hanger. Somehow she managed it. Turning, she noted that Cooper was regarding her curiously. Rather than fabricate a wild excuse about why she couldn't open the closet all the way, she decided to say nothing.

He took the coat from her grasp, holding it open for her to slip her arms into the sleeves. It seemed as if his hands lingered longer than necessary on her shoulders, but it could have been her imagination. He had never been one to display affection openly.

"Where are we going?" she asked, and her voice trembled slightly, affected by even the most impersonal touch.

"I chose an Italian restaurant not far from here. I hope that suits you."

"Sounds delicious. I love Italian food." Her tastes in food were wide and varied, but it wouldn't have mattered. If he had suggested hot dogs, she would have been thrilled. The idea of Cooper eating anything with his fingers produced a quivering smile. If he noticed it, he said nothing.

Cooper parked outside the small, family-owned restaurant and came around to her side of the car, opening the door for her. It was apparent when they were seated that he had never been there before. The thought flashed through her mind that he didn't want to be seen with her where he might be recognized. But she quickly dismissed the idea. If he didn't want to be with her, then he wouldn't have asked her out. Those thoughts were unworthy of Cooper, who had always been good to her.

"Is everything all right?" As he stared across the table at her, a frown drew his brows together.

"Yes, of course." She looked down at her menu, guiltily forcing a smile on her face. "I wonder how long it'll be before we know if Claudia will be coming for Christmas," she said, hoping to resume the even flow of conversation.

"Time's getting close. I imagine we'll know soon."

Thanksgiving was the following weekend, but Christmas displays were already up in stores; some had shown up as early as Halloween. Doubtless Seth and Claudia would let them know by the end of next week. The prospect of sharing the holiday with her friend—and therefore Cooper—produced a glow of happiness inside Ashley.

The waiter took their order, then promptly delivered their fresh green salads.

"It's been exceptionally chilly for this time of the year," Cooper commented, lifting his fork, his gaze centered on his plate.

Ashley thought it was a sad commentary that their only common ground consisted of Claudia and the weather. "Yes, it has." She looked up to note that a veiled look had come over his features. Perhaps he was thinking the same thing.

The conversation during dinner seemed stiff and strained to her. Cooper asked her about school and politely inquired if she liked teaching. In return she asked him about the business supply operation he owned and was surprised to learn how much it had grown over the past few years. The knowledge should have pleased her, but instead it only served to remind her that he was a rich man and she was still struggling financially.

When they stepped out of the restaurant, she was pleased to discover that it was snowing.

"Oh, Cooper, look!" she cried with delight. "I love it when it snows. Let's go for a walk." She couldn't keep the excitement out of her voice. "There's something magical about walking in the falling snow."

"Are you sure that's what you want?" He glanced at the thin layer of white powder that covered the ground, then he looked up, his expression odd as his eyes searched hers.

"I'd forgotten, you'll have to drive back in this stuff. Maybe it wouldn't be such a good idea," she commented, unable to hide her disappointment.

His hand cupped her elbow, bringing her near, and when she slipped on the slick sidewalk he quickly placed his arm around her waist, preventing her from falling. He left his arm there, holding her protectively close to his side. Her spirits soared at being linked this way with Cooper.

"Where would you like to walk?" An indiscernible expression clouded his eyes.

"There's a marina a couple of blocks from here, and

I love to watch the snow fall on the water, but if you'd rather not, I understand."

"By all means, let's go to the marina." The smile he gave her was the first genuine one she'd witnessed the entire evening.

"Doesn't this make you want to sing?" she asked, and started to hum "White Christmas" even before he could answer.

"No," he said, and chuckled. "It makes me want to sit in front of a roaring fireplace with a warm drink."

She clucked and pressed her lips together to keep from laughing.

"What was that all about?"

"What?" she asked, feigning ignorance.

"That silly little noise you just made."

"If you must know, I don't think you've done anything impulsive or daring in your entire life, Cooper Masters." She said it all in one giant breath, then watched as a shocked look came over his face.

"Of course I have," he insisted righteously.

"Then I dare you to do something right now."

"What?" He looked unsure.

"Make a snowball and throw it at me," she demanded. Breaking from his hold, she ran a few steps ahead of him. "Bet you can't do it," she taunted, and waved her hands at him.

With marked determination, Cooper stuffed his hands inside his coat pockets. "This is silly."

"It's supposed to be crazy, remember?" she chided him softly.

"But it's not right for a man to throw snowballs at a woman."

"Will this make things easier for you?" she shouted, bending over to scoop up a handful of snow. With an accuracy that astonished her, she threw a snowball that hit him directly in the middle of his chest. If she was surprised, the horrified look on Cooper's face sent her into peals of laughter. Losing her balance on the ice-slickened sidewalk, she went sprawling to the cement with an undignified plop.

"That's what you get for hurling snow at courteous gentlemen," Cooper called once he was sure she wasn't hurt. As he advanced toward her, he shifted a tightly packed snowball from one hand to the other.

"Cooper, you wouldn't—would you?" She gave him her most defenseless look, batting her eyelashes. "Here, help me up." She extended a hand to him, which he ignored.

A wicked gleam flashed from the dark depths of his eyes. "I thought you said I never did anything crazy or daring?"

"You wouldn't!" Her voice trembled with laughter as she struggled to stand up.

"You're right, I wouldn't," he murmured, dropping the snowball and reaching for her. Surprise rocked her as he pulled her into his arms. He hesitated momentarily, as if expecting her to protest. When she didn't, he gently brushed the hair from her temple and just as softly pressed his mouth over hers. The kiss should have been tender, but the moment their lips met it became hungry and needy. The effect was jarring, as if a bolt of awareness were flashing through them. They broke apart, shocked and breathless. The oxygen was trapped in her lungs, making it impossible to breathe.

"Did I hurt you?" he asked, his voice thick with concern.

A shake of her head was all she could manage. "Cooper?" Her voice was a mere whisper. "Would you mind doing that again?"

"Now?"

She nodded.

"Here?"

Again she nodded.

He pulled her back into his embrace, his eyes drinking deeply from hers. This time the kiss was gentle, as if he, too, needed to test these sensations. Lost in the swirling awareness, Ashley felt as if he had touched the deep inner part of her being. For years she had dreamed of this moment, wondered what effect his touch would have on her. Now she knew. She felt a free-flowing happiness steal over her. He had taken her heart and touched her spirit. When he entwined his fingers in the curling length of her hair, she pressed her head against his shoulder and breathed in deeply. A soft smile lifted her lips at the sound of his furiously pounding heart.

"This is crazy," he murmured hoarsely.

"No," she swiftly countered. "This is wonderful."

Carefully he relaxed his hold, easing her from his embrace. His features were unnaturally pale as he smoothed the hair at the side of his head with an impatient movement. "I'm too old for you." His mouth had thinned, and his look was remote.

Her bubble of happy contentment burst; he regretted kissing her. What had been so wonderful for her was a source of embarrassment for him. "I dared you to do something impulsive, remember?" she said with forced gaiety. "It doesn't mean anything. I've been kissed before. It happens all the time."

"I'm sure it does," he replied stiffly. His gaze moved pointedly to his watch. "I think it would be best if I took you home now. Perhaps we could see the marina another time."

"Sure."

His touch was impersonal as they strolled purposefully back toward the restaurant parking lot. To hide her discomfort, Ashley began to hum Christmas music again.

"Rushing the season a bit, aren't you?"

She concentrated on moving one foot in front of the other. "I suppose. But the snow makes it feel like Christmas. Christ wouldn't mind if we celebrated His birth every day of the year."

"The shopping malls would love it if we did," he remarked cynically.

"You're speaking of the commercial aspect of the holiday, I'm talking about the spiritual one."

Cooper didn't comment. In fact, neither one of them spoke until he pulled up to the curb in front of her apartment building.

"Would you like to come in and warm up? It would only take a minute to heat up some cocoa." Although the offer was sincere, she knew he wouldn't accept.

"Perhaps another time."

There wouldn't be another time. He wouldn't ask her out again; the whole evening had been a fiasco. Cooper Masters was a powerful, influential man, whereas she was a high school English Lit teacher.

"You'll let me know if you hear anything from Seth and Claudia?"

"Of course."

He came around to her side of the car, opening the door. "You don't need to walk me all the way to my door," she mumbled miserably.

"There's every need." Although his voice was level, she could tell he was determined to live up to what he felt a gentleman should be.

She didn't argue when he took the keys out of her hand and opened the door of her first-floor apartment for her. "Thank you," she murmured. "The evening was…"

"Crazy," he finished for her.

Wonderful, her mind insisted in return. Afraid of what her eyes would reveal, she lowered her head and her blond curls fell forward, wreathing her face. "Crazy," she repeated.

A finger placed under her chin lifted her eyes to his. His were dark and unreadable, hers soft and shining. Slowly his hand moved to caress the soft, smooth skin of her cheek. The gentle caress sent the blood pulsing through her veins, flushing her face with telltale color.

"If ever you're in trouble or need someone, I want you to contact me."

Although he had never verbally said as much, she had always been aware that she could go to him if ever she needed help.

"I will." Her voice sounded irritatingly weak.

"I want you to promise me." He unbuttoned his coat pocket and took out a business card. Using the door as a support, he wrote down a phone number. "You can reach me here any time of the day."

"I'm not going to trouble you with—"

"Promise me, Ashley."

He was so serious, his look demanding. "Okay," she agreed, accepting the card. "But why?"

A long moment passed before he answered her. "I have a vested interest in you," he said, and shrugged, the indifferent gesture contradicting his words. "Besides, I'd hate to have anything happen to Johnny's godmother."

"Nothing's going to happen to me."

"In case it does, I want you to know I'll always be there."

The business card seemed to sear her hand. In his own way, Cooper cared about her. "Thank you." Impulsively, she raised two fingers to her lips, then brushed them across his mouth. His hand stopped hers, gripping her wrist; his look branded her. Slowly he lowered his mouth to hers in a gentle, sweet kiss.

"Good night, Ashley."

"Good night." Standing in the open doorway, she watched until he drove into the dark night. A solitary figure illuminated by the falling snow.

Expelling her breath in a long quivering sigh, she tucked the card in her purse. Why did she have to love Cooper Masters? Why couldn't she feel for Webb what she did for Cooper? Webb was nice and almost as unpredictable as she was. Maybe that was why they got along so well. Yet it was Cooper who occupied her thoughts. Cooper who made her heart sing. Cooper who filled her dreams. The time had come to wake up and face reality. She was at the age when she should start thinking about marriage and a family, because she definitely wanted children. Cooper wasn't going to be interested in someone like her. He might care about her, even feel some affection for her, but she wasn't the type of woman he would ever ask to be his wife.

Troubled and confused, Ashley made herself a cup of cocoa and sat on the sofa, her feet tucked under the cushion next to her. Things had been so easy for her friends, even Claudia. They met someone, fell in love, got married and started a family. Maybe God had decided He didn't want her to marry. The thought seemed intolerable, but she had learned long ago not to second-guess her heavenly Father. She'd given Him her life, her will, even Cooper's safekeeping. Now she had to learn to trust.

She rinsed out the cup, placed it in the kitchen sink and turned out the lights. Her eyes fell on her purse, hanging on the closet doorknob. She wondered if the day might come when she would need to use the card, not that she intended to.

That same thought ran through her mind several days later when the police officer directed her to the phone. She didn't want to contact Cooper, so she'd tried phoning her family first, hoping she would catch her father at home. But there had been no answer.

"Is there anyone else, miss?" the tall, uniformed man asked.

"Yes," she answered tightly, opening her purse and taking out the card. Her fingers actually trembled as she dialed the number.

"Cooper Masters."

As she suspected, he'd given her his private cell number. "Oh, hi...it's Ashley."

"Ashley." His voice carried clearly over the line. "What's wrong?"

"It isn't an emergency or anything," she began, feeling incredibly silly. "I mean, I don't think they'll keep me."

"Ashley," he heaved her name on an angry sigh. "What's going on?"

"It's a long story."

"All right, tell me where you are. I'll come to you, and then we'll straighten everything out."

She hesitated, swallowing past the lump forming in her throat. "I'm in jail."

Two

"Jail!" Cooper's voice boomed over the line. "I'll be there in ten minutes."

"But, Cooper, Kent's a good thirty minutes from downtown Seattle."

"Kent?" The anger in his voice was barely controlled.

"If you're going to get so mad…" Ashley let the rest of the sentence fade, realizing that the phone line had already been disconnected.

Casting a glance at the police officer beside her, she gave him a wary smile. "A friend's coming."

A smile quivered at one corner of the older man's mouth. "I heard." Looking away, he asked, "Would you like a cup of coffee while you wait?"

"No thanks."

Ashley heard Cooper's voice several minutes before she saw him. By the time he was brought into the area where she was waiting, there wasn't a person in the entire police station who hadn't heard him. She had always known him to be a calm, discreet person. That he would react this way to a minor misunderstanding shocked her.

Although…a lot of things about Cooper had surprised her lately. She was standing, her face devoid of color, when he was escorted into the room.

"Can you tell me what's going on here?" he demanded.

His look did little to encourage confidences; she swallowed tightly and waved her hand helplessly. "Well, apparently someone took the license plate off Milligan."

"Who the heck…?" He paused and took a deep, calming breath. "Who's Milligan?"

"Not who," she corrected, "but what. Milligan's my moped. I parked it outside the Mexican restaurant where I work odd hours, and someone apparently took off with my license plate."

"That isn't any reason to arrest you!" he shouted.

"They haven't arrested me!" she yelled in return, and was humiliated when her voice cracked and wavered. "And if you won't quit shouting at me, then you can just leave."

Raking his fingers roughly through his hair, Cooper stalked to the other side of the room. His mouth was tightly pinched, and he said nothing for several long moments. "All right, let's try this again," he replied in a deceivingly soft tone. "Start at the beginning, and tell me everything."

"There's not much to tell. Someone took the license plate, and, since I don't have the registration on me, the police need some evidence that I own the bike. I haven't been arrested or anything. In fact, they've been very nice." In nervous reaction she looped a long strand of curly hair around her ear. "All I need for you to do is go to my apartment and bring back the registration for Milligan. Then I'll be free to leave." She opened her purse and took out her key ring, then extracted the key to the apartment. "Here," she said, handing it to him. "The registration's in the kitchen, in the silverware drawer, stuck under the aluminum foil. I keep all my important papers there."

If he thought her record storage system was a bit unusual, he said nothing.

"There's a lawyer on his way here, I'll leave word at the front desk for him." Without another word, he turned and left the room.

Within twenty minutes she heard him talking to the officer who had offered her the coffee. A few moments later they both entered the waiting area.

"You're free to go," the policeman explained. "Although I'm afraid we can't let you drive the moped until you have a new license plate."

Before she could protest Cooper inserted, "No need to worry. I've already made arrangements for the bike to be picked up." He turned and directed his words to Ashley. "It'll be delivered to your place sometime tomorrow afternoon."

Rather than argue, Ashley mutely agreed.

"If you're ready, I'll take you home," Cooper said.

Shoving her knit cap onto her head, she stood and swung her backpack over her shoulder, then gave the kind officer a polite smile. She wasn't pleased with the way things were working out. If she didn't have Milligan, she would have to take a series of busses to and from work, with a long trek between stops. Surely something could be done to enable her to ride her moped until she could replace the plate. One look from Cooper discouraged her from asking.

His hand cupped her elbow as they walked to the parking lot. Her attention was centered on the scenery outside the car window as they crossed the Green River and connected with the freeway. Wordlessly, he took the first exit and a couple of minutes later pulled into the parking lot to her apartment building.

He turned off the engine, then called his office. "Gloria, cancel the rest of my appointments for today," he said stiffly, his voice clipped and abrupt. Without waiting for a confirmation, he promptly ended the call, and then turned to Ashley. "Invite me in for coffee."

Her heart lodged someplace near her throat. "Yes, of course." She didn't wait for him to come around to her side of the car and let herself out. He gave her a disapproving look as they met in front of the vehicle. He opened the apartment door and returned the key to her. She placed it back on the key ring and took off her jacket, carelessly tossing it across the top of the sofa. He removed his black overcoat and neatly folded it over the back of the chair opposite the sofa.

"I'll put on the coffee." She moved into the kitchen, pouring water into the small, five-cup pot. She could hear Cooper agitatedly pacing the floor behind her.

"Why are you so angry with me?" she asked. She couldn't look at him, not when he was so obviously furious with her. "I couldn't help it if someone stole my license plate. I never should have phoned you, I'm sorry I did."

"I'm not mad at you," he stormed. "I'm angry that you were put through that ordeal, that you were treated like a criminal, that…" He left the rest unsaid.

"It's not the policeman's fault. He was only doing his

job," she tried to explain, still not facing him. Her fingers trembled as she added the grounds to the pot, placed the lid on top and set it to brew.

A large masculine hand landed on her shoulder, and she had to fight not to lay her cheek on it. A subtle pressure turned her around. With both hands behind her, she gripped the oven door for support. Slowly she raised her eyes to meet his. She was surprised at the tenderness she saw in the dark depths of his gaze, which seemed to be centered on her mouth. Nervously she moistened her dry lips with the tip of her tongue. She hadn't meant to be provocative, but when Cooper softly groaned she realized what she'd done. When he reached for her, she went willingly into his embrace.

He held her against him, breathing in deeply as he buried his face in the curve of her neck. His hands roamed her back, arching her as close as humanly possible. Ashley molded herself to him, savoring the light scent of musk and man; she longed for him to kiss her. She silently pleaded with him to throw common sense to the wind and crush his mouth over hers. Just being held by him was more happiness than she'd ever hoped to experience. Happiness and torment all rolled into one. An embrace, a light caress, a longing look, could never satisfy her, not when she wanted so much more. Gently he kissed the crown of her head and released her. She wanted to cry with disappointment.

The coffee had begun to perk, and to disguise her emotions, Ashley turned and reached for two cups, waiting for the pot to finish before pouring.

While she dealt with the coffee, Cooper sat in the living room waiting for her. He stood when she entered, taking one cup from her hand.

"I'm sorry, Ashley," he said, his eyes probing hers.

He didn't need to elaborate. He was sorry for his anger, sorry he'd overreacted in the police station, but mostly he regretted throwing aside his self-control and taking her in his arms.

Unable to verbally acknowledge his apology she simply shook her head, letting him know that she understood what he was saying.

"So you work at a Mexican restaurant?" he asked, after taking a sip from the steaming cup.

She wasn't fooled by the veiled interest. He'd commented on the fact she'd taken a second job once before, and he hadn't been pleased then.

"I only work odd hours, less now that I've paid off the loan," she answered, her finger making lazy loops around the rim of her cup.

He pinched his mouth tightly shut, and she recognized that he was biting back words. She wondered how he managed in business confrontations when she found him so easy to read.

Taking another sip of coffee, he stood and moved into the kitchen to put the half-full cup into the sink. "I should go."

She followed his movements. "I haven't thanked you. I… I don't know what I would have done if you hadn't come."

Her appreciation seemed to embarrass him, because his mouth thinned. He lifted his coat off the back of the chair. "I said I wanted you to call me if you needed help. I'm glad you did."

She walked him to the door. "How'd you get to Kent so fast?" Asking him questions helped delay the time when he would leave.

"I was already in the car when you phoned. It was simply a matter of heading in the right direction."

"Oh," she said in a small voice. "I apologize if I inconvenienced you."

"You didn't," he returned gruffly. His eyes met hers then, and again she found herself drowning in those dark depths.

Clenching her hands at her sides, she gave him a falsely cheerful smile. "Thanks again, Cooper. God go with you."

He turned. "And you," he murmured, surprising her.

"Have a nice Thanksgiving."

"I'm sure I will. Are you spending the day with your family?"

"Yes, Mom's making her famous turkey stuffing, and Jeff and his wife, Marsha, are coming." Jeff was her younger brother. John, the youngest Robbins, was working in Spokane and had decided not to make the long drive over the Cascade Mountains in uncertain weather.

Cooper didn't elaborate on his own plans for the holiday, and she didn't ask. "Goodbye, and thanks again."

"Goodbye, Ashley."

As she watched him walk away, she had the strongest desire to blow him a kiss. Immediately she quelled the impulse, but she couldn't help feeling disappointed and frustrated. Closing the front door, she leaned against it and breathed in deeply. She was filling her head with fanciful dreams if she dared to hope Cooper would ever come to love her. Wasting her time and her life. But her heart refused to listen.

* * *

As Cooper promised, her moped was delivered safely to her apartment the following afternoon. Webb drove her home from school, and once she dropped off her things, he took her to the Department of Motor Vehicles, where she applied for new license plates. Granted a temporary plate, she was relieved to learn she could now ride Milligan. The moped might not be much, but it got her where she needed to go in the most economical way.

Webb was tall and thin, his facial features almost gaunt, but he was one of the nicest people Ashley had ever known. When he dropped her off at her apartment, she invited him inside. He accepted with a smile.

"Got plans for the weekend?" he asked over a cup of cocoa.

She shrugged. "Not really. I wanted to do some Christmas shopping, but I dread fighting the crowds."

"Want to go skiing Saturday afternoon? I understand the slopes are open."

"I didn't know you skied?" Ashley questioned, her eyes twinkling.

"I don't," Webb confirmed. "I thought you'd teach me."

"Forget that, buddy. You can take lessons like everyone else, then we'll talk about skiing," she said with a laugh. "You could invite me to dinner instead," she suggested hopefully.

"Fine, what are you cooking?"

"Leftovers."

"I'll bring the egg nog," he said with a sly grin.

"Honestly, Webb, how do you do it?" she asked, laughing.

"Do what?"

"Invite me out to dinner, and I end up cooking?"

"It's all in the wrist, all in the wrist," he told her, flexing his hand, looking smug.

Thinking about their conversation later, she couldn't help laughing. Webb was a fun person, but what she felt for Cooper was exciting and intense and couldn't compare with the friendship she shared with her co-worker.

With Cooper she felt vulnerable in a way that couldn't be explained. But then she was in love with Cooper Masters, and that was simply pointless.

Disturbed by her thoughts, she went to change clothes. As part of her preparation for the coming holidays and the extra calories she would consume, she had started to work out. Following the instructions on the DVD she'd purchased, she practiced a routine that used Christian music for an aerobic dancercise program. Dressed in purple satin shorts, pink leg-warmers and a gray T-shirt, she placed her hands on her hips in the middle of the living room and waited for the warm-up instructions. Just as she completed the first round of exercises, the doorbell rang.

She paused, and with her breath deep and ragged, she turned off the player and checked the peephole in the door. She wasn't expecting anyone. To her horror, she saw it was Cooper.

The doorbell buzzed again, and for a fleeting second she was tempted to let him think she wasn't home, but overriding her embarrassment at having him see her dressed in shorts and a T-shirt was her desire to know why he'd come.

"Hello," she said as she opened the door.

He walked into the apartment, his brow marred by

a puzzled frown as he glanced at her. "Maybe I should come back later."

"Nonsense," she mumbled, dismissing the suggestion. She grabbed a towel to wipe the perspiration from her face. "I was just doing some aerobics. Care to join me?"

"No thanks." The corners of his mouth formed deep grooves as he suppressed a smile. "But don't let me stop you."

His attempt at humor amazed her. It was the first time she could remember him bantering with her—or anyone. "I think I'll skip the rest of the program," she said and laughed.

"Is that coffee I smell?" he asked as he sat on the edge of the sofa.

"No, cocoa. Want some? If you want coffee, though, it'd only take me a minute to brew a pot."

He shook his head.

Looping the towel around her neck, she sat cross-legged opposite him. Her face was glowing and red from the exertion, and she noted the way Cooper couldn't keep his eyes off her. Her heart was pounding fiercely, but she wasn't sure if it was the effects of seeing him again or the aerobics.

For a long moment silence filled the room. "Did you get Madigan back?" he eventually asked.

"Milligan," she corrected.

"How'd you happen to name a moped Milligan?"

"It was the salesman's name. We went out a couple of times afterward, and I couldn't think of the bike without thinking of Milligan, so I started calling it by his name."

Cooper's mouth narrowed slightly. "What do you do when it rains?"

"Wear rain gear," she returned casually. "It's a bit of a hassle, but I don't mind." Why was he so curious about Milligan? Certainly he'd known—or at least known of—someone who rode a moped before now?

"They're not the safest thing around, are they?"

"I suppose not, but I'm careful." This line of questioning was beginning to rankle. "Why all the curiosity?"

Leaning forward, he rested his elbows on his knees, then quickly shifted position, placing his ankle across one knee as if to give a casual impression. "The more I thought about you riding that moped, the more concerned I became. In checking statistics I discovered—"

"Statistics?" she interrupted him. "Honestly, Cooper, I'm perfectly safe."

He closed his eyes for a moment in apparent frustration, then opened them again. "I knew this wasn't going to be easy. You're as stubborn as Claudia," he said, and expelled his breath slowly. "I'm going to worry about you riding around on that silly bit of chrome and rubber."

"I've had Milligan for almost two years," she inserted, feeling the color drain from her face.

"Ashley," he said, his gaze lingering on her. "I want you to accept these and promise me you'll use them." He took a set of keys from his pocket and held them out to her.

"What are they?" Her voice trembled slightly.

"The keys to a new car. If you don't like the color we can—"

"The keys to a new car?" she echoed in shocked disbelief. "You don't honestly expect me to accept that, do you?"

"No," he acknowledged with a heavy sigh, "knowing you, I didn't think you would. If you insist on paying me—"

"Paying you!" she cried, leaping to her feet. "I just cleared one loan—I'm not about to take on another." Her arms cradling her waist, she paced the floor directly in front of him. "Don't you realize how many enchiladas I had to serve to pay off the last loan? I can't understand you. I can't understand why you'd do something like this."

He inhaled deeply, his look full of trepidation. "I don't want you riding around on a stupid moped and getting yourself killed."

"You know, Cooper, you're beginning to sound like my father. I don't need another parent. I'm a capable twenty-six-year-old woman, not a half-wit teenager. What I ride to work is my prerogative."

"I'm only trying to…"

"I know what you're trying to do," she stormed. "Run my life! I have to admit, I was fooled." Her hand flew to her face and she wiped a thin layer of moisture from her brow. "You gave me your phone number and told me to call, but you didn't tell me there were strings attached."

"You're overreacting!" Although he appeared outwardly calm, she knew he was as unsettled as she was. Bright red color was creeping up his neck, but she doubted that he would vent his emotions in front of her.

"I'm not overreacting!" she exclaimed at fever pitch. "You think that because I phoned you, it gives you the right to step into my life. Keep the car, because I assure you I don't need it."

"As you wish," he murmured, his voice tight and controlled. Standing, he returned the keys to his pocket, his expression a stoic mask. "If you'll excuse me, I have an appointment."

"I hope the car isn't in the apartment parking lot, because the manager will have it towed away." The minute the words were out, she regretted having said them.

"It's not," he assured her coldly. Brushing past her, he let himself out, leaving her feeling deflated and depressed. The nerve of the man... He seemed to think... Her thoughts faded as she felt a hard knot form in her stomach. Now she'd done it, really done it.

"Happy Thanksgiving, Mom." Ashley laid the freshly baked pie on the kitchen countertop and leaned over to kiss her mother on the cheek.

"Hello, sweetheart." Sarah Robbins placed an arm around Ashley's waist and hugged her close. "I'm glad you're early, dear, would you mind peeling the potatoes?"

"Sure, Mom," she agreed, pulling open the kitchen drawer and taking out the peeler. Ashley had hoped for some time to talk to her mother privately. "How's work?" she asked in what she hoped was a casual tone. "Is Mr. Masters cracking the whip?" Her mother would have thought it disrespectful if she'd called Cooper anything but Mr. Masters, but the formal title nearly stuck in her throat.

"Oh, hardly." Sarah wiped the back of her hand across her apron. "He's always been wonderful to work for. I must say, he certainly loves those nephews of his. There are pictures of John and Scott all over that house, and I swear the only reason he moved out of the condominium was so those boys would have a decent yard to play in when they came to visit. That's all he ever talks about."

Opening the oven door, she pulled out the rack to baste the turkey with a giblet broth simmering on the top of the stove. "Have you heard from Claudia and Seth?"

Ashley was chewing on a stalk of celery, and she waited until she'd swallowed before answering. "We chat all the time. I'm hoping she'll be here for Christmas."

"That'll please Mr. Masters. I think he needs a bit of cheering up. He's been in the blackest mood the last couple of days."

"He has?" She hoped to disguise her attentiveness. Her family, especially her mother, wouldn't approve of her interest in Cooper. Her feelings for her mother's employer had never been discussed, but she had sensed her mother's subtle disapproval of even their shared role as godparents more than once. In some ways Sarah Robbins and Cooper Masters were a lot alike. Her mother would view it as inappropriate for Ashley to be interested in an important man like Cooper.

"Did you cook a turkey for him this year?"

"No, he said he'd fix himself something, said he didn't want me fussing, when I had a family to tend to," she said on a soft sigh. "He really is the nicest man."

"I think he's wonderful," Ashley agreed absently, without thinking, and colored slightly when she turned to find her mother staring at her with questioning eyes. She was saved from answering any embarrassing questions by her sister-in-law, Marsha, who breezed through the door full of the joy of the season. She was grateful that she and her mother were never alone after that, and soon the meal was on the table.

Everything was delicious, as all her mother's cooking was. As they sat around the table, Ashley's father asked the blessing, then opened the Bible to Psalms and read several praises aloud. After a moment's silence he asked each family member to verbally state one of the blessings they were most thankful for this year. Tears shimmered in Marsha's eyes as she announced that she and Jeff were going to have a baby. The news brought shouts of delight from Ashley's parents. When it came to her turn she thanked God for the rich Christian heritage she had received from her parents and also that she was going to be an aunt at last.

Later, as she helped with the dishes, Ashley's thoughts again drifted to Cooper. Here she was, with a loving family surrounding her, and he was probably alone in his large house. No, she told herself, most likely he was sharing the day with friends or business associates. But she wasn't convinced.

Hounded by constant self-recrimination since their last meeting, she had berated her quick temper a hundred times. He had only been concerned about her safety, and she'd acted as if he'd accosted her.

"Mom," she said and swallowed tightly. "Would you mind if I took a plate of food over to a friend who has to spend the day alone?"

"Of course not, dear, but why didn't you say something earlier? You could have invited them to dinner."

"I wish I'd thought of it," she said.

When she was all set with a large cooler overflowing with turkey and all the extras, Ashley's father loaned her the family car.

Her heartbeat raced frantically as she pulled into Cooper's driveway in the exclusive Redondo area of south Seattle. She wouldn't blame him if he closed the door on her. He'd purchased the house with the surrounding two acres of prime view property shortly after Claudia had given birth to John. Ashley had never seen the house although her mother had told her about it several times.

Now the large, two-story brick structure loomed before her, elegant and impressive. Adjusting her red beret, she rang the doorbell and waited. Several minutes passed before Cooper answered. He wore a suit, and she couldn't recall ever seeing him look more distinguished.

"Happy Thanksgiving, Cooper," she said with a trembling smile. If he didn't invite her inside, she was afraid she would burst into tears and humiliate them both.

"Ashley." He sounded shocked to see her. "Come in. For heaven's sake you didn't ride that deathtrap moped over here, did you?"

"No." She smiled and cast a glance over her shoulder to the older model car parked in the driveway. "Dad loaned me his car."

"Come in, it's cold, and it looks like rain," he offered again. He held out his hand, gesturing her inside.

Ashley didn't need a second invitation. "Here." She handed him the cooler. "I didn't know if you..." She hesitated. "Mom sent this along." Might as well jump in with both feet. Being underhanded about anything went against her inherent streak of honesty, but if her mother questioned her later, she would explain then.

Cooper took the cooler into the kitchen. She followed close behind, awestruck by every nook of the impressive home. The kitchen was a study in polished chrome and marble. It looked as clean as a hospital, yet welcoming. That was her mother's gift, she realized.

"Let me fix you something to drink. Coffee okay?" His eyes pinned hers, and she nodded.

After he poured her a mug, she followed him into a room with a fireplace and book-lined walls. His den, she decided. Two dark leather chairs with matching ottomans sat obliquely in front of the fireplace. He took her hat and red wool coat, hung them in a closet and motioned for her to sit in the chair opposite him.

Centering her attention on the steaming coffee, Ashley paused before speaking again. "I came to apologize."

A movement out of the corner of her eye attracted her gaze, and she watched as Cooper relaxed against the back of the chair.

"Apologize? Whatever for?" he asked.

Her head shot up, and she swallowed the bitter taste in her mouth. He wasn't going to make this easy for her. "I was unforgivably rude the other day, and I have no excuse. You were being thoughtful, and..."

He didn't allow her to finish. Instead he gestured with his hand, dismissing her regret. "Nonsense."

Scooting to the very edge of her cushion, she inhaled a quivering breath. "Will you please stop waving at me as though you find my apology amusing?" she said, fighting to keep a grip on her rising irritation. She bolted to her feet and walked to the far side of the room, pretending to examine his collection of books while struggling to keep her composure. Without turning around she mumbled miserably, "I'm sorry, I didn't mean that."

His soft chuckle sounded remarkably close, and when she turned she discovered that only a few inches separated them.

"Oh, Cooper." Her eyes drank in the heady sight of

him. "I've felt wretched all week. Please forgive me for the way I acted the other day."

"Have you decided to accept my offer?" The laughter drained from his eyes.

Sadly she shook her head. "Please understand why I can't."

He raked his hands through his hair, ruining the well-groomed effect.

Ashley's finger itched to smooth down the sides, to follow the proud line of his jaw, to touch him. Of its own volition her hand rose halfway to his face before she realized what she was doing.

Their eyes holding one another, Cooper captured her hand and held her motionless. Even his touch had the power to shoot sparks of awareness up her spine. When he raised her fingers to his mouth, his lips gently caressed her knuckles. Trapped in a whirlpool of sensation, she swayed toward him.

Her movement seemed to snap something within him, and he roughly pulled her into his embrace.

"Cooper." His name was a bittersweet sigh that was muffled as his mouth crushed hers. His hold was so tight that for a moment it was difficult to breathe, not that it mattered when she was in his arms.

Automatically, she raised her hands and linked them behind his neck as their mouths strained against one another. It was as if they couldn't get close enough, couldn't give enough. Ashley's lithe frame was flooded with a warm excitement, a glowing happiness that stole over her. A soft, whispering sigh escaped as he moved his face against her hair, brushing against her like a cat seeking contentment.

"Why is it you bring out the—"

The phone interrupted him, the sharp ringing shattering the tender moment. With a low, protesting groan he kissed the tip of her nose and moved across the room to answer the insistent call.

Ashley watched him, her heart swelling with pride and love. Their eyes met, and she noticed a warm light she had never seen in him before.

"Yes," he answered abruptly, then stiffened. "Claudia, this is a surprise."

Three

"Wonderful." Cooper continued speaking into the receiver, his eyes avoiding Ashley's. "Of course you're welcome, you know that. Plan to stay as long as you like."

The conversation lasted several more minutes, but it didn't take Ashley long to realize that Cooper wasn't going to let her friend know she was with him. She couldn't help wondering if she was a source of embarrassment to him. How could he hold her and kiss her one minute, then pretend that she wasn't even there with him the next? The promise of happiness she had savored so briefly in his arms left a bitter aftertaste. He must have sensed her confusion, because he turned away as the conversation with Claudia continued and kept his back to her until it ended a few minutes later.

"That was Claudia and Seth," he told her unnecessarily. "He's got a conference coming up in Seattle the second week of December. They've decided to fly down for that, then stay for the holidays."

He sounded so genuinely pleased that Ashley quickly quelled the spark of hurt. She didn't know why he'd chosen to ignore her, but she was going to put it out of her mind, and she certainly wouldn't ask.

"That's great."

"It is, isn't it?" He moved back to her side, gently easing her into his arms. "This is going to be a wonderful Christmas," he murmured against the softness of her hair.

His voice was like that of an eager child, and it rang a chord of compassion within her. He had taken over his brother's business when he was barely into his twenties. Over the years he had built up the supply operation that extended into ten western states. Claudia had once told her that his goal was to have the business go nationwide. But at what price? she wondered. His health? His personal life? What drove a man like Cooper Masters? she wondered. Could it be the desire for wealth? He was already richer than anyone she knew. Recognition? Yet he was careful to keep a low profile, and from what her mother and Claudia told her, he seemed to jealously guard his privacy. The man was a mystery she might never understand, a puzzle she might never solve.

What did it matter, as long as he held her like this? she asked herself. Her arms around his waist, she laid her head against his solid, muscular chest. The steady beat of his heart sounded in her ear, and she smiled with contentment.

"I feel like doing something crazy," he said, and tipped his head back, laughter dancing in his eyes. "Usually that means taking you in my arms and kissing you like there's no tomorrow."

"I'm game." The urge to wrap her arms around his neck and abandon her pride was almost overwhelming.

What pride? her mind echoed. That had been lost long ago where Cooper was concerned.

"Let's go for a walk," he suggested.

Ashley stifled a protest. "It's raining," she warned. A torrential downpour would have been a more accurate description of the turn the weather had taken. She moistened her lips. For once she would have been content to sit in front of the fireplace.

"I'll get us an umbrella," he said, a smile softening the sharp, angular lines of his face.

When he returned, he'd changed clothes and shoes, and was wearing a dark overcoat. A black umbrella dangled from his forearm.

"Ready?" he asked, regarding her expectantly.

He took her red beret and matching wool coat from the closet. He held the coat open for her to slip her arms into the silk-lined sleeves. As he pulled the coat to her shoulders, he paused to gently kiss the slim column of her neck from behind. The tiny kiss shot a tingling awareness over her skin, and she sighed.

"Doesn't this make you want to sing?" he teased as they stepped outside. Rain pelted the earth in an angry outburst.

"No." She laughed. "It makes me want to sit in front of a warm fireplace and drink something warm."

Cooper tipped back his head and howled with laughter. She was only echoing his words to her the night it had snowed. It hadn't been that funny. She watched him sheepishly, trying to recall a time she had ever heard him really laugh.

One arm tucked around her waist, he brought her close

to his side. "Why is it when I'm with you I want to laugh and sing and behave totally irrationally?"

Wrapping her arm around his waist, she looked up into his sparkling eyes. "I seem to bring out that quality in a lot of people."

He chuckled and opened the umbrella, which protected them from the worst of the downpour. He led her along a cement walkway that meandered around the property, finally ending at a chain link fence that was built at the top of a bluff that fell sharply into Puget Sound. The night view was spectacular. Ashley could only imagine how much more beautiful it would be during the day. An array of distant lights illuminated the sky and cast their reflective glow into the dark waters of the Sound.

"That must be Vashon Island," she said without realizing she had spoken out loud.

"Yes, and over there's Commencement Bay in Tacoma." He pointed to another section of lights. But his gaze wasn't on the city. Instead she felt it lingering, gently caressing her. When she turned her head, their eyes locked and time came to a screeching halt. Later she wouldn't remember who moved first. But suddenly she was tightly held in his arms, the umbrella carelessly tossed aside as they wrapped one another in a feverish embrace. The kiss that followed was the most beautiful she had ever received, filled with some unnamable emotion, deep, tender, sweet and all-consuming.

Rain bombarded them, drenching her hair until it hung in wet ringlets. He looked down at her, his breathing uneven and hoarse. Gently he smiled, wiping the moisture from her face. With a laugh, he tugged her hand, and together they ran back to the safety and warmth of the house.

It was the memory of his kiss and that night that sustained Ashley through the long, silent days that followed. Every night she hurried home from work hoping Cooper would contact her in some way. Each day led to bitter disillusionment. When her mother phoned Wednesday afternoon, Ashley already knew what she was going to say.

"Mr. Masters thanked me for the Thanksgiving dinner you brought him. Why didn't you say he was the friend you were going to see?" Her tone hinted of disapproval.

"Because I knew what you would have said if I did," Ashley countered honestly.

"I had no idea you've been seeing Mr. Masters."

"We've only gone out once."

A short, stilted silence followed. "He's too old for you, dear. He's forty, you know."

Closing her eyes, Ashley successfully controlled the desire to argue. "I don't think you need to worry, Mother," she said soothingly. "I doubt that I'll be seeing him again."

"I just don't want to see you get hurt," her mother added on a gentler note.

"I know you don't."

They chatted for a few minutes longer and ended the conversation on a happy note, talking about Marsha and the coming baby, her mother's first grandchild.

Replacing the phone, Ashley released a long, slow breath. Cooper's image returned to trouble her again. Everything about him only served as a confirmation of her mother's unspoken warning. He wore expensively tailored suits, his hair was professionally styled and he seemed to be stamped with an unmistakable look of refinement. Something she would never have. And he was almost fourteen years older than she was, but why should that bother him or her parents when it had never mattered to her? At least she didn't need an explanation for why he hadn't contacted her. After talking to her mother, he had undoubtedly been reminded of their differences. Once again he would shut himself off from her, and who knew how long it would be before she could break through the thick wall of his pride?

Sunday morning during church the pastor lit the first candle of the Advent wreath. Ashley listened attentively as the man of God explained that the first candle represented prophecy. Then he read Scripture from the Old Testament that foretold the birth of a Savior.

Ashley left church feeling more uplifted than she had the entire week. How could she be depressed and miserable at the happiest time of the year? Claudia, Seth and the boys were coming, and Cooper wouldn't be able to avoid seeing her. Perhaps then she could find a way to prove that their obvious differences weren't all that significant.

An email from Claudia was waiting for her after work Monday afternoon. It read:

Ashley,

I'm sorry it's taken me so long to write. I can't believe how busy my boys manage to keep me. I've got some wonderful news! No, I'm not pregnant again, although I don't think Seth would mind. Cooper, either, for that matter. He's surprised both of us the way he loves the boys. The good news is that we'll be arriving at Sea/Tac Airport, Saturday, December 12th at 10 A.M. and plan to stay with Cooper through to the first of the year. That first week Seth will be involved in a series of meetings, but the remainder of the time will be the vacation we didn't get the chance to take this summer.

I can't tell you how excited I am to be seeing you again. I've missed you so much. You've always been closer to me than any sister. You'll hardly recognize John. At three, he's taller than most four-year-olds, but then what can we expect, with Seth being almost six-six? There's so much I want to tell you that it seems impossible to put in an email or speak about over the phone. Promise to block out the holidays on your calendar, because I'm dying to see you again. The Lord's been good to me, and I have so much to tell you.

Scotty just woke from his nap and he never has been one to wake in a happy mood. Take care. I'm counting the days until the 12th.
Love,
Claudia, Seth, John and Scott

Ashley read the message several times. Of course, Claudia didn't realize that she already knew they were coming. Again the hurt washed over her that Cooper had pretended she wasn't there when Claudia had phoned on Thanksgiving Day.

She circled the day on her calendar and stepped back wistfully. When Scott had been born that spring, Cooper had flown up to Nome to spend time with Claudia,

Seth and John. Ashley had yet to see the newest Lessinger. Cooper had said it earlier, and now Ashley added her own affirmation. This was going to be the most wonderful Christmas yet.

Ashley's alarm buzzed early the morning of the twelfth. She groaned defiantly until she remembered that she would have to hurry and shower if she was going to meet Claudia's plane as she intended.

A little while later, wearing jeans and a red cable-knit sweater, she tucked her pant legs into her boots. Thank goodness it wasn't raining.

She parked Milligan in the multistory circular parking garage, then hurried down to baggage claim, her heels clicking against the tiled surface.

Cooper was already waiting when she arrived. He didn't notice her, and for a moment she enjoyed just watching him. He looked fresh and vital. It hardly seemed like more than two weeks since she'd last seen him, and yet they'd been the longest weeks of her life.

The morning sunlight filtered unrestrained through the large plate glass windows, glinting on his dark hair. He was tall and broad shouldered. Seeing him again allowed all her pent-up feelings to spill over. It took more restraint than she cared to admit not to run into his arms. Instead she adjusted her purse strap over her shoulder, stuffed her hands in her pockets and approached him with a dignified air.

"Good morning, Cooper." She gave him a bright smile, although the muscles at the corners of her mouth trembled with the effort. "It's a beautiful day, isn't it?"

If he was surprised to see her, he hid the shock well.

"Ashley," he said, and stood. "Did you bring Madigan with you?" Concern laced his voice.

"Milligan," she corrected and laughed. "You never give up, do you?"

"Not if I can help it." He seemed to struggle with himself for a moment. "How have you been?"

"Sick," she lied unmercifully. "I was in the hospital for several days, doctors said I could have died. But I'm fine now. How about you?" she asked with a flippant air.

"Don't taunt me, Ashley," he warned thickly.

She was deliberately provoking him, but she didn't care. "For all you know it could be true. It's been more than two weeks since I've heard from you."

Turning his gaze to the window, he stood stiffly, watching the sky. "It seems longer," he murmured so low she had to strain to hear.

"Why?" she challenged, standing directly beside him, her own gaze cast toward the heavens.

"How's Webber?" He answered her question with one of his own.

"Webber?" she repeated, her face twisted into a puzzled frown. "You mean Webb?"

"Whoever." He shrugged.

"How do you know about Webb? Oh, wait. Mom." She answered her own question before he had the chance. "Webb and I are friends, nothing more." So this was the way her mother had handled the situation. For a moment fiery resentment burned in her eyes. She loved her mother, but there were times when Sarah Robbins's actions incensed her.

"Your mother mentioned that you and he see a lot of

one another." His words were spoken without emotion, as if the subject bored him.

"Friends often do," she returned defensively. "But then, I doubt you'd know that."

She could feel the anger exude from him as he bristled.

"I'm sorry," she whispered, her tone contrite. "I didn't mean that the way it sounded." When she turned her head to look at him, she saw the cold fury leave his eyes. She placed her hand gently on his forearm, drawing his attention to her. "I don't want to argue. Seth and Claudia will know something's wrong, we won't be able to hide it."

He placed his hand on top of hers and squeezed it momentarily. "I don't want to argue, either," he finished. "According to the notice board, their flight has landed."

Ashley's heart fluttered with excitement. "Cooper," she mouthed softly. "My school is having a Christmas party next weekend. Would you…" Her tongue stumbled over the words. "I mean, could you…would you consider going with me?"

His shocked look cut through her hopes. "Next weekend?"

"The nineteenth…it's a Friday night. A dinner party, I don't think it'll be all that formal, just a faculty get together. It's the last day of school, and the dinner is a small celebration."

"Will you be wearing your red cowboy boots?"

"No, I was going to borrow Dad's fishing rubbers," she shot back, then immediately relented. "All right, for you, I'll wear a dress, pantyhose, the whole bit."

Unbuttoning his coat, Cooper took out his cell phone from inside his suit pocket. He punched a few buttons.

A frown brought thick brows together. "It seems I've already got plans that night."

Disappointment settled over Ashley. Somehow she'd known he wouldn't accept, that he would find an excuse not to attend.

"I understand," she murmured, but her voice wobbled dangerously.

The silence between them lasted until she saw Claudia, Seth and the boys descending the escalator. As soon as they reached the bottom John broke loose from his father's hand and ran into Cooper's waiting arms.

"Uncle Coop, Uncle Coop!" he cried with childish delight and looped his arms around Cooper's neck. John didn't seem to remember Ashley at first until she offered him a bright smile. "Auntie Ash?" he questioned, holding out his arms to her.

She held out her own arms, and Cooper handed the boy to her. Immediately John spread moist kisses over her cheek. When she glanced over she noticed that Seth and Cooper were enthusiastically shaking hands.

"Ashley," Claudia chimed happily. "I didn't know whether you'd make it to the airport or not. I love your hair."

"So does Webb," she laughed, and had the satisfaction of seeing Cooper's eyes narrow angrily. "And this little angel must be Scott." With John's legs wrapped around her waist, Ashley leaned over to examine the eight-month-old baby in Claudia's arms. "And I bet John's a wonderful big brother, aren't you, John?"

The boy's head bobbed up and down. Both of the Lessinger boys had Seth's dark looks, but their eyes were as blue as a cloudless sky. Claudia's eyes.

Ashley didn't get a chance to talk to her friend until later that afternoon. Both boys were down for a nap, Seth and Cooper were concentrating on a game of chess in Cooper's den, while Ashley and Claudia sat enjoying the view from a bay window in the formal dining room.

"I can't get over how good you look," Claudia said, blowing into a steaming coffee mug. "Your hair really is great."

"The easiest style I've ever had." Ashley ran her fingers through the bouncing curls and shook her head, and her blond locks fell naturally into place.

"Do you see much of Cooper?" Claudia delivered the question with deceptive casualness.

"Hardly at all," Ashley replied truthfully. "Why do you ask?"

"I don't know. You two were giving one another odd looks at the airport. I could tell he wasn't pleased with your riding that moped. I thought maybe something was going on between the two of you."

Ashley dismissed Claudia's words with a short shake of her hand. "I'm sure you're mistaken. Can you imagine Cooper Masters being interested in anyone like me?"

"In some ways I can," Claudia insisted. "You two balance one another. He takes everything so seriously, while you finagle your way in and out of anything. I know one thing," she said. "He thinks very highly of you. He has for years."

"You're kidding!"

"I'm not. I don't know that he would have been as happy about me marrying Seth if it hadn't been for you."

"Nonsense," Ashley countered quickly. "I knew you and Seth were right for one another from the first moment I saw you with him. I don't know of any couple who belong together more than you two. And it shows, Claudia, it shows. Your face is radiant. That kind of inner happiness only comes with the deep love of a man."

Claudia's face flushed with color. "I know it sounds crazy, but I'm more in love with Seth now than when I married him four years ago. I never thought that would be possible. I don't understand how I could have doubted our love and that God wanted us together. My priorities are so different now."

"What about your degree? Do you think you'll ever go back to school?"

"I don't know. Maybe someday, but my life is so full now with the boys I can't imagine squeezing another thing in. I wouldn't want to. John and Scott need me. I suppose when they're older and in school full time I might think about finishing my doctorate, but that's years down the road. I do know that Seth will do whatever he can to help me if I decide to go ahead and get my degree." Pausing, she took another drink from her mug. "What about you? Any man in your life?"

"Several," Ashley teased, without looking at her friend. "None I'm serious about, though."

"What about Webb? You've written about him."

Before Ashley could assure Claudia her relationship with Webb didn't extend beyond a convenient friendship, a dark shadow fell into the room, diverting their attention to the two men who had just entered.

Seth's smile rested on his wife as he crossed the room and placed a loving arm across her shoulders. Cooper remained framed in the archway.

"As usual, Cooper beat the socks off me. I don't know why I bother to play. I can't recall ever beating him."

"What about you, Claudia?" Cooper asked. "You used to play a mean, if a bit unorthodox, game of chess."

Standing, Claudia looped her arm around her husband's waist. "Not me, I'm too tired to concentrate. If everyone will excuse me, I think I'll join the boys and take a nap."

Clenching her mug with both hands, Ashley stood. "I'd better rev up Milligan and get home before the weather—"

"No," Claudia interrupted. "You play Cooper, Ash. You always were a better chess player than me."

Ashley threw a speculative glance toward Cooper, awaiting his reaction. He arched his thick brows in challenge. "Would you care for a game, Miss Robbins?" he asked formally.

Wickedly fluttering her eyelashes, she placed both hands over her heart. "Just what are you suggesting, Mr. Masters?"

Claudia giggled. "You know, suddenly I'm not the least bit tired."

"Yes, you are," Seth murmured, tightening his grip on his wife's waist. "You and I are going to rest and leave these two to a game of chess."

Claudia didn't object when Seth led her from the room.

"Shall we?" Cooper asked, long strides carrying him to her side. He extended his elbow, and when Ashley placed her arm in his, he gave her a curt nod.

The thought of playing chess with Cooper was an opportunity too good to miss. She was an excellent player and had been the assistant coach for the school's team the year before.

The two leather chairs were pushed opposite one another with a mahogany table standing between. An inlaid board with ivory figures sat atop the table.

"I would like to suggest a friendly wager." The words were offered as a clear challenge.

"Just what are you suggesting?" she asked.

"I'm saying that if I win the match, then you'll accept the new car."

"Honestly, Cooper, you don't give up, do you?"

"Accept the car without any obligation to reimburse me," he continued undaunted, "plus the promise that you'll faithfully drive it to and from work daily."

"And just what do I get if *I* win?" she countered.

"That's up to you."

She released a weary sigh. "I don't think you can give me what I want," she mumbled, lowering her gaze to her hands, laced tightly together in her lap.

"I think I can."

"All right," she added, straightening slightly. "If I win, you must promise never to speak derogatorily of Milligan again, or in any way insinuate that riding my moped is unsafe." He opened and closed his mouth in mute protest. "And in addition I would ask that a generous donation be made to the school's scholarship fund. Agreed?" She could tell he wasn't pleased.

"Agreed." The teasing light left his eyes as he viewed the chess board with a serious look. Taking both a black and a white pawn, he placed them behind his back, then extended his clenched fists for her to choose.

She mumbled a silent prayer, knowing she would have

the advantage if she were lucky enough to pick white. Lightly, she tapped his right hand.

Cooper relaxed his fist and revealed the white pawn. Her spirits soared. He would now be on the defensive.

Neither spoke as they positioned the pieces on the board. A strained, tense air filled the den, and the only sound was the occasional crackle from the fireplace.

Her first move was a standard opening, pawn to king four, which he countered with an identical play. She immediately responded with a gambit, pawn to king's bishop four.

It didn't take her long to impress him with her ability. A smug smile lightly brushed her mouth as she viewed his shock as she gained momentum and dominated the game.

Bending forward, he rubbed a hand across his forehead and then his eyes. Ashley was forced to restrain another smile when he glanced up at her.

"Claudia was right, you *are* a good player."

"Thank you," she responded, hoping to hide the pleasure his acknowledgement gave her.

He made his next move, and she paused to study the board.

"Claudia was right about something else, too," he said softly.

"What's that?" she asked absently, pinching her bottom lip between her thumb and index finger, her concentration centered on the chess board.

"I don't think I've ever told you what an attractive woman you are."

His husky tone seemed to reach out and wrap itself

around her. "What'd you say?" Her concentration faltered, and she lifted her gaze to his.

His eyes were narrowed on her mouth. "I said you're beautiful."

The current of awareness between them was so strong that she would gladly have surrendered the game right then and there. She felt close to Cooper, closer than she had to any other person. They had so little in common, and yet they shared the most basic, the strongest, emotion of all. If he had moved or in any way indicated that he wanted her, she would have tossed the chess game aside and wrapped herself in his arms. As it was, her will to win, the determination to prove herself, was quickly lost in the power of his gaze.

"It's your move."

Her eyes darkened with anger as she seethed inwardly. He was playing another game with her, a psychological game in which he had proved to be the clear winner with the first move. Using the attraction she felt for him, he'd hope to derail her concentration. His game read Cooper one, Ashley zilch.

She jumped to her feet and jogged around the room. Pausing to take a series of deep breaths, she took in his cynical look with amusement.

"I hate to appear ignorant here, but just what are you doing?"

"What does it look like?" she countered sarcastically.

"Either you're training for the Olympics or you're sorely testing my limited patience."

"Guess again," she returned impudently, beginning a series of jumping jacks.

"I thought we were playing chess, not twenty questions."

Hands resting challengingly on her hips, she paused and tossed him a brazen glare. "It was either vent my anger physically or punch you out, Cooper Masters."

"Punch me out?" he echoed in disbelief. "What did I do?"

"You know, so don't try to deny it." The anger had dissipated from her blue eyes as she returned to her chair and resumed her study of the board. As the blood pounded in her ears, she knew she'd made a mistake the minute she lifted her hand from the pawn. But would Cooper recognize her error and gain the advantage?

"Cooper?" she whispered.

"Hmm," he answered absently.

"Do you remember the last time I was here?"

He lifted his gaze to hers. "I'm not likely to forget it. After the cold I caught, I coughed for a week."

"Sometimes doing something crazy and irrational has a price." She leaned forward, her chin supported by the palm of her hand.

"Not this time, Ashley Robbins," he gloated, making the one move that would cost her the game. "Check."

Four

Ashley stared at the chess board with a sense of unreality. There was only one move she could make, and she knew what would happen when she took it.

"Checkmate."

She stared at him for a long moment, unable to speak or move. Cooper stood and crossed the room to a huge oak desk that dominated one corner. She watched as he opened a drawer and took out some papers. When he returned to her side, he gave her the car keys.

Her hand was shaking so badly she nearly dropped them.

"This is the registration," he told her, handing her a piece of paper. "After what happened not so long ago, I suggest you keep it in the glove compartment."

Unable to respond with anything more than a nod, she avoided his eyes, which were sure to be sparkling with triumph.

"These are the insurance forms, made out in your name. I believe there's a space for you to sign at the bottom of the policy." He pointed to the large "X" marking the spot, then handed her a pen.

Mutely Ashley complied, but her signature was barely recognizable. She returned the pen.

"I believe that's everything."

"No," she protested, unable to recognize the thin, high voice as her own. "I insist upon paying for the car."

"That wasn't part of our agreement."

"Nonetheless, I insist." She had to struggle to speak clearly.

"No, Ashley," he insisted, "the car is yours."

"But I can't accept something so valuable, not over a silly chess game." She raised her eyes to meet his. Their gazes held, his proud and determined, hers wary and unsure. A muscle moved convulsively at the side of his jaw, and she realized she had lost.

"The car is a gift from me to you. There isn't any way on this earth that I'll accept payment. You were aware of the terms before you agreed to the game."

A painful lump filled her throat, and when she spoke her voice was hoarse. "You have so much," she murmured, her voice cracking. "Must you take my pride, too?" Tears shimmered in the clear depths of her eyes. Wordlessly she left the den, took her coat and walked out the front door. Without a backward glance she climbed aboard Milligan and rode home.

Her mood hadn't improved the next morning as she dressed for church. The sky was dark and threatening, mirroring her temper. How could she love someone as headstrong and narrow minded as Cooper Masters? No wonder his business had grown and prospered over the years. He was ruthless, determined and obstinate.

After tucking her Bible into her backpack, she stepped outside to lock her apartment door. A patch of red in the parking lot caught her attention and she noted that a shiny new car was parked beside Milligan in front of her apartment. As she seethed inwardly, it took great restraint not to vent her anger by kicking the gleaming new car.

The first drops of rain fell lazily to the ground. Even God seemed to be on Cooper's side, she thought, as she heaved a troubled sigh. Either she had to change into her rain gear or drive the car. She chose the latter. Pulling out of the parking lot, she was forced to admit the car handled like a dream. Ashley was prepared to hate the car, but it didn't even take the full five miles to church for her to acknowledge she was going to love this car. Just as much as she loved the man who had given it to her.

As the Sunday School teacher for the three-year-olds, she was excited that John Lessinger would be in her class.

Claudia dropped him off at the classroom, Scotty resting on her hip, the diaper bag dangling from her arm.

"Morning." Ashley beamed warmly. "How's Johnny?" She directed her attention to the small boy who hid behind Claudia's skirts.

"He's playing shy today," Claudia warned.

"I don't blame him," Ashley whispered in return. "A lot's happened in the last couple of days."

"I'll drop Scotty off at the nursery and come back to see how John does."

"He'll be fine," Ashley assured her. "Did you see the playdough, Johnny?" she asked, directing his attention to the low table where several other children were busy playing. "Come over here and I'll introduce you to some of my friends."

John's look was unsure, and he glanced over his shoulder at his retreating mother. His lower lip began to quiver as tears welled in his blue eyes. Kneeling down to his level, Ashley placed her hands on his small shoulders. "Johnny, it's Auntie Ash. You remember me, don't you? There's nothing to frighten you here. Come over and meet Joseph and Matthew. You can tell them all about Alaska."

John was playing nicely with the other children when Claudia returned. She sighed in relief. "Now I can relax," she whispered. "I don't know what it is about men and Sunday mornings, but it takes Seth twice as long as me to get ready. Then I'm left to carry Scott, steer John, haul the diaper bag, the Bibles and my purse, while Seth can't manage anything more than his car keys."

Ashley stifled a giggle. She allowed the children to play for several more minutes, chatting with Claudia, who insisted on staying for the first part of Sunday School to be sure John was really all right.

Ashley gathered the children in a circle and had them sit on the patch of carpet in the middle of the floor. As she sat cross-legged on the floor with them, one of the shyer children came over and seated herself in Ashley's lap. "I'm glad we're all together, together, together," the little girl sang in a sweet, melodious voice. "Because Jesus is here, and teacher's here, and—"

"Cooper's here," Claudia chimed in softly.

The song died on the girl's lips as everyone looked over at the tall, compelling figure standing in the open door. His attention was centered on Ashley and the little girl in her lap. For a moment he seemed to go pale, and the muscles in his jaw jerked, and Ashley wondered what she had done now to anger him. Without a word, he pivoted and left the room.

"I'd better see what he wanted," Claudia said, following him out of the room.

Ashley didn't see either of them again until it was time for the morning worship service. The four adults sat together, Claudia between her and Cooper. A hundred questions whirled in her mind. How had Claudia gotten Cooper to attend church? It wasn't all that long ago that he had scoffed at her friend's newfound faith. She wondered if Seth had some influence on Cooper's decision to attend church. More than likely John had said something, and Cooper had been unable to refuse.

Just as the pastor stepped in front of the congregation to light the third candle of the Advent wreath, a loud cry came from the nursery.

Claudia emitted a low groan. "Scotty." She leaned over and whispered to Ashley, "I wasn't sure I'd be able to leave him this long." She stood and made her way out of the pew. Cooper closed the space separating them.

Never had Ashley been more aware of a man's presence. As his thigh lightly touched hers, she closed her eyes at the potency of the contact. Nervously she scooted away, putting some space between them. When he turned and looked at her an unfamiliar quality had entered his eyes. He smiled, one of those rare smiles that came from his heart and nearly stopped hers. Its overwhelming force left her exposed and completely vulnerable. Undoubtedly he would be able to read the effect he had on her and know her thoughts. Quickly turning her face away, she squeezed her eyes closed, and then the pastor, the service, everything, everyone, was lost as Cooper closed his hand firmly over hers.

In all the years she had loved Cooper, Ashley had never dared to dream that he would sit beside her in church or share her strong faith. The intense sensations of having him near touched her so dramatically that for a moment she was sure her heart would burst with un-restrained happiness.

His grip remained tight and firm until Claudia returned to the pew and sat beside Seth. Immediately Cooper released Ashley's hand. The happiness that had filled her so briefly was gone. He seemed content to hold her hand only as long as no one knew. The minute someone came, he let her go.

Once again she was forcefully reminded of the huge differences that separated them. He was a corporate manager, a powerful, wealthy man. She was a financially struggling schoolteacher. In some ways she was certain he cared for her, but not enough to admit it openly. She sometimes feared she was an embarrassment to him, a fear that had dogged her from the beginning.

"Did you win the Irish Sweepstakes?" Webb asked Ashley as she pulled into the school parking lot and climbed out of the shining new car.

"No," she said and sighed unhappily. "I lost a chess game."

He gave her a funny look. "Let me make certain I've got this straight. You *lost* the chess game and won the car?"

"You got it."

Rubbing the side of his chin with one hand, he stared at her with confused eyes. "I know there's logic in this someplace, but for the moment it's escaped me."

"I wouldn't doubt it," she said, and nodded a friendly greeting to the school secretary as she walked through the door.

"What would you have gotten if you'd *won?*" Webb asked as he followed on her heels.

"Milligan and my pride."

"That's another one of those answers that seems to have gone right over my head." He waved his hand over the top of his blond head in illustration. Confusion clouded his eyes. "All I really want to know is whether this person likes chess and plays often? It wouldn't be hard for me to lose. I don't even like the game."

"You wouldn't want to play this person," she mumbled under her breath, heading toward the faculty room.

"Don't be hasty, Ashley," he countered quickly. "Let me be the judge of that."

Tossing him a look she usually reserved for rowdy students was enough to quell his curiosity.

"We're going to the Christmas party Friday night, aren't we?" he asked, steering clear of the former topic of discussion.

Releasing a slow breath, Ashley cupped a coffee mug with both hands. Her enthusiasm for the party had disappeared with Cooper's excuse not to attend. Probably because she believed that the previous appointment he claimed to have was merely a pretext to avoid refusing her outright.

"I don't know, I have a friend visiting from Alaska,"

she said before sipping. "We may be doing something that night."

"Sure, no problem," he said with a smile. "Let me know if you change your mind."

No pleading, no hesitation, no regrets. The least he could do was show some remorse over her missing the party. As she watched him saunter out of the faculty room, she threw imaginary daggers at his back. Unhappy and more than a little depressed, she finished her coffee and went to her homeroom.

"Is there something drastically wrong with me?" Ashley asked Claudia later that afternoon. She'd stopped by after school for a short visit with Claudia and the boys before Cooper returned from his office.

When Claudia looked up from bouncing Scotty on her knee, her eyes showed surprise. "Heavens, no. What makes you ask?"

"I mean, you'd tell me if I had bad breath or something, wouldn't you?"

"You know me well enough to answer that."

As Johnny weaved a toy truck around the chair legs, then pushed it under the table to the far side of the room, Ashley's eyes followed the movement of her godson. Lowering her face, she took a deep breath, afraid she might do something stupid like cry. "I want to get married and have children. I'm twenty-six and not getting any younger."

"I'm sure there are plenty of men out there who'd be interested. Only yesterday Seth was saying how pretty you've gotten. Surely there's someone—"

"That's just it," Ashley interrupted, knowing she

couldn't mention Cooper. "There isn't, and I found a gray hair the other day. I'm getting scared."

"You and Cooper both. Have you noticed how he's getting gray along his sideburns? It really makes him look distinguished, doesn't it?"

Ashley agreed with a smile, but her eyes refused to meet her friend's, afraid she wouldn't be able to disguise her feelings for Cooper.

"Oh, before I forget, Seth and I have been invited to a dinner party this Friday night, and we were wondering if you could watch the boys. If you have plans just say so, because I think your mother might be able to do it."

Some devilish impulse made her ask, "What about Cooper?"

"He's got some appointment he can't get out of."

For a startled second the oxygen seemed trapped in Ashley's lungs. He had been telling the truth. He *did* have an appointment. In that brief second the sun took on a brighter intensity; it was as if the birds began to chirp.

"I'd love to stay with John and Scott," she returned enthusiastically. "We'll have a wonderful time, won't we, boys?" Neither one looked especially pleased. Glancing at her watch, Ashley quickly stood. "I've gotta scoot, I'll see you Friday. What time do you want me?"

"Is six too early? I'll try to get the boys fed and dressed."

"Don't do that," Ashley admonished with a laugh. "It'll be good practice for me. I need to learn all this motherhood stuff, you know."

"Don't rush off," Claudia said. "Cooper will be home any minute."

"I can't stay. Tell him I said hello—no, don't," she

added abruptly. He might have been telling the truth about being busy Friday night, but it didn't lessen the hurt of his rejection. "Mid-year reports go home this Friday, and I want to get a head start."

Claudia regarded her quizzically as she walked her to the door. "Thanks again for Friday. I don't like to leave the boys with strangers. It's bad enough for them to be away from home."

"Happy to help," Ashley said sincerely. Giving a tiny wave to both boys, she smiled when Scotty raised his chubby hand to her. Johnny ran to the front window to look out, and Ashley played peek-a-boo with him. The small head had just bobbed out from behind the drapes when Cooper spoke from behind her.

"Hello, Ashley."

She stiffened at the sound of his voice, her heartbeat racing double time. Last Sunday at church had been the last time she'd seen him.

"Hello." Her voice was devoid of any warmth or welcome. He looked dignified in his suit and silk tie. Childishly she was upset at him all the more for it.

"Is something the matter?" he asked in a quiet voice.

"No," she answered, her gaze stern and unyielding. "I'm just surprised that you'd taint your image by being seen with me."

"What are you talking about?"

"If you don't know, then I'm not going to tell you."

His gaze narrowed. "What's wrong? Obviously something's troubling you."

"The man's a genius," she replied flippantly. "Now, if you'll excuse me, I'll be on my way."

Cooper's eyes contained a hard gleam she had never

seen. His hand shot out and gripped her upper arm. "Tell me what's going on in that unpredictable mind of yours."

Defiance flared from her as she stared pointedly at his hand until he relaxed his hold. Breaking free, she took a few steps in retreat, creating the breathing space she needed to vent her frustration. "I'll have you know, Cooper Masters, I'm not the least bit ashamed of who or what I am. My mother may be your housekeeper, but she has served you well all these years. My father's a skilled sheet metal worker, and I'm proud of them both. I don't have a thing to be ashamed about. Not in front of you or anyone." Having finished her tirade, she avoided looking at him and walked straight to her car.

She never made it. A strong hand on her shoulder swung her around, pinning her against the side of the car. "What are you implying?" The tone of his voice made Ashley shudder. His nostrils flared with barely restrained fury.

Tears shimmered in her eyes until his face was swimming before her. She bit her bottom lip. Suddenly she could feel the anger drain out of him.

"What's the matter with us?" he demanded hoarsely, then expelled an impatient breath.

"Everything!" she cried, her voice trembling. "Everything," she repeated. When she struggled, he released her and didn't try to stop her again. He stepped back as she climbed inside the car, revved the engine and drove away.

If Ashley was miserable then, it was nothing compared to the way she felt later. To soothe away her emotional turmoil and frustration, she filled the bathtub with hot water and bubble bath, and soaked in it until the water became tepid. In an attempt to pray, she tried the conversational approach that had come so naturally to her in the past, but even that was impossible in her present state of mind.

Sleep was a long time coming that night. She couldn't seem to find a comfortable position, and when she did drift off she found herself trapped in a dream of hopelessness. Waking early the next morning, she rose before the alarm sounded, put on the coffee and sat in the dark, shadow-filled room waiting for the first light.

Lackadaisically, she reached for her devotional and discovered the suggested reading for the day was the famous love chapter in First Corinthians, Chapter Thirteen. *Love is very patient and kind*, verse four stated.

Had she been patient? Ten years seemed a long time to her, and that was how long it had been since she first realized she'd loved Cooper. Since the tender age of sixteen. Glancing back to her Bible, she continued reading. *Love doesn't demand its own way. It isn't irritable or touchy. It doesn't hold grudges and will hardly notice when others do wrong.... If you love someone you will always believe in him, always expect the best of him and always stand your ground in defending him.*

Closing her Bible, Ashley released an uneven breath. It looked as though she had a long way to go to achieve the standards God had set.

When it came time for her to pray, she got down on her knees, meditating first on the words she had read. Ever since Sunday she'd expected the worst from Cooper, thought the worst of him. She'd wanted to explain how hurt she was, but it sounded so petty to accuse him of being ashamed of her because he'd quit holding her hand. In voicing her thoughts, the whole incident sounded ludicrous. It seemed she was building things in her own mind because she was insecure. The same thoughts had come to her the night he'd taken her to the Italian restaurant, and the night Claudia had phoned from Alaska. She'd never thought of herself as someone with low self-esteem before Cooper.

"Oh, ye of little faith," she said aloud. *No*, her heart countered, *ye of little love*.

Ashley hummed cheerfully as she pulled into the school parking lot. She was proud of the fact that she had worked things out in her own mind—with God's help, of course. The next time she saw Cooper, she would apologize for her behavior and ask that they start again. Poor man, he wouldn't know what to think. One minute she was ranting and raving, and the next she was apologizing.

Today was a special day for her Senior Literature class. They'd been reading and studying the Western classic *The Oxbow Incident* by Walter Van Tilburg Clark. As part of her preparation for their final exam, Ashley dressed up as one of the characters in the book. Portraying the part as believably as possible, she was usually able to draw out heated discussions and points that might otherwise have been glossed over.

Today she was dressing as Donald Martin, one of the three men accused of cattle rustling in the powerful narrative. This was always Ashley's favorite part of the quarter, and her classroom antics were well known.

Her afternoon students were buzzing with speculation when the bell rang. She waited until everyone was seated before she came through the door to be greeted by laughter and cheers. She was wearing a ten-gallon hat. Her cowboy boots had silver spurs, and her long, slim legs were disguised by leather chaps. Two toy six-shooters were holstered at her hips. With her hair tucked under the hat, she'd made a token attempt toward realism by smearing dirt over her creamy smooth cheeks and pasting a long black mustache across her upper lip.

The class loved it, and immediate speculation arose about what character she was portraying.

"I'm here today to talk about mob justice," she began, sitting on the corner of her desk and dangling one foot over the edge.

"She's Gil," one of the boys in the back row called out.

"Good guess, David," she said, pointing to him. "But I'm no drifter. I own my own spread at Pike's Hole. Me and the missus are building up our herd."

"It's Mex," someone else shouted.

"No way," Diana Crosby corrected. "Mex wasn't married."

"Good girl, Diana." She twirled both six-shooters around a couple of times and by pure luck happened to place them in the holsters right side up. When her class applauded she bowed, her hat falling off her head. As she bent to pick it up she noticed a face staring at her from the small glass portion of the class door. The face was lovingly familiar. Cooper.

"If you'll excuse me a minute, I have to check my horse," she said, quickly making up a pretense to escape into the hallway.

"What are you doing here?" she demanded in a low tone.

A smile danced in his eyes as he attempted to hide

his grin by rubbing his thumb across the angular line of his jaw. "Butch Cassidy, I presume."

"Cooper, I'm in the middle of class," she muttered with an exaggerated sigh, both hands gripping his arms. "But I'm so glad to see you. I feel terrible about the way I acted yesterday. I was wrong, terribly wrong."

The laughter faded from his features as he regarded her seriously. "I had no idea the dinner party meant so much to you."

"What dinner party?" He was talking in riddles.

"The one you asked me to attend with you. I assumed that was what upset you yesterday."

She shook her head in wry dismay. "No...that wasn't it."

"Then what was?"

Casting an apprehensive glare over her shoulder, she turned pleading eyes to him. "I can't talk now."

He rubbed a weary hand over his face. "Ashley, I rearranged my schedule. I'll be happy to take you to the school Christmas party."

She groaned softly. "But I can't go now."

"What do you mean, you can't go?" His dark, steely eyes narrowed.

He didn't need to say another word for her to know how much it had inconvenienced him to readjust his schedule.

"Cooper, I'm sorry, but I..."

"Invited someone else," he finished for her, his eyes as cold as a blast of arctic wind. "That Webber fellow, I imagine."

"I haven't got time to stand in the hall and argue with you. My class is waiting."

"And so, I imagine, is Webber."

Fury blazed in her eyes as she slashed him a cutting look. "You do that on purpose."

"Do what?" His voice was barely civil.

"Call Webb 'Webber,' the same way you call Milligan 'Madigan.' I find the whole denial thing rather childish," she snapped resentfully. By now she was too incensed to care if she was making sense.

"I find that statement unworthy of comment."

"You would." She spun away and stalked back into the classroom, restraining the impulse to slam the door.

Claudia was dressed in a mauve-colored chiffon evening gown that was a stunning complement to her auburn hair and cream coloring. Seth, too, looked remarkably attractive in his suit and tie.

"Okay, I showed you where everything is in the bedroom, and here's the phone number of the restaurant." Claudia laid the pad near the phone in the kitchen. "I've left a baby bottle in the refrigerator, but I've already nursed Scotty, so he probably won't need it."

"Okay," Ashley said, following Claudia out of the kitchen.

"Both boys are dressed for bed, and don't let either of them stay up past eight-thirty. You may need to rock Scotty to sleep."

"No problem, I got my degree in rocking chair."

Checking her reflection in the hallway mirror, Claudia tucked a stray hair back into her coiled French coiffure. "You didn't happen to have an argument with Cooper, did you?" The question came out of the blue.

Ashley could feel the blood rush from her face, then just as quickly flood back. "What makes you ask?"

"Seth and I have hardly seen him the last couple of days, and he's been in the foulest mood. It's not like him to behave like this. I can't understand it."

"What makes you think I have anything to do with it?" she asked, doing her best to conceal her reaction.

"I know it sounds crazy, and I wouldn't want to offend you, Ash, but I still think something's stirring between you two. I may be an old married fuddy-duddy, but I recognize the looks he's been giving you. What I can't understand is why the two of you work so hard at hiding it. As far as I'm concerned, you're perfect for one another."

"Ha," Ashley said harshly. "We can't spend two minutes together lately without going for each other's jugular."

Seth took Claudia's wrap from the hall closet and placed it over her shoulders. "Sounds like the way it was with us a few times, doesn't it, Honey?" he asked, and tenderly kissed the creamy smooth slope of Claudia's neck.

"Call if you have any problems, won't you?" Claudia said, suddenly sounding worried. "Scotty will cry the first few minutes after we've left, but he should quiet down in a little bit, so don't panic."

"I never panic," Ashley assured her with a cheeky grin.

True to his mother's word, Scott gave a hearty cry the minute the door was closed.

"It's all right. Look, here's your teddy."

Scotty took the stuffed animal, threw it across the room and cried all the louder.

Ten minutes passed and nothing seemed to calm his frantic cries. Even John looked as if he was ready to give way and start howling.

"Come on, sweetie, not you, too."

"I want my mommy."

"Let's pretend I'm your mommy," Ashley offered, "and then you can tell me how to make Scotty happy."

"Will you hold me like my mommy?" Johnny asked, a tear running down his pale face.

"Sure, join the crowd," Ashley laughed, lifting him so that she had a baby on each hip. Johnny cried in small whimpering sounds and Scott in large howling sobs.

Pacing the floor, she glanced up to find Cooper standing in the entryway watching her, a stunned look on his face.

Five

"Look, Johnny, Scott," Ashley said cheerfully. "Uncle Cooper's here."

Both boys cried harder. Scotty buried his face in her neck, his stubby hands tangled in her blond hair. When he pulled a long strand, she cried out involuntarily, "Ouch."

The small protest spurred Cooper into action. He hung his overcoat in the hall closet and entered the living room, taking John from Ashley.

"What's the matter, fella?" he asked in a reassuring tone.

"I want my mommy!" John wailed.

"They went out for the evening," Ashley explained, both hands supporting Scott as she paced the floor, making cooing sounds in his ear. But nothing seemed to comfort the baby, who continued to cry pitifully.

"What about Webber and your party?" Cooper asked stiffly.

"I tried to tell you that I wasn't going," she explained,

and breathed in deeply. "I didn't say a thing about attending the party with Webb. You assumed I was."

"Are you telling me the reason you didn't go tonight is because you'd promised to baby-sit John and Scotty?"

Ashley silently confirmed the statement with a weak nod. His dark eyes narrowed with self-directed anger.

"Why do you put up with me?" he asked.

She didn't get the opportunity to answer, because Scotty began bellowing even louder.

A troubled frown broke across Cooper's expression. "Is he sick? I've never heard him cry like that."

"No, just unhappy. Claudia said she'd left a bottle for him. Maybe we should heat it up."

All four moved into the kitchen. With Scotty balanced on her hip, Ashley took the baby bottle out of the refrigerator. "It needs to be heated." She held it out to him.

"If you say so," he said, shrugging his broad shoulders. "How does your mommy do it?" he asked Johnny, who seemed more secure now that his uncle had arrived.

"She nurses Scotty."

Slowly Cooper's dark eyes met hers, amusement flickering across his face. She giggled, and soon they were both laughing. Scotty cried all the harder, clinging to Ashley.

The humor broke the terrible tension that had existed between them for days.

Cooper smiled warmly into her eyes, trying to hold back his laughter. He walked across the room and took a large pan out of the bottom cupboard, then filled it with hot water. "I don't want to chance the microwave. What if I melt the bottle? It's plastic, after all." By the time he'd set the pan on the stove and turned on the burner, he'd regained his composure.

Ashley placed the baby bottle in the water. "Is it supposed to float?"

"I don't know." He shook his head briefly, the look in his eyes unbelievably tender.

"Oh well, we'll experiment, won't we, boys?"

"What's an experiment?" Johnny asked. He was sitting on top of the counter, his short legs dangling over the edge.

"It's a process by which we examine the validity of a hypothesis and determine the nature of something as yet unknown."

"Cooper..." Ashley laughed at the way the three-year-old's mouth and eyes rounded as he tried to understand what Cooper was saying. "Honestly! Let me explain." She turned to Johnny. "An experiment is trying something you've never done before."

"Oh!" Johnny's clouded expression brightened, and he eagerly shook his head. "Mommy does that a lot with dinner."

"That's right." Ashley beamed.

"Smart aleck," Cooper whispered under his breath, his gaze lingering on her for a heart-stopping moment.

Ashley found herself drowning in the dark depths of his eyes and quickly averted her head. The water in the pan was coming to a boil, the baby bottle tossing back and forth in the bubbling liquid.

"It must be ready by now," she commented as she turned off the burner.

Cooper went out to the back porch and returned with

a huge pair of barbeque tongs. He quickly lifted the bottle from the hot water, setting it upright on the counter.

"Nicely done," she commented, and waited a few minutes before testing the milk's temperature. Once she was sure it wouldn't burn Scotty's tender mouth, she led the way into the living room.

Remembering what Claudia had said about rocking the baby, Ashley sat in the polished wooden rocker and gently tipped back and forth. Scotty reached for the bottle and held it himself, sucking greedily. Her eyes filled with tenderness. She brushed the fine hair from his face and cupped his ear. The room was blissfully silent as John and Cooper sat across from her.

Johnny crawled into Cooper's lap and handed him a book that he wanted read. Cooper complied, his voice and face expressive as he turned page after page, reading quietly.

Ashley found her attention drawn again and again to the man and the young boy. A surge of love filled her, so strong and overpowering that tears formed in her eyes. Hurriedly she looked away, batting her eyelashes to forestall the moisture.

Losing interest in the bottle, Scotty began chewing the nipple and watching Ashley. His round eyes held a fascinated expression as he studied her hair and reached out to grab her blond curls.

Carefully, she brushed her hair back. As she did her eyes met Cooper's. His gaze had centered on her mouth with a disturbing intensity. The power he had over her produced an aching tightness in her throat.

"You'll make a good mother someday." His voice was low and husky.

"I was just thinking the same thing about you," she murmured, then realizing what she'd said and hastened to correct herself. "I mean a good father."

"I know what you meant."

"Uncle Cooper." Johnny tugged at Cooper's arm. "You're supposed to be reading."

"So I am," he agreed in a lazy drawl. "So I am."

Finished now, Scotty tossed the bottle aside, then struggled to sit up. "I know I should burp him," Ashley said, "but I'm not sure of the best way to hold him."

Cooper stood. "Claudia left a baby book lying around here somewhere. Maybe it would be best to look it up."

The small party moved into Cooper's den. Ashley carried Scotty on her hip. He didn't make a sound, having apparently become accustomed to her, and that pleased her.

Cooper found the book and set it on his desk, flipping the pages. As soon as Ashley bent over next to him to read a paragraph, Scotty burped loudly.

"Well I guess that answers that, doesn't it?" she said, laughing.

"Uncle Coop, can I have a piggyback ride?" Johnny climbed onto the chair and held out his hands entreatingly.

Cooper looked unsure for a moment but agreed with a good-natured nod. "Okay, partner."

Johnny climbed onto Cooper's back, looped his legs around his uncle's waist and clung tightly with his chubby arms. "Gitty-up, horsey," he commanded happily.

Cooper grinned. "How come this is called a piggyback ride and you say 'Gitty-up, horsey'?"

Johnny chuckled. "It's an experiment."

"He's got you there." Ashley flashed him a cheeky grin.

Cooper mumbled something unintelligible and trotted into the next room.

Ashley followed, enjoying the sight of Cooper looking so relaxed. Scotty clapped his hands gleefully, and Ashley trotted after the others.

After a moment Cooper paused. "I smell something."

"Not…" She didn't finish.

"I think it must be."

Three pairs of eyes centered on the baby. Dramatically, Johnny plugged his nose. "Scotty has a messy diaper," he announced with the formality of a judge.

"Well, he's still a baby, and they're expected to do that sort of thing. Isn't that right, Scotty?"

Unconcerned, Scotty cooed happily, chewing on his pajama sleeve.

"Claudia showed me where everything is, this shouldn't take long."

"Ashley." Cooper stopped her, his face tight. "I think I should probably be the one to change him."

"You? Why? Are you saying it's the proper thing to do, since he's a boy?"

"I'm saying it's not a lot of fun and I've done it before, so…"

Unsuccessfully disguising a grateful smile, she handed him the baby. Scotty protested loudly as Cooper supported him with his hands under the baby's armpits, holding him as far away as possible.

"Call me if you need help."

Johnny led the way up the stairs, the large wooden steps almost more than he could manage. Cooper glanced down, his brow marred by a frown, then followed his nephew down the hall.

Ashley waited at the foot of the stairs, one shoe positioned on the bottom step, in case Cooper called.

"Auntie Ash." Johnny came running down the wide hallway and stopped at the top of the stairs. "Uncle Cooper says he needs you."

A tiny smile formed lines at the edges of her mouth. Somehow the words sounded exceedingly beautiful. She yearned to hear them from Cooper himself, though not exactly in this context.

She entered the bedroom and saw that his frown had deepened. He extended a hand to stop her as she entered the nursery. "I need a washcloth or something...you can give it to John."

Ashley ran the water in the bathroom sink until it was warm and soaked the washcloth in it. After wringing out most of the moisture, she handed it to Johnny, who ran full speed into the bedroom.

Loitering outside the room, Ashley impatiently stuck her head inside the door. "Cooper, this is silly."

"I'm almost finished," he mumbled. "This was just a little...more than I'm used to dealing with." His expensive silk tie was loosened, and the long sleeves of his crisp business shirt had been rolled up to his elbows.

Ashley watched from the doorway, highly amused.

"Voilà," he said, pleased with himself, as he stood Scotty up on the table.

Ashley dissolved into fits of laughter. The disposable diaper stuck out at odd angles in every direction. Had he really done this before, or had he just been trying to spare her an unpleasant task? As she was giggling, the diaper began to slide down Scotty's legs, stopping at knee level. She laughed so hard that her shoulders shook.

"Here, let me try," she insisted after a moment, swallowing her amusement as best she could.

Cooper looked almost grateful when she took the baby and laid him back onto the changing table. She did the best she could, but her efforts weren't much better than Cooper's. He was kind enough not to comment.

When she had finished, she paused to look around the room for the first time. Claudia had told her about the bedroom Cooper had decorated for the boys, but she hadn't had a chance to take it all in earlier. Now she could stand back and marvel. The walls were painted blue, with cotton candy clouds floating past and a huge multicolored rainbow with a pot of gold.

Johnny, who had apparently noticed her appreciation, tugged at her hand. "Come look."

Obligingly, Ashley followed.

He closed the door, and flipped the light switch, casting the room into darkness. "See," he said, pointing to the ceiling.

Ashley looked up and noticed a hundred glittering stars illuminated on the huge ceiling. What had been an attractive, whimsical room with the light on became a land of fantasy with the light off.

"It's great," she murmured, her voice slightly thick. Over and over again Claudia had commented on how much Cooper loved the boys. Ashley had seen it herself. He wasn't lofty or untouchable when he was with John and Scott. His affinity for children showed he could be human and vulnerable. He was so warm and loving with the boys that it was all she could do to keep from running into his arms.

Cooper made a show of checking his wristwatch. "Isn't it about time for you boys to go to bed?"

"Can I wear your watch again?" Johnny asked eagerly.

Cooper didn't hesitate, slipping the gold band from his wrist and placing it on his godson's arm.

Ashley couldn't help but wonder at the ease with which Cooper relinquished a timepiece that must have cost thousands of dollars.

Scotty cried when she placed him in the crib. She stayed for several minutes, attempting to comfort him, but to no avail. She would just get him to lie down and tuck him under the blanket when he would pull himself upright, hold onto the bars and look at her with those pleading blue eyes. She couldn't refuse, and finally gave in and lifted him out of the crib.

"Claudia said something about rocking him to sleep."

"No problem," Cooper said with a sly grin. He left and returned a minute later with the wooden rocker from downstairs.

"Will you pray with me, Uncle Cooper?" Johnny—who was also still wide awake—requested, kneeling at his bedside.

Cooper joined the little boy on the plush navy blue carpet.

For the second time that night Ashley was emotionally stirred by the sight of this man with a child.

"God bless Mommy, Daddy and Scotty," John prayed, his head bowed reverently, his small hands folded. "And God bless Uncle Cooper, Auntie Ash and all the angels. And I love you, Jesus, and amen."

"Amen," Cooper echoed softly.

Scotty had his eyes closed as he lay securely in Ashley's arms. Gently she stood to lay him in the crib, but both eyes flew open anxiously and he struggled to sit up. With a short sigh of acquiescence, she sat back down and began to rock again. Content, Scotty watched her, but with every minute his eyes closed a little more. She wouldn't make the mistake of getting up too early a second time. Gently, she brushed the wisps of hair from his brow.

Cooper was sitting on the mattress beside Johnny, who was playing with the wristwatch, his gaze fixed on the lighted digits. Cooper pushed a variety of buttons, which delighted the boy. After a few minutes, Cooper tucked Johnny between the sheets and leaned over to kiss his brow.

"Night, night, Auntie Ash," Johnny whispered.

She blew him a kiss. Johnny pretended to catch it, then tucked his stuffed animal under his arm and rolled over.

The moment was serene and peaceful. Finally sure that Scotty was asleep, she stood and gently put him into the crib. Cooper came to stand at her side, a hand cupping her shoulder as they looked down on the sleeping baby.

Neither spoke, afraid of destroying the tranquility. When they finally stepped back, he removed his hand. Immediately, Ashley missed the warmth of his touch as they headed back downstairs.

He paused at the bottom of the stairs, a step ahead of her. He turned, halting her descent.

"Ashley," he whispered on a soft trembling breath, his look dark and troubled.

A tremor ran through her at the perplexing expression she saw in his eyes. Spontaneously she slipped her arms around his neck without even being aware of what she was doing.

"Ashley," he repeated, the husky sound a gentle caress. He crushed her to him, his arms hugging her waist as his lips sought hers. The kiss was like it had always been between them. That jolt of awareness so strong it seemed to catch them both off guard. When his mouth broke from hers, she could hear his labored breathing and the heavy thud of his heart.

He loosened his hold, bringing his hands up to her neck, weaving long fingers through her hair. His lips soothed her chin and temple, and she gloried in the tingling sensations that spread through her. She continued to lean against him, needing his support, because her legs felt weak and wobbly.

"I'm sorry about the party tonight," he murmured, and she couldn't doubt the sincerity in his voice.

"No, I'm the one who should be sorry. I said so many terrible things to you." Tipping her head back so she could gaze into his impassioned eyes, she spoke again. "I'm amazed you put up with me." Lovingly, she traced the proud line of his jaw, a finger paused to investigate the tiny cleft in his chin. Unable to resist, she kissed him there and loved the sound of his groan.

"Ashley," he warned, "please, it's hard enough keeping my hands off you."

"It is? Really? Oh, Cooper, really?"

"Yes, so don't tease."

"I think that's the nicest thing you've ever said to me."

His hand curved around her waist as he brought her down the last step. "Have you eaten dinner?"

"No, I didn't have time. You?"

"I'm starved. Maybe we can dig up something in the kitchen."

She couldn't see why they needed to look for anything. Her mother did the cooking for him, and there were bound to be leftovers. "Mom—"

"I gave her the rest of the month off," he explained before she could finish.

"Well, in that case, I vote for pizza."

"Pizza?" He glanced at her, aghast.

"All right, you choose." She placed an arm around him and smiled deeply into his dark eyes.

"Let's look." Together they rounded the corner that led to the kitchen. He checked the refrigerator and turned, shaking his head. "I don't know how we'd manage to make pizza from any of this."

"Not make," she corrected. "Order. All we need to do is phone and wait for the delivery guy."

"Amazing." He tilted his head at an inquiring angle. "Is this something you and this Webber fellow do often?"

A denial rose automatically to her lips, but she successfully swallowed it back. "Sometimes. And his name is Dennis Webb."

The corner of his mouth lifted in a half smile. "Sorry." But he didn't look the least bit repentant.

"Do you want me to order?"

He straightened and leaned against the kitchen counter. "Sure, whatever you want."

"Canadian bacon, pineapple and olives."

His dark eyes widened questioningly, but he nodded his agreement.

She couldn't help laughing. "It tastes great, trust me."

"I'm afraid I'll have to."

She used the phone in the kitchen. Cooper regarded her suspiciously when she punched in the number without looking it up in the directory.

"You know the number by heart? Just how often do you do this?"

"I'm good with numbers."

After placing their order, she turned and smiled seductively. "Shall we play a game of chess while we're waiting?"

His look was faintly mocking. "I have a feeling I'd better not."

"Why?" she asked, batting her long lashes.

"If I say yes, then no wagers," he insisted.

"You take all the fun out of it," she said, and feigned a pout. "But I'll manage to whip you anyway."

He chuckled and took her hand, leading them into his den.

While she set up the game board, Cooper lit the logs in the fireplace. Within minutes flickering shadows played across the walls.

His eyes were serious as he sat down opposite her. As before, each move was measured and thought-filled. At mid-game the advantage was Ashley's. Then the doorbell chimed, interrupting their concentration.

Cooper answered and returned with a huge flat box, his look slightly abashed. "You ordered enough for a family of five," he chastised her.

"You said you were hungry," she argued, not lifting her gaze from the game. Her eyes brightened as she moved and captured his knight, lifting it from the board.

"How'd you do that?" His expression turned serious

as he set the pizza on the hearth to keep warm. "I don't want to stop now. We can eat later."

"I'm hungry," she insisted slyly.

He waved her away with the flick of his hand, his attention centered on the board. "You go ahead and eat, then."

She left the room and returned a minute later with a plate and napkin, sitting on the floor in front of the fire. The aroma of melted cheese and Canadian bacon filled the room when she lifted the lid. "Yumm, this is delicious," she said after swallowing her first bite.

A frown drove three wide creases into his brow as he glanced up. "You're eating in here," he said, as if noticing her for the first time.

"I'm not supposed to?" Color invaded her face until her cheeks felt hot. She was always doing something she shouldn't where Cooper was concerned. Her actions had probably shocked him. No doubt he had never in his entire life eaten any place but on a table with a linen cloth. Pizza on the floor made her look childish and gauche.

His expression softened. "It's fine, I'm sure. It's just that I never have."

"Oh." She felt ridiculously close to tears and bowed her head. The pizza suddenly tasted like glue. She closed the lid, then set her plate aside. "The carpet is probably worth a fortune. I wouldn't want to ruin it," she said with total sincerity.

He put a finger under her chin and raised her eyes to his. "Shh," he whispered, and gently laid his mouth over hers.

His kiss had been unexpected, catching her off guard, but quickly she became a willing victim.

"You're right," Cooper murmured, then chuckled. "The pizza does taste good." He lowered himself onto the floor beside her and helped himself to a piece. "Delicious," he agreed, his eyes smiling.

"Can I have a taste?" she asked, a faint smile curving her mouth.

He held out the triangular wedge. She leaned forward and carefully took a bite.

"Thank you," she told him seriously.

With slow, deliberate movements, he placed the pizza box, plates and napkins aside, and reached for her.

Ashley moved willingly into his arms. Sliding her hands around his neck, she raised her face, eager for his attention. Her mouth was trembling in anticipation when he claimed it. A feeling of warmth wove its way through her and seemed to touch Cooper as the kiss deepened.

Somewhere, a long way in the distance, a bell began to chime. Fleetingly, she wondered why it had taken so long to hear bells when Cooper kissed her.

Abruptly, he broke away, grumbling something unintelligible. He briefly touched his mouth to her cheek before he stood and answered the phone.

Six

"It's Claudia," Cooper said, holding out the receiver.

Ashley stood, her movements awkward as the lingering effects of Cooper's kiss continued to stir her senses. "Hello."

"Ash, I'm sorry," Claudia began. "I didn't know Cooper was going to show up. Is everything okay?"

"Wonderful."

"You two aren't arguing, are you?"

"Quite the contrary," Ashley murmured, closing her eyes as Cooper cupped her cheek with his hand. A kaleidoscope of emotions rippled through her.

"Are the boys down?" Claudia inquired.

"The boys?" Ashley jerked her eyes open and straightened. "Yes, they're both asleep."

"Seth and I may be several hours yet. If everything's peaceful, then don't feel like you need to stay. I'm sure Cooper can handle things if the boys wake up. But they probably won't."

"Okay," she agreed. "I'll talk to you later. Don't worry about anything."

The sound of Claudia's soft laugh came over the line. "I don't think I need to. Take care."

"Bye," Ashley said, and replaced the phone. "That was Claudia checking on the boys," she explained unnecessarily.

"I thought it might be," he said, and nuzzled the top of her head. "Let's finish our dinner," he suggested, taking her by the hand and leading her back to the fireplace.

They ate in contented silence. His look was thoughtful as he paused once to ask, "Do you pray?"

The question was completely unexpected.

"Yes," she responded simply. "What makes you ask?"

He shrugged indifferently, and she had the impression he was far more interested than he wanted to admit. "This is the first time I've eaten pizza on the floor with a beautiful woman."

"Beautiful woman?" she teased. "Where?"

His eyes were more serious than she had ever seen them. "You," he answered, and looked away. The steady tone of his voice revealed how sincere he was.

"There are a lot of things I haven't done in my life. Prayer is one of them. Tonight when Johnny had me get down on my knees with him…" He let the rest of what he was going to say fade. "It felt right." He glanced back at her. "Do you kneel down, too, or is that just something for children?"

"I do on occasion, but it certainly isn't necessary."

Cooper straightened, leaning back against the ottoman. "How do you pray?"

Ashley was surprised by the directness of his question. "Whole books have been written on the subject. I don't know if I'm qualified to answer."

"I didn't ask about anyone else, only you," he countered.

"Well," she began, unsure on how best to answer him. "I don't know that anyone else does it like me."

"I've noted on several occasions that you're a free spirit," he muttered, doing his best to hide his amusement. "Okay, let's go at this from a different angle. When do you pray?"

Answering questions was easier for her. "Mostly in the morning, but any time throughout the day. I pray for little things, parking places at the grocery store, and before I pay bills, and over the mail, and also for the big ones, like everyone in my life staying healthy and happy."

"Why mostly in the morning?" He regarded her steadily.

"That's when I do my devotions," she explained patiently.

"What are devotions?"

"Bible reading and praying," she told him. "My private time with the Lord. My day goes better when I've had a chance to discuss things with Jesus."

"You talk to Him as if He were a regular person?"

"He is," she said, more forcefully than she intended.

He paused and appeared to consider her words thoughtfully. "Do you speak to Him conversationally, then?"

"Yes and no."

"You don't like talking about this, do you?"

"It isn't that," she tried to explain, a soft catch in her voice. "If I tell you… I guess I'm afraid you'll think it's silly."

"I won't." The wealth of tenderness in his voice assured her he wouldn't.

"Usually I set aside a formal time for reading my Bible, other devotional books and praying. After I do my Bible reading, I get down on my knees, close my eyes and picture myself on a beautiful beach." She glanced up hesitantly, and Cooper nodded. The warmth in his look seemed to caress her, and she continued. "The scene is perfectly set in my mind. The waves are crashing against the sandy shore and easing back into the sea. I envision the tiny bubbles popping against the sand as the water ebbs out. This is where I meet Christ."

"Does He talk to you?"

"Not with words." She looked away uneasily. "I don't know how to explain this part. I know He hears me, and I know He answers my prayers. I see the evidence of that every day. But as for Him verbally speaking to me, I'd have to say no, though I hear His voice in other ways."

"I don't understand."

"I'm not sure I can explain, I just *do*."

Cooper seemed to accept that. "Then all you do is talk. You make it sound too easy." He seemed unsure, and she hastened to arrest his doubts.

"No, I spend part of the time thanking Him or...praising Him would be a better description, I guess. Another part is spent going over the previous day and asking His forgiveness for any wrongs I've done."

"That shouldn't take a lot of time," he teased.

"Longer than I care to admit," she informed him sheepishly and mentally added that the time had increased since she'd been seeing Cooper. "I also keep a list of requests that I pray about regularly and go down each one."

"Am I on your list?" The question was asked so softly that she wasn't sure he'd even spoken.

"Yes," she answered. "I pray for you every day," she admitted, her voice gaining intensity. She didn't add that all the people she loved were on her list. To avoid other questions she continued speaking. "For a while I wrote out my prayers. That was years ago, and it became a journal of God's faithfulness. But I can't write as fast as I can think, so I found that often I'd lose my train of thought. But I've saved those journals and sometimes read over them. When I do, I'm amazed again at God's goodness to me."

A baby's frantic cry broke into their conversation. "Scotty," Ashley said, bounding to her feet. "I'll go see what's wrong."

Scotty was standing in the crib, holding onto the sides. His crying grew louder and more desperate as she hurried into the room.

"What's wrong, Scotty?" she asked soothingly. Soft light from the hallway illuminated the dark recess of the bedroom. She lifted him out of the crib and hugged him close. Checking his diaper, she noted that he didn't seem to be wet. Probably he'd been frightened by a nightmare. Settling him in her arms, she sat in the rocking chair and rocked until she was sure he was back to sleep. With a kiss on the top of his head, she placed him back in his crib.

Cooper was waiting for her at the bottom of the stairs.

"He's asleep again," she whispered.

"I made coffee, would you like a cup?"

She smiled her appreciation. He curved an arm around her narrow waist, bringing her close to his side as he led her back into the den. A silver tea service was set on his desk. She saw that the remains of their dinner had been cleared away, along with their chess game. Biting into her bottom lip to contain her amusement, she decided not to comment on what a neat-freak he was.

He poured the steaming liquid into the china cups, then offered her one. Her hand shook momentarily as she accepted it. Dainty pieces of delicate china made her nervous, and she would have much preferred a ceramic mug.

"This set is lovely," she said, holding the cup in one hand. Tiny pink rosebuds, faded with age, decorated the teacup. She balanced the matching saucer in the palm of her other hand.

"It was my grandmother's," he said proudly. "There are only a few of the original pieces left."

"Oh." Her index finger tightened around the porcelain handle. In her nervousness, her hand wobbled and the boiling hot coffee sloshed over the side onto her hand and her lap, immediately soaking through her thin corduroy jeans. With a gasp of pain, she jumped to her feet. The saucer flew out of her lap and smashed against the leg of the desk, shattering into a thousand pieces.

"Ashley, are you all right?" Cooper bounded to his feet beside her.

Stunned, she couldn't move, her eyes fixed on the broken china as despair filled her. "I'm so sorry," she mumbled. Her voice cracked, and she swallowed past the huge lump building in her throat.

"Forget the china," he said, and took the teacup out of her hand. "It doesn't matter, none of it matters."

"It does matter!" she cried, her voice wobbling uncontrollably. "It matters very much."

"You've got to get that hand in ice water. What about your leg? Is it badly burned?" He tugged at her elbow, almost dragging her into the kitchen. He brought her to the sink and stuck her hand under the cold water. She looked down to see an angry red patch on the back of her left hand, where the coffee had spilled. Funny, she didn't feel any pain. Nothing. Only a horrible deep regret.

"Cooper, please, listen to me. I'm so sorry...your grandmother's china is ruined because of me."

"Keep that hand under the water," he said, ignoring her words. Then he went to get ice from the automatic dispenser on the refrigerator door.

Ashley looked away rather than face him. She heard the water splash as he dumped the ice into the sink.

"What about your leg?" he demanded.

"It's fine." She tilted her chin upward and closed her eyes to forestall the tears. The burns didn't hurt; if anything, her hand was growing numb with cold. How could she have been so stupid? His grandmother's china...only a few pieces left. His earlier words echoed in her ears until they were nearly deafening.

"Ashley," he whispered, a hand on her shoulder. "Are you all right? You've gone pale. Is the pain very bad? Should I take you to a doctor?"

Talking was impossible, because her throat felt raw and painful, so she shook her head. "Your grandmother's china," she said at last, her voice barely above a tortured whisper.

"Would you quit acting like it's some great tragedy? You've been burned, and that's far more important than some stupid china."

"Do you know what my mother uses for fancy dinners?" she asked in a hoarse voice, then didn't wait for him to answer. "Dishes she picked up at the grocery store. With every ten dollar purchase she could buy another plate at a discount price."

"What has that go to do with anything?" he demanded irritably.

"Nothing. Everything. I swear I'll replace the saucer. I'll contact an antique dealer, I promise..."

"Ashley, stop." His firm hands squeezed her shoulders. "Stop right now. I don't care about a stupid saucer. But I do care about you." His grip tightened. "The saucer means nothing. Nothing," he repeated. "Do you understand?"

Her throat muscles had constricted so that she couldn't speak. Miserably, she hung her head, and her soft curls fell forward, wreathing her face.

She started to tremble, and with a muted groan Cooper hauled her into his arms.

"Honey, it doesn't matter. Please believe me when I tell you that."

She held on to him hard, because only the warmth of his touch was capable of easing the cold that pierced her heart. A lone tear squeezed past her lashes. She loved Cooper Masters so much it had become a physical pain. Never before had she realized how wrong she was for him. He needed someone who...

She wasn't allowed to complete the thought as Cooper's hand touched her face, turning her to meet his gaze. Her tortured eyes tried to avoid him, but he held her steady.

"Ashley, look at me." He sounded gruff, impatient.

But she was determined, and she shook herself loose,

then swayed against him, her fingers spread against his shirt. He found her lips and kissed her with a desperation she hadn't experienced from him. It was as if he needed to confirm what he was saying, to comfort her, reassure her. She knew she shouldn't accept any of it. But one minute in Cooper's arms and it didn't matter. All she could do was feel.

His hands roamed her back as he buried his face in the hair at the side of her face. "Let's sit down."

He took her into the living room and set her down in the soft comfort of the large sofa. Next he opened the drapes and revealed the same view of Puget Sound that they'd enjoyed on Thanksgiving Day, when they'd walked on his property in the rain.

Hands in his pockets, he paused to admire the beauty. "Sometimes in the evening I sit here, staring into the sky, counting the stars." He spoke absently, standing at the far corner of the window, gazing into the still night. "Looking at all that magnificence makes me feel small and very insignificant. One man, alone." His back was to her. "It's times like this that make me regret not having a wife and family. I've worked hard, and what do I have to show for it? An expensive home and no one to share it with." He stopped and turned, their eyes meeting. For a breathless moment they stared at one another. Then he dropped his gaze and turned slowly back to the window.

Confused for a moment, she watched as he turned away from her, as if trying to block her out of his mind. His action troubled her. He stood alone, across the room, a solitary figure silhouetted against the night. What was he telling her? She didn't understand, but she did realize that he had revealed a part of himself others didn't see.

Unfolding her long legs from the sofa, she joined him at the window. Standing at his side, she slipped an arm around his waist as if she'd done it a thousand times.

He smiled at her then, and she couldn't remember ever seeing anything transform a face more. His dark eyes seemed to spark with something she couldn't define. Happiness? Contentment? Pleasure? His smile widened as he looped his arm over her shoulders, and then he brushed her temple with a light kiss.

"Do you have your Christmas tree up yet?"

"No," she whispered, afraid talking normally would destroy the wonderful mood. "I thought I'd put it up tomorrow."

"Would you like some help?"

The offer shocked her. "I'd... I'd love some."

"What time?"

"Probably afternoon." Her sigh was filled with a sense of dread. "I've got to get some shopping done. There are only a few days left, and I've hardly started."

"Me, either, and I still need to get something for the boys."

"I'm afraid I haven't had the chance to shop. The last days of school were so hectic. I hate leaving everything to the last minute like this."

"Why don't we make a day of it?" he suggested. "I'll pick you up, say around ten. We can do the shopping, go for lunch and decorate your tree afterward."

"That sounds wonderful. I'd like that. I'd like it very much."

"And, Ashley..." Cooper said, looking away uncomfortably.

"Yes?"

"I was thinking about buying myself a pair of cowboy boots and wanted to ask your advice about the best place to go."

"I know just the store, in the Pavilion near Southcenter. But be warned, they're expensive." As soon as the words were out, she regretted them. Cooper didn't need to worry about money.

He chuckled and gave her a tiny squeeze. "I wish other people were as reluctant to spend my money."

"We'll see how reluctant I am tomorrow," she murmured with a small laugh.

Seven

Ashley changed clothes three times before the doorbell chimed, announcing Cooper's arrival. Her final choice had been a soft gray wool skirt and a white bouclé-knit sweater. The outfit, with knee-high black leather boots, was one she usually reserved for church, but she wanted everything to be perfect for Cooper.

A warm smile lit up her face as she opened the door. "Morning, you're right on…" She didn't finish; the words died on her lips. Cooper in jeans! Levis so new and stiff they looked as if they would stand up on their own. Her lashes fluttered downward to disguise her shock.

"Morning. You look as beautiful as ever."

"Thank you," she whispered, somewhat bewildered. "Do you want a cup of coffee or something before we go?"

"No, I think we'd better get started before the crowds get too bad."

She lounged back in her seat, content to let him drive. He flipped a switch, and immediately the interior was filled with classical music. She savored the gentle sounds of the string section and glanced up, surprised when the music abruptly changed to a top forty station.

"Why'd you do that?" she asked, her blue gaze sweeping toward him, searching his profile.

"I thought this would probably be more to your liking." His gaze remained on the freeway, the traffic surprisingly heavy for early morning.

"It's not," she murmured, a little of her earlier happiness dissipating with the thought that Cooper assumed she preferred more popular music to the classics. *But don't you?* her mind countered.

They took the exit for Southcenter, a huge shopping complex south of Seattle, but didn't stop there. The area's largest toy store was situated nearby, and they had decided earlier that it would be the best place to start.

The parking lot was already full, so Cooper had to drive around a couple of times before locating a spot at the far end.

His hand cupped her elbow as they hurried inside. Only a few shopping carts were left, and she glanced around, doing her best to squelch a growing sense of panic. The store had barely opened, and already there was hardly room to move through the aisles.

"My goodness," she murmured impatiently. They were forced to wait to move past the throng of shoppers entering the first aisle. "Do you want to come back later?" she asked, glancing at him anxiously.

"I don't think it's going to get any better," he muttered darkly.

"I don't think it will, either. Maybe we should decide

now what we want to buy the boys. That would at least streamline the process. We're going together, aren't we?" At Cooper's questioning glance, she added, "I mean, we'll split the cost."

"I'll pay," he insisted.

"Cooper," she groaned. "Either we divide the cost or forget it."

His mouth thinned slightly. "All right, I should know better. You and that pride of yours."

He looked as if he wanted to add something more, but the crowd moved, and she pushed the cart forward.

"Okay, what should we get Johnny?" Her eyes followed the floor-to-ceiling display of computer games. On the other side of the aisle were more traditional games and puzzles.

"I've thought of something perfect," Cooper announced proudly. "I'm sure you'll agree."

"What?"

"A computer chess game. I saw one advertised the other day."

"He's too young for that," Ashley declared. She hated to stifle Cooper's enthusiasm, but Johnny wasn't interested in chess.

"He's not," Cooper shot back. "I've been teaching him a few moves. It's the perfect gift—educational, too."

"Good," she said emphatically. "Then you get him that, but I want to buy him something he'll enjoy."

Cooper's soft chuckle caught her unaware. "What's so funny?" she asked.

"You." He paused and looked around before lightly kissing her cheek. "I can't think of a thing in the world that you and I will ever agree on. Our tastes are too different." His gaze seemed to be fixed on her softly parted lips. "Do men often have to restrain themselves from kissing you?"

A happy light shimmered from her deep blue eyes. "Hundreds," she teased. Immediately she realized it had been the wrong thing to say. She could almost visualize the wall that was going up between them.

He straightened and pretended an interest in one of the displays.

"Cooper," she whispered, and laid her hand across his forearm. "That was a dumb joke."

"I imagine it was closer to the truth than you realize."

"Oh, hardly," she denied with a light laugh.

An hour and a half later, their packages stored in the booth beside them, Ashley exhaled a long sigh.

"Coffee," Cooper told the waitress, who quickly returned and filled their mugs.

"I can't remember a time when I needed this more," Ashley murmured and took an appreciative sip.

"Me, either. Could you believe that checkout line?"

"But Johnny's going to love his fire truck and hat."

"And his computer chess game."

"Of course," she agreed, grinning.

"At least we agreed on Scotty's gift. That wasn't so difficult, was it?"

Ashley's gaze skipped from Cooper to the stuffed animal beside him, and she burst into peals of laughter. "Oh, Cooper, if only your friends could see you now with that gorilla next to you."

"Yes, I guess that would be cause for amusement."

Digging through her purse, Ashley brought out her Bible, flipping through the worn pages.

"What are you doing now?" he asked in a hushed whisper.

"Don't worry, I'm not going to stand on the seat and start a crusade. I want to find something."

"What?"

"A verse." She paused, a finger marking the place. "Here it is. First Peter 1:4."

"Honestly, you've got to be the only woman in the world who whips out her Bible in a restaurant."

Unaffected by his teasing tone, she laid the book open on the tabletop, turned it sideways and pointed to the passage she wanted him to read. "After what we just went through, I decided I wanted to be sure heaven has reserved seating. It does, look." Aloud she read a portion of the text. "'To obtain an inheritance which is reserved in heaven for you.'"

A hint of a smile quivered at the edges of his mouth. "You're serious, aren't you?"

"Sure I am. I've seen pictures of riots that looked more organized than that mess we were in."

He laughed loudly then, attracting the curious glances of others. "Ashley Robbins, I find you delightful."

Pleased, she beamed and placed the small Bible back inside her purse.

"Where do you want to go next?" he asked as he glanced at his wristwatch.

"Do you need to be back for something?"

He raised his eyes to meet hers. "No," he said, and shook his head to emphasize his denial.

"If you feel like you could brave the maddening crowd a second time, we could tackle the mall."

He looked unsure for a moment. She couldn't blame him. The thought of facing thousands of last-minute shoppers wasn't an appealing one, but she did still have gifts to buy—and he wanted those boots.

"Sure, why not?" he agreed.

Ashley could think of forty thousand hectic reasons why not, but she didn't voice a single one, content simply being with Cooper.

"However, I hope you don't object if we store Tarzan's friend in the trunk of the car," he added, and glanced wryly at the stuffed animal.

The crowds at the mall proved to be even worse than the toy store, but a couple of hours later, their arms loaded with packages, they finally retreated to the car.

Even Cooper, who was normally so calm and reserved, looked a bit ashen after fighting the chaos. They hadn't even stopped for lunch, eating caramel apples instead as they walked from one end of the mall to the other.

"Do you think Claudia will like the necklace?" he asked as he joined her in the front seat and inserted the key into the ignition.

"Of course." Ashley had picked out the turquoise necklace and knew her friend would love it, but he was still skeptical. "Trust me."

"There's something about that phrase that makes me nervous."

"But you didn't buy two. Now I'm curious," she ventured, not paying attention to what he'd said.

"Two? Two what?"

"Necklaces." She gave him an impatient look. Sometimes they seemed to be speaking at complete cross purposes.

"Do you think Claudia would want two?" He gave her a curious glance.

"Of course not," she said with a sigh. "But you always buy me the same thing as Claudia." She didn't add that it had been perfume for the past three Christmases.

"Not this year."

"Really?" Her interested piqued, she asked, "What are you getting me?"

"Like John and Scott, you'll have to wait until Christmas morning."

She was more pleased than she dared show. Not that she would be forced to wait until Christmas, but that she'd moved beyond the same safe category as Claudia. It thrilled her to know that their relationship had evolved to the point that he wanted to get her something different this year.

Cooper played with the radio until he found some Christmas music.

Again Ashley could feel the comforting music float around her, soothing her tattered nerves. "Doesn't that make you want to sing?"

"Every time you say that we have a storm," he complained.

"Killjoy," she muttered under her breath.

A large hand reached over and squeezed hers. "Ready to decorate the tree?"

"More than ready," she agreed. Much of her shopping remained to be done, but she'd promised Claudia that they would head out early Monday morning so there would be plenty of time to finish.

The remainder of the short drive to her apartment was accomplished in a companionable silence. Her mind wandered to the first time Cooper had asked her to dinner after she'd paid off the loan. At the time she would have doubted she could ever sit at his side without being nervous. Now she felt relaxed, content.

Although nothing had ever been openly stated, their relationship had come a long way in the past couple of months. She could only pray that this budding rapport would continue after Claudia, Seth and the boys returned to Alaska.

Ever the gentleman, Cooper took the apartment key away from her and unlocked the door. Men didn't usually do that sort of thing for her, but then again, she probably wouldn't have let anyone but Cooper.

"I put the tree on the lanai until it was time to decorate," she told him, and took his coat, hanging it with hers in the closet. When she turned around Cooper was helping himself to a handful of popcorn.

"I wouldn't eat that if I were you, it's a week old."

He dropped the kernels back into the bowl and wrinkled his nose.

"Quit giving me funny looks like I'm a terrible housekeeper. You're supposed to leave the popcorn out to get stale. It strings easier that way."

"Strings?"

"For the tree."

"Of course, for the tree," he echoed.

She had the uneasy sensation that he didn't know what she meant. Lightly, she shrugged her shoulders. He would learn soon enough.

"Are you hungry?" she asked on her way into the kitchen. "I can make us pastrami sandwiches with dill pickles and potato chips."

"That sounds good, except I'll have my potato chips on the side."

"Cute," she murmured, sticking her head around the corner.

"With you I never know," he complained with a full smile.

While she made lunch, Cooper brought the Christmas tree inside. Since it was already in the stand, all he had to do was find a place to set it in the living room. When he'd finished he joined her in the compact kitchen.

Working contentedly with her back to him, she hummed softly and cut thin slices of pickle.

"You can have one of the chocolates I bought if you like," she told him, as she spread a thick layer of mustard across the bread.

"I thought you said chocolates weren't meant to be shared."

She laughed softly. "I was only teasing."

"Ashley..."

Just the way he spoke her name caused her to pause and turn around.

"I think we should do this before we eat."

"Do what?" Her heart was chugging like a locomotive at the look he was giving her.

"This." He took the knife out of her hand and laid it on the counter. His gaze centered on her mouth.

She gave a soft welcoming moan as his lips fit over hers. All day she'd yearned for his touch. It was torture to be so close to him and maintain the friendly facade, when in her heart all she wanted was to be held and loved by him.

When he dragged his mouth from hers, she knew he felt as unsatisfied as she did. Kissing was quickly becoming insufficient to satisfy either of them. His hands roamed possessively over her back, arching her closer. Again his mouth dipped to drink from the sweetness of hers. With a shuddering breath he released her.

Sensation after sensation swirled through her. These feelings he stirred within her were what God had intended her to feel toward the man she loved, and she couldn't doubt the rightness of them. But what was *he* feeling? Certainly he wasn't immune to all this.

His smile was gentle when he asked, "Did you say something about lunch?"

"Lunch," she repeated like a robot, then lightly shook her head, irritated that she was reacting like a lovesick teenager. No, she mused, Cooper couldn't help but be aware of the powerful physical attraction between them. He was simply much more in control of himself than she was.

A few minutes later she carried their meal into the living room on a tray. He was sorting through her ornaments and looked up. A frown was creasing his brow.

"What's wrong?" she asked, setting their plates on the coffee table and glancing over at him.

"There's something written across these glass ornaments."

"I know," she answered simply.

"But what is it and why?"

A soft smile touched her mouth as she lifted half of her sandwich and prepared to take the first bite. "Remember how I mentioned that I dated the man who sold me Milligan a couple of times?"

"I remember."

The tightness in his voice sent her searching gaze to him a second time. "Unfortunately, Jim was decidedly not a Christian. We saw one another a couple of times in December, and he couldn't understand why I didn't want to do certain things."

"What things?" Cooper's tone had taken on an arctic chill.

"It doesn't matter," she said, and smiled, dismissing his curiosity. The past was over, and she didn't want to review it with him. "But one thing I *am* grateful for is the fact Jim told me the Christmas tree is a pagan custom. He found it interesting that I professed this deep faith in Christ yet chose to allow a pagan ritual to desecrate my home." She set the sandwich aside and knelt beside Cooper on the carpet. "You know, he's right. I was shocked, so I decided to make my Christmas tree Christ centered."

"But how?"

"It wasn't that difficult. The tree is an evergreen, constant, never changing, just as my faith in Christ is meant to be. And Christ died upon a tree. The lights were the easiest part. Jesus asks that each one of us be the light of the world. But when it came to the ornaments, I had to be a little inventive, so I took glitter glue—"

"Glitter glue?" he interrupted.

"Glue that has glitter already in it. It's much easier to write out the fruits of the Holy Spirit that way."

"Hold on, you've lost me."

"Here." She stood and retrieved her Bible from the oak end table. Flipping the pages, she located the verses she wanted. "Paul wrote in his epistle to the Galatians about the fruits of the Christian life."

"Love, joy, peace," he read from each of the pink glass ornaments. "I get it now."

"Exactly," she stated excitedly.

"Clever girl." His thick brows arched expressively.

"Thank you."

"I'm very curious now about how you tie in the popcorn."

"Yes, well…" Frantically, her mind searched for a plausible reason. She hadn't thought about the decorative strings she added each year.

"I've got it," he said. "White and spotless like the Christ child."

"Very good," she congratulated him.

There was a disconcerted look in his eyes as they met hers. "Your commitment to Christ is important to you, isn't it?"

"Vital," she confirmed. "One's relationship with God is a personal thing. But Christ is the most important person in my life. He has been for several years."

"You stopped seeing Madigan because he didn't have the same belief system as you."

"More or less. In some ways we hit it off immediately.

I liked Jim, I still do. But our relationship was headed for a dead end, so I cut it off before either one of us got serious."

"Because he didn't believe the same way as you? Isn't that narrow minded?"

"To me it isn't, and that wasn't the only reason. Cooper…" She paused and held her breath when she saw his troubled look. "Why all the questions? Do you think I'm wrong in the way I believe?"

"It doesn't matter what I think."

"Of course, it matters." *Because you do,* she added silently.

He rose and walked to the far side of the room. "I don't believe the same way you do. Oh, I acknowledge there's a God. I couldn't look at the heavens and examine our world and not believe in a Supreme Being. I accept that Christ was born, but I never have understood salvation, justification and all the rest of it. Everyone talks about the free gift, but—"

A loud knock on her door interrupted him.

She glanced at him and shrugged. She wasn't expecting anyone. She got to her feet, crossed the room and checked the peephole.

"It's Webb," she told Cooper before opening the door.

"Hello, Sweet Thing. How's your day been?" He sauntered into the room whistling "White Christmas" and paused long enough to brush his lips across her cheek. The song died on his lips when he spotted Cooper.

"Webb," Ashley said stiffly, folding her hands tightly together in front of her. "This is Cooper Masters. I believe I've mentioned him."

She watched as the two men exchanged handshakes. "Cooper, this is Dennis Webb."

Ashley wanted to shout at her friend. Webb couldn't have picked a worse time to pop in for one of his spontaneous visits.

"No, I can't say that I recall you mentioning him," Webb announced as he glanced back to Ashley.

She seethed silently and somehow managed a weak smile.

"I can't say the same about you," Cooper muttered in the stiff, formal tone she'd come to hate.

"Would you like to sit down, Webb?" She motioned toward the sofa and glared at him, desperately hoping he would get the message and leave.

"Thanks." He plopped down on the couch and crossed his legs. "You missed a great party last night. Hardly seemed right without you there, Ash. Next time I won't take no for an answer."

Cooper lowered himself onto the far end of the sofa. His back remained rigid.

"I'll make coffee," Ashley volunteered as she left the room, thinking the atmosphere back there was so thick she could taste it.

"I'll see if I can help in the kitchen," she heard Webb say, and a second later he was at her side.

"Who is this guy?" he hissed.

"What do you mean?" she demanded in a hushed whisper, then didn't wait for an answer. "He's my best friend's uncle, and what do you mean I've never mentioned him? I talk about him all the time."

"You haven't," Webb insisted. "Unless he's the one you played chess with and lost?"

"That's him." Her fingers refused to work properly, and coffee grounds spilled across the counter. "Darn, darn, darn."

"I don't care who he is, if he calls me Webber one more time, I'm going to punch him."

"Webb," she expelled her breath and noticed that Cooper was watching her intently from the doorway. She stopped talking and forced a beguiling smile onto her face. Her teeth were clenched so tight her jaw hurt. "Can't you see it's not a good time?" she hissed beneath her breath.

"Are you saying you want me to leave?"

"Yes." She nearly shouted the one word.

Cooper stepped closer. "Is everything all right, Ashley?" he asked in a formal tone, but his burning gaze was focused on Webb.

The look was searing. She had never seen such disapproval illuminated so clearly on anyone's features. Cooper's mouth was pinched, his eyes narrowed. For a crazy second she wanted to laugh. The two men were eyeing one another like bears who had encroached on each other's territory.

"I'm fine. Webb was just saying that he has to go."

"I do?" he said. "Oh, yes, I guess I do." He walked out of the kitchen with Ashley on his heels. "I'll talk to you soon," he told her, his gaze full of meaning.

"Right." She held open the door for him. "Sorry you have to leave so soon."

The look Webb gave her nearly sent her into peals of laughter. "I'll phone you soon," she promised.

"Nice meeting you, Cooper," Webb said graciously.

"Now that I recall, Ash *has* mentioned you. I understand you play a mean game of chess."

"I play," Cooper admitted with a look of indifference.

"I dabble in the game myself," Webb said, tossing Ashley a teasing glance.

"See you later, Webb," she said firmly, and closed the door. The lock clicked shut, and she paused, her eyes closed, and released a long, slow breath.

"Nice fellow, Webber," Cooper said from behind her.

"He's a friend." She had to be certain Cooper understood that her relationship with Webb didn't go any further than that of congenial co-workers.

"I imagine he's the kind of Christian who fits right into that cozy picture you have built in your mind." His tone was almost harsh.

Ashley did her best to ignore it. "Webb's a wonderful Christian man."

"You probably should marry someone like him," he stated with a sharp edge. His gaze narrowed on her. It wasn't difficult to tell that he was angry, but she didn't know why.

"You're upset, aren't you?" she asked, confronting him. Her back was against the door, her hands clenched at her side.

Cooper's long strides carried him to the far side of the room. He tried to ram his hands in his pockets, apparently forgetting he was wearing jeans. That seemed to irritate him all the more.

"We never did eat our lunch," she said shakily.

He glared at the thick sandwich and then back to her. "I'm not hungry."

"Let's decorate the tree, then." She hugged her middle to ward off the cold she felt beginning to surround her. Cooper was freezing her out, and she didn't know what to say or do to prevent him from doing that.

He stared at her blankly, as if he hadn't heard a word she'd said. Helplessly, she watched as he opened the closet door and took out his coat.

"Cooper?" she whispered, but he didn't hesitate, slipping his arms into the sleeves and starting on the buttons.

She was still standing in front of the door, and she decided she wouldn't move, wouldn't let him walk out as if she wasn't there. What had happened? Everything had been so beautiful last night and today, and now, for no apparent reason, he was pushing her away. She felt as if their relationship had taken a giant step backward.

His drawn expression didn't alter as he came to stand directly in front of her. His hand brushed a blond curl off her face and lingered a second to trace a finger across her cheek.

"You really should marry someone like Webber."

"No." The sound was barely audible. "I won't." How could she marry Webb when she loved Cooper?

"Funny how we never seem to do the things we should," he muttered cryptically.

"Cooper?" Her voice throbbed with a feeling she couldn't identify. Agony? Need? Desperation? "What's wrong?" she tried again.

"Other than the fact you and I are as different as night and day?"

"We've always been different, why should it matter now?"

"I don't know," he told her honestly.

"I had a wonderful time today," she whispered, and hung her head to avoid his searching look. Her lashes fluttered wearily. She knew she was losing, but not why. "I don't want it to end like this. I didn't know Webb was coming."

"It isn't Webber," Cooper admitted harshly. "It's everything." An ominous silence followed his announcement. "I like to pretend with you."

"Pretend?" She lifted her gaze, uncertain of what he was admitting.

"You're warm and alive, and you make me yearn for things that were never meant to be."

"Now you're talking in riddles. And I hate riddles, because I can never understand them. I don't understand *you.*"

"No," he murmured, and rubbed a hand across his face. "I don't suppose that's possible."

Ashley didn't know what directed her, perhaps instinct. Of their own volition her arms slipped around his neck. At first he held himself stiff and unyielding against her, but she refused to be deterred. Her exploring fingers toyed with the dark hair at the back of his head. She applied a gentle pressure, urging his mouth to hers. His resistance grew stronger, forcing her to stand on her tip toes and mold herself to him. Gradually, she eased her mouth over his.

He didn't want her kiss, but she could feel the part of him that unwillingly reached out to her.

Abruptly he broke the contact and pulled himself away. Both hands cupped her face, tilting it up at an angle. A smoldering light of something she couldn't decipher burned in his eyes.

"Ashley." The husky tone of his voice betrayed his desire, yet she marveled at his control.

"Hmm?" she answered with a contented whisper.

"Next time I start acting like a jerk, promise me you'll bring me out of my ill temper just like this."

She gave a glad cry and kissed him again. "I promise," she said after a long while.

Eight

"Was Cooper with you Saturday?" Claudia asked as she laid the menu aside.

Most of Monday morning and half the afternoon had been spent finishing up their Christmas shopping. For the past two hours Ashley had dragged Claudia to every antique store she could find.

Her index finger made a lazy circle around the rim of her water glass. "What makes you ask?" A peculiar pain knotted her stomach. It happened every time she suspected Cooper didn't want anyone to know they were seeing one another. She had spent the entire day with him. After decorating the tree they'd gone out to dinner and a movie. It was midnight before he kissed her good night. Yet he hadn't told Claudia anything.

"What makes me ask?" Claudia repeated incredulously. "You mean besides the fact that he mysteriously disappeared for the entire day? Then he saunters in about midnight with a sheepish look. Gets up early Sunday morning whistling. Cooper. Whistling. He even went to church with us again, which surprised both Seth and me."

"What makes you think I had anything to do with it?"

"What is it with you two? You'd think you were ashamed to be seen with one another."

"You're being ridiculous."

"I'm not. Look at how elusive you're being. Were you or were you not with Cooper Sunday?"

"Yes, I was with him."

"Just part of the time?"

"No," she admitted and breathed in heavily. "All day."

"Ash?" Claudia hesitated as if searching for the right words. "I know you're probably going to say this is none of my business, but I've never seen you act like this."

"Act like what?" she returned defensively.

"All our lives you were the fearless one. There didn't seem to be anything you weren't willing to try. I've never seen you so reticent."

Ashley shrugged one shoulder slightly.

"You're in love with Cooper, aren't you?"

A small smile played over Ashley's mouth. "Yes." It felt good to finally verbalize her feelings. "Very much."

Claudia's eyes glinted with an inner glow of happiness. "Who would ever have guessed you'd fall in love with Cooper?"

"I don't know. Probably no one."

"Has he told you he loves you yet?" Claudia asked, obviously doing her best to contain her excitement.

"No, but then I'm not exactly an 'uptown girl,' am I?" The words slipped out more flippantly than she'd intended.

"Ashley," Claudia snapped, "I can't believe you'd say something like that. You're closer to me than any sister could ever—"

"It's not you," Ashley interrupted, lowering her gaze to her half-full water glass. "Cooper's ashamed to be seen with me."

"That's pure nonsense," Claudia insisted.

"I wish it was," Ashley said in a serious tone.

Any additional discussion was interrupted by the waitress, who arrived to take their order.

"Promise me one thing," Claudia asked as soon as the woman was gone, her eyes pleading.

"What?"

"That you won't drag me to any more antique shops. Cooper doesn't care about that saucer, so I don't see why you should."

"But I do," Ashley said forcefully. "I'm going to replace it if I have to look for the rest of my life."

"Honestly, Ash, it's not that big a deal. Cooper would feel terrible if he knew the trouble you're putting yourself through."

"Don't you dare tell him."

Their Cobb salads arrived, and the flow of conversation came to a halt as they began to eat.

"You're planning to come with us Wednesday, aren't you?" Claudia asked, looking up from her salad.

"Is that the day you're taking the boys to Seattle Center Enchanted Forest?" Every Christmas the Food Circus inside the Center created a fantasyland for young children. The large open area was filled with tall trees and a train that enthralled the youngsters. Clowns performed and handed out balloons. "That's Christmas Eve day."

"Brilliant deduction," Claudia teased. "Cooper's going," she added, as if Ashley needed an inducement.

Ashley's blond curls bounced as she laughed. "I'd be

excited about it even if Cooper wasn't coming along. We're going to have a wonderful time. The boys will love it."

"Cooper's been asking Seth a lot of questions," Claudia announced unexpectedly.

"Questions? About what?"

"The Bible." Claudia placed her fork beside her plate. "They spent almost the entire afternoon on Sunday discussing things. When I talked to Seth about it later, he told me that he felt inadequate because some of Cooper's questions were so complicated. Personally, I don't know where Cooper stands with the Lord, but he seems to be having a difficult time with some of the basic concepts." She paused, then added, "He can't seem to accept that salvation is not something we can earn with donations or good works."

"I can understand that," Ashley defended him. "Cooper has worked hard all his life. Nothing's been free. I can see that the concept would be more difficult for him to accept than for others."

Claudia lounged back, a smile twinkling in her eyes. "You really *do* love him, don't you?"

"I'll tell you something else that'll shock you." Ashley nervously smoothed her pant leg. "I've loved him from the time I was sixteen. It's just been…harder to hide lately."

Claudia's expression softened knowingly. "I think I guessed how you felt almost as soon as I saw the two of you together at the airport when Seth and I arrived with the boys. And then, when I thought back, I realized how long it had been going on, at least for you."

"How did you know?" Ashley's eyes narrowed thoughtfully.

"From the time we were teens, it was you who defended Cooper when he did something to irritate me. You were always ready to leap to his defense."

"Was I so obvious?"

"Not at all," Claudia assured her. "Now, are you ready for something else?" She didn't wait for a response. "Cooper's been in love with you since before I married Seth."

"That I don't believe," Ashley argued. She picked up her fork and put it back down twice before finally setting it aside.

"Think about it," Claudia challenged, a determined lift to her chin. "Seth asked me to marry him, and I was so undecided. I knew I loved him, but moving to Alaska, leaving school and all my dreams of becoming a doctor, made the decision difficult. You were telling me to follow my heart, and at the same time Cooper was unconditionally opposed to the whole idea."

"I remember how miserable you were."

"I was more than miserable. I was at the airport wanting to die, I loved him so much, yet I felt it would never work for Seth and me. You told me if I loved him to go after him." Her blue eyes glimmered with the memory, and a soft smile played at the corners of her mouth. "Still, I was undecided, and I looked to Cooper, wanting him to make up my mind for me. It's funny how clearly I can recall that scene now. Cooper glanced from me to you. At the time I didn't recognize the look in his eyes, but I do now. After so many bitter arguments, Cooper looked at you and told me the decision was mine."

"I think you've blown the whole thing out of proportion." Ashley felt safer in denying what her friend thought than placing any faith in it.

"Don't you see?" Claudia persisted. "Cooper changed his mind because, for the first time in his life, he knew what it was to be in love with someone."

"I wish it were true," Ashley murmured sadly, "but if he felt that way four years ago, why didn't he make an effort to go out with me?"

A wayward lock of auburn hair fell across Claudia's cheek. "Knowing Cooper, that isn't so difficult to understand."

"I wish I could believe it, I really do."

Claudia reached across the small table and squeezed Ashley's forearm. "I've been waiting four years to give you the kind of advice you gave me. Go for him, Ash. Cooper needs you."

Ashley's eyes were filled with determination. "I have no intention of letting him go."

Claudia's laugh was almost musical. "In some ways I almost pity my uncle."

Ashley was sitting on the floor with Scott on her lap when Johnny crawled in beside him. "Can we play a game, Auntie Ash?"

Ashley looked into his round blue eyes, unsure. She'd told Claudia she'd watch the boys while her friends wrapped Christmas presents, and she didn't want to get Johnny all wound up.

"What kind of game?"

"Horsey. Uncle Cooper let me ride him, and Scotty and Daddy were the other horsey."

The picture that flashed into her mind produced a

warm smile. "But I wouldn't be a good horse for both you *and* Scotty," she told him gently.

A disappointed look clouded his expressive face, but he accepted her decision. "Can you read?" he asked next, and handed her a book.

"Sure." With her natural flair for theatrics, she began to read from the *Bible Story Book.*

"How many days until Jesus's birthday?" Johnny asked when she'd finished.

"Only a few now. Are you excited to open all your presents?"

Eagerly he shook his head. "If Jesus hadn't been born, would we have Christmas?" He cocked his head at a curious angle so he could look at her.

"No. We wouldn't have any churches or Sunday School, either."

"What else wouldn't we have?"

"If Jesus hadn't come, our world would be a very sad place. Because Jesus wouldn't live in people's hearts, and they wouldn't love one another the way they should."

"We wouldn't have a Christmas tree," Johnny added.

"Or presents, or Easter."

The young boy's eyes grew wide. "Not even Easter?"

"Nope."

Johnny sat quietly for a minute. "Then the best gift of all at Christmas is Jesus."

A rush of tenderness warmed Ashley's heart. "You said it beautifully."

Scotty squirmed out of her arms and onto the thick carpet, crawling with all his might toward the Christmas tree. Ashley hurriedly intercepted him and, with a laugh, swept him from the carpet and into the air high above her head.

Scotty gurgled with delight. "You like this funny looking tree, don't you?" she asked him, laughing. "I bet if you got the opportunity, every present here would be torn to shreds."

The front door closed, and she turned with Scotty in her arms to find Cooper shaking the rain from his hat.

"Hi."

He didn't see her immediately, and as he turned a surprised look crossed his dark features. Almost as quickly the look was replaced with one of welcome that sent her heart beating at an erratic pace.

"Claudia and Seth left you to the mercies of these two again?"

"No, they're wrapping presents. My duty is to keep the boys out of trouble."

He hung his coat in the hall closet and joined her, lifting Johnny into his arms. The boy squeezed Cooper's neck and gave him a moist kiss on the cheek.

"You know what Auntie Ash said?" John leaned back to look at his uncle.

"I can only guess," Cooper replied, his eyes brightening with a smile. Lovingly he searched her face.

"She said if Jesus hadn't been born, we wouldn't have Christmas."

"No, we wouldn't," Cooper agreed.

"I know something else we wouldn't have," she murmured and moistened her lips.

Johnny's gaze followed hers, and he shouted excitedly, "Mistletoe."

Cooper's eyes hadn't left hers, although his narrowed slightly as if he couldn't take them off her.

"Mistletoe," she repeated, her invitation blatant.

Motionless, Cooper held her look, but gave her no indication of what he was thinking.

Two quick strides carried him to her side. Her senses whirled as he placed Johnny on the ground and gathered her in his arms. Half of her pleasure came from the fact that he didn't look around to see if anyone was watching.

Cooper's gaze skidded to the baby she was still holding between them, and he let out a long exaggerated sigh. "No help for this. I can't kiss you properly while you're holding the baby."

"I'll take a rain check," she teased.

"But I won't," he announced, then removed Scotty from her arms and gently set him on the floor.

Ashley started to protest, but before she could utter a sound, Cooper's mouth was over hers. Winding her arms around his neck, she reveled in the feel of him as his hands gripped her narrow waist.

The sound of someone clearing their throat had barely registered with her when he abruptly broke off the kiss and breathed in deeply.

"You two forget something?" Claudia demanded, hands on her hips as she watched them with a teasing smile.

"Forget?" Ashley was still caught in the rapture; clear thinking was almost impossible. Cooper's warm breath continued to caress her cheek, and she knew he was as affected as she was.

"Like Scotty and John?"

"Oh." Ashley gasped and looked around, remembering how the baby had been enthralled with the Christmas tree.

Seth had lifted the baby by the seat of his pants and was holding him several inches off the ground.

"I think we've been found out," Ashley whispered to Cooper.

"Looks that way," he said releasing her.

Seth handed his wife the baby, who cooed happily, and the two men left the room.

"I've been meaning to ask you all day what you're wearing tomorrow," Claudia said, tucking her son close to her side.

"Wearing tomorrow?" Ashley echoed. "I don't understand?"

"To the party." Claudia looked at her as if she had suddenly developed amnesia.

"The party?"

"Cooper's dinner party tomorrow night, of course," Claudia said, laughing lightly.

The world suddenly seemed to come to an abrupt stop. Ashley's heart pounded frantically; the blood rushed to her face. In that instant she knew what it must feel like to be hit in the stomach. Claudia continued to elaborate, giving her the details of the formal dinner party. But Ashley was only half listening; the words drifted off into nothingness. The only sound that penetrated the cloud of hurt and disappointment were the words *family...friends*. She was neither. She was the cook's daughter, nothing more.

She heard footsteps, and her breathing became actively painful as her gaze shifted to meet Cooper's eyes. Standing there, Ashley prayed she would find something in his look that could explain why she had been excluded from the party. But all she saw was regret. He hadn't wanted her to know.

"Ashley, are those tears?" Claudia asked in a shocked whisper. "What did I say? What's wrong?"

In a haze, Ashley looked beyond the concerned face of her friend. Seth was standing with Johnny at his side, a troubled look on his face. Everyone she loved was there to witness her humiliation. Without a word, she turned and walked out of the house.

"Ashley." There was a pleading quality in Cooper's voice as he followed her out of the house. She quickened her pace, ignoring his demand that she wait. By the time he reached her, she was inside her car, the key in the ignition.

"Will you stop?" he shouted, his mouth tight. "At least give me the chance to explain."

Nothing was worth her staying and listening; he'd said everything without having uttered a word. She wanted to tell him that, but it was all she could do to swallow back the tears.

When she started the engine, Cooper tried to yank open the car door, but she was quicker and hit the lock. Jerking the car into reverse, she pulled out of the driveway. One last glance in Cooper's direction showed him standing alone, watching her leave. His shoulders were hunched in defeat.

Her cell phone was ringing even before she reached her small apartment. She knew without looking that it was Cooper. She also knew he would refuse to give up, so finally, in exasperation, she answered.

"Yes," she snapped.

A slight pause followed. "Miss Robbins?"

"Yes?" Some of the impatience left her voice.

"This is Larry Marshall, of Marshall's Antiques. You talked to me this morning about that china saucer you were looking for."

"Did you find one?"

"A friend of mine has the piece you're looking for," he told her.

"How soon can I pick it up?"

"Tomorrow, if you like. There's only one problem," he continued.

"What's that?"

"My friend's shop is in Victoria, Canada."

Ashley wouldn't have cared if it was in Alaska. Replacing Cooper's china saucer was of the utmost importance. He need never know it had come from her. She could give it to Claudia. After writing down the dealer's name and address, she thanked the man and told him she would put a check in the mail to cover his finder's fee.

Immediately after she replaced the receiver, the phone rang again. She stared at it dumbfounded, unable to move as Cooper's name came up on the screen. She stared at it for a long moment, unwilling to deal with him. After several rings she muted the phone and stuck it back inside her purse.

Silence followed, and she exhaled, unaware until then that she'd been holding her breath. Her palms hurt, and she turned her hand over and saw that her long nails had made deep indentations in the sensitive skin of her palm.

For weeks she'd tried to convince herself that Cooper wasn't ashamed to be seen with her, but the love she felt had blinded her to the truth. Even what Claudia had explained to her over lunch couldn't refute the fact that he hadn't invited her to the dinner party.

Twenty minutes later the doorbell chimed.

"Ashley!" Cooper shouted and pounded on the door. "At least let me explain."

What could he possibly say that hadn't already been said more clearly by his action?

Her heart was crying out, demanding that she listen, but she'd been foolish in the past and had learned from her mistakes. She'd been too easily swayed by her love, but not again.

"Please don't do this," he said.

Her resolve weakened. Cooper had never sounded more sincere. She jerked open the hall closet door and whipped her faux fur jacket off the hanger, put it on and zipped it up all the way to her neck. Then she threw open the front door, crossed her arms and stared at a shocked Cooper with defiance flashing from her blue eyes.

"You have three minutes." Unable to look at him, she held up her wrist and pretended an acute interest in her watch.

"Where are you going?" he demanded.

"Two minutes and fifty seconds," she answered stiffly. "But if you must know, I'm going to see Webber. He happens to like me. It doesn't matter to him that my mother's some rich man's cook, or that my father's a laborer."

"It's Webb."

"Dear heaven," she said, and laughed almost hysterically. "You've got me doing it now."

"Ashley," he said, his voice softening. "It doesn't matter to me who your mother is or where your father works.

I'm sorry about the party. I wouldn't want to hurt you for the world."

She bit into the soft skin of her inner lip to keep from letting herself be affected by his words. Her back rigid, she glared at the face of the watch, her body frozen. "Two minutes even," she murmured.

"I didn't think you'd want to come," he began again. "Mostly it's business associates—"

"Don't make excuses. I understand, believe me," she interrupted.

"I'm sure you don't," he countered sharply.

"But I do. I'm the kind of girl who enjoys pizza on the floor in front of a fireplace. I wouldn't fit in, that's what you're saying isn't it? It would be terribly embarrassing for all involved if I showed up wearing red cowboy boots. I might even break a piece of china or, worse yet, use the wrong spoon. No, I understand. I understand all too well." Her eyes and throat burned with the effort of suppressing tears. "Your time's up. Now, if you'll excuse me…" She stepped outside and closed the door.

"I want you to be there tomorrow night," he told her as she turned her key in the lock.

"I don't see any reason to make an issue over it. I couldn't have come anyway, I'm working tomorrow night."

"That's not true," he said harshly.

"You don't stop, do you? Does it give you pleasure to say these things to me…to call me a liar?" she whispered. "I suppose I should have learned how stubborn you are when I was forced to accept the car." She turned her stricken eyes to his. "I'm not lying."

"You told me school's out," he said with calculated anger.

"It is," she said. "This is my second job, the menial one. I'm a waitress, remember?"

Frustration marked his features as he followed her into the parking lot. "Ashley..."

"I'd like to stay and chat, but I have to be on my way." She paused and laughed mirthlessly. "I appreciate what you're trying to do, but you're the last person on God's green earth I ever want to see again. Goodbye, Cooper."

"Try to understand." The glimpse of pain she witnessed in his eyes couldn't be disguised. Despite what he'd done, she hadn't meant to hurt him, but in her own anguish she had lashed back at him. It was better that she leave now, before they said more hurtful things to one another.

A tight smile lingered on her mouth as she stared into his hard features. "I do understand," she whispered in defeat.

"I doubt that," he mumbled, as he opened the car door for her and stepped back.

She could see him in the side mirror, standing stiff and proud, his look angry, arrogant. He almost fooled her, until he lifted a hand and wiped it across his face. When he dropped his arm, she noted the pain and frustration that glittered from his eyes. The sight made her ache inside, but she wouldn't let herself be influenced, not after what he'd done.

Ashley pulled out of the parking lot, intent on doing as she'd said. Webb would know what to say to comfort her. He was her friend, and she needed him. Tears blinded her vision, and she had to wipe them aside at every traffic signal. Tears would shock Webb; he'd never seen her cry.

Webb's car was in the driveway as she pulled in. He must have seen her arrive, because he opened the front door before she'd had time to ring the bell.

"Ashley." He sounded surprised, but his amazement quickly turned to apprehension. "Are you all right? You look upset. You're not crying, are you?"

All she could do was nod. "Oh, Webb," she sobbed, and walked into his arms.

He hugged her and patted her back like a comforting big brother, which was just what she needed. "I don't suppose this has anything to do with that Cooper character, does it?"

Miserably, she nodded. "How'd you know?"

He led her into the house and closed the door. "Because he just pulled up and parked across the street."

Ashley's head snapped up. "You're kidding! You mean he followed me here?" She took a tissue from her purse and blew her nose. "He probably followed me to find out if I was telling the truth."

"The truth?"

"I told him I was coming to see you. Do you mind?" She glanced up at him anxiously.

"Of course I don't mind." Webb's enthusiasm sounded forced. "Cooper's only four inches taller than I am and outweighs me by fifty pounds. Do you think he'll give me a choice of weapons?"

"You're being silly." She laughed, and then, to her supreme embarrassment, she hiccupped.

"Hang on," he said, and disappeared into the kitchen.

A moment later he was back. "Here, drink this." He handed her a bottle of water.

She accepted because it gave her something to do with her hands. Tipping her head back, she took a large swallow.

"You're in love with him, aren't you?"

"Don't be ridiculous. I thoroughly dislike the man," she countered quickly.

"Now that's a sure sign. I wasn't positive before, but that clinched it."

"Webb, don't tease," she pleaded.

"Who's joking?" He led her to a chair, then sat across the room from her. "I've seen it coming on for the last couple of weeks. Other than the fact that he thinks I'm his arch rival and can't seem to get my name right, I like your Cooper."

"He's not mine," she said, more forcefully than she'd meant to.

"Okay, I won't argue. But if you love each other and really want things to work out, then whatever's wrong can be cleared up. If it doesn't, then you have to believe God has other plans for you."

Ashley closed her eyes for a long moment, then opened them and released a weary sigh. "You know, one of the worst things about you is that you're so darn logical. I can't stand it. I've always said an organized desk is the sign of a sick mind."

"And that, my friend, is one of the nicest things you've ever said to me."

They talked for a bit longer, and Webb did his best to raise her spirits. He joked with her, coaxing her to smile. Later they ordered pizza and played a game of Scrabble.

He won royally and refused to discount the fact that her mind wasn't on the game. When he walked her to the car, he kissed her lightly and waved as she backed out of the driveway.

Ashley slept fitfully, her heart heavy. The alarm went off at four-thirty, and she doubted that she'd gotten any rest. Cold water took the sleep out of her eyes, but she looked wan and felt worse. Connecting with the early ferry still meant a five-hour ride across Puget Sound to Victoria, British Columbia. The schedule gave her an hour to locate the antique shop, buy the saucer and connect with the ferry home. The trip would be tiring, and she would barely have enough time to shower and change clothes before leaving for her job at Lindo's Mexican Restaurant.

She had visited the Victorian seaport many times, and its beauty had never failed to enthrall her. Usually she came in summer when the Butchart Gardens were in full bloom. She found it amazing how a city tucked in the corner of the Pacific Northwest could have the feel, the flavor and the flair of England. Even the accent was decidedly British.

Without difficulty she located the small antique shop off one of the many side streets that catered to the tourists. When Larry Marshall phoned she'd been so pleased to have found the saucer that she'd forgotten to ask about the price. She paled visibly when the proprietor cheerfully informed her how fortunate she was to have found this rare piece and she read the sticker. Her mind balked, but her pride made two hundred dollars for one small saucer sound like a bargain.

On the return trip, she stood at the rail. A demon wind whipped her hair across her face and numbed her with its cold. But she didn't leave, her eyes following the narrow strip of land until it gradually disappeared. Only when a freezing rain began to pelt the deck did she move inside. Surprisingly, she fell asleep until the foghorn blast of the ferry woke her as they eased into the dock in Seattle.

An hour later she smiled at Manuel, Lindo's manager, as she stepped in the back door. After hanging her coat on a hook in the kitchen, she paused long enough to tie an apron around her waist.

"There's someone to see you," Manuel told her in a heavy Spanish accent.

She looked up, perplexed.

"Out front," he added.

She peered around the corner to see a stern-faced Cooper sitting alone at a table. His steel-hard eyes met and trapped her as effectively as a vice.

Nine

Carrying ice water and the menu, Ashley approached Cooper. What was he doing here? What about the party?

Dark, angry sparks flashed from his gaze, and a muscle twitched along the side of his jaw as his eyes followed her. "Where have you been all day?" he asked coldly.

Ashley ignored the question. "The daily special is chili verde." She pointed it out on the menu with the tip of her pencil. "I'll be back to take your order in a few minutes." Her voice contained a breathless tremor that betrayed what seeing him was doing to her. She hated herself for the weakness.

"Don't walk away from me," he warned. The lack of emotion in his voice was almost frightening.

"Are you ready to order now?" She took out the small pad from the apron pocket. Her fingers trembled slightly as she paused, ready to write down his choice.

"Ashley." His look was tight and grim. "Where were you?"

"I could say I was with Webb," she said, and swallowed tightly at the implication she was trying to give.

"Then you'd be lying," he added flatly.

"Yes, I would."

"Okay, we'll do this your way. It doesn't matter where you were or what sick game you've been playing with me…"

"Sick game?" she echoed, remarkably calm. A sad smile touched her mouth as she averted her gaze.

"I didn't mean that," he muttered.

"It doesn't matter." She lowered her chin. "You'd think by now that we could accept the fact that we're wrong for one another. Forcing the issue is only going to hurt us." She paused and swallowed past the growing tightness in her throat. "I'm not willing to be hurt anymore."

His narrowed eyes searched hers. "I want you to come to the party with me."

Sadly, she hung her head. "No."

"I've already talked to the manager. He says he doesn't think tonight's going to be all that busy anyway."

"I won't go," she repeated insistently.

"Then I'm not leaving. I'll sit here all night if that's what it takes." The tight set of his mouth convinced her the threat wasn't idle.

"But you can't, your guests…" She stopped, angry at how easily she'd fallen into his plan. "I won't be blackmailed, Cooper. Sit here all night if you like." Her pulse raced wildly.

"All right." His head shifted slightly to one side as he studied the menu. "I'll take a plate of nachos and the special you mentioned."

Furiously, she wrote down the order.

"You stay?" Manuel asked after she called Cooper's

order into the kitchen. "I already call my cousin to come in and work for you. You can go to this important party."

"I'm here to work, Manuel," she explained in a patient tone. "I'm sure there will be enough work for both your cousin and me."

Nothing seemed to be going right. Cooper watched her every action like a hawk studying its prey before the kill. By seven o'clock Manuel's cousin had served nearly every customer. Only two customers were seated in her section. Ashley was convinced Cooper had somehow arranged that. She wanted to cry in frustration.

"Cooper," she pleaded, "won't you please leave? It's almost seven."

"I won't go without you," he told her calmly.

"Talk about sick games," she lashed back, and to her consternation a sensuous smile curved his mouth.

"I'm not playing games," he stated firmly.

"Then if you miss your own party it's your problem." She tried to sound nonchalant.

By seven-fifteen she was pacing the floor, her resolve weakening. Cooper couldn't offend his associates this way. It could hurt him and his business.

Using the need to refill his coffee cup as an excuse, she avoided his gaze as she said, "I don't have anything to wear."

"Cowboy boots are fine. I'll wear mine, if you like." Her hand was suddenly captured between his. "Nothing in the world means more to me than having you at my side tonight."

"Oh, Cooper," she moaned. "I don't know. I don't belong there."

He studied her slowly, his eyes focused on her soft mouth. "You belong with me."

She felt the determination to defy him drain out of her. "All right," she whispered in defeat.

"Thank God." As he hurried out of the booth he added, "I'll meet you at your place."

Numbly she nodded. As it worked out, he pulled into the apartment parking lot directly behind her.

"While you change, I'll phone Claudia."

Ashley wanted to kick herself for being so weak. Examining the contents of her closet, she pulled out a wool blend dress with a Victorian flair. The antique lace inserts around the neck, bodice and cuffs gave the white dress a formal look. The glittering gold belt matched the high heels she chose.

Her fingers shook as she applied a light layer of makeup. After a moment of hurried effort, she gripped the edge of the small bathroom sink as she stopped to pray. It wasn't the first time today that she'd turned to God. She'd tried to pray standing on the deck of the ferry, the wind whipping at her, but somehow the words wouldn't come. The pain of Cooper's rejection had been too sharp to voice, even to God. Now, having finished, she lifted her head and released a shuddering breath. More confident, she added a dab of perfume to the pulse points at her wrists and neck, and stepped out to meet Cooper.

He turned around as she entered the room. A shocked look entered his eyes. "You're beautiful."

"Don't sound so surprised. I can dress up every now and then."

"You're a little pale. Come here, I can change that."

Before she was aware of what he was doing, he pulled her into his arms and kissed her. The demand of his mouth tilted her head back. His hand pressed against her back, arching her against him.

Ashley's breath caught in her lungs at the unexpectedness of his action. Her hands were poised on the broad expanse of his chest, his heartbeat hammering against her palm.

"There." He tilted his face to study her. "Plenty of color now." Releasing her, he held her coat open so she could easily slip her arms inside. "I'm afraid we're going to make something of a grand entrance. Everyone's arrived. Claudia sounded frantic. She said the hors d'oeuvres ran out fifteen minutes ago."

"Is my mother...?" She let the rest of the question fade, sure Cooper would know what she was asking.

"No, it's being catered." With a hand at the back of her waist, he urged her out the door.

"Oh, Cooper." She hurried back inside. "I almost forgot." Her heels made funny little noises against the floor as she rushed into her bedroom and came out with the wrapped package. "Here." She gave it to him.

"Do I have to wait for Christmas?"

"No. It's a replacement for the saucer I broke, the one from your grandmother's service."

"I can't believe... Where did you ever find it?"

"Don't ask."

"Ashley..." He set his hands on her shoulders and turned her around so she was facing him. "Is this what you were up to today?"

She nodded silently.

His mouth thinned as his look became distant. "I think

I went a little crazy looking for you." He slipped an arm around her waist. "We'll talk about that later. If we keep Claudia waiting another minute, she's likely to disown us both."

The street and driveway outside Cooper's house looked like a high performance car showroom. Ashley felt her nerves tense as she clenched her hands in her lap.

"Ashley, stop."

"Stop?"

"I can feel you tightening up like a coiled spring. Every man here is going to be envious of me. Just be yourself."

The front door flew open before they were halfway up the walk. Claudia stood there like an avenging warlord, waving her arms and glaring at them.

"Thank goodness you're here!" she exclaimed forcefully. "If you ever do this to me again, I swear I'll…" Her voice drifted away. "Don't stand out here listening to me, get inside. Everyone's waiting." Her gaze narrowed on Cooper. "And I do mean everyone."

Ashley didn't need to be reminded that some of the most important people in Seattle would be there.

Claudia gave her an encouraging smile, winked and took her coat.

His hand at her elbow, Cooper led Ashley into the living room. The low conversational hum rose as a few guests called out his name. Apparently the champagne had been flowing freely, because no one seemed to mind that Cooper was late to his own party.

He introduced her to several couples, though she knew she couldn't hope to remember all the names. After twenty minutes the smile felt frozen on her face. Someone handed her a glass of what she assumed was wine, but she didn't drink it. Tonight she would need to keep her wits about her in a room full of intimidating people. There was hardly room to maneuver, and she felt as if the walls were closing in around her.

"Is this the little lady who kept us waiting?" A distinguished, middle-aged man with silver streaks at his temples asked Cooper for an introduction.

"I am," she admitted with a weak smile. "I hope you'll forgive me."

"I find it very easy to forgive someone as pretty as you. Maybe we could get together later, so I can listen to your excuse."

"Whoa, Tom," Cooper teased, but his voice contained an underlying warning. "The lady's with me."

With a good-natured chuckle, Tom slapped him across the shoulder. "Anything you say."

Ashley spotted Claudia at the far side of the room. "If you'll both excuse me a minute...?" she whispered.

Claudia caught her eye and arched her delicate brows.

"Boy, am I glad to see a familiar face," Ashley said, and released a slow sigh as she leaned against the wall for support.

"What took you two so long?" Claudia demanded. "I was frantic. You wouldn't believe some of the excuses I gave. Dear heavens, Ash, where were you today? I thought Cooper was going to go mad."

"Canada."

"Canada?" Claudia shot back. "Well, I must admit, that was one place he didn't look. Have you talked to your mother yet? I don't know what he said to her, but he was closed up in his den for an hour afterward. Believe me, he didn't look happy. No one, not even the boys, could get near him."

"I know he feels miserable about the whole thing, but I understand better than he realizes. I wouldn't have invited me to this party, either. Look at me. I stick out like a sore thumb."

"If you do, it's because you're the prettiest woman here."

Ashley's light laugh was forced. "You're a better friend than I thought."

"I *am* your friend, but don't underestimate yourself." A hush came over the room as someone in a caterer's apron made the announcement that dinner was ready. "I don't know why Cooper wouldn't invite you tonight. He wasn't overly pleased with me for letting the cat out of the bag, I can tell you that."

"No, I imagine he wasn't." How much simpler things would have been if she'd stayed innocently unaware. "But I'm glad you did," she murmured, and hung her head. "Very glad." When she glanced up she saw the object of their conversation weaving his way toward her. Progress was slow, as people stopped to chat or ask him a question. Although he smiled and chatted, his probing gaze didn't leave her for more than a moment.

"I don't want you hiding in a corner," he muttered when he finally got to her, and gripped her elbow, then led her toward the huge dining room.

"I'm not hiding," she defended herself. "I just wanted to talk to Claudia for a minute."

"It was far longer than a minute," he said between clenched teeth.

"Honestly, Cooper, are you going to start an argument now? I'm here under protest as it is."

"You're here because I want you here. It's where you belong." His control over his temper seemed fragile.

Rather than say anything she would regret later, Ashley pinched her mouth tightly closed.

The dining room table had been extended to accommodate forty guests. Ashley looked at the china and sparkling crystal, and the fir and candle centerpiece that extended the full length of the table. Everything was exquisite, and she was filled with a sense of awe. She didn't belong here. What was she doing fooling herself?

Cooper sat at the head of the table, with Ashley at his right side. Under normal circumstances she would have enjoyed the meal. The caterers had also supplied four waitresses, and she found herself watching their movements instead of involving herself in idle conversation with Cooper or the white-haired man on her right. Once the salad plates were removed, they were served prime rib, fresh green beans and new potatoes. Every bite and swallow was calculated, measured, to be sure she would do nothing that would call attention to herself. For dessert a cake in the shape of a yule log was carried into the room. She only took one bite, afraid she would end up spilling frosting on her white dress. Once, when she glanced up, she found Cooper watching her, his look both foreboding and thoughtful. If this was a test, she was certain she was failing miserably, and his look did nothing to boost her confidence.

When the meal was finished, she couldn't recall ever being more relieved.

Cooper's hand was pressed to her waist, keeping her at

his side, as they moved into the living room. She didn't join the conversation, only smiled and nodded at the appropriate times. An hour later, her face felt frozen into a permanent smile.

A few people started to leave. Grateful for the opportunity to slip away, she murmured a friendly farewell and left Cooper to deal with his guests.

"I don't know how much more of this I can take," she whispered to Claudia.

"Don't worry, you're doing great. Not much longer now."

"Where's Seth?"

"Checking the boys. He's not much for this kind of thing, either. Haven't you noticed the way he keeps loosening his tie? By the time the evening's over, the whole thing will be missing."

"What time is it?" Ashley muttered.

"Just after eleven."

"How much longer?"

"I don't know. Don't look now, but Cooper's headed our way."

His stern expression hadn't relaxed. He was obviously displeased about something. "I want to talk to you in my den when everyone's gone." His look was ominous as he turned and left.

Primly, Ashley clasped her hands together in front of her. "Heavens, what did I do now?" she asked Claudia.

Claudia shrugged. "I don't know, but for heaven's sake, humor him. Another day like today, and Seth and I are packing our bags and finding a hotel."

By the time the last couple had left, Ashley's stomach was coiled into a hard lump.

The caterers were clearing away glasses and the last of the dishes from the living room when Cooper found her in the corner talking to Seth and Claudia. As Claudia had predicted, Seth's tie had mysteriously disappeared. His arm was draped across his wife's shoulders.

Seth looked over to Cooper. "You don't mind if we head upstairs, do you?"

"No, no, go ahead." Cooper's answer sounded preoccupied. He gestured toward his den. "We'll be more comfortable in there," he said to Ashley.

She tossed Claudia a puzzled look. Cooper didn't look upset anymore, and she didn't know what to think. His face was tight and drawn, but not with anger. She couldn't recall ever seeing him quite like this.

"Oh!" Claudia paused halfway up the stairs and turned around. "Don't forget tomorrow morning. We'll pick you up around ten. The boys are looking forward to it."

"I am, too," Ashley replied.

They entered the familiar den, and he closed the door, leaning against the heavy wood momentarily. He gestured toward a chair, and she sat down, her back straight.

Again he paused. He rubbed the back of his neck, and when he glanced up, it struck Ashley couldn't remember ever having seen him look more tired.

"Cooper, are you feeling all right? You're not sick, are you?"

"Sick?" he repeated slowly. "No."

"What's wrong, then? You look like you've lost your best friend."

"In some ways, I think I have." He moved across the room to his desk, rearranging the few items that littered the top.

Impatiently, Ashley watched him. He'd said he wanted to talk to her, yet he seemed hesitant.

"How do you feel about the way things went tonight?" he asked finally.

"What do you mean? Was the food good? It was excellent. Do I like your friends? I found them to be cordial, if a bit overwhelming. Cooper, you have to remember I'm just an ordinary schoolteacher."

The pencil he'd just picked up snapped in two. "You know, I think I'm sick of hearing how ordinary you are."

"What do you mean?" She watched as his mouth formed a brittle line.

"You ran to a corner to hide every chance you got. You wouldn't so much as lift a fork until you'd examined the way three other people were holding theirs to be sure you did it the same way."

"Is that so bad?" she flared. "I felt safe in a corner."

"And not with me?"

"No!"

"I think that tells me everything I want to know."

"You forced me into coming tonight," she accused him.

"It was a no-win situation. You understand that, don't you?"

She stood and moved to the far side of the room. Cooper was talking down to her as if she was a disobedient child, and she hated it. "No, I don't. But there's very little I understand about you anymore."

"I didn't invite you tonight for a reason!" he shouted.

"Do you think I don't already know that?" she flashed bitterly. "I don't fit in with this crowd."

"That's not why," he insisted loudly.

"If you raise your voice to me one more time, I'm leaving." Tears welled in her eyes. How she hated to cry. Her eyes stung, and her throat ached. "It's not the first time, either, is it?"

"What are you talking about?" He tossed her a puzzled look.

"For a while I thought it was just my overactive imagination. That I was thinking like an insecure schoolgirl. But it's true."

"What are you talking about?" What little patience he had was quickly evaporating.

"The first time we went out, you chose a small Italian restaurant, and I thought you didn't want to be seen with me."

"You can't honestly believe that?" His eyes filled with disbelief.

"Then Claudia phoned on Thanksgiving Day and I was there, but you didn't say a word." She paused long enough to swallow back a sob. "I knew you didn't want Claudia or Seth or anyone else to know I was with you. Even in church when you held my hand, it was done secretively and only when there wasn't a possibility of anyone seeing us."

A tense silence enclosed them.

"You've thought that all this time?" The dark, troubled look was back on his face.

She nodded. "I don't know about you, but I'm tired. I want to go home."

His dark eyes searched her face. She noted the weariness that wrinkled his brow and the indomitable pride in his stern jaw.

He opened the door wordlessly and retrieved her coat.

He didn't say a word until he pulled up in front of her apartment building. "I find it amazing that you could think all those things, yet continue to see me."

"Now that you mention it, so do I," she returned bitterly.

His mouth thinned, but he didn't retaliate.

She handed him her apartment key, and he unlocked the door. She held out her hand, waiting for him to return the key. He didn't seem to notice, his look a thousand miles away.

When he did glance up, their eyes met and held. The troubled look remained, but with flecks of something she couldn't quite decipher. A softness entered as he lowered his gaze to her soft mouth. "It's not true, Ashley, none of it." With that he turned and left.

Stunned, she stood watching him until he was out of sight.

Her room was dark and still when she turned out the light. She hadn't behaved well tonight. That was what had originally upset Cooper. But she'd been frightened, out of her element. Those people were important, and she was nothing. The four walls surrounding her seemed to close in. Why had he left that way? For once, couldn't he have stayed and explained himself? Tomorrow she would make sure everything was cleared up between them. No more misunderstandings, her heart couldn't take it.

"Are you ready, Auntie Ash?" Johnny asked as he bounded into her apartment excitedly the next morning.

"You bet." She bent over to give her godson a big hug.

"You should hurry, 'cause Daddy's driving Uncle Cooper's car," John added.

Ashley straightened. "Where's Cooper?"

"He decided at the last minute not to come. What happened with you two last night?" Claudia asked.

"Why?"

Claudia glanced at her son, who was impatiently pacing the floor. "We'll talk about it later."

"Uncle Cooper bought the car seat just for Scotty," Johnny told her proudly when she climbed in the back seat. "He said I was a big boy and could use a special one with a real seat belt. Watch." He pulled the belt across his small body, and after several tries the lock clicked into place. "See? I can do it all by myself."

"Good for you." Ashley looped an arm around his shoulders.

"You should put yours on, too," Johnny insisted. "Uncle Cooper does."

"I think you're right," she agreed with a wry smile.

It was all Ashley could do not to quiz her friend about Cooper's absence as Seth maneuvered in and out of the heavy traffic.

"Christmas Eve Day," Johnny said as he looked around eagerly. "It's Jesus's birthday tomorrow, and we get to open all our gifts. Scotty's never opened presents."

"I don't think he'll have any problem getting the hang of it," Seth teased from the front seat.

"You're coming tonight, aren't you, Ash?" Claudia half turned to glance into the rear seat.

"I don't know," Ashley said, trying to ignore the heaviness that weighted her heart.

"But I thought it was already settled. Christmas Eve with us and Christmas with your parents."

Ashley pretended an inordinate amount of interest in

the scenery flashing past outside her window. "I thought it was, too." Cooper was saying several things with his absence today. One of them was crystal clear. "Maybe I'll come for a little while. I want to see the boys open the presents from Cooper and me."

"Do I get to open a present tonight?" Johnny demanded.

Claudia threw Ashley a disgruntled look. "We'll see," she answered her son.

The downtown Seattle area was crowded with last-minute shoppers. Amazingly, Seth found a parking place on the street. While Ashley and Claudia dug through the bottoms of their purses for the correct change for the meter, Seth opened the trunk and retrieved the stroller for Scotty.

"Can I put the money in?" Johnny wanted to know.

Ashley handed him the coins and lifted him up so he could insert them into the slot.

"Good boy," Ashley said, and he beamed proudly.

"Now tell me what happened," Claudia insisted in a low voice. "I'm dying to know."

"Nothing, really. He wasn't pleased with the way the party turned out. Mainly, he was disappointed in me."

"In *you*?" Claudia looked surprised. "What did you do? I thought you were fine."

"I don't understand him, Claudia." She couldn't conceal a sigh of regret. "First, he pointedly doesn't invite me and openly admits he didn't want me there. Then he forcefully insists that I attend. And to make matters worse, he doesn't approve of the way I acted."

"If you ask me, I think he's got a lot of nerve," Claudia admitted. "I hardly spoke to him this morning. But something's wrong. He's miserable. He loves you, I'd bet my life on it. It would be a terrible shame if you two didn't get together."

"I suppose."

"You suppose?" Claudia drawled the word slowly. "If you love one another, then nothing should keep you apart."

"Spoken like a true optimist. But I'm not right for Cooper," Ashley announced sadly. "He needs someone with a little more—I hate to use this word, but…finesse."

"And you need someone more easy-going and fun-loving. Like Webb," Claudia finished for her.

"No, not at all." Ashley's cool blue eyes turned questioningly toward her friend. "I'm surprised you'd even suggest that. Webb's a friend, nothing more."

Clearly pleased, Claudia shook her head knowingly. "I don't think you realize that you bring out the best in Cooper, or that he does the same for you. I don't think I've seen a couple who belong together more than you two."

"Oh, Claudia, I hope we do, because I love him so much."

"Have you ever thought about letting *him* know that?"

A blustery wind whipped Ashley's coat around her, preventing her from answering.

"I think we should catch the monorail," Seth suggested. "It's getting windy out here. Agreed?"

The two women had been so caught up in their conversation they'd hardly noticed.

"Fine." Ashley shook her head.

"Sure," Claudia said, looking a little guilty as Seth handled both boys so she could talk.

For a nominal fee they were able to catch the transport

that had been built as part of the Seattle World's Fair in 1962. The rail delivered them to the heart of the Seattle Center, only a few blocks from the Food Circus.

The boys squealed with delight the minute they spied the Enchanted Forest. Scotty clapped his hands gleefully and pointed to the kiddy size train that traveled between artificial trees.

"Are you hungry?" Seth wanted to know.

"Not me." Ashley's thoughts were on other things.

"I wouldn't object to cotton candy," Claudia confessed.

"I had to ask," Seth teased, and lovingly brushed his lips over his wife's cheek.

Ashley viewed the tender scene with building despair. Someday, she wanted Cooper to look at her like that. More than anything else, she wanted to share her life with him, have his children.

"Ash, are you all right?" Claudia asked.

Quickly, she shook her head. "Of course. What made you ask?"

"You looked so sad."

"I am, I…"

"My goodness, Ash, look, Cooper's here."

"Cooper?" Her spirits soared. "Where?"

"Across the room." Claudia pointed, then waved when he saw them.

His level gaze crossed the crowded room to hold Ashley's, his look discouraging.

"I'm going to do it," Ashley said, straightening. Claudia gave her a funny look, but didn't question her as she started toward him.

They met halfway. He looked tired, but just as determined as she felt.

"Ashley."

"I want to talk to you," she said sternly.

"I want to talk to *you*, too."

"Wonderful. Let me go first."

He looked at her blankly. "All right," he agreed.

"You asked me last night why I continued to see you if I believed all those things I confessed. I'll tell you why. Simply. Honestly. I love you, Cooper Masters, and if you don't love me, I think I'll die."

Ten

"That's not the kind of thing you say to a man in a public place." He studied her face for a tantalizing moment, gradually softening.

"I know, and I apologize, but I couldn't hold it in any longer."

"Why couldn't you have told me that last night?"

Oblivious to the crowds milling around, they stared at one another with only a small space separating them.

"Because I was afraid, and you were so…"

Cooper rubbed a hand across his eyes. "Don't say it. I know how I was."

"When you weren't with Claudia this morning, I didn't know what to think."

"I couldn't come. Not when you believed that I didn't want to be seen with you—that I was ashamed of you. You've carried that inside all these weeks, and not once did you question me."

Her teeth bit tightly into her lower lip. "I was afraid. Sounds silly, doesn't it?" She didn't wait for him to answer. "Afraid if I brought my fears into the open and forced you to admit it, that I wouldn't see you again. I couldn't face the truth if it meant losing you."

"The day you started ranting about your mother being my cook and your father being a steelworker... Was that the reason?"

She looked away and nodded.

Slowly he shook his head. "I can understand how you came to that conclusion, but you couldn't be more wrong. I love you, Ashley, I—"

"Cooper, oh, Cooper," she cried excitedly and threw her arms around him, spreading happy kisses over his face.

His mouth intercepted her as he hungrily devoured her lips. Although she could hear the people around them, she wouldn't have cared if they were in New York City at Grand Central Station. Cooper loved her. She'd prayed to hear those words, and nothing, not even a Christmas crowd in a public place, was going to ruin her pleasure.

When he dragged his mouth from hers, his husky voice breathed against her ear, "Do you promise to do that every time I admit I love you?"

"Yes, oh, yes," she said with a joyous smile.

He cleared his throat self-consciously. "In case you hadn't noticed, we have an audience."

She was too contented to care. A searing happiness was bubbling within her. "I want the whole world to know how I feel."

"You seem to have gotten a good start," he teased with an easy laugh, and kissed the top of her head. "Don't look now, but Claudia and company are headed our way."

Reluctantly, Ashley dropped her arms and stepped

back. Cooper pulled her close to his side, cradling her waist.

"Is everything okay with you two, or do you need more time?" Claudia's gaze went from one of them to the other. "If that embrace was anything to go by, I'd say things are looking much better."

"You could say that," Cooper agreed, his eyes holding Ashley's. The look he gave her was so warm and loving that it seemed to burst free and touch her heart and soul.

"But there are several things we need to discuss," Cooper continued. "If you don't mind, I'm going to take Ashley with me. We'll all meet back at the house later."

Claudia and Seth exchanged knowing looks. "We don't mind," Seth answered for them.

"But… Seth has your car," Ashley said, confused. "How will we…?"

He smiled. "I have a second car, since I can't afford to be without transportation. We'll be fine."

"Do I still get to open a present tonight? Because Auntie Ash said we could," Johnny quizzed anxiously, not the least bit interested in the logistics of the grownups' plans.

Cooper's eyes met Claudia's, and she shrugged.

"I think that will be fine, if that's what your Auntie Ash said," Seth interrupted.

"Uncle Cooper?" John's head tilted up at an inquiring angle.

"Yes?" He squatted down so that he was eye level with his godson.

"Is there mistletoe here, too?"

Briefly Cooper scanned the interior of the huge building. "I don't see any, why?"

"'Cause you were kissing Auntie Ash again."

"Sometime I like to kiss her even when there isn't any reason."

"You mean like Daddy and Mommy?"

"Exactly," he said, and smiled as his eyes caught Ashley's.

"I think it's time we left and let these two talk. We'll meet you later," Seth announced. Claudia lifted Johnny into her arms and turned around, then looked back and winked.

"Are you hungry?" Cooper asked.

She hadn't eaten all day. "Starved. I hardly touched dinner last night."

"I noticed." His tone was dry.

She ignored it. "And then this morning I was too miserable to think about food. But now I could eat a cow."

"We're at the right place. Choose what you want, and while you find us a table, I'll go get it."

The Food Circus had a large variety of booths that sold every imaginable cuisine. The toughest decision was making a choice from everything that was available.

They hardly spoke as they ate their chicken. Ashley licked her fingers. Cooper carefully unfolded one of the moistened towelettes that had been provided with their meal and carefully cleaned his own hands.

He glanced up and found her watching him. A tiny smile twitched at the corner of her mouth. "What's so funny?" he asked.

"Us." She opened her own towelette and followed his example. "Claudia told me she didn't know any two people more meant for one another."

Cooper acknowledged the statement with a curt nod. "I know I love you, whether we're right or wrong for one another doesn't seem to be the question." He reached across the table and captured her hand. "But then, you're an easy person to love. You're warm and alive, and so unique you make my heart sing just watching you."

"And you're so calm and dignified. Nothing rattles you, and so many times I've wished I could be like that."

"We balance one another." His eyes searched hers in a room that seemed filled with only them.

A burst of applause diverted Cooper's attention to the antics of a clown. "Let's get out of here."

Ashley happily agreed.

They stood, dumped their garbage in the proper receptacles and linked their arms around one another's waists as they strolled outside.

A chill raced over her forearms, and she shivered.

Cooper brought her closer to his side. "Cold?"

"Only when you close me out," she whispered truthfully. "If you hadn't admitted to loving me, I don't know that I could have withstood the cold."

He drank deeply from her eyes, perhaps realizing for the first time how strong her emotions rang. "We need to talk," he murmured, and quickened his pace.

A half hour later he pulled into the driveway of his home.

"Coffee?" he suggested as he hung her coat in the hall closet.

"Yes." She nodded eagerly. "But, Cooper, could I have it in a mug? I'd feel safer."

His mouth thinned slightly, and she knew her request had troubled him. "I'm not the dainty teacup type," she said more forcefully than she wanted to. "What I mean is..."

"I know what you mean." Lightly he pressed a kiss on her cheek, then against the hollow of her throat. "Do you have any idea how difficult it's been this week to keep my hands off you?"

"Not half as difficult as it's been not to encourage you to touch me," she admitted, and felt color suffuse her cheeks.

A few minutes later he carried two ceramic mugs into the den on a silver platter.

A soft smile danced from Ashley's eyes. "Compromise?"

"Compromise," he agreed, handing her one of the mugs.

She held it with both hands and stared into its depths. "I have a feeling I know what you're going to say."

"I doubt that very much, but go ahead."

"No." She shook her head, then nervously tugged a strand of hair around her ear. "I've put my foot in my mouth so many times that for once I'm content to let you do the talking."

"We seem to have a penchant for saying the wrong things to each other, don't we?" His gaze searched hers, and the silence was broken only by an occasional snap and pop from the logs in the fireplace.

His look was thoughtful as he straightened in his chair. Nervously, she glanced around the den she had come to love—the books and desk, the chess set. One of the most ostentatious rooms in the house and, strangely, the one in which she felt the most comfortable. Maybe it was because this was the room Cooper used most often.

"I think it's important to clear away any misunderstandings, especially about the party. Ashley, when I saw how hurt you were to be excluded, well… I can't remember ever feeling worse. Believe this, because it's the truth. I wanted you there from the first. But I felt you would be uncomfortable. Those people are a lot like me."

"But I love you," she said, keeping her gaze on her coffee.

"I didn't know that at the time. I didn't want to do anything that was going to make you feel ill-at-ease. Thrusting you into my world could have destroyed our promising relationship, and that was far more important to me. Now I realize what a terrible mistake that was."

"And the other things?" She had to know, had to clear away any reasons for doubt.

"Thinking over everything you've told me, your point of view makes perfect sense." He set his cup aside and sat on the ottoman in front of her chair. Holding her face with both hands, he tilted her gaze to meet his. Ashley couldn't doubt the sincerity of his look. "I did those things because I thought you wouldn't want to be associated with me. I didn't let Claudia know you were here on Thanksgiving when she phoned to protect you from speculation and embarrassing questions. The same with what happened in church."

"Oh, Cooper…" She groaned at her own stupidity. "I was so miserable. I know it was stupid not to say anything, but I was afraid of the truth."

His kiss was sweet and filled with the awe of the discovery of her love. "Things being what they are, maybe you should open your Christmas gift now."

"Oh, could I?"

"I think you'd better." He opened the closet and brought out a large, beautifully wrapped box.

Much bigger than an engagement ring, Ashley mused thoughtfully, fighting to overcome her disappointment. Cowboy boots? She'd tried on a couple of pairs when they'd bought his, but she'd decided against them because of the expense. But if her present was cowboy boots, why would Cooper feel it was important to give it to her now?

He placed it on her lap, and she untied the red velvet bow, then hesitated. "My gift to you is at home." It was important that he know he'd meant enough to her to buy him something special. "But I'm making you wait until Christmas."

"Maybe I should make *you* wait, too," he teased, ready to take back the gaily wrapped present.

"No you don't," she objected, and gripped the package tightly.

"Actually," he said, and the teasing light left his eyes, "it's important that you open this now." He smiled huskily and kissed her. His lips were a light caress across her brow.

Ashley's fingers shook as she pulled back the paper and lifted the lid of the box. Inside, nestled in white tissue, was a large family Bible. Her heart was thumping so loudly she could barely hear Cooper speaking above the hammering beat.

"A Bible," she murmured and looked up at him, her gaze probing his.

"I've thought about what you said about your relationship with Christ, and how important it was to you. I wanted to have a strong faith for you, because of my love. But that wasn't good enough. There were so many things I didn't understand. If Christ paid the price for my salvation with His life, then how can my faith be of value if all

I have to do is ask for it?" He stood and walked across the room, pausing once to run his hand through his hair. "I talked to Seth about it several times. He always had the answers, but I wasn't convinced. Last Sunday I was in church, sitting in the sanctuary waiting for the service to begin, and I asked God to help me. On the way out of church after the service I saw the car I had given you in the parking lot. Suddenly I knew."

Ashley had been at church, but she had taught Sunday School and then helped in the nursery during the worship service. She had talked only briefly to Claudia and hadn't seen Cooper at all.

"My car? How did my car help?"

"It sounds crazy, I know," he admitted wryly. "But I gave it to you because I love you. Freely, without seeking reimbursement, knowing that you couldn't afford a car. It was my gift to you, because I love you. It suddenly occurred to me that was exactly why Christ died for me. He paid the price because I couldn't."

Unabashed tears of happiness clouded her eyes as her hands lovingly traced the gilded print on the cover of the Bible.

"I've made my commitment to Christ," he told her, his voice rich and vibrant. "He's my Savior."

"Oh, Cooper." She wiped a tear from her cheek and smiled up at him.

"That's not all."

An overwhelming happiness stole through her. She couldn't imagine anything more wonderful than what he'd just finished explaining.

"Do you recall the first Sunday Claudia and Seth arrived?"

Ashley nodded.

"I stepped into your Sunday School class." He looked away as a glossy shine came over his dark eyes. "You were on the floor with a little girl sitting in your lap."

"I remember. You turned around and walked out. I thought I'd done something to upset you."

"Upset me?" he repeated incredulously. "No. Never that. You looked up, and your blue eyes softened, and in that moment I imagined you holding another child. Ours. Never have I felt an emotion so strong. It nearly choked me, I could hardly think. If I hadn't turned around and walked away, I don't know what I would have done."

Ashley thought her heart would burst with unrestrained joy. "Our child."

"Yes." Cooper knelt on the floor beside her, took the Bible out of its box and set the box on the floor. Reverently, he opened the first pages of the holy book. "I got this one for a reason. I've written our names here, and I'm asking that we fill the rest out together."

Ashley looked down at the page, which had been set aside to record a family history. Both their names were entered under "Marriage," the date left blank.

"Will you marry me, Ashley?" he asked, an unfamiliar humble quality in his voice.

The lump of joy in her throat prevented her from doing anything but nodding her head. "Yes," she finally managed. "Yes, Cooper, yes." She flung her arms around his neck and spread kisses over his face. She laughed with breathless joy as the tears slid down her cheeks.

His arms went around her as he pulled her closer. His mouth found hers in a lingering kiss that cast away all doubts and misgivings.

She lovingly caressed the side of his face. "I don't know how you can love me. I always seem to think the worst of you."

"Not anymore you won't," he whispered against her temple as he continued to stroke her back. "I won't ever give you reason to doubt again. I love you, Ashley."

She linked her hands behind his neck and smiled contentedly into his eyes. "I do want children. Just being with Johnny and Scott has shown me how much I want babies of my own."

"We'll fill the house. I can't wait to tuck them into bed at night and listen to their prayers."

"What about horsey rides?"

"Those, too."

"Cooper…" She paused and swallowed tightly. "Why were you so angry with me after the party?" She wanted everything to be right and needed to know what she'd done to displease him.

Some of the happiness left his face. "I love you so much, Ashley. It hurt me to see you so uncomfortable, afraid to make a move. Your fun-loving, outgoing nature had been completely squelched. I wanted you to be yourself. Later—" He sat on the ottoman and took both her hands in his. "—I had already gotten the Bible with the hope of asking you to marry me, and you listed off all the things I had done to make you believe I was ashamed to be seen with you. I don't mind telling you that it shook me up. I was on the verge of asking you to be my wife, and you didn't even know how much I loved you."

"I won't have that problem again," she told him softly.

"I know you won't, because you'll never have reason to doubt again. I promise you that, my love."

The sound of footsteps in the hall brought their attention to the world outside the door.

Cooper stood, and extended a hand toward her. "I don't think either Claudia or Seth will be surprised by our announcement. Or your family, for that matter."

"My family?"

"I talked to your mother and father yesterday. They've given us their blessing. I was determined to have you, Ash. I wouldn't want to live my life without you now." He hugged her tightly and curved an arm around her waist. "Christmas. It's almost too wonderful to believe. God gave His Son in love. And now He's given me you."

* * * * *

THE MATCHMAKERS

One

"Danny, hurry up and eat your cereal," Dori Robertson pleaded as she rushed from the bathroom to the bedroom. Quickly pulling on a tweed skirt and a sweater, she slipped her feet into black leather pumps and went back into the kitchen.

"Aren't you going to eat, Mom?"

"No time." As fast as her fingers would cooperate, Dori spread peanut butter and jelly across two pieces of bread for a sandwich, then opened the refrigerator and took out an orange. She stuffed both in a brown paper sack with a cartoon cat on the front. Lifting the lid of the cookie jar, she dug around and came up with only a handful of crumbs. Graham crackers would have to do.

"How come we're always so rushed in the mornings?" eleven-year-old Danny wanted to know.

Dori laughed. There'd been a time in her life when everything had fit into place, but not anymore. "Because your mother has trouble getting out of bed."

"Were you always late when Dad was still alive?"

Turning, Dori leaned against the kitchen counter and

crossed her arms. "No. Your father used to bring me a cup of coffee in bed." Brad had had his own special way of waking her with coffee and kisses. But now Brad was gone and, except for their son, she faced the world alone. Still, the rushed mornings were easier to accept than the long lonely nights.

"Want me to bring you coffee? I could," Danny offered. "I've seen you make it lots of times."

A surge of love for her son constricted the muscles of her throat, and Dori tried to swallow. Every day Danny grew more like his father. Tenderly she looked down at his sparkling blue eyes and the freckles that danced across his nose. Brad's eyes had been exactly that shade of bottomless blue, though the freckles were all hers. Pinching her lips together, she turned back to the counter, picked up a cup and took her first sip of lukewarm coffee. "That's very thoughtful of you," she said.

"Then I can?"

"Sure. It might help." Anything would be better than this insane rush every morning. "Now brush your teeth and get your coat."

When Danny moved down the hallway, Dori carried his empty cereal bowl to the sink. The morning paper was open, and she folded it and set it aside. Danny used to pore over the sports section, but recently he'd been reading the want ads. He hadn't asked for anything in particular lately, and she couldn't imagine what he found so fascinating in the classified section. Kids! At his age, she remembered, her only interest in the paper had been the comics and Dear Abby. Come to think of it, she didn't read much more than that now.

Danny joined her in the kitchen and together they went

out the door and into the garage. While Dori backed the Dodge onto the narrow driveway, Danny stood by and waited to pull the garage door shut.

"One of these days," she grumbled as her son climbed into the front seat, "I'm going to get an automatic garage-door opener."

Danny gave her a curious look. "Why? You've got me."

A smile worked its way across Dori's face. "Why, indeed?"

Several minutes followed while Danny said nothing. That was unusual, and twice Dori's eyes sought his. Danny's expression was troubled, but she didn't pry, knowing her son would speak when he was ready.

"Mom, I've been wanting to ask you something," he began haltingly, then paused.

"What?" Dori said, thinking the Seattle traffic got worse every morning. Or maybe it wasn't that the traffic got heavier, just that she got later.

"I've been thinking."

"Did it hurt?" That was an old joke of theirs, but Danny didn't have an immediate comeback the way he usually did.

"Hey, kid, this is serious, isn't it?"

Danny shrugged one shoulder in an offhand manner. "Well, I know you loved Dad and everything, but I think it's time you found me another dad."

Dori slammed on her brakes. The car came to a screeching halt at the red light as she turned to her son, eyes wide with shock. "Time I did *what?*" she asked incredulously.

"It's been five years, Mom. Dad wouldn't have wanted

you to mope for the rest of your life. Next year I'm going to junior high and a kid needs a dad at that age."

Dori opened her mouth, searching for words of wisdom that didn't come.

"I can make coffee in the morning, but that's not enough. You need a husband. And I need a dad."

"This is all rather…sudden, isn't it?" Her voice was little more than a husky murmur.

"No, I've been thinking about it for a long time." Danny swiveled his head and pointed behind him. "Hey, Mom, you just missed the school."

"Darn." She flipped on her turn signal and moved into the right lane with only a fleeting glance in her rearview mirror.

"Mom…watch out!" Danny shrieked just as her rear bumper barely missed the front end of an expensive foreign car. Dori swerved out of its path, narrowly avoiding a collision.

The driver of the other car blared his horn angrily and followed her when she pulled into a side street that would lead her back to the grade school.

"The guy you almost hit is following you, Mom, and, boy, does he look mad."

"Great." Dori's fingers tightened around the steering wheel. This day was going from bad to worse.

Still looking behind him, Danny continued his commentary. "Now he's writing down your license plate number."

"Wonderful. What does he plan to do? Make a citizen's arrest?"

"He can do that?" Danny returned his attention to his flustered mother.

"Yup, and he looks like the type who would." Judging by the hard, uncompromising face that briefly met hers in the rearview mirror... The deep-set dark eyes had narrowed, and the thick, equally dark hair was styled away from his face, revealing the harsh contours of his craggy features. He wasn't what could be called handsome, but his masculinity was blatant and forceful. "A man's man" was the term that came to mind.

"I recognize him," Danny said thoughtfully. "At least I think I do."

"Who is he?" Dori took a right-hand turn and eased to a stop in front of Cascade View Elementary. The man in the BMW pulled to a stop directly behind her and got out of his car.

"He looks familiar," Danny commented a second time, his wide brow furrowed in concentration, "but I don't know from where."

Squaring her shoulders, Dori reluctantly opened the car door and climbed out. She brushed a thick swatch of auburn hair off her shoulder as she walked back to meet the tall formidable man waiting for her. His impeccable suit and expensive leather shoes made him all the more intimidating. His eyes tracked her movements. They were interesting and arresting eyes in a face that looked capable of forging an empire—or slicing her to ribbons—with one arch of a brow. Dori was determined not to let him unnerve her. Although she indicated with her hand that Danny should stay by the car, he seemed to think she'd need him for protection. She didn't have time to argue.

"I don't appreciate being followed." She decided taking the offensive was her best defense.

"And I don't appreciate being driven off the road."

"I apologize for that, but you were in my blind spot and when I went to change lanes—"

"You didn't even look."

"I most certainly did," Dori said, her voice gaining volume. For the first time she noticed a large brown stain on his suit jacket. The beginnings of a smile edged up the corners of her mouth.

"Just what do you find so amusing?" he demanded harshly.

Dori cast her eyes to the pavement. "I'm sorry. I didn't mean to be rude."

"The most polite thing you can do is stay off the road."

Hands on her hips, Dori advanced one step. "In case you weren't aware of it, there's a law in Washington state against drinking any beverage while driving. You can't blame me if you spilled your coffee. You shouldn't have had it in the car in the first place." She prayed the righteous indignation in her tone would be enough to assure him she knew what she was talking about.

"You nearly caused an accident." He, too, advanced a step and a tremor ran through her at the stark anger in his eyes.

"I've already apologized for that," Dori said, knowing that if this confrontation continued she'd come out the loser. Discretion was the better part of valor—at least that was what her father always claimed, and for once Dori was willing to follow his advice. "If it'll smooth your ruffled feathers, I'll pay to have your suit cleaned."

The school bell rang, and Danny hurried back to the car for his books and his lunch. "I've got to go, Mom."

Dori was digging around the bottom of her purse for a

business card. "Okay, have a good day, hon." She hoped one of them would; hers certainly didn't look promising.

"Don't forget I've got soccer practice after school," he reminded her, walking backward toward the steps of the school.

"I won't."

"And, Mom?"

"Yes, Danny?" she said irritably, the tight rein on her patience slackening.

"Do you promise to think about what I said?"

Dori glanced at him blankly.

"You know, about getting me another dad?"

Dori could feel the hot color creep up her neck and invade her face. Diverting her gaze from the unpleasant man standing beside her, she expelled her breath in a low groan. "I'll think about it."

A boyish grin brightened Danny's face as he turned and ran toward his classmates.

Searching for a business card helped lessen some of Dori's acute embarrassment. Another man might have said something to ease her chagrin, but not this one. "I'm sure I've got a card in here someplace."

"Forget it," the man said gruffly.

"No," she argued. "I'm responsible, so I'll pay." Unable to find the card, after all, Dori wrote her name and address on the back of her grocery list. "Here," she said, handing him the slip of paper.

He examined it briefly and stuck it in his suit pocket. "Thank you, Mrs. Robertson."

"It was my fault."

"I believe you've already admitted as much." Nothing seemed likely to crack this man's granite facade.

"I'll be waiting for the bill, Mr...?"

"Parker," he said grudgingly. "Gavin Parker." He retreated toward his car.

The name was strangely familiar to Dori, but she couldn't recall where she'd heard it. Odd. Danny had recognized him, too.

"Mr. Parker," Dori called out.

"Yes?" Irritably he turned to face her again.

"Excuse me, but I wonder if I could have another look at the paper I gave you."

His mouth tightened into an impatient line as he removed the slip from his pocket and handed it back.

She scanned the grocery list, hoping to commit it to memory. "Thanks. I just wanted to make sure I remembered everything."

He looked at her coldly, and by the time Dori was in her car and heading for the insurance office, she'd forgotten every item. Just the memory of his eyes caused a chill to race up her spine. His mouth had been interesting, though. Not that she usually noticed men's mouths. But his had been firm with that chiseled effect so many women liked. There was a hard-muscled grace to him— Dori reined in her thoughts. How ridiculous she was being. She refused to spend one extra minute on that unpleasant character.

The employee parking lot was full when she arrived and she was forced to look for a place on the street, which was nearly impossible at this hour of the morning. Luckily, she found a narrow space three blocks from the insurance company where she was employed as an underwriter for homeowner policies.

By the time she got to her desk, she was irritated, exhausted and ten minutes late.

"You're late," Sandy Champoux announced as Dori rolled back her chair.

"I hadn't noticed," Dori returned sarcastically, dropping her purse in a bottom drawer and pretending an all-consuming interest in the file on her desk as her boss, Mr. Sandstrom, sauntered past.

"You always seem to make it to your desk on time," Sandy said, ignoring the sarcasm. "What happened this morning?"

"You mean other than a near-accident with a nasty man in an expensive suit or Danny telling me I should find him a new father?"

"He's right, you know."

Purposely being obtuse, Dori batted her thick lashes at her friend and smiled coyly. "Who's right? Danny or the man in the suit?"

"Danny! You *should* think about getting married again. It's time you joined the world of the living."

"Ah—" Dori pointed her index finger at the ceiling "—you misunderstand the problem. Danny wants a father the same way he wanted a new bike. He's not interested in a husband for me...." She paused and bit her bottom lip as a thought flashed into her mind. "That's it." Her eyes lit up.

"What's it?" Sandy demanded.

"The bike."

"You're going to bribe your son so he'll forget his need for a father?" Sandy was giving Dori the look she usually reserved for people showing off pictures of their children.

"No, Sandy." Dori groaned, slowly shaking her head. "You don't want to know."

Frowning, Sandy reached for a new policy from her basket. "If you say so."

Despite its troubled beginnings, the day passed quickly and without further incident. Dori was prepared to speak to her son when he stomped into the house at five-thirty, his soccer shoes looped around his neck.

"Hi, Mom, what's there to eat?"

"Dinner. Soon."

"But I'm starved *now*."

"Good, set the table." Dori waited until Danny had washed his hands and placed two dinner plates on the round oak table before she spoke. "I've been thinking about what you said this morning."

"Did it hurt?" Danny asked and gave her a roguish grin, creating twin dimples in his freckled face. "What did you decide?"

"Well…" Dori paid an inordinate amount of attention to the cube steak she was frying, then said, "I'll admit I wasn't exactly thrilled with the idea. At least not right away."

"And now?" Danny stood at the table, watching her keenly.

She paused, gathering her resolve. "The more I thought about it," she said at last, "the more I realized you may have a valid point."

"Then we can start looking?" His voice vibrated with eagerness. "I've had my eye on lots of neat guys. There's Jason—he helps the coach with the soccer team. He'd be real good, but I don't think he's old enough. Is nineteen too young?"

This was worse than Dori had thought. "Not so fast," she said, stalling for time. "We need to go about this methodically."

"Oh, great," Danny mumbled. He heaved a disgusted sigh. "I know what that means."

"It means we'll wait until the dinner dishes are done and make up a list, just like we did when we got your bike."

Danny brightened. "Hey, that's a great idea."

Dori wasn't as sure of that as Danny was. He bolted down his dinner, and the minute the dishes were washed and put away, he produced a large writing tablet.

"You ready?" he asked, pausing to chew on the tip of the eraser.

"Sure."

"First we should get someone as old as you."

"At least thirty-three," Dori agreed, pulling out a chair.

"And tall, because Dad was tall and it'd look funny if we got a short guy. I don't want to end up being taller than my new dad."

"That makes sense." Again Dori was impressed by how seriously her son was taking this.

"He should like sports 'cause I like sports. You try, Mom, but I'd like someone who can throw a football better than you."

That was one duty Dori would relinquish gladly. "I think that's a good idea."

"And it'd be neat if he knew karate."

"Why not?" Dori agreed amicably.

Danny's pencil moved furiously over the paper as he added this latest requirement to the growing list. "And

most important—" the blues eyes grew sober "—my new
dad should love you."

"That would be nice," Dori murmured in a quavering voice. Brad had loved her. So much that for a while
she'd thought she might die without him. Even after all
these years, the capacity to love another man with such
intensity seemed beyond her.

"Now what?" Danny looked up at her expectantly.

"Now," she said, taking a giant breath. "Now that we
know what we're looking for, all we need to do is wait
for the right man to come along."

Danny seemed doubtful. "That could take a long
time."

"Not with both of us looking." She took Danny's list
and attached it to the refrigerator with a large strawberry
magnet. "Isn't it time for your bath, young man?"

Danny shoved the pad and pencil into the kitchen
drawer and headed down the hall that led to his bedroom.

Dori retired to the living room, took out her knitting and turned on the television. Maybe Danny was
right. There had to be more to life than work, cooking
and knitting. It wasn't that she hadn't tried to date; she
had. Sandy had fixed her up with a friend of a friend at
the beginning of summer. The evening had turned out
to be a disaster, and Dori had refused her friend's at-
tempts to match her up again. Besides, there hadn't been
any reason to date. She was fairly content and suffered
only occasionally from bouts of loneliness, usually late
at night. Danny filled her life. He loved sports and she
loved watching him play.

But Danny did need a father figure, especially now as
he reached adolescence. Dori didn't see how any other

man could replace Brad. Danny had been too young to remember much about his father, since Brad had died when Danny was just six. Her own memories of that age were vague and distant, and she wondered how much she would have remembered of her father if she'd been in Danny's place.

The house was unusually quiet. Danny was normally in and out of the bath so quickly that she often suspected he didn't get completely wet.

Just as she was about to investigate, Danny ran into the room, clutching a handful of sports cards. "Mom, that was Gavin Parker you nearly ran into today!"

Dori glanced up from her knitting. "I know."

"Mom—" his voice was filled with awe "—why didn't you *say* something? I want his autograph."

"His autograph?" Suddenly things were beginning to add up. "Why would you want that?"

"Why?" Danny gasped. "He's only the greatest athlete in the whole world."

Dori decided to ignore her son's exaggeration. Gavin Parker might be a talented sportsman of some kind, but he was also rude and arrogant. He was one man she instinctively wanted to avoid.

"Here, look." Danny shoved a football card under her nose.

Indeed, the name was the same, but the features were younger, smoother, more subdued somehow. The dark piercing eyes in the picture merely hinted at the capacity for aggression. Gavin Parker's appearance had altered over the years and the changes in him were due to more than age. The photo that stared back at her was of an intense young man, full of enthusiasm and energy for life.

The man she'd met today was angry and bitter, disillusioned. Of course, the circumstances of their meeting hadn't exactly been conducive to a friendly conversation.

The back of the card listed his height, weight and position—quarterback. According to the information, Gavin had played for the Raiders, leading his team to two Super Bowl championships. In the year he'd retired, Gavin had received the Most Valuable Player award.

"How did you know who he was?" Dori asked in a tone of surprise. "It says here that he quit playing football six years ago."

"Mom, Gavin Parker was one of the greatest players to ever throw a football. *Everyone* knows about him. Besides, he does the commentary for the Vikings' games on Sundays."

Every Sunday afternoon, Dori and Danny joined her parents for dinner. Vaguely, Dori recalled the football games that had captured the attention of the two men in her life: her father and her son. It was a sport that had never interested her very much.

"Can we ask him for his autograph?" Danny asked hopefully.

"Danny," Dori said with a sigh, yanking hard on the wool, "I sincerely doubt we'll ever see Mr. Parker again."

His shoulders sagged with defeat. "Darn. Now the guys won't believe me when I tell 'em my mom nearly ran Gavin Parker off the road."

"You may find this hard to believe," Dori admitted softly, "but I'd rather not have the world know about our little mishap this morning, anyway."

"Aw, Mom."

"Haven't you got homework?"

"Aw, Mom."

She felt her lips curve and her resolve not to smile vanished. "The room seems to have developed an echo."

Head drooping, Danny returned to his bedroom.

The following morning, in the early dawn light, Dori was awakened by a loud knock on her bedroom door. Struggling to lift herself up on one elbow, she brushed the wild array of springy auburn curls from her face.

"Yes?" The one word was all she could manage.

Already dressed in jeans, Danny entered the bedroom, a steaming cup of coffee in his hand.

"Morning, Mom."

"My eyes are deceiving me," she mumbled, leaning back against the pillow. "I thought I saw an angel bearing me tidings of joy and a cup of java."

"Nope," Danny said with a smile. "This is coffee."

"Bless you, my child."

"Mom?"

"Hmm?" Still fighting off the urge to bury her face in the pillow and sleep, Dori forced her eyes open.

"Do... I mean, do you always look like this when you wake up?"

Dori blinked self-consciously and again smoothed the unruly mass of curls. "Why?"

Clearly uneasy, Danny shuffled his feet and stared at the top of his tennis shoes. "If someone saw you with your hair sticking out like that, I might never get a new dad."

"I'll try to do better," she grumbled.

"Thanks." Appeased, Danny left, giving Dori the opportunity to pout in private. Muttering to herself, she threw back the sheets and climbed out of bed. A glance in the bathroom mirror confirmed what Danny had said. And her hair wasn't the only thing that needed improvement.

By the time Dori arrived in the kitchen, she'd managed to transform herself from the Wicked Witch of the West to something presentably feminine.

One look at his mother, and Danny beamed her a radiant smile of approval. "You're really pretty now."

"Thanks." She refilled her cup with coffee and tried to hide her grimace at its bitterness. Later, with the utmost tact and diplomacy, she'd show Danny exactly how much ground coffee to use. Any more of this brew, she thought, would straighten her naturally curly hair.

"Do you think we might see Gavin Parker on the way to school?" her son asked brightly as they pulled out of the driveway.

"I doubt it," Dori answered. "In fact, I doubt Mr. Parker lives in Seattle. He was probably just visiting."

"Darn. Do you really think so?"

"Well, keep your eyes peeled. You never know."

For the remainder of the ride to the school, Danny was subdued, studying the traffic. Dori was grateful he didn't catch a glimpse of Gavin Parker. If he had, she wasn't sure what Danny would've expected her to do. Running him off the road again was out of the question. She felt lucky to have come away unscathed after yesterday's encounter.

Danny didn't mention Gavin again that day or the next, and Dori was convinced she'd heard the last about "the world's greatest athlete." But the following Monday a cleaning bill arrived in the mail.

The envelope was typed, and fleetingly Dori wondered if Mr. Gavin Parker had instructed his secretary to mail the bill. In addition to the receipt from a downtown dry cleaner, Gavin had sent back her grocery list. Hot color blossomed in Dori's cheeks as she turned it over and saw the bold handwriting. At the bottom of her list Gavin had added "Driving lessons." Dori crumpled the paper and tossed it into the garbage.

The sooner she ended her dealings with this rude man the better. She'd just finished writing the check when Danny wandered into the room.

"What can I have for a snack?" he asked as he looked over her shoulder.

"An apple."

"Can I have some cookies, too?"

"All right, as long as you promise to eat a decent dinner." Not that there was much worry. Danny had developed a perpetual appetite of late. The refrigerator door opened behind her.

"Hey, Mom, what's this?"

Dori glanced over her shoulder at the yellow nylon bag Danny was holding up, pinched between forefinger and thumb. "Tulip bulbs. For heaven's sake, don't eat one."

He ignored her attempt at humor. "How long are they going to be in here?"

Dori flushed slightly, recalling that she'd bought them on special six weeks earlier. "I'll plant them soon," she said.

Loudly crunching a crisp red apple, Danny pulled up the chair across from her. "What are you doing?"

"Paying a bill." Guiltily she looked down at her checkbook, deciding to leave well enough alone and not mention *whose* bill she was paying. Another one of her discretion-and-valor decisions.

Saturday morning, Dori came out of her bedroom, sleepily tying the sash of her housecoat. The sound of cartoons blaring from the living room assured her that Danny was already up. An empty cereal bowl on the table was further testimony. The coffee was made, and with a soft smile she poured a cup and diluted it with milk.

"You're up." Danny came into the kitchen and grinned approvingly when he saw she'd combed her hair.

"Don't get hooked on those cartoons," she warned. "I want us to get some yard work done today."

Danny's protest was immediate. "I've got a soccer game."

"Not until eleven-thirty."

"Aw, Mom, I hate yard work."

"So do I," she said, although planting the tulip bulbs was a matter of pride to her. Otherwise they'd sit in the vegetable bin for another year.

Twenty minutes later, dressed in washed-out jeans and a faded sweatshirt that had seen better days, Dori got the hand trowel from the garage.

The day was glorious. The sun had broken through and splashed the earth with golden light. The weather was unseasonably warm for October; the last days of an Indian summer graced Seattle.

Danny was content to rake the leaves that had fallen from the giant maple tree onto the sidewalk, and Dori was surprised to hear herself humming. The scarf that held her hair away from her face slipped down and she pushed it back with one hand, smearing mud on her cheek.

She was muttering in annoyance when Danny went into peals of excitement.

"You came, you came!" Danny cried enthusiastically.

Who came? Stripping off her gloves, Dori rose to find Gavin Parker staring at her from across the yard.

"This had better be important," he said as he advanced toward her.

Two

"Important?" Dori repeated, not understanding. "What?"

"This." Impatiently Gavin shoved a slip of paper under her nose.

Not bothering to read the message, Dori shrugged. "I didn't send you anything other than the check."

His face reddening, Danny stepped forward, the bamboo rake in his hand. "You didn't, Mom, but I... I did."

Dori's response was instinctive and instant. "What?" She jerked the paper from Gavin's fingers. "I MUST TALK TO YOU AT ONCE—D. ROBERTSON" was typed in perfect capital letters. "In person" was written beneath.

"You see," Danny went on to explain in a rushed voice, "Mom said we'd probably never see you again and I want your autograph. So when Mom put the envelope on the counter to go in the mail, I opened it and stuck the note inside. I *really* want your autograph, Mr. Parker. You were the greatest quarterback ever!"

If Gavin felt any pleasure in Danny's profession of undying loyalty, none was revealed in the uncompromising line of his mouth. From the corner of her eye, Dori glimpsed a blonde fidgeting in the front seat of his car, which was parked in the street. Obviously Gavin Parker had other things on his mind.

Placing a protective arm around her son's shoulders, Dori met Gavin's unflinching gaze. "I apologize for any inconvenience my son has caused you. I can assure you it won't happen again."

Taking his cue from the barely restrained anger vibrating in his mother's voice, Danny dropped his head and kicked at the fallen leaves with the toe of his tennis shoe. "I'm sorry, too. I just wanted your autograph to prove to the guys that Mom really did almost drive you off the road."

A car door slammed and Dori looked up. Shock mingled with disbelief. It wasn't a woman with Gavin Parker, but a young girl. No more than thirteen and quite pretty, but desperately trying to hide her femininity.

"What's taking so long?" The girl strolled up in faded blue jeans and a Seahawks football jersey. The long blond hair was pulled tightly away from her face and tied at her nape. A few curls had worked themselves free and she raised a disgruntled hand to her head, obviously displeased with the way they'd sprung loose.

A smile lit her eyes as she noticed that Danny was wearing a football jersey identical to her own. "Hey, do you like the Seahawks?"

"You bet. We're gonna make it to the play-offs this year," Danny boasted confidently.

"I think so, too. My dad used to play pro ball and he says the Hawks have a good chance."

Dimples appeared on Danny's freckled face as he smiled, nodding happily.

"Get back in the car, Melissa." Gavin's tone brooked no argument.

"But, Dad, it's hot in there and I'm thirsty."

"Would you like a glass of orange juice?" Danny offered enthusiastically. "Gosh, I didn't think girls liked football."

"I know everything there is to know about it and I throw a good pass, too. Just ask my dad."

Before either Gavin or Dori could object, Melissa and Danny were walking toward the house.

Dori raised her brows in question. "I'll trade you one cup of coffee for an autograph," she said resignedly. A cup of Danny's coffee was poetic justice, and a smile hovered at the corners of her mouth.

For the first time since their dubious beginning, Gavin smiled. The change that simple movement made in his austere expression was remarkable. Deep lines fanned out from his eyes and grooves that suggested smiles and even laughter bracketed his mouth. But the transformation didn't stop with his face. Somehow, in some way, the armor he wore had cracked as she was given a rare dazzling smile.

Unfortunately his good humor didn't last long, and by the time he'd followed her into the house the facade was back in place.

Melissa and Danny were at the kitchen table, sipping from tall glasses filled with orange juice.

"Dad—" Melissa looked up eagerly "—can Danny go to the Puyallup Fair with us? It's no fun to go on the rides by myself and you hate that kind of stuff."

"I'm afraid Danny's got a soccer game this afternoon," Dori said.

"I'm the center striker," Danny inserted proudly. "Would you like to come and watch me play?"

"Could we, Dad? You know I love soccer. When the game's over we could go to the fair." Melissa immediately worked out their scheduling.

It was all happening so fast that Dori didn't know what to think.

"Mrs. Robertson?" Gavin deferred to her for a decision.

"What time would Danny be home tonight?" Dori asked, stalling for time. Gavin Parker might be a famous football player, but he was a stranger and she wasn't about to release her child to someone she didn't know. If she had to come up with an excuse, she could always use church the following morning and their weekly dinner with her parents.

"You have to come, too," Melissa insisted. "Dad would be bored to tears with Danny and me going on all the rides."

"Could we? Oh, Mom, could we?"

Needing some kind of confirmation, Dori sought Gavin's eyes.

Gavin said quietly, "It would make Melissa happy."

But not him. It didn't take much for Dori to tell that Gavin wasn't pleased with this turn of events. Not that she blamed him. The idea of spending an afternoon with two children and a dirt-smudged mom wouldn't thrill her, either.

Apparently seeing the indecision in her eyes, Gavin added, "It would solve several problems for me."

"Oh, Mom, could we?" repeated Danny, who seemed

to have become a human pogo stick, bouncing around the kitchen.

"Who could refuse, faced with such unabashed enthusiasm?" Dori surrendered, wondering what she was letting herself in for. She gave Gavin the address of the nearby park where the game was to be played and arranged to meet him and Melissa there.

Granted a new audience, Danny was in top form for his soccer game. With boundless energy he ran up and down the field while Dori answered a multitude of questions from Melissa. No, Dori explained patiently, she wasn't divorced. Yes, her husband was dead. Yes, she and Danny lived alone. Danny was eleven and in the sixth grade.

Then Melissa said that her parents were divorced and her dad had custody. She boarded at a private school in Seattle because her dad traveled so much. As the vice president in charge of sales in the whole northwest for a large computer company, her dad was really busy. In addition, he did some television commentaries for pro football games on Sunday afternoons, and she couldn't always go with him.

Standing on the other side of his daughter, Gavin flashed her a look that silenced the girl immediately. But her father's censure didn't intimidate Melissa for long, and a few minutes later she was prodding Dori with more questions.

Danny kicked two of his team's three goals and beamed proudly when Gavin complimented him on a fine game. A couple of the boys followed the small group back to the car, obviously hoping one or the other would get up enough courage to ask Gavin for his autograph. Since even the discouraging look he gave them wasn't enough to dissuade the boys, Gavin spent the next five minutes scribbling his name across a variety of slips of paper, hurriedly scrounged from jacket pockets.

The party of four stopped at the house so Danny could take another of his world-record-speed baths and change clothes. While they were waiting, Melissa watched Dori freshen her makeup. When Dori asked the girl if she'd like to use her cologne, Melissa looked at her as though she'd suggested dabbing car grease behind her ears.

"Not on your life. No one's going to get me to use that garbage. That's for sissies."

"Thanks, anyway," Gavin murmured on the way out to the car.

"For what?"

"I've been trying for months to turn this kid into a girl. She's got the strongest will of any female I've yet to meet."

Dori couldn't imagine Gavin losing any argument and was quick to conceal her surprise that his daughter had won this battle.

The Puyallup Fair was the largest agricultural fair in Washington state. Situated in a small farming community thirty miles southwest of Seattle, the fair attracted visitors from all over western Washington and presented top Hollywood entertainment.

As a native Seattleite, Dori had been to the fair many times in the past and loved the thrill and excitement of the midway. The exhibits were some of the best in the country. And the food was fabulous. Since Gavin had paid for their gate tickets, Dori treated everyone to hush puppies and cotton candy.

"Can we go to the rides now?" Melissa asked eagerly, her arms swinging at her side.

The crowds were thick, especially around the midway, giving Dori reason for concern.

"I think I'd rather look at some of the exhibits before you two run loose," she said, turning to Gavin. His stoic expression told her he didn't care either way.

If Melissa was disappointed at having to wait, she didn't show it. Spiritedly she ran ahead, pointing out the displays she and Danny wanted to see first.

Together they viewed the rabbits, goats and pigs. Despite herself, Dori laughed as Melissa and Danny ran through the cow barn holding their noses. Gavin, too, seemed to be loosening up a little, and his comments regarding Melissa's and Danny's behavior were quite amusing, to Dori's surprise.

"Dad, look." Melissa grabbed her father's arm as they entered the chicken area and led him to an incubator where a dozen eggs were set under a warm light. A tiny beak was pecking its way through the white shell, enthralling everyone who watched.

The bee farm, its queen bee marked with a blue dot, was another hit. Fascinated, Danny and Melissa studied the inner workings of a hive for several minutes. As they left, Dori stopped to hear a ten-minute lecture from a wildlife group. Gavin and the kids weren't nearly as interested, but they all stood and listened to the plight of the American bald eagle.

From the animal barns, they drifted to the 4-H displays and finally to the agricultural center.

Two hours later, Dori and Gavin sat drinking coffee

at a picnic table on the outskirts of the midway while the two kids lined up for rides.

"You don't like me much, do you?" Gavin's direct approach shocked her a little.

It wasn't that she actually disliked him. In fact, she'd discovered she enjoyed his sharp wit. But Dori didn't try to fool herself with the belief that Gavin had actively sought her company. Having her and Danny along today simply made this time with his daughter less complicated.

"I haven't made up my mind yet." She decided to answer as straightforwardly as he'd asked.

"At least you're honest."

"I can give you a lot more honesty if you want."

A slow smile crinkled around his eyes. "I have a feeling my ears would burn for a week."

"You're right."

A wariness was reflected on Gavin's face. "I've attracted a lot of gold diggers in my day. I want you to understand that I have no intention of remarrying."

What incredible conceit! The blood pounded angrily through Dori's veins. "I don't recall proposing marriage," she snapped.

"I didn't want you to get the wrong idea. You're a nice lady and you're doing a good job of raising your son. But he's looking for a father, or so he's said, and you're looking for a husband. Just don't try to include me in your rosy little future."

Dori's hand tightened around the cup of coffee as she fought back the urge to empty the contents over his head.

She noticed the beginnings of a smile. "You have the most expressive eyes," he said. "There's no doubt when you're angry."

"You wouldn't be smiling if you knew what I was thinking."

"Temper, temper, Mrs. Robertson."

"Far be it from me to force myself on you, Mr. Parker." The derision in her voice was restrained to a minimum. Dori was astonished that she'd managed this much control. Standing, she deposited her half-full coffee cup in a nearby bin. "Shall we synchronize our watches?"

He stared at her blankly.

"Three hours. I'll meet you back here then."

With his attitude, she'd enjoy herself more alone. There were still a lot of exhibits to see. Staying with Gavin was out of the question now. Undoubtedly he'd spend the entire time worrying that she was going to slip a wedding ring on his finger.

Standing hastily, Gavin followed her, confusion narrowing his eyes. "Where are you going?"

"To enjoy myself. And that's any place you're not."

Stopping in his tracks, Gavin looked stunned. "Wait a minute."

Dori jerked the strap of her purse over her shoulder. "Forget it." Rarely had a man evoked so much emotion in her. The worst part, Dori thought, was that given the slightest encouragement, she could come to like Gavin Parker. He was a mystery—and she always enjoyed a mystery. Melissa was an impressionable young girl, desperately in need of some female guidance. It was obvious the girl was more than Gavin could handle. From their conversation during Danny's soccer game, Dori had learned that Melissa spent very few weekends with her father. Dori could only speculate as to the whereabouts of the girl's mother, since Melissa hadn't mentioned her. And Dori didn't want to pry openly.

"You know what your problem is, Gavin Parker?" Dori stormed, causing several people to turn and stare curiously.

Gavin cleared his throat and glanced around self-consciously. "No, but I have a feeling you're going to tell me."

Having worked herself up to a fever pitch, Dori hardly heard him. "You've got a chip on your shoulder the size of a California redwood."

"Would it help if I apologized?"

"It might."

"All right, I'm sorry I said anything. I thought it was important that you understand my position. I don't want you to go home smelling orange blossoms and humming 'The Wedding March.'"

"That's an apology?" Dori yelped.

People were edging around them as they stood, hands on their hips, facing each other, their eyes locked in a fierce duel.

"It's the best I can do!" Gavin shouted, losing his composure for the first time.

A vendor who was selling trinkets from a nearby stand apparently didn't appreciate their arguing in his vicinity. "Hey, you two, kiss and make up. You're driving away business."

Gavin tucked her arm in his and led her away from the milling crowd. "Come on," he said, then took a deep breath. "Let's start over." He held out his hand for her to shake. "Hello, Dori, my name is Gavin."

"I prefer Mrs. Robertson." She accepted his hand with reluctance.

"You're making this difficult."

"Now you know how I feel." She bestowed her most chilling glare on him. "I hope you realize I have no designs on your single status."

"As long as we understand each other."

Dori was incredulous. If he wasn't so insulting, she would have laughed.

"Well?" He was waiting for some kind of response.

"I'm going to look at the farm equipment. You're welcome to join me if you like. Otherwise, I'll meet you back here in three hours." It simply wasn't a real fair to Dori if she didn't take the time to check out the latest in farm gear. She supposed that was a throwback to her heritage. Her grandfather had owned an apple orchard in the fertile Yakima Valley—often called the apple capital of the world.

Gavin rubbed the side of his clean-shaven face and a fleeting smile touched his mouth. "Farm equipment?"

"Right." If she told him why, he'd probably laugh and she wasn't making herself vulnerable to any more of his attacks.

As it turned out, they walked from one end of the grounds to the other, admiring a variety of exhibits as they went. Several times people stopped to stare curiously at Gavin. If he was aware of their scrutiny, he gave no indication. But no one approached him and they continued their leisurely stroll undisturbed. Dori assumed the reason was that no one would expect the great Gavin Parker to be with someone as ordinary as she. Someone over thirty, yet.

At the arcade, Dori made a serious effort to restrain

her smile, which hovered on the edge of laughter, as Gavin tried to pitch a ball and knock over three milk bottles. With his pride on the line, the ex-football hero was determined to win the stuffed lion. An appropriate prize, Dori felt, although he could've purchased two for the amount he spent to win one.

"You find this humorous, do you?" he muttered, carrying the huge stuffed beast under his arm.

"Hilarious," she admitted.

"Well, here." He handed the lion to her. "It's yours. I feel ridiculous carrying this around."

Feigning shock, Dori placed a hand over her heart. "My dear Mr. Parker, what could this mean?"

"Just take the stupid thing, will you?"

"One would assume," Dori said as she stroked the orange mane, "that an ex-quarterback could aim a little better than that."

"Ouch." He put out his hands and batted off invisible barbs. "That, Mrs. Robertson, hit below the belt."

She bought some cotton candy, sharing its sticky pink sweetness with him. "Now you know what 'smelling orange blossoms and humming "The Wedding March"' felt like."

Masculine fingers curved around the back of her neck as his eyes smiled into hers. "I guess that did sound a little arrogant, didn't it?"

Smiling up at him, Dori chuckled. "Only a little."

The sky was alight with stars and a crescent moon in full display before they left the fairgrounds and drove back to Seattle. The BMW's cushioned seats bore a number of accumulated prizes, hats and other goodies. By the time they located the freeway, both Danny and Melissa were asleep, exhausted from eight solid hours of recreation.

Forty minutes later, Gavin parked in front of Dori's small house. Suppressing a yawn, she offered him a warm smile. "Thank you for today."

Their eyes met above the stuffed lion's mane. He released her gaze by looking down at her softly parted lips, then quickly glancing up.

Flushed and a little self-conscious, Dori directed her attention to her purse, taking out her house keys.

"I had fun." Gavin's voice was low and relaxed.

"Don't act so surprised."

At the sound of their voices, Danny stirred. Sitting upright, he rubbed his eyes. "Are we home?" Not waiting for an answer, he began gathering up his treasures: a mirrored image of his favorite pop star and the multicolored sand sculpture he'd built with Melissa.

Undisturbed, Gavin's daughter slept on.

"I had a great time, Mr. Parker." The sleepy edge remained in Danny's voice.

Gavin came around to open her door. With her keys in one hand and the stuffed lion in the other, Dori climbed out. Then she helped Danny from the backseat. "Thanks again," she whispered. "Tell Melissa goodbye for me."

"I will." Gavin placed a hand on Danny's shoulder. "Good night, Danny."

"Night." The boy turned and waved, but was unsuccessful in his attempt to hold back a huge yawn.

Dori noted that Gavin didn't pull away until they were safely inside the house. Danny went directly into his bedroom. Setting the lion on the carpet, Dori moved to the window to watch the taillights fade as Gavin disappeared into the night. She doubted she'd ever see him again. Which was just as well. At least that was what she told herself.

"Time to get up, Mom." A loud knock at her bedroom door was followed by Danny's cheerful voice.

Dori groaned and propped open one eye to give her son a desultory glance. Mondays were always the worst. "It can't be morning already," she moaned, blindly reaching out to turn off the alarm before she realized it wasn't ringing.

"I brought your coffee."

"Thanks." Danny's coffee could raise the dead. "Set it on my nightstand."

Danny carefully put down the mug, but instead of leaving as he usually did, he sat on the edge of the bed. "You know, I've been thinking."

"Oh, no." Dori wasn't ready for any more of Danny's insights. "Now what?"

"It's been a whole week and we still haven't found me a new dad."

After spending Sunday afternoon arguing that Gavin Parker wasn't husband material, Dori couldn't handle another such conversation. Besides, someone like her wasn't going to interest Gavin. In addition, he'd made his views on marriage quite plain.

"These things take time," she murmured, struggling into a sitting position. "Give me a minute to wake up before we do battle. Okay?"

"Okay."

Dori grimaced at her first sip of strong coffee, but the jolt of caffeine started her heart pumping again. She rubbed a hand over her weary eyes.

"Can we talk now?" Danny asked.

"Now?" Whatever was troubling her son appeared to be important. She sighed. "All right."

"It's been a week and other than Mr. Parker we haven't met any guys."

"Danny." Dori reached over to rest a hand on his shoulder. "This is serious business. We can't rush something as important as a new father."

"But I thought we should add bait."

"Bait?"

"Yeah, like when Grandpa and I go fishing."

Another sip of coffee confirmed that she was indeed awake and not in the middle of a nightmare. "And what exactly did you have in mind?"

"You."

"Me?" Now she knew what the worm felt like.

"You're a neat mom, but you don't look like the moms on TV."

Falling back against the pillows, Dori shook her head. "I've heard enough of this conversation."

"Mom."

"I'm going to take a shower. Scoot."

"But there's more." Danny looked crestfallen.

"Not this morning, there's not."

His face sagged with discouragement as he got off the bed. "Will you think about exercising?"

"Exercising? What for? I'm in great shape." She patted her flat stomach as proof. She could afford to lose a few pounds, but she wouldn't be ashamed to be seen in a bikini. Well, maybe a one-piece.

Huge doubting eyes raked her from head to foot. "If you're sure…"

After scrutiny like that, Dori was anything but sure. Still, she was never at her best in the mornings; Danny knew that and had attacked when she was weakest.

By the time Dori arrived at the office, her mood hadn't improved. She'd begun to attack the latest files when Sandy walked in, holding a white sack.

"Good morning," her friend greeted her cheerfully.

"What's good about Mondays?" Dori demanded, not meaning to sound as abrupt as she did. When she glanced up to apologize, Sandy was at her side, setting a cup of coffee and a Danish on her desk. "What's this?"

"A reason to face the day," Sandy replied.

"Thanks, but I'll skip the Danish. Danny informed me this morning that I don't look like a TV star."

"Who does?" Sandy laughed and sat on the edge of Dori's desk, one foot dangling. "There are the beautiful people of this world and then there are the rest of us."

"Try telling Danny that." Dori pushed back her chair and peeled the protective lid from the cup. "I'm telling you, Sandy, I don't think I've ever seen this child more serious. He wants a father and he's driving me crazy with these ideas of his."

A smile lifted the corners of Sandy's mouth. "What's the little monster want now?"

"Danny's not a monster." Dori felt obliged to defend her son.

"All kids are monsters."

Sandy's dislike of children was well-known. More than once she'd stated emphatically that the last thing she ever wanted was a baby. Dori couldn't understand her attitude, but Sandy and her husband were entitled to their own feelings.

"Danny's decided I need to start an exercise program to get into shape," she said, her hands circling the coffee cup as she leaned back in her chair. A slow smile grew on her face. "I believe his exact words were that I'm to be the *bait*."

"That kid's smarter than I gave him credit for." Sandy finished off her Danish and reached for Dori's.

Dori had yet to figure out how anyone could eat so much and stay so thin. Sandy had an enormous appetite, but managed to remain svelte no matter how much she ate.

"I suppose you're going to give in?" Sandy asked, wiping the crumbs from her mouth.

"I suppose," Dori muttered. "In some ways he's right. I couldn't run a mile to save my soul. But what jogging has to do with finding him a father is beyond me."

"Are you honestly going to do it?"

"What?"

"Remarry to satisfy your kid?"

Dori's fingers toyed nervously with the rim of the coffee cup. "I don't know. But if I do marry again it won't just be for Danny. It'll be for both of us."

"Jeff's brother is going to be in town next weekend. We can make arrangements to get together, if you want."

Dori had met Greg once before. Divorced and bitter, Greg didn't make for stimulating company. As she recalled, the entire time had been spent discussing the mercenary inclinations of lawyers and the antifather prejudices of the court. But Dori was willing to listen to another episode of *Divorce Court* if it would help. Danny would see that she was at least making an effort, which should appease him for a while, anyway.

"Sure," Dori said with a nod of her head. "Let's get together."

Sandy didn't bother to hide her surprise. "Danny may be serious about this, but so are you. It's about time."

Dori regretted agreeing to the date almost from the minute the words left her lips. No one was more shocked than she was that she'd fallen in with Sandy's latest scheme.

That afternoon when Dori returned home, her mood had not improved.

"Hi, Mom." Danny kissed her on the cheek. "I put the casserole in the oven like you asked."

In a few more years, Danny would be reluctant to demonstrate his affection with a kiss. The thought produced a twinge of regret. All too soon, Danny would be gone and she'd be alone. The twinge became an ache. *Alone.* The word seemed to echo around her.

"Are you tired?" Danny asked, following her into the bedroom where she kicked off her shoes.

"No more than usual."

"Oh." Danny stood in the doorway.

"But I've got enough energy to go jogging before dinner."

"Really, Mom?" His blue eyes lit up like sparklers.

"As long as you're willing to go with me. I'll need a coach." She wasn't about to tackle the streets of Seattle without him. No doubt Danny could run circles around her, but so what? She wasn't competing with him.

Dori changed out of her blue linen business suit and dug out an old pair of jeans and a faded T-shirt.

Danny was running in place when she came into the kitchen. Dori groaned inwardly at her son's display of energy.

As soon as he noticed her appearance, Danny stopped. "You're not going like that, are you?"

"What's wrong now?" Dori added a sweatband.

"Those are *old* clothes."

"Danny," she groaned. "I'm not going to jog in a dress." No doubt he'd envisioned her in a skintight leotard and multicolored leg warmers.

"All right," he mumbled, but he didn't look pleased.

The first two blocks were murder. Danny set the pace, his knobby knees lifting with lightning speed as he sprinted down the sidewalk. With her pride at stake, Dori managed to meet his stride. Her lungs hurt almost immediately. The muscles at the back of her calves protested such vigorous exercise, but she succeeded in moving one foot in front of the other without too much difficulty. However, by the end of the sixth block, Dori realized she was either going to have to give up or collapse and play dead.

"Danny," she gasped, stumbling to a halt. Her breath was coming in huge gulps that made talking impossible. Leaning forward, she rested her hands on her knees and drew in deep breaths. "I don't…think… I…should… overdo it…the first…day."

"You're not tired, are you?"

She felt close to dying. "Just…a little." Straightening, she murmured, "I think I have a blister on my heel." She was silently begging God for an excuse to stop. The last time she'd breathed this deeply, she'd been in labor.

Perspiration ran down her back. It took all the energy she had to wipe the moisture from her face. Women weren't supposed to sweat like this, were they? On second thought, maybe those were tears of agony on her cheeks. "I think we should walk back."

"Yeah, the coach always makes us cool down."

Dori made a mental note to give Danny's soccer coach a rum cake for Christmas.

Still eager to show off his agility, Danny continued to jog backward in front of Dori. For good measure she decided to add a slight limp to her gait.

"I'm positive I've got a blister," she said, shaking her head for emphasis. "These tennis shoes are my new ones. I haven't broken 'em in yet." In all honesty she couldn't tell whether she had a blister or not. Her feet didn't ache any more than her legs did, or her lungs.

The closer they came to the house, the more real her limp became.

"Are you sure you're all right, Mom?" Danny had the grace to show a little concern.

"I'm fine." She offered him a feeble smile. The sweat-band slipped loose and fell across one eye, but Dori didn't have the energy to secure it.

"Let me help you, Mom." Danny came to her side and placed an arm around her waist. He stared at her flushed and burning face, his brows knit. "You don't look so good."

Dori didn't know what she looked like, but she felt on the verge of throwing up. She'd been a complete idiot to try to maintain Danny's pace. Those six blocks might as well have been six miles.

They were within a half block of the house when Danny hesitated. "Hey, Mom, look. It's Mr. Parker."

Before Dori could stop him, Danny shouted and waved.

Standing in the middle of the sidewalk, hands on his hips, stood Gavin Parker. He didn't bother to hide his amusement, either.

Three

"Are you okay?" Gavin inquired with mock solicitude.

"Get that smirk off your face," Dori warned. She was in no mood to exchange witticisms with him. Not when every muscle in her body was screaming for mercy.

"It's my fault," Danny confessed, concerned now. "I thought she'd attract more men if they could see how athletic she is."

"The only thing I'm attracting is flies." She ripped the sweatband from her hair; the disobedient curls sprang out from her head. "What can I do for you, Mr. Parker?"

"My, my, she gets a bit testy now and then, doesn't she?" Gavin directed his question to Danny.

"Only sometimes." At least Danny made a halfhearted attempt to be loyal.

There was no need for Gavin to look so smug. His grin resembled that of a cat with a defenseless mouse trapped under its paws.

"Aren't you going to invite me in?" he asked dryly.

Clenching her jaw, Dori gave him a chilly stare. "Don't press your luck, Parker," she whispered for his ears only. Hobbling to the front door, she struggled to retrieve her house key from the tight pocket of her jeans.

"Need help?" Gavin asked.

The glare she flashed him informed him she didn't.

With a mocking smile he raised his arms. "Hey, just asking."

The front door clicked open and Danny forged ahead, running to the kitchen and opening the refrigerator. He stood at the entrance, waiting for Dori to limp in—closely followed by Gavin—and handed her a cold can of root beer.

With a hand massaging her lower back, Dori led the way to the kitchen table.

"Do you want one, Mr. Parker?" Danny held up another can of soda.

"No, thanks," Gavin said, pulling out a chair for Dori. "You might want to soak out some of those aches and pains in a hot bath."

It was on the tip of her tongue to remind him that good manners wouldn't let her seek comfort in a hot bath while he still sat at her kitchen table.

Danny snapped open a can and guzzled down a long swig. Dori restrained herself to a ladylike sip, although her throat felt parched and scratchy.

"I found Danny's jacket in the backseat of the car the other day and thought he might need it," Gavin said, explaining the reason for his visit. He handed Danny the keys. "Would you bring it in for me?"

"Sure." Danny was off like a rocket, eager to obey.

The front screen slammed and Gavin turned his attention to Dori. "What's this business about jogging to make you more attractive to men?"

Some of the numbness was beginning to leave Dori's limbs and her heartbeat had finally returned to normal. "Just that bee Danny's got in his bonnet about me remarrying. Rest assured you're out of the running."

"I'm glad to hear it. I'm rotten husband material."

A laughing sigh escaped as Dori's eyes met his. "I'd already determined that."

"I hung the jacket in my room," Danny told his mother, obviously wanting to please her. "It was nice of you to bring it back, Mr. Parker."

For the first time, Dori wondered if the jacket had been left intentionally so Gavin would have an excuse to return. She wouldn't put it past her son.

Gavin held out his palm to collect the keys.

"How come Melissa isn't here?" Danny wanted to know. "She's all right for a girl. She wasn't afraid to go on any of the rides. She even went on the Hammer with me. Mom never would." A thoughtful look came over Danny as if he was weighing the pros and cons of being friends with a girl. "She did scream a lot, though."

"She's at school." Gavin stood up to leave, the scrape of his chair loud in the quiet kitchen. "She thought you were all right, too…for a boy." He exchanged teasing smiles with Danny.

"Can we do something together again?" Danny asked as he trailed Gavin into the living room. Dori hobbled a safe distance behind them, pressing her hand to the ache at the small of her back. Who would've believed a little run could be this incapacitating?

"Perhaps." Gavin paused in front of the television and lifted an ornate wooden frame that held a family portrait taken a year before Brad's death. It was the only picture of Brad that Dori kept out. After a silent study, he replaced the portrait and stooped to pat the stuffed lion, now guarding the window. "I'll get Melissa to give you a call the next weekend she's not at school."

"Not at school?" Danny repeated incredulously. "You mean she has to go to school on Saturdays, too?"

"No," Gavin said. "She boards at the girls' school she attends and spends the weekends with me if I'm not broadcasting a game. Things get hectic this time of year, though. I'll have her give you a call."

"Danny would like that," Dori said, smiling sweetly, assured that Gavin had understood her subtle message. Having Melissa call Danny was fine, but Dori didn't want anything to do with Gavin.

As Gavin had suggested, a leisurely soak in hot water went a long way toward relieving her aching muscles. Her parting shot had been childish, and Dori regretted it. She drew in a deep breath and eased down farther in the steaming water. It felt sinful to be so lazy, so relaxed.

"The table's set and the timer for the oven rang," Danny called.

With her hair pinned up and her lithe—but abused— body draped in a cozy housecoat, Dori ambled into the kitchen. Danny was standing by the refrigerator, rereading the list of prerequisites for a new father.

"Dinner smells good. I'll bet you're hungry after all that exercise."

Danny ignored her obvious attempt to divert his attention. That kid was getting wise to her ways.

"Did you realize Mr. Parker knows karate? I asked him about it."

"That's nice." Dori hoped to play down the information. "I'll take out the casserole and we should be ready to eat."

"He's tall and athletic and Melissa said he's thirty-six—"

"Danny," she snapped, "no! We went over this yesterday. I have veto power, remember?"

"Mr. Parker would make a great dad," he argued.

Her glass made a sharp clang as it hit the table. "But not yours."

To his credit Danny didn't bring up Gavin Parker's name again. Apparently the message had sunk in, although Dori knew her son genuinely liked Gavin and Melissa. As for herself, she still hadn't made up her mind about Gavin. Melissa was a sweet child but her father was another matter. No one exasperated Dori more than he did. Gavin Parker was arrogant, conceited and altogether maddening.

Another week passed and Danny marked off the days on their calendar, reminding her daily of his need for a new dad. Even the promise of a puppy wasn't enough to dissuade him. Twice he interrupted her while they did the weekly shopping to point out men in the grocery store. He actually wanted her to introduce herself.

The date with Sandy's brother-in-law, Greg, did more harm than good. Not only was she forced to listen to an updated version of *Divorce Court*, but Danny drilled her with questions the next morning until she threatened to drop the new father issue entirely.

The next few days, her son was unusually subdued. But Dori knew him well enough to suspect that although she'd won this first battle, he was out to win the war. The situation was weighing on her so heavily that she had a nightmare about waking up and discovering a stranger in her bed who claimed Danny had sent him.

Monday evening, when Danny was supposed to be doing homework, she found him shaking money from his piggy bank onto his bed. She'd purposely given him a bank that wouldn't open so he'd learn to save his money. He dodged her questions about the need to rob it, telling her he was planning a surprise.

"That kid's got something up his sleeve," Dori told Sandy the following day.

"Didn't you ask?"

"He said he was buying me a present." This morning Dori had brought in the coffee and Danishes, and she set a paper sack on Sandy's desk.

"Knowing Danny, I'd say it's probably a jar of wrinkle cream."

"Probably," she murmured and took a bite of the Danish.

"I thought you were on a diet."

"Are you kidding? With all the aerobics and jogging Danny's got me doing, I'm practically wasting away."

Sandy crossed one shapely leg over the other. "And people wonder why I don't want kids."

The phone was ringing when Dori let herself into the house that evening. She tossed her purse on the kitchen table and hurried to answer it, thinking the caller was most likely her mother.

"Hello."

"I'm calling about your ad in the paper."

Dori frowned. "I'm sorry, but you've got a wrong number." The man on the other end of the line wanted to argue, but Dori replaced the receiver, cutting him off.

He sounded quite unpleasant, and as far as she was concerned, there was nothing more to discuss.

Danny was at soccer practice at the local park, six blocks from the house. The days were growing shorter, the sun setting at just about the time practice was over. On impulse, Dori decided to bicycle to the field and ride home with him. Of course, she wouldn't let him know the reason she'd come. He'd hate it if he thought his mother was there to escort him home.

When they entered the house twenty minutes later, the phone was ringing again.

"I'll get it," Danny shouted, racing across the kitchen.

Dori didn't pay much attention when he stretched the cord around the corner and walked into the hall closet, seeking privacy. He did that sometimes when he didn't want her to listen in on his conversation. The last time that had happened, it was because a girl from school had phoned.

Feeling lazy and not in a mood to fuss with dinner, Dori opened a package of fish sticks and dumped them on a cookie sheet, shoving them under the broiler with some French fries. She was chopping a head of cabbage for coleslaw when Danny reappeared. He gave her a sheepish look as he hung up the phone.

"Was that Erica again?"

Danny ignored her question. "Are you going to keep on wearing those old clothes?"

Dori glanced down at her washed-out jeans and Irish cable-knit sweater. "What's wrong with them?" Actually, this was one of her better pairs of jeans.

"I just thought you'd like to wear a dress for dinner or something."

"Danny—" she released an exasperated sigh "—we're having fish sticks, not filet mignon."

"Oh." He stuck his hands in his pockets and yanked them out again as the phone rang. "I'll get it."

Before Dori knew what was happening, he was back in the closet, the phone cord stretched to its farthest. Within minutes, he was out again.

"What's going on?"

"Nothin'."

The phone rang and the doorbell chimed simultaneously. "I'll get it," Danny hollered, jerking his head from one direction to the other.

Drying her hands on a dish towel, Dori gestured toward the living room. "I'll get the door."

Gavin Parker stood on the other side of screen, the morning paper tucked under his arm.

"Gavin." Dori was too surprised to utter more than his name.

Laugh lines fanned out from his eyes, and he had that cat-with-the-trapped-mouse look again. "Phone been ringing a lot lately?"

"Yes. How'd you know? It's been driving me crazy." Unlatching the screen door, she opened it, silently inviting him inside. What a strange man Gavin was. She hadn't expected to see him again and here he was on her doorstep, looking inexplicably amused.

Gavin sauntered in and sat on the sofa. "I don't suppose you've read the morning paper?"

Dori had, at least the sections she always did. Dear Abby, the comics, a trivia column and the front page, in that order. "Yes. Why?"

Making a show of it, Gavin pulled out the classified

section and folded it open, laying it across the coffee table. Idly, he moved his index finger down the column of personal ads until he located what he wanted. "I was checking out cars in today's paper and I found something else that was pretty interesting...."

A sick feeling attacked the pit of Dori's stomach, weakening her knees so that she had to lower herself into the maple rocking chair across from him.

"Are you in any way related to the person who ran this ad? 'Need dad. Tall, athletic, knows karate. Mom pretty. 555-5818.'"

It was worse, far worse, than anything Dori would ever have dreamed. Mortified and angry, she supported her elbows on the arms of the rocker and buried her face in the palms of her hands. A low husky sound slipped from her throat as hot color invaded her neck, her cheeks, her ears, not stopping until her eyes brimmed with tears of embarrassment.

"Daniel Bradley Robertson, get in here this minute!" Rarely did she use that tone with her son. Whenever she did, Danny came running.

The closet door opened a crack and Danny's head appeared. "Just a minute, Mom, I'm on the phone." He paused, noticing Gavin for the first time. "Oh, hi, Mr. Parker."

"Hello, Daniel Bradley Robertson." Gavin stood up and took the receiver out of the boy's hand. "I think your mother would like to talk to you. I'll take care of who-ever's on the phone."

"Yeah, Mom?" A picture of innocence, Danny met Dori's fierce gaze without wavering. "Is something wrong?"

Her scheming son became a watery blur as Dori shook her head, not knowing how to explain the embarrassment he'd caused her.

"Mom?" Danny knelt in front of her. "What's the matter? Why are you crying?"

Her answer was a sniffle and a finger pointed in the direction of the bathroom. Danny seemed to understand her watery charade and leaped to his feet, returning with a box of tissues.

"Do you people always use the hall closet to talk on the phone?"

Gavin was back and Danny gave his visitor a searching look. "What's the matter with Mom? All she does is cry."

The phone pealed again and Dori gave a hysterical sob that sounded more like a strangled cry of pain.

"I'll get it," Gavin assured her, quickly taking control. "Danny, come with me into the kitchen. Your mother needs a few minutes alone."

For a moment it looked as though Danny didn't know what to do. Indecision played across his face. His mother was crying and there was a man with an authoritative voice barking orders at him. With a weak gesture of her hand, Dori dismissed her son.

In the next hour the phone rang another twenty times. With every ring, Dori flinched. Gavin and Danny remained in the kitchen and dealt with each call. Dori didn't move. The gentle sway of the rocker was her only solace. Danny ventured into the living room just once, to announce that dinner was ready if she wanted to eat. Wordlessly shaking her head, she let him know she didn't.

After a while her panic abated somewhat and she decided not to sell the house, pack up her belongings and seek refuge at the other end of the world. A less drastic approach gradually came to mind. The first thing she had to do was get that horrible ad out of the personals. Then she'd have her phone number changed.

More composed now, Dori blew her nose and washed her tear-streaked face in the bathroom off the hall. When she walked into the kitchen, she was shocked to discover Gavin and Danny busy with the dinner dishes. Gavin stood at the sink, the sleeves of his expensive business shirt rolled up past his elbows. Danny was standing beside him, a dish towel in his hand.

"Hi, Mom." His chagrined eyes didn't quite meet hers. "Mr. Parker told me that what I did wasn't a very good idea."

"No, it wasn't." The high-pitched sound that issued from her throat barely resembled her voice.

"Would you like some dinner now? Mr. Parker and I saved you some."

She shook her head, then asked, "What's been happening in here?"

In response the phone rang, its jangle almost deafening—or so it seemed to Dori, who immediately cringed.

Not hesitating at all, Gavin dried his hands and went to the wall phone.

"Listen to him," Danny whispered with a giggle. "Mr. Parker figured out a way to answer the phone without having to argue. He's really smart."

Catching Dori's eye, Gavin winked reassuringly and picked up the receiver. After a momentary pause, he mocked the phone company recording. "The number you have reached has been disconnected," he droned in a falsetto voice.

For the first time that evening, the tight line of Dori's mouth cracked with the hint of a smile. Once again, she was forced to admire the cleverness of Gavin Parker.

Grinning, he hung up the phone and sat in the chair next to Dori's. "Are you feeling okay now?"

"I'm fine." She managed a nod. The confusion and anger she'd experienced earlier had only been made worse by Gavin's gloating. But now she felt grateful that he'd stepped in and taken charge of a very awkward situation. Dori wasn't sure what would have happened otherwise.

A finger under her chin tilted her face upward. "I don't believe you're fine at all. You're as pale as a sheet." A rush of unexpected pleasure shot through her at the contact, impersonal though it was.

His finger ventured over the smooth line of her jaw in an exploratory caress. The action was meant to soothe and reassure, but his touch was oddly sensual and highly arousing. Bewildered, Dori raised her eyes to his. They stared at each other as his hand slipped to her neck, his fingers tangling with her shoulder-length hair. Dori could see the rise and fall of his chest and noted that the movement increased slightly, as if he too had been caught unawares by these emotions. His eyes narrowed as he withdrew his hand. "You need a drink. Where...?"

With a limp arm, Dori motioned toward the cupboard that held her small stock of liquor. As he poured a shot of brandy into a glass, Gavin said quietly, "Danny, haven't you got some homework that needs to be done?"

"No." Danny shook his head, then hurriedly placed

his fingers over his mouth. "Oh... I get it. You want to talk to my mom alone."

"Right." Gavin exchanged a conspiratorial wink with the boy.

As Danny left the room, Gavin deposited the brandy in front of Dori and sat beside her again. "No arguments. Drink."

"You like giving orders, don't you?" Whatever had passed between them was gone as quickly as it had come.

Gavin ignored the censure in her voice. "I have an idea that could benefit both of us."

Dori took a swallow of the brandy, which burned her throat and brought fresh tears to her eyes. "What?" was all she could manage.

"It's obvious that Danny's serious about this new father business and to be truthful, Melissa would like me to remarry so she won't have to board at the school anymore. She hates all the restrictions."

Dori sympathized with the young girl. Melissa was at an age when she should be testing her wings and that included experimenting with makeup and wearing the latest fashions.

"You're not humming 'The Wedding March,' are you?" Dori asked.

Gavin sent her a look that threatened bodily harm, and she couldn't contain a soft laugh. She loved turning the tables on this impudent man.

"I've already explained that I have no intention of remarrying. Once was enough to cure me for a lifetime. But I am willing to compromise if it means Melissa will let up on the pressure."

"How do Danny and I fit into this picture?"

Eager now, Gavin shifted to the edge of his seat and leaned forward. "If the two of us were to start going out on a steady basis, Melissa and Danny would assume we're involved with each other."

Dori drew in a slow trembling breath. Much as she hated to admit it, the idea had promise. Melissa needed a woman's influence, and all Danny really cared about was having a man who'd participate in the things she couldn't. Dori realized her son was already worried about the father-son soccer game scheduled for the end of the season. For years his grandfather had volunteered for such events, but her dad was close to retirement and these days playing soccer would put a strain on him.

"We could start this weekend. We'll go to dinner Friday night and then on Sunday I'll take Danny to the Seahawks game if you'll take Melissa shopping." His mouth slanted in a coaxing smile.

Dori recognized the crooked grin as the one he probably used on gullible young women whenever he wanted his own way. Nibbling her lower lip, Dori refused to play that game. She wasn't stupid; he was willing to tie up Friday and Sunday, but he wanted Saturday night free. Why not? She didn't care what he did. As long as he didn't embarrass her in front of Danny and Melissa.

"Well?" Gavin didn't look nearly as confident as he had earlier, and that pleased Dori. There was no need for him to assume she'd fall in with his plans so easily.

"I think you may have stumbled on to something."

His smile returned. "Which, translated, means you doubt I have more than an occasional original thought."

"Perhaps." He'd been kind and helpful tonight. The

least she could do was be a little more accommodating in exchange. "All right, I agree."

"Great." A boyish grin not unlike Danny's lit up his face. "I'll see you Friday night about seven."

"Fine." Standing, she clasped her hands behind her back. "And, Gavin, thank you for stepping in and helping tonight. I do appreciate it. I'll phone the paper first thing in the morning to make sure the ad doesn't appear again and contact the phone company to have my number changed."

"You know how to handle any more calls that come in tonight?"

Dori plugged her nose and imitated the telephone company recording.

The laugh lines around his eyes became prominent as he grinned. "We can have a good time, Dori. Just don't fall in love with me."

So he was back on that theme. "Believe me, there's no chance of that," she snapped. "If you want the truth, I think you may be the—"

She wasn't allowed to finish as he suddenly hauled her into his arms and kissed her soundly, stealing her breath and tipping her off balance. With her hands pushing against his chest, Dori was able to break off the unexpected attack.

"Shh," Gavin whispered in her ear. "Danny's right outside the door."

"So?" She still wasn't free from his embrace.

"I didn't want him to hear you. If we're going to convince either of those kids, we've got to make this look real."

She felt herself blush. "Give me some warning next time."

Gavin eased her away, studying the heightened color of her face. "I didn't hurt you, did I?"

"No," she assured him, thinking the worst thing about being a redhead was her pale coloring, which meant the slightest sign of embarrassment was more pronounced.

"Well, how'd I do?"

"On what?"

"The kiss." He shook his head as though he expected her to know what he was talking about. "How would you rate the kiss?"

This, Dori was going to enjoy. "On a scale of one to ten?" She let a lengthy pause follow as she folded her arms and quirked her head thoughtfully at the ceiling. The time had come for someone to put this overconfident male in his place. "If I take into consideration that you're an ex-quarterback, I'd say a low five."

His mouth twitched briefly. "I was expecting you to be a little less cruel."

"And from everything you say," she went on, "I don't expect your technique to improve."

"It might," he chuckled, "but I doubt it."

Danny chose that moment to wander into the kitchen. "I'm not interrupting anything, am I?"

"You don't mind if I take your mom out for dinner on Friday night, do you?"

"Really, Mom?"

Dori would willingly have given her son double his allowance not to have sounded quite so eager.

"I guess," she said dryly. Gavin ignored her lack of enthusiasm.

"But I thought you said Mr. Parker was a—"

"Never mind that now," she whispered pointedly, as another flood of color cascaded into her cheeks.

"I'll see you at seven on Friday." Gavin rolled down the sleeves of his shirt and rebuttoned them at the wrist. "It's a date."

Dori had hardly ever seen Danny happier about anything. He quizzed her on Friday from the moment she walked in the door after work. As she drove him to her parents' place—they were delighted to have their grandson for the night—he wanted to know what she was going to wear, what kind of perfume, which earrings, which shoes. He gave her advice and bombarded her with football statistics.

"Danny," she said irritably, "I don't think Gavin Parker expects me to know that much about football."

"But, Mom, it'll impress him," he pleaded in a sing-song voice.

"But, Danny." Her twangy voice echoed his.

Back at her own house, an exhausted Dori soaked in the tub, then hurriedly dried herself, applied some makeup—why was she doing it with such care? she wondered—and dressed. She wasn't surprised that Gavin was fifteen minutes late, nor did she take offense. The extra time was well spent adding a last coat of pale pink polish to her nails.

Gavin looked rushed and slightly out of breath as he climbed the porch steps. Dori saw him coming and opened the front door, careful not to smear her polish. "Hi." She didn't mention the fact that he was late.

Gavin's smile was wry. "Where's Danny?"

"My mom and dad's."

"Oh." He paused and raked his fingers through his hair, mussing the carefully styled effect. "Listen, tonight isn't going exactly the way I planned. I promised to do a favor for a friend. It shouldn't interfere with our date."

"That's okay," Dori murmured and cautiously slipped her arms into the coat Gavin held for her. She hadn't the faintest idea what he had in mind, but knowing Gavin Parker, it wasn't moonlight and roses.

"Do you mean that?" Already he had his car keys out and was fiddling with them, his gaze lowered. "I ran into some complications at the office so I'm a bit late."

"Don't worry about it, Gavin. It's not like we're madly in love." She couldn't restrain a bit of sarcasm. Thank goodness Danny wasn't there to witness her "date."

While she locked the front door, Gavin sprinted down the porch steps and started the engine. Dori released an exasperated sigh as he leaned across the seat and opened the passenger door. With a forced smile on her lips, she slid inside. So much for any pretense of gallantry and romance.

It wouldn't have shocked her if there was another woman waiting for him somewhere. What did surprise her was that he pulled into a local fast-food place, helped her out of the car and seated her, then asked what she wanted to eat. She told him, and he lined up with the schoolkids and young parents to order their meals. She didn't know what he had up his sleeve or if he expected some kind of reaction to the choice of restaurant, but she didn't so much as blink.

"I did promise you dinner," he said, handing her a wrapped cheeseburger, fries and a chocolate shake.

"That you did," she returned sweetly.

"Whatever else happens tonight, just remember I fed you."

"And I'm grateful." Not for the first time, she had difficulty keeping the sarcasm out of her voice. Good grief, where could he be taking her?

"The thing is, when I asked you to dinner I forgot about a…previous commitment."

"Gavin, it's fine. For that matter you can take me back to my house—it's not that big a deal. In fact, if there's another woman involved it would save us both a lot of embarrassment." Not him, but the two women.

Gavin polished off the last of his hamburger and crumpled the paper. "There isn't another woman." He looked horrified that she'd even suggest such a thing. "If you don't mind coming, I don't mind bringing you. As it is, I had a heck of a time getting an extra ticket."

"I'm game for just about anything." Fleetingly Dori wondered what she was letting herself in for, but learning that it involved a ticket was encouraging. A concert, maybe? A play?

"Is it a performance?" she asked brightly.

"You could say that," he replied. "Sometimes these things can go on quite late."

"Not to worry. Danny's staying the night with my parents."

"Great." He flashed her a brilliant smile. "As Danny would say, for a girl, you're all right."

He made it sound exactly like her son. "I'm glad you think so."

After dumping their leftovers in the garbage, Gavin escorted her to the car and drove out of the parking space. He took the freeway toward Tacoma. Dori still wasn't sure precisely where they were going, but she wasn't turning back now.

Several other cars were parked outside a dimly lit part of downtown Tacoma. Gavin stepped out of the car and glanced at his wristwatch. He hurried around the front of the car to help her out. His hand grasped her elbow as he led her toward a square gray building. The streetlight was too dim for Dori to read the sign over the door, not that Gavin would have given her time. They were obviously late.

They entered a large hall and were greeted by shouts and cheers. As Dori scanned the audience, the automatic smile died on her lips and she turned furiously to Gavin.

"I promised a friend I'd take a look at his latest prodigy," he explained, studying her reaction.

"You mean to tell me that you brought me to the Friday-night fights?"

Four

"Is that a problem?" Gavin asked defensively, his gaze challenging hers.

Dori couldn't believe this was her "date" with the handsome and popular Gavin Parker. She'd never gone to a boxing match in her life, nor had she ever wanted to. But then, sports in general didn't interest her much— unless they were her son's soccer games. Despite that, her "No, I guess not," was spoken with a certain amount of honesty. Danny would be thrilled. Little else would convince the eleven-year-old that Gavin was serious about her.

Following Gavin into the auditorium and down the wide aisle, Dori was a little hesitant when he ushered her into a seat only a few rows from the ring. Whatever was about to happen she would see in graphic detail.

Apparently Gavin was a familiar patron at these matches. He introduced Dori to several men whose names floated past her so quickly that she could never hope to remember them. Glancing around, Dori noted that there were only a few other women present. In her little black dress and wool coat, she was decidedly over-dressed. Cringing, Dori huddled down in her seat while Gavin carried on a friendly conversation with the man in the row ahead of them.

"You want some peanuts?" He bent his head close to hers as he asked.

"No, thanks." Her hands lay in her lap, clutching her purse and an unread program she'd received at the door. People didn't eat while they watched this kind of thing, did they?

Gavin shrugged and stood up, reaching for some loose change in his pocket. He turned back to her. "You're not mad, are you?"

Dori was convinced that was exactly what he'd expected her to be. Perhaps it was even what he wanted. Her anger would be just the proof he needed that all women were alike. Based on everything that had occurred between them, Dori realized Gavin didn't particularly *want* to like her. Any real relationship would be dangerous to him, she suspected—even one founded on friendship and mutual respect.

"No." She gave him a forced but cheerful smile. "This should be very interesting." Already she was fashioning a subtle revenge. Next time they went out, she'd have Gavin take her to an opera.

"I'll be back in a minute." He left his seat and clambered over the two men closest to the aisle.

Feeling completely out of her element, Dori sat with her shoulders stiff and squared against the back of the folding wooden seat. She was mentally bracing herself for the ordeal.

"So you're Dori." The man who'd been talking to Gavin turned to her.

They'd been introduced, but she couldn't recall his name. "Yes." Her smile was shy as she searched her memory.

"This is the first time Gavin's ever brought a woman to the fights."

Dori guessed that was a compliment. "I'm honored."

"He was seeing that gorgeous blonde for a while. A lot of the guys were worried he was going to marry her."

A blonde! Dori's curiosity was piqued. "Is that so?" Gavin hadn't mentioned any blonde to her. If he was going to see someone else regularly it would ruin their agreement. Gavin took her to the Friday-night fights, while he probably wined and dined this blonde on the sly. Terrific.

"Yeah," the nameless man continued. "He was seeing her pretty regularly. For a while he wasn't even coming to the fights."

Obviously Gavin and the blond woman had a serious relationship going. "She must've been really something for Gavin to miss the fights." Smiling encouragingly, Dori hoped the man would tell her more.

"He doesn't come every week, you understand."

Dori nodded, pretending she did.

"Fact is, during football season we're lucky to see him once a month."

Dori was beginning to wonder just how "lucky" she was. The man grinned and glanced toward the aisle. Dori's gaze followed his and she saw Gavin coming down the crowded center aisle, carrying a large bag of peanuts.

As soon as he sat down, Dori absently helped herself to a handful.

"I thought you said you didn't want any," Gavin said, giving her the bag.

"I don't," she mumbled, cracking one open with her teeth. "I don't even like peanuts."

"Then why did you grab them out of my hand the minute I sat down?"

"I did?" When she was agitated or upset, the first thing she usually did was reach for something to eat. "Sorry," she said, returning the paper sack. "I didn't realize what I was doing."

"Is anything bothering you?" Gavin asked. His eyes darkened as though he was expecting an argument.

Dori hated being so easy to read. She'd thought that sometime during the evening she'd casually bring up his liaison with this...this other woman who was jeopardizing their tentative agreement.

"Nothing's bothering me," she answered. "Not really."

His glittering eyes mocked her.

"It's just that your friend—" she gestured with her hand toward the row in front of them "—was saying that you were seeing a blonde and..."

"And you jumped to conclusions?"

"Yes, well...it isn't exactly in our agreement." What upset Dori the most was that it mattered to her if Gavin was seeing another woman. She had no right to feel anything for him—except as far as their agreement was concerned. But if Danny heard about this other woman, she might slip in her son's estimation, she told herself. He might decide that Gavin wasn't interested in her and redouble his search for a new husband-and-father candidate.

"Well, you needn't worry. I'm not seeing her anymore."

"What's the problem," Dori taunted in a low whisper, "was she unfortunate enough to smell orange blossoms?"

"No." He pursed his lips and reached for a peanut, cracking it open with a vengeance. "Every time she opened her mouth, her brain leaked."

Dori successfully hid a smile. "I'd have thought that type of girlfriend was the best kind." *For someone like you,* she added mentally.

"I'm beginning to have the same feeling myself," he said dryly, his gaze inscrutable.

Feeling a growing sense of triumph, Dori relaxed and didn't say another word.

Soon cheers and loud hoots rose from the auditorium as the young boxers paraded into the room with an entourage of managers and assistants.

The announcer waited until the two men had parted the ropes and positioned themselves in their appropriate corners. Glancing at her program, Dori read that these first two were in the lightweight division.

Pulling down a microphone that seemed to come from nowhere, the announcer shouted, "Ladies and gentlemen, welcome to the Tacoma Friday-night fights. Wearing white trunks and weighing 130 awesome pounds is Boom Boom Bronson."

The sound echoed around the room. Cheers and whistles followed. Boom Boom hopped into the middle of the ring and punched at a few shadows, to the delight of the audience, before he returned to his corner. Even when he was in a stationary position, his hands braced against the ropes, Boom Boom's feet refused to stop moving.

Then the other boxer, Tucker Wallace, was introduced. Tucker hopped in and out of the middle ring, punching all the way. The crowd went crazy. The man beside Dori stormed to his feet, placed two fingers in his mouth and pierced the air with a shrill whistle. Dori grabbed another handful of peanuts.

The two fighters met briefly with the announcer and spoke with the referee before returning to their respective corners. The entourages formed around each fighter again. Probably to decide a strategy, Dori mused.

The bell clanged and the two men came out swinging. Dori blinked twice, stunned at the fierce aggression between the men. They might have been listed in the lightweight division, but their corded muscles told her that their stature had little to do with their strength or determination.

Gavin had shifted to the edge of his seat by the end of round one. The bell brought a humming silence to the room.

Dori knew next to nothing about boxing. She hated fighting, but the competition between Boom Boom and Tucker seemed exaggerated and somehow theatrical. Despite her dislike of violence, Dori found herself cheering for Boom Boom. When he was slammed to the ground by Tucker's powerful right hand, Dori jumped to her feet to see if he was hurt.

"Oh, goodness," she wailed, covering her forehead with one hand as she sank back into her seat. "He's bleeding."

Gavin was looking at her, his compelling dark eyes studying her flushed, excited face as if he couldn't quite believe what he saw.

"Is something wrong?" Boldly her gaze met his and a shiver of sensual awareness danced over her skin. "I'm cheering too loud?" She'd become so engrossed in what was happening between the two boxers that she must have embarrassed him with her vocal enthusiasm.

"No," he muttered, shaking his head. "I guess I'm surprised you like it."

"Well, to be honest," she admitted. "I didn't think I would. But these guys are good."

"Yes." He gave her a dazzling smile. "They are."

The adrenaline pumped through Dori's limbs as Boom Boom fought on to win the match in a unanimous decision. At the end of three bouts the evening was over and Gavin helped her on with her coat. The night had turned rainy and cold, and Dori shivered as they walked to the car.

The moment they were settled, Gavin turned on the heater. "You'll be warm in a minute."

Dori stuck her bare hands deep in her pockets. "If it gets much colder, it'll probably snow."

"It won't," Gavin stated confidently. "It was hot in the auditorium, that's all." He paused to snap his seat belt into place. Dori averted her face to check the heavy flow of traffic. They wouldn't be able to get out of their parking spot for several minutes, but there wasn't any rush. Although she was reluctant to admit it, she'd enjoyed the evening. Being taken to the fights was the last thing she'd expected, but Dori was quickly learning that Gavin was a man of surprises.

"Here," Gavin said, half leaning across her. "Buckle up." Before Dori could free her hand to reach for the seat belt, Gavin had pulled it across her waist. He hesitated, his eyes meeting hers. Their mouths were close, so close. Dori swallowed convulsively. Her heart skipped a beat, then hammered wildly. She stared at him, hardly able to believe what she saw in his eyes or the feelings that stirred in her own breast. A strange, inexplicable sensation came over her. At that moment, she felt as if she and Gavin were good friends, two people who shared a special bond of companionship. She liked him, respected him, enjoyed his company.

She knew when he lowered his head that he was going to kiss her, but instead of drawing away, she met him halfway, shocked at how much she wanted him to do exactly this. His mouth fit easily, expertly, over hers in a tender, undemanding caress. One hand smoothed the hair from her temple as he lifted his mouth from hers and brushed his lips over her brow.

"Feeling warmer?" he asked in a husky murmur.

Her body was suffused by an unexpected rush of heat, her blood vigorously pounding through her veins. Unable to find her voice, she nodded.

"Good." He clicked her seat belt into place, and with utter nonchalance, checked the rearview mirror before pulling onto the street.

Silently Dori thanked God for the cover of night. Her

face burned at her own imprudence. Gavin had kissed her and she'd let him. Worse, she'd enjoyed it. Enjoyed it so much that she'd been sorry when he'd stopped.

"I give you a six, maybe a low seven," she challenged, struggling to disguise his effect on her.

"What?"

"The kiss," she returned coolly, but there was a brittle edge to her airy reply. Her greatest fear was that he might be secretly amused by the ardor of her response.

"I'm pleased to know I'm improving. As I recall, the last kiss was a mere five." He merged with the moving traffic that led to the main arterial, halted at a stoplight and chuckled. "A seven," he repeated. "I'd have rated it more of an eight."

"Maybe." Dori relaxed and a light laugh tickled her throat. "No, it was definitely a seven."

"You're a hard woman, Dori Robertson."

Her laugh would no longer be denied. "So I've been told."

Instead of heading for the freeway as she expected, Gavin took several turns that led indirectly to the waterfront.

"Where are we going?"

"For something to eat. I thought you might be hungry."

Dori had to stop and think about it before deciding that yes, she probably could eat. "One thing."

"Yeah?" Gavin's eyes momentarily left the road.

"Not another hamburger. That's all Danny ever wants when we go out."

"Don't worry, I have something else in mind."

Gavin's "something else" turned out to be The Lobster Shop, an elegant restaurant overlooking the busy Tacoma harbor. Dori had often heard about the restaurant but had never been there. It was the kind of place where reservations were required days in advance.

"You were planning this all along," she said as he drove into the parking lot in front of the restaurant. She studied the strong, broad face and thick dark hair with silver wings fanning out from the temples.

"I thought I might have to appease you after taking you to the fights."

"I enjoyed myself."

His soft chuckle filled the car. "I know. You really surprised me, especially when you flew to your feet and kissed Boom Boom."

"It's so different from seeing it on television. And I blew him a kiss," she said on a note of righteous indignation. "That's entirely different from flying to my feet and kissing him. I was happy he won the bout, that's all."

"I could tell. However, next time you feel like kissing an athlete, you might want to try me."

"You must be joking!" She brought her hand to her heart and feigned a look of shock. "What if you rated me?"

Gavin was still chuckling when he left the car and came around to her side. There was a glint of admiration in his eyes as he escorted her into the restaurant.

The food was as good as Dori had expected. They both had lobster and an excellent white wine; after their meal, they sat and talked over cups of coffee.

"To be truthful," Dori said, staring into the depths of her drink, "I didn't have much hope for our 'date.'"

"You didn't?" A crooked smile slid across Gavin's mouth.

"But to my utter amazement, I've enjoyed myself. The best thing about this evening is not having to worry about making any real commitment or analyzing our relationship. So we can just enjoy spending this time together. We both know where we stand and that's comfortable. I like it."

"I do, too," Gavin agreed, finishing his coffee. He smiled absently at the waitress as he paid their bill.

Dori knew they should think about leaving, but she felt content and surprisingly at ease. When another waitress refilled their cups, neither objected.

"How long have you been a widow?" Gavin asked.

"Five years." Dori's fingers curved around the cup as she lowered her gaze. "Even after all this time I still have trouble accepting that Brad's gone. It seems so…unreal. Maybe if he'd had a lingering illness, it would've been easier to accept. It happened so fast. He went to work one morning and was gone the next. A year later I was still reeling from the shock. I've thought about that day a thousand times. Had I known it was going to be our last morning together, there would've been so many things to say. As it was, I didn't even get a chance to thank him for the wonderful years we shared."

"What happened?" Gavin reached for her hand. "Listen, if this is painful, we can drop it."

"No," she whispered and offered him a reassuring smile. "It's only natural for you to be curious. It was a freak accident. To this day I'm not sure exactly what happened. Brad was a bricklayer and he was working on a project downtown. The scaffolding gave way and a half ton of bricks fell on him. He was gone by the time they could free his body." She swallowed to relieve the tightness in her throat. "I was three months pregnant with our second child. We'd planned this baby so carefully, building up our savings so I could quit my job. Everything seemed to fall apart at once. A week after Brad's funeral, I lost the baby."

Gavin's fingers tightened on hers. "You're a strong woman to have survived those years."

Dori felt her throat muscles constrict and she nodded sadly. "I didn't have any choice. There was Danny, and his world had been turned upside down along with mine. We clung to each other, and after a while we were able to pick up the pieces of our lives. I'm not saying it was easy, but there really wasn't any choice. We were alive, and we couldn't stay buried with Brad."

"When Danny asked for a new father it really must've thrown you."

"It certainly came out of left field." Her eyes sparkled with silent laughter. "That boy thinks up the craziest ideas sometimes."

"You mean like the want ad?"

Dori groaned. "That has to be the most embarrassing moment of my life. You'll never know how grateful I am that you stepped in when you did."

"If you can persuade Melissa to buy a dress, I'll be forever in your debt."

"Consider it done."

Strangely, her answer didn't seem to please him. He

gulped down the last of his coffee, then pushed back his chair and rose. "You women have ways of getting exactly what you want, don't you?"

Dori bit back an angry retort. She didn't understand his reaction; she hadn't done anything to deserve this attack. But fine, let him act like that. She didn't care.

As he held open her car door, he hesitated. "I didn't mean to snap at you back there. I apologize."

An apology! From Gavin Parker! Dori stared at him. "Accepted," she murmured, hiding her astonishment as she concentrated on getting into the car.

On the return drive to Seattle, Dori rested her head against the seat and closed her eyes. It had been a long, difficult week and she was tired. When Gavin stopped in front of her house, she straightened and tried unsuccessfully to hide a yawn.

"Thank you, Gavin. I had a good time. Really."

"Thank *you*." He didn't turn off the engine as he came around to her side of the car. Dori experienced an odd mixture of regret and relief. She'd toyed with the idea of inviting him in for a nightcap or a final cup of coffee. But knowing Gavin, he'd probably assume the invitation meant more. In any case, he'd left the engine running, so he was ready to be on his way. Dori found she was disappointed that their time together was coming to an end.

With a guiding hand at her elbow, Gavin walked her to the front porch. She fumbled in her purse for her key, wondering if she should say anything. It hadn't slipped her notice that he'd asked about Brad yet hadn't offered any information regarding his ex-wife. Dori was filled with questions she didn't want to ask.

She hesitated, the key in her hand. "Thanks again." She didn't think he was going to kiss her, but she wouldn't object if he tried. The kiss they'd shared earlier had been pleasant, more than pleasant—exciting and stirring. Even now the taste of his mouth clung to hers. Oh, no! Why was she feeling like this? Dori's mind whirled. It must be the wine that had caused this light-headed feeling, she decided frantically. It couldn't have been his kiss. Not Gavin Parker. Oh, please, don't let it be Gavin.

He was standing so close that all she had to do was sway slightly and she'd be in his arms. Stubbornly, Dori stood rigid, staying exactly where she was. His finger traced the delicate line of her chin as his eyes met hers in the dim glow of her porch light. Dori's smile was weak and trembling as she realized that he *wanted* to kiss her but wouldn't. It was almost as though he was challenging her to make the first move—so he could blame her for enticing him.

Dori lowered her eyes. She wouldn't play his game. "Good night," she said softly.

"Good night, Dori." But neither of them moved. "I'll pick up Danny about noon on Sunday," he added.

"Fine." Her voice was low and slightly breathless. "He'll be ready." Knowing Danny, he was ready now. Her quavering smile was touched by her amusement at the thought.

"I'll bring Melissa at the same time," Gavin murmured, and his gaze shifted from the key clenched in her hand to her upturned face.

"That'll be fine."

He took a step in retreat. "I'll see you on Sunday then."

"Sunday," she repeated, purposefully turning around and inserting the key in her lock. When the door opened, she looked back at him over her shoulder. "Good night, Gavin."

"Good night." His voice was deep and smooth. She recognized the message in his eyes, and her heart responded while her nerve endings screamed a warning. Hurrying now, Dori walked into the house and closed the door. He hadn't kissed her, but the look he'd given her as he stepped off the porch was far more powerful than a mere kiss.

The next morning the front door slammed shut as Danny burst into the house. "Mom! How did it go? Did Mr. Parker ask you any football questions? Did he try to kiss you good-night? Did you let him?"

Dori sat at the kitchen table, dressed in her old bathrobe with the ragged hem; her feet rested on the opposite chair. Glancing up from the morning paper, she held out her arms for Danny's hug. "Where's Grandma?"

"She has a meeting with her garden club. She wanted me to tell you she'd talk to you later." Pulling out a chair, Danny straddled it backward, like a cowboy riding a wild bronco. "Well, how'd it go?"

"Fine."

Danny cocked his head to one side. "Just fine? Nothing *happened*?" Disappointment made his voice fall dramatically.

"What did you think we were going to do?" Amusement twitched at the edges of her mouth, and her eyes twinkled. "Honey, it was just a date. Our first one, at that. These things take time."

"But how long?" he demanded. "I thought I'd have a new dad by Christmas, and Thanksgiving will be here soon."

Dori set the paper aside. "Danny, listen to me. We're dealing with some important issues here. Remember when we got your bike? We shopped around and got the best price possible. We need to be even more careful with a new father."

"Yeah, but I remember that we went back and bought my bike at the very first store we looked at. Mom, Mr. Parker will make a perfect dad." His arm curled around the back of the chair. "I like him a lot."

"I like him, too," Dori admitted, "but that doesn't mean we're ready for marriage. Understand?"

Danny's mouth drooped and his shoulders hunched forward. "I bet you looked pretty last night."

"Thank you."

"Did Mr. Parker see how pretty you looked?"

Dori had to think that one over. To be honest, she wasn't sure Gavin was the type to be impressed by a new dress or the fact that she was wearing an expensive perfume. "Do you want to hear what we did?"

"Yeah." Danny's spirits were instantly buoyed and he didn't seem to notice that she hadn't answered his question.

"First we had hamburgers and fries."

"Wow."

Dori knew that would carry weight with her son. "But it wasn't even the best part. Later we went to a boxing match in Tacoma."

Danny's eyes rounded with excitement.

"If you bring me my purse, I'll show you the program."

He bounded into the other room and grabbed her handbag. "Mom—" he hesitated before passing it to her, staring pointedly at her feet "—you didn't let Mr. Parker know that you sometimes sleep with socks on, did you?"

Dori could feel the frustration building inside her. "No," she said, keeping her eyes on her purse as she pulled out the program. "The subject never came up."

"Good." The relief in his voice was evident.

"Gavin wants you to be ready tomorrow at noon. He's taking you to the Seahawks football game."

"Really?" Danny's eyes grew to saucer size. "Wow! Will I get to meet any players?"

"I don't know, but don't ask him about it. All right? That would be impolite."

"I won't, Mom. I promise."

Danny was dressed and ready for the game hours before Gavin arrived on Sunday morning. He stood waiting at the living room window, fidgeting anxiously. But the minute he spotted the car, Danny was galvanized into action, leaping out the front door and down the steps.

Dori followed and stood on the porch steps, her arms around her middle to ward off the early-November chill. She watched as Melissa and Gavin climbed out of the car, then smiled at the way Danny and Melissa greeted each other. Like conquering heroes on a playing field, they ran to the middle of the lawn, then jumped up and slapped their raised hands in midair in a gesture of triumph.

"What's with those two?" Gavin asked, walking toward Dori.

"I think they're pleased about…you know, our agreement."

"Ah, yes." A frown puckered his brow as he gave her a disgruntled look and stepped past her into the house.

Dori's good mood did a nosedive, but she turned and followed him inside. "Listen, if this is too much of an inconvenience we can do it another week." Somehow she'd have to find a way to appease Danny. The last thing she wanted was for Gavin to view his agreement to spend time with her son as an annoying obligation. For that matter, she could easily take Danny and Melissa to a movie if Gavin preferred it. She was about to suggest doing just that when Danny and Melissa entered the house.

"Hi, Mr. Parker," Danny greeted him cheerfully. "Boy, I'm really excited about you taking me to the game. It's the neatest thing that's ever happened to me."

Gavin's austere expression relaxed. "Hi, Danny."

"Mom packed us a lunch."

"That was nice of your mom." Briefly, Gavin's gaze slid to Dori. Although he offered her a quick smile, she wasn't fooled. Something was bothering him.

"Yeah, and she's a really great cook. I bet she's probably one of the best cooks in the world."

"Danny," Dori warned in a low voice, sending him an admonishing look.

"Want a chocolate chip cookie?" Danny switched his attention to Melissa instead. "Mom baked them yesterday."

"Sure." Gavin's daughter accompanied Danny into the kitchen.

Dori turned to Gavin. "You know, you don't have to do this. I'll take Danny and Melissa to a movie or something. You look worn out."

"I am." He jammed his hands deep inside his pockets and marched to the other side of the room.

"What's wrong?"

"Women."

Dori recognized the low murmuring that drifted out from the kitchen as the sound of Melissa talking nonstop and with great urgency. Whatever was wrong involved Gavin's daughter.

"In the plural?" Dori couldn't hide a knowing grin as she glanced toward the children.

"These are the very best cookies I've ever had in my whole life," Melissa's voice sang out from the kitchen.

Shaking her head, Dori broke into a soft laugh. "Those two couldn't be any more obvious if they tried."

"No, I suppose not." Gavin shifted his gaze and frowned again. "Melissa and I had an argument last night. She hasn't spoken to me since. I'd appreciate it if you could smooth things over for me."

"Sure, I'll be happy to try."

Gavin lapsed into a pensive silence, then stooped to pat the stuffed lion he'd won for her at the fair. "Aren't you going to ask what we fought about?"

"I already know."

As he straightened, Gavin's dark eyes lit with amused speculation. "Is that a fact?"

"Yes."

"All right, Ms. Know-It-All, you tell me."

Dori crossed the living room and stopped an inch away from him. "The next time you go out with another woman, you might want to be a bit more discreet." Deftly she lifted a long blond hair from his shoulder.

Five

"It wasn't my fault," Gavin declared righteously. "Lainey showed up last night uninvited."

Dori's eyebrows arched expressively. How like a man to blame the woman. From the beginning of time, this was the way it had been. It had started in the Garden of Eden when Adam blamed Eve for enticing him to partake of the forbidden fruit, Dori thought, and it was still going on. "Uninvited, but apparently not unwelcome," she murmured, doing her best to hide a smile.

Gavin rubbed the back of his neck in an agitated movement. "Don't you start on me, too." His angry response cut through the air.

"Me!" It was all she could do to keep from laughing outright.

"No doubt I'm sentenced to a fifteen-minute lecture from you, as well."

Feigning utter nonchalance, Dori moved to the other side of the room and sat on the sofa arm. With relaxed grace she crossed her legs. "It wouldn't be fair for me to lecture you. Besides, I have a pretty good idea of what happened."

"You do?" He eyed her speculatively.

"Sure. This gorgeous blonde showed up...." She paused to stroke her chin as if giving the matter deep thought. "Probably with two tickets to something she knew you really wanted to see."

"Not tickets but—" He stopped abruptly. "Okay. You're right, but I was only gone an hour and Melissa acted like I'd just committed adultery or worse." His defensiveness returned. Stalking over to stand by the television set, he whirled around, asking, "Are you mad at me, too?"

"No." Amused was more the word.

Gavin expelled his breath and looked visibly relieved. "Good. I swear this arrangement is almost as bad as being married."

"Even if I was upset, Melissa's scolded you far more effectively than I ever could."

A smile touched his eyes, revealing tiny lines of laughter at their outer corners. "That girl's got more of her mother in her than I realized."

"One thing, Gavin."

"Yes?" His gaze met hers.

"Is this Lainey the one whose brain leaks?"

"Yeah, she's the one."

"So you went out with her again although you claimed you weren't going to?" She wanted to prove to him that he wasn't as stouthearted or strong-willed as he'd wanted her to believe.

He surveyed her calmly. "That's right."

"Then what does that make you?" Dori hated to admit how much she was enjoying this.

His eyes were locked on her face. "I knew you'd get back at me one way or another."

Blinking her lashes wickedly, Dori gave him her brightest smile. It was obvious that Gavin was angrier with himself than with anyone else and that he didn't like his susceptibility to the charms of this blonde. And to be honest, Dori wasn't exactly pleased by it, either, although she'd rather have choked than let him know.

"Don't worry, all is forgiven," she said with a heavy tone of martyrhood. "I'll be generous and overlook your faults. It's easy, since I have so few of my own."

"I hadn't asked for your forgiveness," he returned dryly.

"Not to worry, I saved you the trouble."

A barely suppressed smile crossed his face. "I can't remember Melissa ever being so angry."

"Don't worry, I'll talk to her."

"What are you going to say?"

Not for the first time, Dori noticed how resonant his voice was. She shrugged one shoulder and glanced out the window. "I'm not sure, but I'll think of something," she assured him.

"I know what'll help."

"What?" She raised her eyes to his.

He strode over to her and glanced into the kitchen. "Danny, are you about ready?" Before Danny had a chance to answer, Gavin pulled Dori to her feet, enfolded her in his arms and drew her so close that the outline of his body was imprinted on hers.

"Ready, Mr. Parker," Danny said as he flew into the living room with Melissa following sluggishly behind. Before Dori could say anything, Gavin's warm mouth claimed hers, moving sensuously over her lips, robbing her of thought. Instinctively her arms circled his neck as his fiery kiss burned away her objections.

"Gavin!" The word vibrated from her throat. Somehow she managed to break the contact and, bracing her hands against his chest, separated her body from his. She was too stunned to say more than his name. The kiss had been so unexpected—so good—that she could only stare up at him with wide disturbed eyes.

"Danny and I should be back about five. If you like, we can all go to dinner afterward."

Mutely, Dori nodded. If he'd asked her to swim across Puget Sound naked, she would have agreed. Her mind was befuddled, her senses numb.

"Good." Gavin buried his mouth in the curve of her neck and Dori's bewildered eyes again widened with shock. As he released her, she caught a glimpse of Melissa and Danny smiling proudly at each other. Dori had to smother an angry groan.

"See you at five." With a thoughtful frown, Gavin ran his index finger down the side of her face.

"Bye, Mom," Danny interrupted.

"Bye." Dori shook her head to clear her muddled thoughts and calm her reactions. "Have a good time."

"We will," Gavin promised. He hesitated, studying his daughter. "Be good, Melissa."

The brilliant smile she gave him forced Dori and Gavin to hide a tiny, shared laugh.

"Okay, Dad, see you later."

Gavin's astonished eyes sought Dori's and he winked boldly. Parents had their own forms of manipulating. Again, Dori had difficulty concealing her laughter.

The front door closed and Melissa plopped down on the sofa and crossed her arms. "Dad told you about *her*, didn't he?"

"He mentioned Lainey, if that's who you mean."

"And you're not mad?" The young girl leaned forward and cupped her face in her hands, supporting her elbows on her knees. "I thought you'd be furious. I was. I didn't know Dad could be so dumb. Even I could see that she's a real phony. Ms. Bleached Blonde was so gushy last night I almost threw up."

Dori sat beside the girl and took the same pose as Melissa, placing her bent elbows on her knees. "Your dad doesn't need either of us to be angry with him."

"But…" Melissa turned to scrutinize Dori, her smooth brow furrowed in confusion. "I think we should both be mad. He shouldn't have gone out with her. Not when he's seeing you."

Throwing an arm around the girl's shoulders, Dori searched for the right words. Explaining his actions could get her into trouble. "Your father was angrier at himself than either of us could be. Let's show him that we can overlook his weaknesses and…love him in spite of them." Dori knew immediately that she'd used the wrong word.

"You love Dad?"

A shudder trembled through Dori. "Well, that might have been a little too strong."

"I think he's falling in love with you," Melissa said fervently. "He hardly talks about you, and that's a sure sign."

Dori was unconvinced. If he didn't talk about her, it was because he wasn't thinking about her—which was just as well. She wasn't going to fool herself with any unwarranted emotions. She and Gavin had a dating agreement and she wasn't looking for anything more than a way of satisfying Danny's sudden need for a father. Just as Gavin was hoping to appease his daughter.

"That's nice," Dori said, reaching for the Sunday paper. "What would you like to do today?" Absently she flipped the pages of the sales tabloids that came with the paper.

The girl shrugged and reclined against the back of the sofa. "I don't know. What would you like to do?"

"Well." Dori eased herself into a comfortable position and pretended to consider the possibilities. "I could do some shopping, but I don't want to drag you along if you'd find it boring."

"What are you going to buy?"

Remembering the way Melissa had watched her put on makeup sparked an idea. "I thought I'd stop in at Northgage plaza and sample a few perfumes at Macy's. You can help me decide which one your father would like best."

"Yeah, let's do that."

Two hours later, before she was even aware of Dori's scheme, Melissa owned her first cosmetics, a new dress and shoes. Once Dori had persuaded the girl that it was okay to experiment with some light makeup, progressing to a dress and shoes had been relatively easy.

Back at the house Melissa used Dori's bedroom to try on the new outfit. Shyly she paraded before Dori, her intense eyes lowered to the carpet as she walked. The dress was a lovely pink floral print with a calf-length skirt that swung as she moved. The ballet-style shoes were white and Melissa was wearing her first pair of nylons. Self-consciously she held out her leg to Dori. "Did I put them on right?"

"Perfect." Dori smiled with pride. Folding her hands together, she said softly, "Oh, Melissa, you're so pretty."

"Really?" Disbelief made her voice rise half an octave.

"Really!" The transformation was astonishing. The girl standing before her was no longer a defiant tomboy but a budding young woman. Dori's heart swelled with emotion. Gavin would hardly recognize his own daughter. "Come and look." Dori led her into the bathroom and closed the door so Melissa could see for herself in the full-length mirror.

The girl breathed a long sigh. "It's beautiful," she said in a shaking voice. "Thank you." Impulsively she gave Dori a hug. "Oh, I wish you were my mother. I really, really wish you were."

Dori hugged her back, surprised at the emotion that surged through her. "I'd consider myself very lucky to have you for a daughter."

Melissa stepped back for another look at herself. "You know, at first I was really hoping Dad would marry Lainey." She pursed her lips and tilted her head mockingly. "That's how desperate I am to get out of that school. It's not that the teachers are mean or anything. Everyone's been really nice. But I really want a family and a regular, ordinary life."

Dori hid a smile. *Really* was obviously Melissa's word for the day.

"But the more I thought about it, the more I realized Lainey would probably keep me in that stupid school until I was twenty-nine. She doesn't want me hanging around. If Dad marries her, I don't know what I'd do."

"Your father isn't going to marry anyone..." Dori faltered momentarily. "Not someone you don't like, anyway."

"I hope not," Melissa said heatedly. Turning sideways, she viewed her profile. "You know what else I'd really like to do?"

"Name it." The day had gone so well that Dori was ready to be obliging.

"Can I bake something?"

"Anything you like."

The spicy aroma of fresh-baked apple pie filled the house by the time Danny burst in the front door. "Mom!" he screamed as if the very demons of hell were in pursuit. "The Seahawks won. The score was 14 to 7."

Dori had been so busy it hadn't occurred to her to turn on the television. "Did you have a good time?"

"Mr. Parker bought me a hot dog and a soda pop and some peanuts."

Dori cast an accusing glare at Gavin, who shrugged, then grinned sheepishly.

"What about the lunch I packed you?"

"We couldn't bring it into the stadium. Mr. Parker says it's more fun to buy stuff at the game, anyway."

"Oh, he did, did he?" Amused, Dori found her laughing eyes meeting Gavin's.

The bedroom door opened a crack. "Can I come out yet?"

Guiltily Dori glanced at the hallway. "Oh, goodness, I nearly forgot. Sit down, you two. Melissa and I have a surprise."

Gavin and Danny obediently took a seat. "Ready," Dori called over her shoulder. The bedroom door opened wide and Melissa started down the hallway. Halting her progress for a moment, Dori announced, "While you two were at the game, Melissa and I were just as busy shopping."

Confident now, none of her earlier coyness evident, Melissa strolled into the room and gracefully modeled the dress, turning as she came to a stop in front of the sofa. Smiling, she curtsied and demurely lowered her lashes. Then she rose, folding her hands in front of her, ready to receive their lavish praise.

"You look like a girl," Danny said, unable to disguise his lack of enthusiasm. At the disapproving look Dori flashed him, he quickly amended his hastily spoken words. "You look real pretty, though."

Dori studied Gavin's reaction. A myriad of emotions were revealed in the strong, often stern features. "This can't be my little girl. Not Melissa Jane Parker, my daughter."

Melissa giggled happily. "Really, Dad, who else could it be?"

Gavin shook his head. "I don't know who's wearing that dress, but I can hardly believe I've got a daughter this pretty."

"I made you a surprise, too," Melissa said eagerly. "Something to eat."

"Something to eat?" He echoed her words and looked at Dori, who smiled innocently.

Tugging at his hand, Melissa urged her father off the couch and led him into the kitchen. "Dori helped me."

"Not that much. She did most of the work herself."

"A pie?" Gavin's gaze fell to the cooling masterpiece that rested on the kitchen countertop.

"Apple," Melissa boasted proudly. "Your favorite."

Later that night, Dori lay in bed gazing up at the darkened ceiling, her clasped hands supporting the back of her head. The day had been wonderful. There was no other word to describe it. She'd enjoyed shopping with Melissa, particularly because the girl had been so responsive to Dori's suggestions. Dori didn't like to think about the baby she'd lost after Brad's death. She'd so hoped for a daughter. Today it was almost as if Melissa had been hers. Dori felt such enthusiasm, such joy, in sharing little things, like shopping with Melissa. She loved Danny beyond reason, but there were certain things he'd never appreciate. Shopping was one. But Melissa had enjoyed it as much as Dori had.

Danny's day had been wonderful, too. All evening he'd talked nonstop about the football game and had obviously had the time of his life. Long after Gavin and Melissa had left, Danny continued to recount the highlights of the game, recalling different plays with a vivid memory for detail. Either the two children had superlative—and hitherto unsuspected—acting abilities, or their reactions had been genuine. Dori found it difficult to believe this had all been a charade. She'd had her suspicions when Gavin first suggested their arrangement, but now she thought it might be the best thing to have happened to her in a long time—the best thing for all of them.

The next morning Sandy looked up from her work when Dori entered the office.

"Hi," Dori said absently as she pulled out the bottom drawer of her desk and deposited her purse. When Sandy didn't immediately respond, Dori glanced up. Sandy was studying her, head slightly cocked. "What's with the funny, bug-eyed look?" Dori demanded.

"There's something different about you."

"Me?"

"Yeah. You and this football hero went out Friday night, didn't you?"

Dori couldn't help chuckling. "Yes. To the fights, if you can believe it."

"I don't."

"Well, do, because it's the truth. But first he took me out for a four-star meal of hamburgers, French fries and a chocolate shake."

"And he's alive to tell about it?"

Dori relaxed in her chair and crossed her arms, letting the memory of that night amuse her anew. "Yup."

"From that dreamy look in your eyes I'd say you had a good time."

Dreamy look! Dori stiffened and reached for her pen. "Oh, hardly. You just like to tease, that's all."

Sandy raised her eyebrows in response, then returned to the file she was working on. "If you say so, but you might want to watch where you walk, what with all those stars blinding your eyes."

At about eleven o'clock the phone buzzed. Usually Sandy and Dori took turns answering, but Sandy was away from her desk and Dori automatically reached for the receiver.

"Underwriting," she announced.

"Dori?"

"Gavin?" Her heart began to pound like a jackhammer gone wild. "Hi."

"What time are you free for lunch?" he asked without preamble.

"Noon." From the sound of his voice, he was concerned about something. "Is anything wrong?" Dori probed.

"Not really. I just think we need to talk."

They agreed on an attractive seafood restaurant beside Lake Union. Gavin was already seated at one of the linen-covered tables when Dori arrived an hour later. She noticed that his eyes were thoughtful as he watched the maître d' lead her to his table.

"This is a nice surprise," she said to Gavin, smiling appreciatively at the waiter who held out her chair.

"Yes, although I don't usually take this kind of lunch break." There seemed to be a hidden meaning in his statement.

Gavin always managed to throw her off course one way or another. Whenever she felt she understood him, he'd say or do something that made her realize she hardly knew this man. Her intuition told her it was about to happen again. Mentally she braced herself, and a small sigh of dread quivered in her throat.

To mask her fears, Dori lifted the menu and studied it with unseeing eyes. The restaurant was known for its seafood, and Dori was toying with the idea of ordering a Crab Louis when Gavin spoke. "Melissa had a good time yesterday."

"I did, too. She's a wonderful child, Gavin." Dori set the menu aside, having decided on a shrimp salad.

"Once we got off the subject of you, Danny and I had a great time ourselves," Gavin murmured.

Dori groaned inwardly at the thought of Danny endlessly extolling her virtues. Gavin must have been thoroughly sick of hearing about her. She'd make a point of speaking to Danny later.

"Danny certainly enjoyed himself."

Gavin laid the menu alongside his plate and stared at her in nerve-racking silence.

Instinctively, Dori stiffened. "But there's a problem, right?" she asked with deliberate softness, fighting off a sense of unease.

"Yes. I think you might have laid on this motherhood bit a little too thick, don't you? Melissa drove me crazy last night. First Danny and now my own daughter."

Anger raged within Dori and it was all she could do not to bolt out of the restaurant. To Gavin's twisted way of thinking, she had intentionally set out to convince his daughter that she'd be the perfect wife and mother. On the basis of nothing more than her visit with Melissa the day before, Gavin had cynically concluded that she was already checking out engagement rings and choosing a china pattern. "You know, I was thinking the same thing myself," she said casually, surprised at how unemotional she sounded.

Gavin studied her with amused indifference. "I thought you might be."

His sarcastic tone was her undoing. "Yes, the more I think about it, the more I realize that our well-plotted scheme may be working all *too* well. If you're tired of listening to my praises, then you should hear it from my end."

"Yes, I imagine—"

"That's exactly your problem, Gavin Parker," she cut in, her voice sharp. "The reason Melissa responded to me yesterday was because that child has a heart full of love and no one who seems to want it." Dori fixed her gaze on the water glass as she fought back a rising swell of anger. "I feel sorry for you. Your thinking is so twisted that you don't know what's genuine and what isn't. You're so afraid of revealing your emotions that... that your heart's become like granite."

"And I suppose you think you're just the woman to free me from these despicable shackles?" he taunted.

Dori ignored the derision and the question. "For Melissa's sake I hope you find what you're looking for." She tilted her head back and raised her eyes, meeting his with haughty disdain. "For my part, I want out." She had to go before she became so attached to Melissa that severing the relationship would harm them both. And before she made the fatal mistake of falling for Gavin Parker.

His eyes glittered as cold and dark as the Arctic Sea. "Are you saying you want to cancel our agreement?"

Calmly, Dori placed the linen napkin on her unused plate and stood. "I swear the man's a marvel," she murmured. "It was nice knowing you, Gavin Parker. You have a delightful daughter. Thank you for giving Danny the thrill of his life."

"Sit down," he hissed under his breath. "Please. Let's discuss this like adults."

Still standing, Dori boldly met Gavin's angry eyes. Sick at heart and so miserable that with any provocation at all she would have cried, she slowly shook her head. "I'm sorry, Gavin, but even a phony arrangement can't work with us. We're too different."

"We're not different at all," he argued, then paused to glower at the people whose attention his raised voice had attracted.

"Careful, Gavin," she mocked, "someone might think you're coming on a bit too—"

"Melissa's mother phoned me this morning," he said starkly, and for the first time Dori noticed the deep lines of worry that marred his face.

"What?" she breathed, her pulse accelerating at an alarming rate. She sat down again, her eyes wide and fearful at the apprehension on Gavin's face.

"Our conversation was less than congenial. I need to talk to someone. I apologize if I came at you like a kamikaze pilot."

If, Dori mused flippantly. He'd invited her because he wanted someone to talk to and then he'd tried to sabotage their lunch. "What happened?"

"The usual. Deirdre's in New York and is divorcing her third or fourth husband, I forget which, and wants Melissa to come and live with her."

Dori gasped. She knew nothing about this woman. Until today she hadn't even known her name. But Dori was aware of the pain this woman had inflicted on Gavin's life. "Does she have a chance of getting her?" Already her heart was pounding at the thought of Gavin losing his daughter to a woman he so obviously detested.

Gavin's laugh was bitter. "Hardly, but that won't stop her from trying. She does this at the end of every marriage. She has an attack of guilt and wants to play mommy for a while."

"How does Melissa feel about Deirdre? Does she ever see her mother?" She didn't mean to pry and she didn't want him to reveal anything he wasn't comfortable sharing. But the thought of this young girl being forced into such a difficult situation tore at her heart.

"Melissa spends a month with her every summer. Last year she phoned me three days after she arrived and begged me to let her come home. At the time Deirdre was just as glad to be rid of her. I don't know what happened, but Melissa made me promise that I wouldn't send her there by herself again."

"I realize you're upset, but the courts aren't going to listen to your—"

"I know," Gavin interrupted. "I just needed to vent my frustration and anger on someone. Melissa and I have gone through this before and we can weather another of Deirdre's whims." Gavin's hand gently touched hers. "I owe you an apology for the way I behaved earlier."

"It's forgotten." What wasn't forgotten was that he'd sought her out. Somehow, she'd reached Gavin Parker— and now they were on dangerous ground. This charade became more real every time they saw each other. They'd been convinced they could keep their emotions detached—but they were failing. More and more, Gavin dominated her thoughts, and despite herself, she found excuses to imagine them together. It wasn't supposed to work like this.

"You told me about Brad. I think it's only fair to let you know about Deirdre."

A feeling of gladness raced through Dori. Not because Gavin was telling her about his ex-wife. To be truthful, Dori wasn't even sure she wanted to hear the gory details of his marriage breakdown. But the fact that Gavin was telling her was a measure of his trust. He felt safe enough with her to divulge his deepest pain—as she had with him. "It isn't necessary," she said softly.

"It's only fair that you know." He gripped the icy water glass, apparently oblivious to the cold that must be seeping up his arm. "I don't know where to begin. We got married young, too young I suppose. We were in our last year of college and I was on top of the world. The pros were already scouting me. I'd been seeing Deirdre, but so had a lot of other guys. She came from a wealthy family and had been spoiled by an indulgent father. I liked him. He was a terrific guy, even if he did cater too much to his daughter—but he loved her. When she told me she was pregnant and I was the baby's father, I offered to marry her. I have no difficulty believing that if I hadn't, she would've had an abortion. I went into the marriage with a lot of expectations. I think I was even glad she was pregnant. The idea of being a father pleased me—proof of my manhood and all that garbage." He paused and focused his gaze on the tabletop.

Dori realized how hard this must be for him, and her first instinct was to tell him to stop. It wasn't necessary for him to reveal this pain. But even stronger was her sense that he needed to talk—to get this out of his system.

"Usually people can say when they felt their marriage going bad. Ours went bad on the wedding day. Deirdre hated being pregnant, but worse, I believe she hated me. From the moment Melissa was born, she didn't want anything to do with her. Later I learned that she hated being pregnant so much that she had her tubes tied so there'd never be any more children. She didn't bother to tell me. Melissa was handed over to a nanny and within weeks Deirdre was making the rounds, if you know what I mean. I don't think I need to be any more explicit."

"No." Dori's voice was low and trembling. She'd never known anyone like that and found it impossible to imagine a woman who could put such selfish, shallow pleasures ahead of her own child's needs.

"I tried to make the marriage work. More for her father's sake than Deirdre's. But after he died I couldn't pretend anymore. She didn't want custody of Melissa then, and I'm not about to give up my daughter now."

"How long ago was that?"

"Melissa was three when we got divorced."

Three! Dori's heart ached for this child who'd never experienced a mother's love.

"I thought you should know," he concluded.

"Thank you for telling me." Instinctively Gavin had come to her with his doubts and worries. He was reaching out to her, however reluctantly he'd done so at first. But he'd made a beginning, and Dori was convinced it was the right one for them.

That same week, Dori saw Gavin two more times. They went to a movie Wednesday evening, sat in the back row and argued over the popcorn. Telling Dori about Deirdre seemed to have freed him. On Friday he phoned her at the office again, and they met for lunch at the same restaurant they'd gone to the previous Monday. He told her he was going to be away for the weekend, broadcasting a game.

By the following Monday, Dori was worried. She had so much difficulty keeping her mind on her work, she wondered if she was falling in love with Gavin. It didn't seem possible that this could happen so quickly. Her physical response to his touch was a pleasant surprise. But it had been years since a man had held her the way he did, so Dori had more or less expected and compensated for the physical impact. The emotional response was what overwhelmed her. She cared about him. Worried about him. Thought about him to the exclusion of all else. They were in trouble, deep trouble. But Gavin had failed to recognize it. If they were going to react sensibly, the impetus would have to come from her.

Dori's thoughts were still confused when she stopped at the soccer field to pick up Danny after work that Monday night. She pulled into the parking lot and walked across the lawn to the field. The boys were playing a scrimmage game and she stood on the sidelines, smiling as she watched Danny weave his way through the defenders.

"You're Danny's mother, aren't you?"

Dori switched her attention to the thin, lanky man standing next to her. She recognized him as Jon Schaeffer's dad. Jon and Danny had recently become the best of friends and had spent the night at each other's houses two or three times since the beginning of the school year. From what she understood, Jon's parents were separated. "Yes, you're Jon's father, right?"

"Right." He crossed his arms and nodded at the boys running back and forth across the field. "Danny's a good player."

"Thank you. So is Jon."

"Yeah, I'm real proud of him." The conversation was stilted and Dori felt a little uneasy.

"I hope you won't think I'm being too bold, but did you put an ad in the paper?"

Dori felt waves of color flood her face. "Well, actually Danny did."

"I thought he might have." He chuckled and held out his hand. "My name's Tom, by the way."

Less embarrassed, Dori shook it. "Dori," she introduced herself.

"I read the ad and thought about calling. Despite what I'd hoped, it doesn't look like Paula and I are going to get back together and I was so lonely, I thought about giving you a call."

"How'd you know the number was mine?"

"I didn't," he was quick to explain. "I wrote it down on a slip of paper and set it by the phone. Jon spent last weekend with me and saw it and wanted to know how come I had Danny's phone number."

"Oh." Color blossomed anew. "I've had the number changed since."

"I think Jon mentioned that. So Danny put the ad in the paper?"

"All on his own. It's the first time I've ever regretted being a mother." Involuntarily her voice rose with re-membered embarrassment.

"Did you get many responses?"

He was so serious that Dori was forced to conceal a smile. "You wouldn't believe the number of calls that came the first night."

"That's what I figured."

They lapsed into a companionable silence. "You and your husband split up?"

Tom had a clear-cut view of life, it seemed, and a blunt manner. The question came out of nowhere. "No, I'm a widow."

"Hey, listen, I'm sorry. I didn't mean to be nosy. It's none of my business."

"Don't worry about it," Dori told him softly.

Tom wasn't like most of the men she'd known. He was obviously a hard worker, frank, a little rough around the edges. Dori could tell that he was still in love with his wife and she hoped they'd get back together.

"Jon and Danny are good friends, aren't they?"

"They certainly see enough of each other."

"Could you tolerate a little more togetherness?" His gaze didn't leave the field.

"How do you mean?"

"Could I take you and Danny to dinner with Jon and me?" He looked as awkward as a teenager asking a girl out for the first time.

Dori's immediate inclination was to refuse politely. The last thing she wanted to do was alienate Jon's mother. On the other hand, Dori needed to sort through her own feelings for Gavin, and seeing someone else was bound to help.

"Yes, we'd enjoy that. Thank you."

The smile he beamed at her was bright enough to rival the streetlight. "The pleasure's all mine."

Six

"Mom," Danny pleaded, following her into the bathroom and frantically waving his hand in front of his face while she deftly applied hair spray.

"What?" Dori asked irritably. She'd been arguing with Danny from the minute he'd learned she was going out with Tom Schaeffer.

"Mr. Parker could phone."

"I know, but it's unlikely." Gavin hadn't been in touch with her since their Monday lunch. If he expected her to sit around and wait for his calls, then he was in for a surprise.

Danny's disgruntled look and defiantly crossed arms made her hesitate. "If he does phone, tell him I'm out for the evening and I'll return his call when I get home."

"But I thought you and Mr. Parker were good friends… *real* good friends. You even kissed him!"

"We are friends," she said, feigning indifference as she tucked in a stray hair and examined her profile in the mirror. With a sigh of disgust she tightened her stomach and wondered how long she could go without breathing.

"Mom," Danny protested again, "I don't like this and I don't think Mr. Parker will, either."

"He won't care," she said with more aplomb than she was feeling. Danny assumed that because she was going out on a weeknight, this must be a "hot date." It wasn't. Tom had invited her out after their dinner with the boys and Dori had accepted because she realized that what he really wanted was a sympathetic ear. He was lonely and still in love with his wife. She couldn't have picked a safer date, but Danny wouldn't understand that and she didn't try to explain.

"If you're such good friends with Mr. Parker, how come you're wearing perfume for Jon's dad?"

"Moms sometimes do that for no special reason."

"But you're acting like tonight *is* special. You're going out with Mr. Schaeffer."

Dori placed her hands on her son's shoulders and studied him closely. His face was pinched, his blue eyes intense. "Don't you like Mr. Schaeffer?"

"He's all right, I guess."

"But I thought you had a good time when we went out to dinner Monday night."

"That was different. Jon and I were with you."

Dori knew that Danny wasn't terribly pleased that a high school girl from the neighborhood was coming to babysit. He was at that awkward age—too young to be left completely alone, especially for an evening, but old enough to resent a babysitter, particularly when she was one of his own neighbors.

"I'll be home early—probably before your bedtime," Dori promised, ruffling his hair.

Danny impatiently brushed her hand aside. "But why are you going, Mom? That's what I don't get."

Dori didn't know how she could explain something she didn't completely understand herself. She was worried that her emotions were becoming too involved with Gavin. Tom was insurance. With Tom there wasn't any fear of falling in love or being hurt. But every time she saw Gavin her emotions became more entangled; she cared about him and Melissa. As far as Gavin was concerned, though, the minute he knew she'd fallen for him would be the end of their relationship. He'd made it abundantly clear that he didn't want any kind of real involvement. He had no plans to remarry, and if she revealed any emotional commitment he wouldn't hesitate to reject her as he'd rejected others. Oh, she might hold on to him for a time, the way Lainey was trying to. But Gavin wasn't a man easily fooled—and Dori wasn't a fool.

The doorbell chimed and the sixteen-year-old who lived across the street came in with an armful of books.

"Hello, Mrs. Robertson."

"Hi, Jody." Out of the corner of her eye Dori saw that Danny was sitting down in front of the television. She wasn't deceived by his indifference. Her son was not happy that she was dating Tom Schaeffer, as he'd informed her in no uncertain terms. Dori ignored him and continued her instructions to the sitter. "The phone number for the restaurant is in the kitchen. I shouldn't be much later than nine-thirty, maybe ten." The doorbell chimed again and Danny answered it this time, opening the door for Tom, who smiled appreciatively when he saw Dori.

"Be good," Dori whispered and kissed Danny on the cheek.

He rubbed the place she'd kissed and examined the palm of his hand for any lipstick. "Okay," he agreed with a sad little smile calculated to tug at a mother's heart. "But I'm waiting up for you." He gave her the soulful look of a lost puppy, his eyes crying out at the injustice of being left at the fickle mercy of a sixteen-year-old girl. The emphasis, of course, being on the word *girl*.

If Dori didn't leave soon, he might well win this unspoken battle and she couldn't allow that. "We'll talk when I get back," she promised.

Tom, dressed in a suit, placed a guiding hand at the small of her back as they left the house. "Is there a problem with Danny?"

Dori cast a speculative glance over her shoulder. She felt guilty and depressed, although there was no reason she should. Now she realized how Melissa had made Gavin feel when he'd gone out with Lainey that Saturday night. No wonder he'd been upset on Sunday. Neither of them was accustomed to this type of adolescent censorship. And she didn't like it any more than Gavin had.

"Danny's unhappy about having a babysitter," she answered Tom half-truthfully.

With such an ominous beginning, Dori suspected the evening was doomed before it had even begun. They shared a quiet dinner and talked over coffee, but the conversation was sporadic and when the clock struck nine, Dori fought not to look at her watch every five minutes.

On the drive home, she felt obliged to apologize. "I'm *really* sorry..." She paused, then remembered how often

Melissa used that word and, in spite of herself, broke into a full laugh.

Tom's bewildered gaze met hers. "What's so amusing?"

"It's a long story. A friend of mine has a daughter who alternates *really* with every other word. I caught myself saying it just now and…"

"It suddenly seemed funny."

"Exactly." She was still smiling when Tom turned into her street. Her face tightened and her smile disappeared when she saw a car parked in front. Gavin's car. She clenched her fists and drew several deep breaths to calm her nerves. There was no telling what kind of confrontation awaited her.

As politely as possible, Dori thanked Tom for the dinner and apologized for not inviting him in for coffee.

When she opened the door a pair of accusing male eyes met hers. "Hello, Gavin," Dori said cheerfully, "this is a nice surprise."

"Dori." The glittering harshness of his gaze told her he wasn't pleased. "Did you have a good time?"

"Wonderful," she lied. "We went to a Greek restaurant and naturally everything was Greek to me." She forced a laugh. "I finally ordered exactly what the waiter suggested." Dori hated the way she was rambling like a guilty schoolgirl. Her mouth felt dry and her throat scratchy.

Danny faked a wide yawn. "I think I'll go to bed now."

"Not so fast, young man." Dori stopped him. Her son had played a part in this uncomfortable showdown with Gavin. The least he could do was explain. "Is there something you want to tell me?"

Danny eyed the carpet with unusual interest while his cheeks flushed a telltale red. "No."

Dori was convinced that Danny had called Gavin, but she'd handle that later with a week's grounding. "I'll talk to you in the morning."

"Night, Mr. Parker." Like a rabbit unexpectedly freed from a trap, Danny bolted down the hallway to his bedroom.

It didn't escape Dori's notice that he hadn't wished her good-night. Hanging her coat in the hall closet gave her a moment to collect her thoughts and resolve to ignore the distressing heat that warmed her blood. When she turned to face Gavin, she saw that a cynical smile had quirked up the corners of his stern mouth.

"Don't look so guilty," he muttered.

Dori's cheeks burned, but she boldly met his eyes. "I'm not." She walked into the kitchen and prepared a pot of coffee. Gavin followed her and she automatically took two mugs from the cupboard. Turning, her back pressed against the counter, Dori confronted him squarely. "What happened? Did Danny phone you?"

"I thought we had an agreement."

Involuntarily, Dori flinched at the harshness of his voice. "We do," she said calmly, watching the coffee drip into the glass pot.

"Then what were you doing out with a man? A married one, at that."

"Exactly what has Danny been telling you? Tom and his wife are separated. For heaven's sake, we didn't even hold hands." She studiously avoided meeting his fiery glare, angry now that she'd bothered to explain. "Good grief, you went out with Lainey. I don't see the difference."

"At least I *felt* guilty."

"So did I! Does that make it any better?"

"Yes!" he shouted.

She whirled around, tired of playing mouse to his cat. Her hand shook as she poured hot coffee into the mugs.

"Are we going to fight about it?" she asked as she set his mug on the kitchen table.

"That depends on whether you plan to see him again." His face was impassive, as if the question were of no importance. Dori marveled at his self-control. The hard eyes that stared back dared her to say that she'd be seeing Tom again.

"I don't know." She sat in the chair opposite him. "Does it matter?"

His mouth twisted in a faintly ironic smile. "It could. I don't particularly relish another frantic phone call from your son informing me that I'd better do something quick."

"Believe me, that won't happen again," Dori said, furious with Danny and more furious with herself. She should've known Danny would do something like this and taken measures to avoid it.

"So you felt guilty." His low, drawling voice was tinged with amused mockery.

"I didn't like it any more than you did." She expelled her breath and folded her arms in a defensive gesture. "I don't know, Gavin. Maybe our agreement is working too well." She reached impatiently for the sugar bowl in the middle of the table and stirred a teaspoon into her coffee.

"Before we know it, those two kids are going to have us married and living in a house with a white picket fence."

"Don't worry about that."

"Oh, no—" she waved her hands in the air helplessly "—of course that wouldn't concern you. Mr. Football Hero can handle everything, right? Well, you admitted that Melissa made you miserable when you saw Lainey. Danny did the same thing to me. I think we should bow gracefully out of this agreement while we can." Although Dori offered the suggestion, she hoped Gavin would refuse; she needed to know that the attraction was mutual.

"Is that what you want?" Deftly he turned the tables on her.

In a flash of irritation, Dori pushed back her chair and walked quickly to the sink, where she deposited her mug. She sighed with frustration and returned to the table. "No, unfortunately I don't. Darn it, Parker, in spite of your arrogant ways, I've discovered I like you. That's what scares me."

"Don't sound so shocked. I'm a great guy. Just ask Danny. Of course, it could be my virility that you find so alluring, in which case we're in trouble." Chuckling, he rolled lazily to his feet and took his empty cup to the sink.

"Don't *you* worry," she muttered sarcastically, "your masculinity hasn't overpowered me yet."

"That's probably the best thing we've got going for us. Don't fall in love with me, Dori," he warned, the amusement gone from his eyes. "I'd only end up hurting you."

Her pulse rocketed with alarm. He was right. The problem was that she was already halfway there. And she was standing on dangerous ground, struggling to hold back her feelings.

"I think you've got things twisted here," she told him dryly. "I'm more concerned about you falling for me. I'm not your usual type, Gavin. So the risk could well be of your own making."

Her appraisal didn't appear to please him. "There's little chance of that. One woman's already brought me to my knees and I'm not about to let that happen again."

Dori forced back the words of protest, the assertion that a real woman didn't want a man on his knees. She wanted him at her side as friend, lover and confidant.

"There's another problem coming up, and I think we should discuss it," he continued.

"What?"

He ignored her worried look and leaned casually against the counter. "Melissa and I are going to San Francisco over Thanksgiving weekend. I'm doing the play-by-play of the 49ers game that Saturday. Melissa's been asking me for weeks if you and Danny can come with us."

"But why? This should be a special time for the two of you."

"Unfortunately, that isn't how Melissa sees it. She'll be in the hotel room alone on the Saturday because I'll be in the broadcast booth and I don't want her attending the game by herself. It *is* Thanksgiving weekend, as Melissa keeps pointing out. But I hate to admit that my daughter knows exactly which buttons to push to make me feel guilty."

"I'm not sure, Gavin," Dori hedged. She'd planned to spend the holiday with her parents, but she loved San

Francisco. She'd visited the Bay area as a teenager and had always wanted to return. This would be like a vacation, and she hadn't taken one in years.

"The way I see it," Gavin went on, "this may even suit our needs. The kids are likely to overdose on each other if they spend that much time together. Maybe after three or four days in each other's company, they'll face a few truths about this whole thing."

Dori was skeptical. "It could backfire."

"I doubt it. What do you say?"

The temptation was so strong that she had to close her eyes to fight back an immediate *yes*. "Let…let me think about it."

"Fine," he said calmly.

Dori pulled out a chair and sat down. "Have you heard anything more from Deirdre?"

"No, and I won't."

"How can you be so sure?"

The hard line of his mouth curved upward in a mirthless smile. "Trust me on this."

The manner in which he said it made Dori's blood run cold. Undoubtedly Gavin knew Deirdre's weaknesses and knew how to attack his ex-wife.

"There's no way on this earth I'll hand my daughter over to *her*."

Dori had never seen a man's eyes look more frigid or harsh. "If there's anything I can do…" She let the rest fade. Gavin wouldn't need anything from her.

"As a matter of fact, there is," he said, contradicting her thoughts. "I'm broadcasting a game this Sunday in Kansas City, which means Melissa has to spend the weekend at school. Being there on Saturday and Sunday is the worst, or so she claims."

"She could stay with us. I'd like that immensely." There wasn't anything special planned. Saturday she'd be doing errands and buying the week's groceries, and Danny had a soccer game in the afternoon, but Melissa would enjoy that.

"I was thinking more like one day," Gavin told her. "As it is, you'll hear all about my many virtues for twenty-four hours. Why ask for more?"

"Let her stay the whole weekend," Dori said. "Didn't you just say we should try to 'overdose' the kids?"

Gavin's warning proved to be prophetic. From the moment Dori picked Melissa up at the Eastside Boarding School on Mercer Island, the girl chattered nonstop, extolling her father's apparently limitless virtues—just as he'd predicted.

"Did you know that my father has a whole room full of trophies he won playing sports?"

"Wow," Danny answered, his voice unnaturally high. "Remember our list, Mom? I think it's important that my new dad be athletic."

"What else was on the list?" Melissa asked, then listened attentively as Danny explained each requirement. She launched into a litany of praise for Gavin, presenting him as the ideal father and husband in every respect. However, it hadn't escaped Dori's notice that Melissa didn't mention the last stipulation, that Danny's new father love Dori. Instinctively Melissa recognized that would be overstepping the bounds. Dori appreciated the girl's honesty.

As Melissa continued her bragging about Gavin, Dori had to bite her tongue to keep from laughing. Given the chance, she'd teach those two something about subtlety— later. For now, they were far too amusing. In an effort to restrain her merriment, she concentrated on the heavy traffic that moved slowly over the floating bridge. Friday afternoons were a nightmare for commuters.

The chatter stopped and judging by the sounds she heard from the backseat, Dori guessed that Danny and Melissa were having a heated discussion under their breaths. Dori thought she heard Tom's name but let it pass. With all the problems her date with him had caused, she doubted she'd be seeing Tom again. For his part, he was hoping to settle things with his wife and move back home in time for the holidays. Dori knew that Jon would be thrilled to have his father back, and she prayed Tom's wife would be as willing.

Following the Saturday expedition to the grocery store, the three of them attended Danny's soccer game. To Melissa's delight, Danny scored two goals and was cheered as a hero when he ran off the field at the end of the game. Luckily they arrived back home before it started to rain. Dori made popcorn and the two children watched a late-afternoon movie on television.

The phone rang just as Dori was finishing the dinner dishes. She reached for it and glanced at Danny and Melissa, who were playing a game of Risk in the living room.

"Hello," she answered absently.

"Dori, it's Gavin. How are things going?"

"Fine," she said, unreasonably pleased that he'd

phoned. "They've had their first spat but rebounded re-markably well."

"What happened?"

"Melissa wanted to try on some of my makeup and Danny was thoroughly disgusted to see her behaving like a girl."

"Did you tell him the time will come when he'll ap-preciate girls?"

"No." Her hand tightened on the receiver. Gavin was a thousand miles from Seattle. The sudden warmth she felt at hearing his voice made her thankful he wasn't there to witness the effect he had on her. "He wouldn't have believed it, coming from me."

"I'll tell him. He'll believe me."

Danny would. If there was anything wrong with this relationship, it was that Danny idealized Gavin. One day, Gavin would fall off Danny's pedestal. No man could continue to breathe comfortably so high up, in such a rarefied atmosphere. Dori only hoped that when the crash came, her son wouldn't be hurt. "Are you hav-ing a good time with your cronies?" she asked, leaning against the kitchen wall.

He laughed and the sound produced a tingling rush of pleasure. "Aren't you afraid I've got a woman in the room with me?"

"Not in the least," she answered honestly. "You'd hardly phone here if you did."

"You're too smart for your own good," he chided af-fectionately. He paused, and Dori's heart began to race. "You're going to San Francisco with us, aren't you?"

"Yes."

"Good." No word had ever sounded more sensuous to Dori.

She straightened quickly, frightened by the intensity of her emotions. "Would you like to talk to Melissa?"

"How's she behaving?"

"As predicted."

Gavin chuckled. "Do you want me to say something?"

Gavin was obviously pleased that his daughter's behavior was running true to form. "No. Danny will undoubtedly list my virtues for hours the next time you have him."

"I'll look forward to that."

"I'll bet." Grinning, Dori set the phone aside and called Melissa, who hurried into the kitchen and grabbed the receiver. Overflowing with enthusiasm, she relayed the events of the day, with Danny motioning dramatically in the background, instructing Melissa to tell Gavin about the goals he'd scored that afternoon. Eventually Danny got a chance to report the great news himself. When the children had finished talking, Dori took the receiver back.

"Have they worn your ear off yet?"

"Just about. By the way, I might be able to catch an early flight out of here on Sunday, after the game."

She hadn't seen Gavin since her date with Tom, and much as she hated to admit it, she wanted to spend some time with him before they went to San Francisco. "Do you want us to pick you up at the airport?"

"If you could."

"I'll see if I can manage it."

Before ending the conversation, Dori wrote down Gavin's flight number and his time of arrival.

Late the following afternoon, the three of them were sitting in the arrivals area at Sea-Tac International. They'd come early, and Dori frequently found herself checking her watch, less out of curiosity about the time than out of an unexpected nervousness. She felt she was behaving almost like a love-struck teenager. Even choosing her outfit had been inordinately difficult; she'd debated between a wool skirt with knee-high black leather boots and something less formal. In the end she chose mauve corduroy pants and a pullover sweater the color of winter wheat.

"Dad's plane just landed." Melissa pointed to the monitor and bounded to her feet.

Dori brushed an imaginary piece of lint from her sweater and cursed herself for being so glad Gavin was home and safe. With the children standing at either side, her hands resting lightly on their shoulders, she forced a strained smile to her lips. A telltale warmth invaded her face and Dori raised a self-conscious hand to brush the hair from her temple. Gavin was the third passenger to appear.

"Dad!" Melissa broke formation and ran to Gavin, hugging him fiercely. Danny followed shyly and offered Gavin his hand to shake. "Welcome back, Mr. Parker," he said politely.

"Thank you, Danny." Gavin shook the boy's hand with all the seriousness of a man closing a million-dollar deal.

"How was the flight?" Dori stepped forward, striving to keep her arms obediently at her sides, battling the impulse to greet him as Melissa had done.

His raincoat was draped over one arm and he carried a small carry-on bag in the other hand. Dark smudges under his eyes told her that he was exhausted. Nonetheless he gave her a warm smile. "The flight was fine."

"I thought you said he'd kiss her," Danny whispered indignantly to Melissa. The two children stood a few feet from Dori and Gavin.

"It's too public... I think," Melissa whispered back and turned accusing eyes on her father.

Arching his brows, Gavin held out an arm to Dori. "We'd better not disappoint them," he murmured, "or we won't hear the end of it for the entire week."

That outstretched arm was all the invitation Dori needed. No step had ever seemed so far—or so close. Relentlessly, Gavin held her gaze as she walked into the shelter of his embrace. His hand slipped around the back of her neck, bringing her closer. Long fingers slid into her hair as his mouth made a slow descent to her parted lips. As the distance lessened, Dori closed her eyes, more eager for this than she had any right to be. Her heart was doing a drumroll and she moistened her suddenly dry lips. She heard Gavin suck in his breath as his mouth claimed hers.

Of their own accord, or so it seemed, her hands moved over the taut muscles of his chest and shoulders until her fingers linked behind his neck. In the next instant, his mouth hardened, his touch firm and experienced. The pressure of his hand at the back of her neck lifted her onto the tips of her toes, forcing the full length of her body close to the unyielding strength of his. The sound of Gavin's bag hitting the floor barely registered on her numbed senses. Nor did she resist when he wrapped both arms around her so tightly that she could hardly breathe. All she could taste, feel, smell, was Gavin. She felt as if she'd come home after a long time away. He'd kissed her before, but it had never been like this, like a hundred shooting stars blazing a trail across an ebony sky.

Dori struggled not to give in to the magnificent light show, not to respond with everything in her. She had to resist. Otherwise, Gavin would know everything.

Gavin broke the kiss and buried his face in her hair. "That kiss has to be a ten," he muttered thickly.

"A nine," she insisted, her voice weak. "When we get to ten, we're in real trouble."

"Especially if we're at an airport."

Gavin's hold relaxed, but he slipped his hand around her waist, bringing her closer to his side. "Well, kids, are you happy now?"

"You dropped your bag, Mr. Parker." Danny held it out to him and eyed Melissa gleefully. He beamed from ear to ear.

"So I did," Gavin said, taking his carry-on bag. "Thanks for picking it up."

"Dori put a roast in the oven," Melissa informed him, "just in case you were hungry. I told her how starved you are when you get home from these things."

"Your father's tired, Melissa. I'll have you both over for dinner another time."

"I appreciate that," Gavin told Dori, his gaze caressing her. "I *have* been up for the past thirty hours."

A small involuntary smile raised the corners of Dori's mouth. She hadn't been married to Brad all those years without having some idea of the way a man thought and behaved away from home.

Gavin's eyes darkened briefly as if he expected a sarcastic reply. "No comment?"

"No comment," she echoed cheerfully.

"You're not worried about who I was with?"

"I know—or at least I think I do," she amended.

Gavin hesitated, his eyes disbelieving. "You think you do?" he asked.

"Well, not for sure, but I have a pretty good hunch."

"This I've got to hear." His hand tightened around her waist. "Well?"

Both Danny and Melissa looked concerned. They were clearly disappointed that Dori wasn't showing any signs of jealousy. Obviously, they assumed Gavin had been with another woman. Dori doubted it. If he had, he wouldn't be so blatant about it. Nor would he mention it in front of the children.

"I'd guess that you were with some football friends, drinking beer, eating pretzels and playing poker."

The smug expression slowly faded as a puzzled frown drew his brows together. "That's exactly where I was."

Disguising her pride at guessing correctly was nearly impossible. "Honestly, Gavin, it wasn't that hard to figure out. I'm in my thirties. I've been married. I know how a man thinks."

"And men are all alike," he taunted.

"No," she said, trying desperately to keep a straight face. "But I'm beginning to know *you*. When you stop asking me if I'm concerned about who you were with, then I'll worry."

"You think you're pretty smart, don't you?"

"No." She shook her head. "Men I can understand. It's children that baffle me."

He continued to hold her close as they walked down the long concourse. Melissa and Danny skipped ahead.

"Were they a problem this weekend?" Gavin inclined his head toward the two kids.

"Nothing I couldn't handle."

"I have the feeling there's very little you can't handle."

Self-conscious now, Dori looked away. There was so much she didn't know, so much that frightened her. And the main object of her fears was walking right beside her, holding her as if it were the most natural thing in the world—as if he intended to hold on to her for a lifetime. But Dori knew better.

Seven

The bell of the cable car clanged as Dori, Melissa, Danny and Gavin clung precariously to the side. A low-lying fog was slowly dissipating under the cheerful rays of the early afternoon sun.

"When are we going to Ghiradelli's?" Melissa wanted to know. "I love chocolate."

"Me too," Danny chimed in eagerly.

"Soon," Gavin promised, "but I told Dori we'd see Fisherman's Wharf first."

"Sorry, kids." Although Dori apologized, there was no regret in her voice. The lovely City of Saint Francis was everything she remembered, and more. The steep, narrow streets, brightly painted Victorians, San Francisco Bay and the Golden Gate Bridge. Dori doubted that she'd ever tire of the grace and beauty of this magnificent city.

They'd arrived Thanksgiving Day and gone directly to a plush downtown hotel. Gavin had reserved a large suite with two bedrooms connected to an immense central room. After a leisurely dinner of turkey with all the traditional trimmings, they'd gone to bed, Gavin and

Danny in one room, Dori and Melissa in the other, all eager to explore the city the following morning.

After a full day of viewing Golden Gate Park, driving down Lombard Street with its famous ninety-degree curves and strolling through Fisherman's Wharf, they returned to their hotel suite.

Melissa sat in a wing chair and rubbed her sore feet. "I've got an enormous blister," she complained loudly. "I don't think I've ever walked so much in my life. There's nothing I want to do more than watch TV for a while and then go straight to bed." She gave an exaggerated sigh and looked at Danny, who stared back blankly. When he didn't immediately respond, Melissa hissed something at him that Dori couldn't understand, then jabbed him in the ribs with her elbow.

"Oh. Me too," Danny agreed abruptly. "All I want to do is sleep."

"You two will have to go on without us," Melissa continued with a martyred look. "As much as we'd like to join you, it's probably best if we stay here."

Gavin caught Dori's gaze and rolled his eyes. Dori had difficulty containing her own amusement. The two little matchmakers were up to their tricks again. "But we couldn't possibly leave you alone and without dinner," Dori said in a concerned voice.

"I'm not all that hungry." For the first time Danny looked unsure. He'd never gone without dinner in his life and lately his appetite seemed likely to bankrupt her budget. For Danny to offer to go without a meal was the ultimate sacrifice.

"Don't worry about us—we'll order room service,"

Melissa said with the casual ease of a seasoned traveler. "You two go on alone. We insist. Right, Danny?"

"Right."

By the time Dori had showered and dressed, Danny and Melissa were poring over the room-service menu like two people who hadn't eaten a decent meal in weeks. Gavin appeared to be taking the children's rather transparent scheme in his stride, but Dori wasn't so confident. They'd had two wonderful days together. Gavin had once lived in San Francisco and he gave them the tour of a lifetime. If he'd hoped that Melissa and Danny would overdose on each other's company, his plan was failing miserably. The two of them had never gotten along better.

After checking the contents of her purse, Dori sat on the end of the bed and slipped on her imported leather pumps. Then she stood and smoothed her skirt. Her pulse was beating madly and she paused to place her hand over her heart and inhale a deep, soothing breath. She felt chilled and warm, excited and apprehensive, all at once. Remembering how unemotional she'd been about their first dinner date only made her fret more. That had been the night of the fights, and she recalled how she hadn't really cared what she wore. Ten minutes before Gavin was due to pick her up, she'd added the final coat of polish to her nails. Tonight, she was as nervous as she'd ever been in her life. Twenty times in as many minutes she'd worried about her dress. This simple green silk dress was her finest, but it wasn't high fashion. Gavin was accustomed to women far more worldly and sophisticated than she could ever hope to be. Bolstering her confidence, Dori put on her gold earrings and freshened her lipstick. With fingers clutching the bathroom sink, she forced a smile to her stiff lips and exhaled a ragged breath. No question, she was falling in love with Gavin Parker. Nothing could be worse. Nothing could be more wonderful, her heart responded.

When she reentered the suite's sitting room, Melissa and Danny were sprawled across the carpet in front of the television. Danny gave her a casual look and glanced back at the screen, but Melissa did an automatic double take.

"Wow!" the young girl murmured, then immediately straightened. Her eyes widened appreciatively. "You're—"

"Lovely," Gavin finished for his daughter, his eyes caressing Dori, roving slowly from her lips to the swell of her breasts and downward.

"Thank you." Dori's voice died to a whisper. She wanted to drown in his eyes. She wanted to be in his arms. A long silence ran between them and Dori looked away, her heart racing.

"Don't worry about us," Melissa said confidently.

"We'll be downstairs if you need anything," Gavin murmured, taking Dori by the elbow.

"Be good, Danny."

"Okay," he answered without glancing up from the television screen.

"And no leaving the room for any reason," she warned.

"What about a fire?"

"You know what we mean," Gavin answered for Dori.

"Don't hurry back on our account," Melissa said, propping up her chin with one hand as she lay sprawled on the carpet. "Danny and I'll probably be asleep before the show's even over."

Danny opened his mouth to protest, but closed it at a fierce glare from Melissa.

Gavin opened the door and Dori threw a smile over her shoulder. "Have fun, you two."

"We will," they chorused.

As the door closed, Dori thought she heard a shout of triumph.

Gavin chuckled and slid a hand around her waist, guiding her to the elevator. "I swear those two have all the finesse of a runaway roller coaster."

"They do seem a bit obvious."

"Just a bit. However, this is one time I don't mind being alone with you." His hand spread across her back, lightly caressing the silk of her dress. Slowly his fingers moved upward to rub her shoulder. His head was so close Dori could feel his breath against her neck. She didn't know what kind of game Gavin was playing, but her heart was a far too willing participant.

At the whirring sound of the approaching elevator, Gavin straightened. The hand at her back directed her inside, and he pushed the appropriate button.

Inside the restaurant, the maître d' led them to a linen-covered table in the middle of the spacious room and held out Dori's chair. Smiling her appreciation, she sat, accepted the menu and scanned the variety of dishes offered. Her mouth felt dry, and judging by the way her nerves were acting, Dori doubted she'd find anything that seemed appetizing.

No sooner were they seated and comfortable than the wine steward approached their table. "Are you Mr. Parker?" he asked.

"Yes." Gavin looked up from his menu.

The man snapped his fingers and a polished silver bucket was delivered to the table. Cradled in a bed of ice was a bottle of French champagne.

"I didn't order this." His brow was creased with lines of bewilderment.

"Yes, sir. This is compliments of Melissa and Danny in room 1423." Deftly he removed the bottle from the silver bucket and held it out for Gavin's inspection. As he read the label, Gavin raised his eyebrows. "An excellent choice," he murmured.

"Indeed," the steward agreed. With impressive dexterity he removed the cork and poured a sample into Gavin's glass. After receiving approval from Gavin, he filled both their glasses and left.

Gavin held up his glass for a toast. "To Melissa and Danny."

"To our children." Dori's answering comment was far more intimate than she'd meant it to be.

The champagne slid smoothly down Dori's throat and eased her tension. She closed her eyes and savored the bubbly tartness. "This is wonderful," she whispered, setting her glass aside. "How did Melissa and Danny know how to order such an exquisite label?"

"They didn't. I have a feeling they simply asked for the best available."

Dori's hand tightened around the stem of her glass. "Oh, my goodness, this must cost a fortune." She felt color flooding her face. "Listen, let me pay half. I'm sure Danny had something to do with this and he knows I love champagne. It's my greatest weakness."

"You're not paying for anything," Gavin insisted with

mock sternness. "The champagne is a gift and if you mention it again, you'll offend me."

"But, Gavin, this bottle could cost five hundred dollars and I can't—"

"Are we going to argue?" His voice was low.

Dori felt a throb of excitement at the way he was studying her. "No," she finally answered. "I'll agree not to argue, but under protest."

"Do you have any other weaknesses I don't know about?" he inquired smoothly.

You! her mind tossed out unexpectedly. Struggling to maintain her composure, she shrugged and dropped her gaze to the bubbling gold liquid. "Bouillabaisse."

Something close to a smile quirked his mouth as he motioned for the waiter and ordered the Provençal fish stew that was cooked with at least eight different types of seafood. In addition, Gavin ordered hearts-of-palm salad. Taking their menus, the waiter left the table and soon afterward the steward returned to replenish their champagne.

Relaxing in her chair, Dori propped her elbows on the table. Already the champagne was going to her head. She felt a warm glow seeping through her.

The bouillabaisse was as good as any Dori had ever tasted; the wine Gavin had ordered with their meal was mellow and smooth.

While they lingered over cups of strong black coffee, Gavin spoke freely about himself for the first time since the night he'd described his marriage. He talked about his position with the computer company and the extensive traveling it sometimes involved. The job was perfect for him because it gave him the freedom to continue broadcasting during the football season. Setting his own hours was a benefit of being part-owner of the firm. He spoke of his goals for the future and his love for his daughter; he spoke of the dreams he had for Melissa.

His look was poignant in a way she'd never expected to see in Gavin. A longing showed there that was deep and intense, a longing for the well-being and future happiness of those he loved. He didn't mention the past or the glories he'd achieved on the football field. Nor did he mention Deirdre.

Every part of Dori was conscious of Gavin, every nerve, every cell. Dori had never expected to feel such a closeness with another human being again. She saw in him a tenderness and a vulnerability he rarely exposed. So often in the past months, just when Dori felt she was beginning to understand Gavin, he'd withdrawn. The fact that he was sharing these confidences with Dori told her he'd come to trust and respect her, and she rejoiced in it.

The waiter approached with a pot of coffee and Dori shook her head.

Gavin glanced at his watch. "Do we dare go back to the suite? We've only been gone two hours."

The way she was feeling, there wasn't any place safe tonight, not if she was with Gavin. She wanted to be in his arms so badly that she was almost anticipating his touch. She cast about for an excuse to stay. "They'd be terribly disappointed if we showed up so soon."

"There's a band playing in the lounge," he said. "Would you care to go dancing?"

"Yes." Her voice trembled slightly with renewed awareness. "I'd like that."

Gavin didn't look for a table when they entered the

lounge. A soft, melodious ballad was playing and he led her directly to the dance floor and turned her into his arms.

Dori released a long sigh. She linked her fingers at the back of his neck and pressed the side of her face against the firm line of his jaw. Their bodies were so close that Dori could feel the uneven rhythm of his heartbeat and recognized that her own was just as erratic. They made only the pretense of dancing, holding each other so tightly that for a few seconds breathing was impossible. Dragging air into her lungs, Dori closed her eyes to the fullness of emotion that surged through her. For weeks she'd been fighting her feelings for Gavin. She didn't want to fall in love with him. Now, in the few brief moments since he'd taken her in his arms, Dori knew it was too late. She loved him. Completely and utterly. But admitting her love now would only intimidate him. Her intuition told her that Gavin wasn't ready to accept her feelings or acknowledge his own. Pursuing this tiny spark could well extinguish it before it ever had a chance to flicker and flame.

"Dori." The raw emotion in his voice melted her heart. "Let's get out of here."

"Yes," she whispered.

Gavin led her off the tiny floor, out of the lounge and through the bustling lobby. He hesitated momentarily, apparently undecided about where they should go.

"The children will be in bed," she reminded him softly.

The elevator was empty and just as soon as the heavy doors closed, Gavin wrapped his arms around her.

Yearning shamelessly for his kiss, Dori smiled up at

him boldly. She saw his eyes darken with passion as he lowered his head. Leaning toward him, she met his lips with all the eager longing that this evening had evoked. Gavin kissed her with a fierce tenderness until their breaths became mingled gasps and the elevator came to a stop.

Sighing deeply, Gavin tightened his hold, bringing her even closer. "If you kissed me like this every time we entered an elevator, we'd never get off."

"That's what I'm afraid of," she murmured and looked deeply into his eyes.

He was silent for a long moment. "Then perhaps we should leave now, while we still can." His grip relaxed slightly as they stepped off the elevator.

No light shone from under the door of their suite, but Dori doubted they'd have any real privacy. Undoubtedly Melissa and Danny were just inside the bedroom doors, eager to document the most intimate exchanges between their parents.

Gavin quietly opened the door. The room was dark; what little light there was came from a bright crescent moon that shone in through the windows. They walked into the suite, Gavin's arm around her waist. He turned, closed the door and pressed the full length of her body against it, his gaze holding hers in the pale moonlight.

"I shouldn't kiss you here," he murmured huskily as if he wanted her to refuse.

Dori could find no words to dissuade him—she wanted him so badly. The moment seemed to stretch out. Then, very slowly, she raised her hands to caress the underside of his tense jaw. Her fingertips slid into the dark fullness of his hair and she raised herself onto the tips of her toes to gently place her lips on his. The pressure was so light that their lips merely touched.

Gradually his mouth eased over hers in exquisite exploration, moving delicately from one side of her lips to the other. The complete sensuality of the kiss quivered through Dori. A sigh of breathless wonder slid from the tightening muscles of her throat. The low groan was quickly followed by another as Gavin's mouth rocked over hers in an eruption of passion and desire that was all too new and sudden. She'd thought these feelings, these very sensations, had died with Brad. She wanted Gavin. She couldn't have stopped him if he'd lifted her in his arms and carried her to the bedroom. The realization shocked her.

He stroked the curves of her shoulders as he nibbled at her lips, taking small, sensuous bites. His fingers tangled in her hair, and he slid his mouth over her cheek to her eyes and nose and grazed her jaw. She felt him shudder and held his head close as she took in huge gulps of air. The need to experience the intimate touch of his hands and mouth flowered deep within her. Yet he restrained himself with what Dori believed was great effort.

"If you rate that kiss a ten, then we're in real trouble," he muttered, close to her ear.

"We're in real trouble."

"I thought as much." But he didn't release her.

"Knowing Danny, I'd guess he's probably taken pictures of this little exchange." The delicious languor slowly left her limbs.

"And knowing Melissa, I'd say she undoubtedly lent him the camera." Gradually, his arms relaxed their hold.

"Do you think they'll try to blackmail us?" she asked, hoping to end the evening on a lighter note.

"I doubt it," Gavin whispered. "In any case, I have the perfect defense. I believe we can attribute tonight to expensive champagne and an excellent meal, don't you?"

No, she didn't. But Dori swallowed her argument. She knew that this feeling between them had been there from the time they'd boarded the plane in Seattle. Gavin had wanted to be alone with her tonight, just as she'd longed to be with him. Their kissing was a natural consequence of this awakened discovery.

Deciding that no answer was better than telling a lie, Dori faked an exaggerated yawn and murmured, "I should think about bed. It's been a long day."

"Yes," Gavin agreed far too readily. "And tomorrow will be just as busy."

They parted in the center of the room, going in opposite directions toward their respective rooms. Dori undressed in the dark, not wanting to wake Melissa—if indeed Melissa was asleep. Even if she wasn't, Dori didn't feel up to answering the girl's questions.

Gently lifting back the covers of her twin bed, Dori slipped between the sheets and settled into a comfortable position. She watched the flickering shadows playing on the opposite wall, tormenting herself with doubts and recriminations. Gavin attributed their overwhelming attraction to the champagne. She wondered what he'd say if it happened again. And it would. They'd come too far to go back now.

The following afternoon, Melissa, Danny and Dori sat in front of the television to watch the San Francisco

49ers play the Denver Broncos. Dori wasn't particularly interested in football and knew very little about it. But she'd never before watched a game that Gavin was broadcasting. Now she listened proudly and attentively to his comments, appreciating for the first time his expertise in sports.

Another well-known ex-football player was Gavin's announcing partner and the two exchanged witticisms and bantered freely. During halftime, the television camera crew showed the two men sitting in the broadcast booth. Gavin held up a pad with a note that said, "Hi, Melissa and Danny."

The kids went into peals of delight and Dori looked on happily. This four-day weekend was one she'd never forget. Everything had been perfect—perhaps too perfect.

Gavin came back to the hotel several hours after the end of the game. His broad shoulders were slightly hunched and he rubbed a hand over his eyes. His gaze avoided Dori's as he greeted the children, then sank heavily into a chair.

"You were great!" Danny said with unabashed enthusiasm.

"Yeah, Dad." The pride in Melissa's voice was evident.

"You're just saying that because the 49ers won and you were both rooting for them." Gavin's smile didn't quite reach his eyes.

"Can I get you anything, Gavin?" Dori offered quietly, taking the chair across from him. "You look exhausted."

"I am." His gaze met hers for the first time since he'd returned. The expression that leaped into his eyes made her catch her breath, but just as quickly an invisible shutter fell to hide it. Without a word, he turned his head to the side. "I don't need anything, thanks." The way he said it forced Dori to wonder if he was referring to her. That morning, he'd been cool and efficient, but Dori had attributed his behavior to the football game. Naturally he'd be preoccupied. She hadn't expected him to take her in his arms and wasn't disappointed when he didn't. Or so she told herself.

Melissa sat on the carpet by Gavin's feet. "Danny and I knew you'd be tired so we ordered a pizza. That way, you and Dori can go out again tonight and be alone." The faint stress placed on the last word made Dori blush.

She opened her mouth to protest, then closed it. She certainly wasn't ready for a repeat performance of last night's meal, but she wanted to hear what Gavin thought. His eyes clashed with hers and narrowed fractionally as he challenged her to accept or decline.

"No," Dori protested quickly, her voice low. "I'm sure your dad's much too tired. We'll all have pizza."

"Okay." Melissa shot to her feet, willing to cooperate with Dori's decision. "Danny and I'll go get it. The pizza place is only a couple of blocks from here."

"I'll go with you," Dori said, not wanting the two children walking the streets by themselves after dark.

A hand stopped her, and Dori turned to find Gavin studying her. His mouth twisted wryly; his eyes were chilling. "What's the matter?" he asked.

She searched his face, wondering about the subtle challenge in his question. "Nothing," she replied smoothly, calmly. "You didn't want to go out, did you?"

"No."

"Then why are you looking at me like I committed

some serious faux pas?" Dori inclined her head to one side, not understanding the change in him.

"You're angry because I didn't hold up your name with the kids' this afternoon."

Dori's mouth dropped open in shock. "Of course not! That's crazy." Gavin couldn't believe something that trivial would bother her, could he?

But apparently he did. He released her arm and leaned back in the chair. "Women are all alike. You want attention, and national attention is all the better. Right?"

"Wrong!" She took a step in retreat, stunned by his harshness. She didn't know how to react to Gavin when he was in this mood and judging from the stubborn look on his face, she didn't expect it to change.

Dori's thoughts were prophetic. Gavin seemed withdrawn and unnaturally quiet on the flight home early the next morning. He didn't phone her in the days that followed. During the past month, he'd called her twice and sometimes three times a week. Now there was silence. Even worse was the fact that she found herself waiting for his call. Her own reaction angered her more than Gavin's silence. And yet, Dori thought she understood why he didn't contact her. She also realized that she shouldn't contact him. Maybe he expected her to; maybe he even wanted her to. But Dori wouldn't. She couldn't. Gavin was fighting his feelings for her. He knew that what had happened between them that evening in San Francisco couldn't be blamed on the champagne, and it scared him. He couldn't see her, afraid of what he'd say or do. It was simpler to invent some trumped-up grievance, blame her for some imaginary wrong.

Friday morning, after a week of silence, Dori sat at her desk, staring into space.

"Are you and Gavin going out this weekend?" Sandy asked with a quizzical slant of one delicate brow.

Dori returned her attention to the homeowner's insurance policy on her desk. "Not this weekend."

"Is Gavin announcing another football game?"

"I don't know," she responded without changing her expression.

"Did you two have a fight or something?"

"Or something," Dori muttered dryly.

"Dori." Sandy's eyes became serious. "You haven't ruined this relationship, have you? Gavin Parker is perfect for you. Whatever's happened, make it right. This fish is much too rich and good-looking to throw back. Reel him in very carefully, Dori."

An angry retort trembled on the tip of her tongue, but Dori swallowed it. Not once had she thought of Gavin as a big fish, and she didn't like the cynical suggestion that she should reel him in carefully or risk losing him. Their relationship had never existed on those terms. Neither of them was looking for anything permanent—or at least they hadn't been, not in the beginning.

Dori's mood hadn't improved by the time she got home.

Danny was draped over the sofa, his feet propped up against the back, his head touching the floor. "Hi, Mom."

"Hi." She unwound the scarf from around her neck and unbuttoned her coat. Stuffing her scarf in the sleeve, she reached for a hanger.

"Aren't you going to ask me about school?"

"How was school?" For the first time in years, she

didn't care. A long soak in a hot bath interested her far more. This mood infuriated her.

"Good."

Dori closed the closet door. "What's good?"

Danny untangled his arms and legs from the sofa and sat up to stare at her. "School is." He cocked his head and gave her a perplexed look. "You feeling sick?"

It was so easy to stretch the truth. She was sick at heart, disillusioned and filled with doubts. She never wanted to see Gavin Parker again, and yet she was dying for a word from him. Anything. A Christmas card would have elated her, a business card left on her doorstep, a chain letter. Anything. "I'm a little under the weather."

"Do you want me to make dinner tonight?"

"Sure." Her willingness to let Danny loose in the kitchen was a measure of how miserable she felt. This time last week they'd been in San Francisco....

"You *want* me to cook?" Danny was giving her a puzzled look again.

"There might be a microwave dinner in the freezer. You can have that."

"What about you?"

Dori hesitated before heading down the hallway to her room. "I'm not hungry." There wasn't enough chocolate in the world to get her through another week of not hearing from Gavin.

"Not hungry? You must really be sick."

Dori's appetite had always been healthy and Danny was well aware of it. "I must be," she said softly, and went into the bathroom to fill the tub. On impulse she added some bath-oil beads. While the water was running, she stepped into her room to get her pajamas, the faded blue housecoat with the ripped hem and a pair of thick socks.

Just as she was sliding into the fragrant mass of bubbles, Danny knocked anxiously on the bathroom door.

"Go away," she murmured irritably.

Danny hesitated. "But, Mom—"

"Danny, please," she cried. "I don't feel good. Give me a few minutes to soak before hitting me with all your questions." She could hear him shuffling his feet outside the door. "Listen, honey, if there are any cookies left in the cookie jar, they're yours as long as you don't disturb me for thirty minutes. Understand?"

Dori knew she should feel guilty, but she was willing to bend the rules this once if it brought peace and quiet.

"You sure, Mom?"

"Danny, I want to take a nice, hot, uninterrupted bath. Got that?"

He hesitated again. "Okay, Mom."

Dori soaked in the bath until all the bubbles had disappeared and the hot water had turned lukewarm. This lethargy was ridiculous, she decided, nudging up the plug with her big toe. The ends of her curls were wet; after brushing her hair, Dori let it hang limply around her face. The housecoat should have been discarded long ago, but it suited Dori's mood. The socks came up to her knees and she shoved her feet into rabbit-shaped slippers that Danny had given her for Christmas two years before. The slippers had long floppy ears that dragged on the ground and pink powder-puff tails that tickled her ankles. They were easily the most absurd-looking things she owned.

"Hi, Mom…" Danny frowned when she stepped into

the living room, concern creasing his face. "You look terrible."

Dori didn't doubt it, with her limp hair, ragged old housecoat and rabbit slippers.

"Mr. Parker's never seen you look so awful."

"He won't, so don't worry."

"But, Mom," Danny protested loudly. "He'll be here any minute."

Eight

For a wild instant, Dori resisted the panic. "He's not coming." She'd waited all week for him to call and heard nothing. And now he was about to appear on her doorstep, and she didn't want to see him. She couldn't face him, looking and feeling the way she did. In her heart she was pleading with her son to say that Gavin wasn't really coming. "I'm sure Gavin would phone first." He'd better!

"He did, Mom." Danny's expression was one of pure innocence.

"When?" Dori shouted, her voice shaking.

"While you were running your bath. I told him you had a bad day and you wanted to soak."

"Why didn't you *tell* me?" she cried, giving way to alarm.

The doorbell chimed and Dori swung around to glare at it accusingly. Gripping her son by the shoulders, she had the irrational urge to hide behind him. "Get rid of him, Danny. Understand?"

"But, Mom—"

"I don't care what you have to tell him." It occurred to Dori that she must be crazy to make a suggestion like that.

The doorbell continued to ring in short, impatient bursts. Before either mother or son could move, the front door opened and Gavin walked in. "How come your door's open?"

At Danny's guilty look, he scowled. "Don't you know how dangerous that is? Anyone could…" His words faded to a whisper as he stared at Dori. "Has anyone called a doctor? You look terrible."

"So everyone's been telling me," she snapped, clenching her fists. All week she'd been dying for a word or a glance, anything, from Gavin and now that he was here, she wanted to throw him out of her house. Whirling, she stalked into the kitchen. "Go away."

Gavin followed her there and stood, feet braced, as if he expected a confrontation. "I need to talk to you."

Dori opened the refrigerator door and set a carton of eggs on the counter, ignoring him. She wasn't hungry, but scrambling eggs would give her something to concentrate on.

"Did you hear me?" Gavin demanded.

"Yes, but I'm hoping that if I ignore you, you'll go away."

At that moment Danny strolled into the room, pulled out a kitchen chair and sat down. His eager gaze went from his mother to Gavin and again to Dori; they both frowned at him warningly.

"You two want some privacy, right?"

"Right," Gavin answered.

"Before I go, I want you to know, Mr. Parker, that Mom doesn't normally look like…this bad."

"I realize that."

"Well, I was worried because—"

"Danny, please," Dori hissed. "You're doing more harm than good."

His chair scraped against the kitchen floor as he pushed it away from the table. "Don't worry," he said. "I get the picture."

Dori wondered how her son could claim to know what was going on when she didn't have the slightest idea. For that matter, she suspected Gavin didn't, either.

Taking a small bowl from the cupboard, she cracked two eggs against the side.

"How was your week?" Gavin asked.

Dori squeezed her eyes shut and mentally counted to five. "Wonderful."

"Mine too."

"Great." She couldn't hide the sarcasm in her voice.

"I suppose you wondered why I didn't phone," Gavin said next.

Dori already knew, but she wanted to hear it from him. "It crossed my mind once or twice," she said flippantly, as she whipped the eggs with such a vengeance they threatened to slosh out of the small bowl.

"Dori, for heaven's sake, would you turn around and look at me?"

"No!" A limp strand of hair fell across her cheek and she jerked it aside.

"Please." His voice was so soft and caressing that Dori felt her resistance melt away.

With her chin tucked against her collarbone, she winced at a mental image of herself with limp, lifeless hair, a ragged housecoat and silly slippers. She turned toward him, her fingers clutching the counter as she leaned against it for support.

Gavin moved until he stood directly in front of her and placed his hands on her shoulders. Absurd as it was, Dori noticed that his shoes were shined. Worse, they were probably Italian leather, expensive and perfect. He lifted her chin with one finger, but her eyes refused to meet his.

"I've missed you this week," he whispered, and she could feel his gaze on her mouth. It took all Dori's strength not to moisten her lips and invite his kiss. She felt starved for the taste of him. A week had never seemed so long. "A hundred times I picked up the phone to call you," he whispered.

"But you didn't."

"No." He sighed unhappily and slowly shook his head. "Believe it or not, I was afraid."

His unexpected honesty allowed her to meet his gaze openly. "Afraid?"

"Things are getting a little...intense between us, don't you think?" His voice rose with the urgency of his admission.

"And heaven forbid that you have any feelings for a woman in her thirties." She drew a sharp breath and held out a lifeless strand of auburn hair. "A woman who's about to discover her first gray hair, no less."

"Dori, that has nothing to do with it."

"Of course it does," she argued angrily. "If you're

going to get involved with anyone, you'd prefer a twenty-five-year-old with a perfect body and flawless skin."

"Would you stop!" He shook her shoulders lightly. "What's the matter with you?"

"Maybe this week has given me time to think. Maybe I know you better than you know yourself. You're absolutely right. You *are* afraid of me and the feelings I can arouse in you, and with good reason. You're attracted to me and it scares you. If it hadn't been for the kids last weekend, who knows what would've happened between us?" At his narrowed look, she took another deep breath and continued her tirade. "Don't try to deny it, Gavin. *I* can figure a few things out for myself—that's the problem when you start seeing a woman whose brain doesn't leak. I know darned well what's going on here. I also know what you're about to suggest."

"I doubt that." His brow furrowed with displeasure.

"It's one of two things," she went on, undaunted.

"Oh?" He took a step in retreat, crossed his arms and leaned against the kitchen table. His eyes were burning her, but Dori ignored the heat.

"Either you want to completely abandon this charade now and never see each other again. This, however, would leave you with a disgruntled daughter who's persistent enough to have you seek out a similar arrangement with another woman. Knowing the way you think, I'd say you probably toyed with the idea for a while. However, since you're here, I'm guessing you've decided another mature woman would only cause you more trouble. You're so irresistible that she's likely to fall in love with you," she said scornfully. "So it's best to deal with the enemy you know—namely me."

His mouth was so tight that white lines appeared at the corners of his lips. "Go on."

"Option number two," she said after a breath. "This one, I'll tell you right now, is completely unacceptable and I'm furious with you for even thinking it."

"What hideous crime have I committed in my thought life now?" he inquired on a heavy note of sarcasm.

All week the prospect of his "invitation" had been going through her mind. Oh, he'd undoubtedly deny it, but the intention was there; she'd stake a month's salary on it. "You are about to suggest that we both abandon everything we think of as moral to sample marriage."

"Believe me—" he snickered loudly "—marriage is the last thing on my mind."

"I know that. I said *sample*, not actually do it. You were about to suggest that Danny and I move in with you. This, of course, would only be a trial run—a test drive, you'd probably call it—to see if things go smoothly. Then you'd end it when things got complicated or life was disrupted in any way. My advice to you on that one is don't even bother. I'd never agree and I'll think less of you for asking."

"Less than you already do," he finished for her. "But you can rest assured the thought never entered my mind."

Dori could have misjudged him, but she doubted it. "Take a good look at me," she said and held out the sides of her ragged housecoat. Its tattered blue hem dragged on the kitchen floor. "Because what you see is what you get."

Gavin might not have been angry when he arrived, but he was now. "What I can see is that having any kind of rational discussion with you is out of the question."

Lowering her eyes, Dori released a jagged sigh. "As you may have guessed, I'm not the best of company tonight. I... I didn't mean to come at you with my claws showing." She knew she should apologize, but the words stuck in her throat. She wished he'd leave so she could indulge her misery in private.

"I'll admit to having seen you in better moods."

She decided to ignore that. "As I said, it's been a rough week."

A long moment passed before Gavin spoke again and when he did, Dori could tell that he'd gained control of his anger. "There's a Neil Simon play at the 5th Avenue. Do you think you'll feel well enough to go tomorrow night?"

The invitation was so surprising that it stunned her. The muscles of her throat seemed paralyzed, so she merely gave an abrupt nod.

"I'll pick you up around seven-fifteen. Okay?"

Again, all Dori could manage was a nod.

He turned to leave, then paused in the doorway. "Take care of yourself."

"I... I will."

Dori heard the living room door close, and she shuddered in horror. What was the matter with her? She'd come at Gavin like a madwoman. Even now, she didn't know what he'd actually intended to say.

The recriminations and self-doubts remained with her the following afternoon. Perhaps because of them she splurged and had her hair cut and styled, a rare treat. Dori wanted to tell her stylist to do something new and exciting that would look sexy and sophisticated and make five pounds instantly disappear. But she decided not to bother—the woman did hair, not magic.

Dori couldn't recall any other date that had involved so much planning, not even her high school prom. She bought a sleek jumpsuit that came with a fancy title: "Rhapsody in Purple." The label said it was elegant, dynamic and designed for the free-spirited woman, and tonight, those were all the things she wanted to be. Reminding herself that it was the season to be generous and that she deserved some generosity herself, Dori plunked down her credit card, praying the purchase wouldn't take her over her credit limit.

At home, she hung the outfit on the back of her bedroom door and studied it. The soft, pale lavender jumpsuit was simply cut, with long billowy sleeves, and for what she'd paid, it should have been fashioned out of pure gold. The deep V in the back made it the most daring outfit she owned.

Dori had delivered Danny to her parents' house earlier that afternoon, so she was dressed and ready at seven. While she waited for Gavin, she searched the newspaper, looking for an advertisement for the play. He had told her it was a Neil Simon comedy, but he hadn't mentioned which one. A full-page ad announced it: *The Odd Couple.* Dori nearly laughed out loud; the description fit her and Gavin so aptly. She certainly didn't know any odder couple.

Gavin was right on time and did a double take when Dori opened the door.

"Hi," she said almost shyly, holding her head high. Her dangling gold earrings brushed the curve of her shoulders.

"Hello..." Gavin seemed at a loss for words. He let himself into the living room, his gaze never leaving hers. "For a woman who's not twenty-five, you look pretty good."

"I'll take that as a compliment," she said, recalling yesterday's comments. She prided herself on not rising to the bait. Any reaction from Gavin was a plus, and a positive one was worth every penny of the jumpsuit. "You don't look so bad yourself."

He straightened his tie and gave her another of his dazzling smiles. "So my innumerable female companions tell me."

That was another loaded comment best ignored. Dori reached for her handbag, an antique one beaded with a thousand minute pearls. She tucked it under her arm, eager to leave. From past experience, she knew they'd have trouble finding a parking space if they dallied over drinks.

Gavin hesitated as if he expected her at least to offer him something, but she felt suddenly ill-at-ease, anxious to get to the theater and into neutral territory. "We should probably go, don't you think?" she asked flatly.

Gavin frowned and glanced at her hall closet. "What about your coat?" he asked.

"I don't need one." A woman didn't wear "Rhapsody in Purple" with a full-length navy blue coat. This jumpsuit was created for gauzy silk shawls, not wool.

"Dori, don't be ridiculous! It's just above freezing. You can't go outside without a coat."

"I'll be fine," she insisted.

"You'll freeze."

Grudgingly, Dori stomped across the room, yanked open the hall closet and threw on her winter coat. "Satisfied?"

"Yes," he breathed irritably, burying his hands deep in the pockets of his dark overcoat. Dori suspected he was resisting the urge to throttle her.

"I'm ruining my image," she muttered with ill grace, stalking past him and out the front door.

Their seats at the play were excellent and the performers had received enthusiastic reviews. But Dori had trouble concentrating on the characters and the plot. Although Gavin sat beside her, they could've been strangers for all the notice he gave her. He didn't touch her, hold her hand or indicate in any way that he was aware of her closeness. Nor did he laugh at the appropriate times. His mind seemed to be elsewhere; of course, her own concentration wasn't much better.

During the intermission, it became her goal to make him notice her. After all, she'd spent a lot of time, money and effort to attract his attention. And she intended to get it.

Her plan was subtle. When the curtain rose for the second act, Dori crossed her legs and allowed the strap of her sandal to fall loose. With her heel exposed, she pretended to inadvertently nudge his knee. She knew she'd succeeded when he crossed his own legs to avoid her touch. Part two of her plan was to place her hand on the armrest between their seats. Before he was aware of it, she'd managed to curl her fingers around the crook of his elbow. Almost immediately she could feel the tension drain out of him, as though he'd craved her touch, hungered for it. But that couldn't be. If this was how he felt, why hadn't he simply taken her hand? Gavin was anything but shy. This reluctance to touch her shattered her preconceived ideas about him and why he'd asked her out. When he'd admitted the night before that he was frightened, he hadn't been overstating his feelings. The revelation must have been difficult for him and she'd carelessly tossed it back in his face, then hurled her own accusations at him. He wanted to be with her, enjoyed her company—and perhaps he was even falling in love with her. Earlier he'd said he'd missed her that week, and she'd cut him off with her fiery tirade. Now she wanted to groan and cry at her stupidity.

Dori wanted to take him in her arms and humbly ask him to forgive her. She wanted to plead with him to tell her what he'd really come to say. Regret, doubt and uncertainty all collided in her mind, drowning out the performers onstage.

Oh, heavens! Could Gavin have realized that he loved her? Maybe. Even if he wasn't ready to act on his feelings, he had at least reached the point of discussing them. And she'd blown it. She'd taunted him with her outraged presumptions, condemning him before he'd even spoken. Dori closed her eyes at the agony of her own thoughtlessness.

In that moment, when all the doubts crashed together in her mind, Gavin raised his hand and closed it over hers, holding her slender fingers in his warm grasp.

Dori couldn't breathe; she couldn't move. An eternity

passed before she could turn her face to him and see for herself the wonder she knew would be waiting for her. What she saw nearly brought her to tears. His eyes were gentle and yielding, his look potent enough to bring her to her knees.

The play ended and they applauded politely only because those around them did. When the audience came to its feet, Gavin and Dori rose, but his hand continued to grip hers.

Dori had never felt such deep communication with another person. If he admitted to being frightened, then so was she. Dori hadn't expected Gavin to come to her so easily. She loved him but had assumed it would take him far longer to acknowledge his feelings.

"I enjoyed the play," he said as he helped her into her coat. His voice was only slightly husky.

"Wonderful." Hers was overwhelmed by emotion. But if he noticed, Gavin gave no indication. It took all Dori had not to throw her arms around his neck and kiss him. She smiled a little, reflecting that if he'd known what she was thinking, Gavin would have been grateful for her restraint.

The drive back to her house was accomplished in a matter of minutes. He pulled to a stop at the curb, but kept his hand on the steering wheel. "Is Danny with his grandparents tonight?"

Dori had the impression that he didn't ask it conversationally but out of a desire to be alone with her. Her heart pounded painfully. "Y-yes."

He looked at her oddly. "Are you feeling sick again?"

"No, I'm fine." Dori cursed the fact that life had to be

so complicated. "Would you like to come in for coffee?" They both knew the invitation was a pretense. When Gavin took her in his arms, she didn't want half the neighborhood watching.

The car engine was still running and Gavin made an elaborate show of checking his watch. "Another time," he said. "It's late."

Ten forty-five was not late! If Dori was confused before, it was nothing to the myriad of bewildered emotions that went through her now. "You wanted to say something to me yesterday," she tried again, struggling to sound calm and composed. She forced a smile despite the catch in her voice. "I can't apologize enough for the way I behaved."

"One thing about you, Dori, you're completely unpredictable."

"You did want to tell me something?" she repeated.

"Yes." He paused and she saw the way his fingers tightened around the steering wheel. "As I said, things are getting a little intense between us."

"Yes," she whispered tenderly, her heart in her eyes.

"That's something I hadn't planned on."

"I know." Her throat constricted and she could hardly speak.

"In light of what happened in San Francisco…" He hesitated. "We reached a ten on that last kiss and even you said a ten meant trouble. Heaven only knows where we'd progress from there."

"I remember." Who was he trying to kid? They both knew where they were headed and it wasn't the kitchen. She didn't understand why he was hedging like this.

"Dori," he said, clearing the hoarseness from his throat. "I've been thinking that perhaps we're seeing too much of each other. Maybe it'd be best if we cooled things for a while."

No words could have been more unexpected. All this time she'd been waiting to hear a profession of love and he'd been trying to tell her he wanted out. To her horror, her eyes filled with stinging tears. Fiercely she blinked them away. She grabbed the door handle in her haste to escape. What a fool she'd been!

"Sure," she managed to stammer without disgracing herself. "Whatever you think." The car door swung open and she clambered out in such a frenzied rush that she was fortunate not to trip. "Thank you for the play. As I said before, it was wonderful." Not waiting for any response, she slammed the car door and hurried toward the house. The sound of his door opening and closing made her suck in a savage breath and battle for control.

"I thought you didn't want any coffee," she said, without turning to face him. The porch light was sure to reveal her tears, which would embarrass them both.

"Dori, listen, I'm sorry. But I need time to sort everything out. Whatever is going on between us is happening too fast. Give me some time...."

From the distance of his voice, Dori guessed he was about halfway up the sidewalk. "I understand." She did, far better than he realized. She'd looked at him with adoring eyes and all the while he'd been trying to come up with some way to dump her—or as he'd probably say, let her down gently. Her eyes blinded by tears, she ripped open her purse and searched for the keys. "Don't worry, you've got all the time in the world," she muttered, clutching the house key between stiff fingers.

"A month. All I want is a month." The pause in his voice revealed his uncertainty.

"Take six," she returned impertinently. "Why stop there—make it ten." She wanted to laugh, but the noise that erupted from her throat was a dry, pain-filled sob.

"Dori." His shoe scraped sharply against the porch steps and then there was a tentative moment of silence as he stood there, looking up at her. "Are you crying?"

"Who me?" She laughed, sobbing again. "No way! You don't want to see me again? Fine. I'm mature enough to accept that."

"Turn around and let me see your face."

Her chest heaved with the effort of not sobbing openly. She was such a fool.

"Dori, I didn't mean to hurt you."

"I'm not hurt!" she shouted and leaned her forehead against the screen door. Afraid another sob would escape, she covered her mouth with one hand. When she was finally able to catch her breath, she turned to face him. "I'm fine, so please don't feel obligated to stick around. Danny and I'll be just fine."

"Dori—"

"I'm fine!" she insisted again, wiping away her tears. "See?" Without another word, she turned back to the door, inserted the key and let herself in the house.

"Did you have fun with Mr. Parker last night, Mom?" Danny sat at the kitchen table with Dori, who was sipping from a mug of hot coffee. Her mother had phoned earlier to announce that she'd drop Danny off on her way to do some errands.

"The play was great." Dori felt frail and vulnerable but managed to give her son a wan smile. Her thoughts were darker than they'd been since she lost Brad. She'd have to tell Danny that her relationship with Gavin had come to a standstill, but it wasn't going to be easy. "Did you have a good time with Grandma and Grandpa?"

"Yeah, but I'll be glad when you and Mr. Parker get married 'cause I'd rather be a family. Melissa and I could stay alone and I wouldn't have to have a sitter or go to Grandma's every time you want to go out."

"Danny, listen." Dori struggled to maintain an unemotional facade, although she felt as if her heart was breaking. "Mr. Parker and I have decided it would be best if we didn't see each other for a while."

"What?" Danny's mouth dropped open in utter disbelief. "But why? I thought you really liked each other. I thought you might even be talking about marriage. Melissa was sure…" He let the rest drop as if he'd inadvertently divulged a secret.

"No." She lowered her eyes and swallowed hard. There was no choice but to give Gavin exactly what he'd asked for—time. "Gavin isn't ready for that kind of commitment and this is something you and I have to accept."

"But, Mom—"

"Listen," Dori implored, taking his small hand between her own. "You need to promise me that you won't contact Gavin in any way. Sometimes adults need time to think, just like kids do, and we have to respect that. Promise me, Danny. This is important."

He studied her intently, finally nodding. "What about Melissa? Will we be able to see her?"

The two children had become good friends and Dori hated to punish them for their parents' problems. "I'm sure we could make some kind of arrangement to have her over on weekends when Gavin's broadcasting football games." Gavin probably wouldn't mind, as long as he didn't have to see *her*.

"You love him, don't you?"

Dori's smile was wistful. "Gavin Parker is a very special man and loving him is easy. But it won't be the end of the world if we never see him again."

Danny's eyes widened incredulously, as though he found her words completely shocking. "But Mr. Parker was *perfect*."

"Yes," she agreed, "he met each requirement on your list, but there are lots of other men who will, too."

"Are you going to start looking for another father for me?" Danny rested his chin in the palms of his hands, eyes forlorn.

Immediate protests crowded her mind. "Not right away." Like Gavin, she needed time, but not for the same reasons. For her, it would be a waiting game. In a few weeks, she'd know if her gamble had paid off. Falling for him had been a mistake; he'd warned her often enough. Now she was suffering the consequences.

In the days that followed, Dori was astonished by her own strength of will. It was a struggle, but when thoughts of Gavin invaded her well-defended mind, she cast them aside. He didn't make any effort to get in touch with her and she didn't expect him to. Whatever had happened with Deirdre had hurt him so badly that he might never risk committing himself to another woman. That was his and Melissa's loss…and hers and Danny's.

On Wednesday morning, as Dori stirred hot water into her instant oatmeal, she flipped through the pages of the paper. "Danny," she called over her shoulder. "Hurry, or you'll be late for school."

"Okay, Mom." His muffled voice drifted from his bedroom.

Setting his bowl on the table, Dori leaned against the counter and turned to the society page, looking for the Dear Abby column. At first she didn't recognize the people in the picture on the front page of the city section.

Then her glance fell on Gavin's smiling face and her heart suddenly dropped to her knees. The oxygen became trapped in her lungs, making it painful to breathe. Some unnamed blond-haired beauty who couldn't have been more than twenty-two was grasping his arm and smiling up at Gavin adoringly. Dori knew the look well. Only a few days before she'd gazed at him in exactly the same doting way. She felt a knife twist in her heart as she read the accompanying article, which described the opening of the opera season with a gala performance of Bizet's *Carmen*. So *this* was how Gavin was sorting through his feelings for her. It hadn't taken him long to find a younger woman with flawless skin and a perfect body. *Let him,* her mind shouted angrily. Foolish tears burned her eyes and she blinked them away, refusing to give in to her emotions.

"Mom, what's the matter? You look like you want to hit someone."

"I do?" Hurriedly, she folded the paper. "It's nothing. Okay?"

Danny cocked his head. "Mr. Parker told me that sometimes women act weird. I guess this is one of those times."

"I'm sick of hearing about Mr. Parker." She jerked open the refrigerator and took out bread for her son's lunch. When he didn't respond, she whirled around. "Did you hear me?"

Danny was staring down at his cereal. "Are you going to cry or something?"

"Of course not! Why should I? It's almost Christmas."

His spoon worked furiously, stirring sugar into the cinnamon-and-raisin-flavored oatmeal. "I don't know, but when your mouth twists up like that, it always means you're upset."

"Thanks," she returned flippantly.

The remainder of the day was as bad as the morning had been. Nothing went right. She mislaid a file. Her thoughts drifted during an important meeting and when Mr. Sandstrom asked her opinion, Dori had no idea what they'd been discussing. Sandy had sent her a sympathetic look and salvaged a potentially embarrassing moment by speaking first. As a thank-you Dori bought her friend lunch, though she couldn't really afford it.

The minute she walked into the house, Dori kicked off her shoes and paused to rub her aching feet. Danny was nowhere to be seen and she draped her coat on the back of a kitchen chair, wondering where he'd gone now. He was supposed to stay inside until she got home. She took a package of hamburger out of the refrigerator, but the prospect of coming up with a decent meal was almost more than she could face.

As she turned, she noticed the telephone. The receiver

was off the hook. The cord stretched around the corner and disappeared into the hall closet. Danny. She crossed to the door and pulled it open.

Danny was sitting cross-legged on the floor and at Dori's intrusion, he glanced up, startled, unable to disguise his sudden look of guilt.

"All right, Daniel Robertson, just who are you talking to?"

Nine

"Oh, hi, Mom," he managed awkwardly, struggling to his feet.

"Who's on the phone?" She repeated her question, but her mind was already whirling with possibilities, all of them unpleasant. If it was Gavin, she was likely to do something stupid, such as grab the receiver and drone in a mechanical-sounding voice that the call had just been disconnected. The memory of his helpful little strategy produced a familiar twinge in her heart. She missed Gavin more than she'd ever thought possible. There was no point in trying to fool herself any longer. She was miserable.

"I'm talking to a girl," Danny admitted, color creeping up his neck at being caught.

"Erica?"

"No." He reluctantly handed her the receiver. "Melissa."

Dori entered the closet, pushing aside their winter coats, and sat on the floor. For the past few days, she'd been cranky with Danny. She hoped this gesture would show him that she regretted being such a grouch.

Amused at his mother's actions, Danny sat next to her

and closed the door. Immediately they were surrounded by a friendly darkness. "Hello, Melissa," Dori murmured into the receiver. "How are you?"

"Fine," the thirteen-year-old answered seriously, "I think."

"Why the 'I think' business? It's nearly Christmas and there's lots of stuff going on. A young girl like you shouldn't have a care in the world."

"Yes, I know." Melissa sounded depressed, but Dori didn't know how deeply she should delve into the girl's unhappiness. Where Gavin was concerned—and that included his relationship with his daughter—Dori was particularly vulnerable. She loved Gavin and felt great affection for Melissa.

Danny was whispering furiously from his end of the closet.

"Excuse me a minute, Melissa. It seems Danny has something extremely important to tell me." She placed her palm over the receiver. "Yes, Danny?"

"Melissa's got a mother-daughter fashion thing at her school and she doesn't have anyone to bring."

Dori nodded. "Danny says your school's having a fashion show."

"My Family Studies class is putting it on. I sewed a dress and everything. It's almost as pretty as the outfit you helped me buy. The teacher gave me an A."

"Congratulations. I'm sure you did a good job to have rated such a high grade." Already Dori knew what was coming and she dreaded having to turn the girl down. But with the way things stood between her and Gavin, Dori couldn't very well offer to go.

"I sewed it superbly," Melissa admitted with a charming lack of modesty. "It's the best thing I ever made. Better than the apron, but then I had to take the waistband off four times. I only made one minor mistake on the dress," she continued, her voice gaining volume and speed with each word. "I sewed the zipper in backward, you know, so the tab was on the inside. I thought it was all right, it still went over my head and everything, but I had to take it out and do it again. I was mad at myself for being so dumb." She paused to draw in a giant breath, then hurried on. "Will you come and pretend to be my mother? Please, Dori? Practically everyone has someone coming. Even the other girls who board…"

"Oh, Melissa." Dori's shoulders slumped forward as she sagged against the wall. "Honey, I don't know." Her stomach started churning frantically. She hated to refuse the girl, but Gavin was likely to read something unintended into her acceptance.

"Dori, please, I won't ask anything of you ever again. I need a pretend mother for just one night. For the fashion show."

The soft, pleading quality of the girl's voice was Dori's undoing. She briefly considered suggesting that Melissa ask Lainey, until she recalled the girl's reaction to the blonde. Despite her misgivings, Dori couldn't ignore the yearning in Melissa's request. "I'll do it on two conditions," she agreed cautiously.

"Anything." The girl's voice rose with excitement.

"First, you mustn't tell any of your friends that I'm your mother. That would be wrong. As much as I wish

I had a daughter like you, Melissa, I can never be your mother."

"Okay," she agreed, slightly subdued. "What else?"

"I don't want your father to know I've done this." Gavin would be sure to see more in this simple act of kindness than there was. "I'm not asking you to lie to him, but I don't want him assuming the wrong thing. Okay, Melissa?"

"Okay. He won't even need to know because everything's taking place at the school and he never goes there on weekdays. And I promise not to tell him."

"Then I guess all I need to know is the date and time."

"Next Monday at seven-thirty. May I talk to Danny again?"

"Sure." Dori handed the receiver back to her son and got awkwardly to her feet, hitting the top of her head on the rod positioned across the small enclosure. "Ouch," she muttered as she gingerly opened the door, seeking a safe passage out.

A few minutes later Danny joined her in the kitchen, where Dori was frying the hamburger. "That was nice of you, Mom."

"I'm happy to do it for Melissa. I'm very fond of her." Gavin loved his daughter—that much Dori didn't doubt—but she hoped he appreciated her, as well.

"Melissa was really worried about the fashion show. I thought it was tough not having a dad, but I guess it's just as bad without a mom."

"I'm sure it is," she replied smoothly. "Now how about if you set the table?"

"What are we having for dinner?"

Dori looked at the sautéing meat and shrugged. "I don't know yet."

"Aw, Mom, is it another one of *those* meals?"

On Friday morning, Dori overslept. Danny woke her almost twenty minutes after her alarm should have gone off.

"Mom," he murmured, rubbing the sleep from his face. "Aren't we supposed to be up? This isn't Saturday, is it?"

Dori took one look at the silent clock radio, gasped and threw back the covers. "Hurry and get dressed! We're late."

Feeling a little like the rabbit in *Alice in Wonderland*, Dori dashed from one room to the next, exclaiming how late they were. Her shower rivaled Danny's thirty-second baths for a new speed record. She brushed her teeth with one hand and blow-dried her hair with the other. The result was hair that looked as if it had been caught in an eggbeater and a toothpaste stain on the front of her blouse.

"Should I buy lunch today?" Danny wanted to know, shoving his arms into a sweatshirt and pulling his head through to gaze at her inquisitively.

"Yes." There was no time to fix a sandwich now. "Take some money out of my purse."

Danny returned a minute later with her billfold. "All you've got is a twenty-dollar bill."

"Oh, great." As she slipped her feet into soft leather pumps, her mind raced frantically. "What about your piggy bank?"

"But, Mom…"

"It's a loan, Danny. I'll pay you back later."

"Okay," he agreed with all the charity of an ill-tempered loan shark.

"Hurry up now. I'll get the car out of the garage."

Dori was parked in the driveway, revving the cold engine, when Danny ran through the garage. He slammed the door and climbed into the car.

"I got four dollars."

"Good." She looked over her shoulder as she backed out of the driveway. Traffic was heavy and driving took all her concentration.

"Mom," Danny said after a few minutes. "About that four dollars."

"Danny, good grief, I'll pay you back tonight. Now quit worrying about it." She slowed to a full stop at a traffic light.

"But I'm going to need it! It's almost Christmas and I can't afford to be generous."

Dori paused to think over his words before turning to stare at her son. "Did you hear what you just said?"

"Yeah, I shouldn't have to pay for my own lunch. I want my money back."

"Danny." She gave him an incredulous look. Her son couldn't afford to be generous because it was Christmas? The time of year when love and human goodness were supposed to be at their peak. A low rumbling sound escaped Dori's throat. Then she began to giggle. The giggles burst into full laughter until her whole body shook and she had to hold her side to keep from laughing harder. Still engrossed in the pure irony of his statement, Dori reached over, despite the seat belt, and hugged her son. "Thanks." She giggled. "I needed that."

"It's not that funny," Danny objected, but he was laughing, too. Suddenly he sobered, his hand raised. "Mom, look! It's Mr. Parker. He's in the car right beside us."

Unable to resist, Dori glanced over at the BMW stopped next to her. Her laughter fled as she recognized Gavin. He hadn't seen her and Danny, or if he had, he was purposely looking in the opposite direction. Just when she was wondering what, if anything, she could do, Gavin's eyes met hers. Dori's heart gave a wild leap and began to thump madly as the dark, thoughtful eyes looked straight into hers. Stunned, she recognized an aching tenderness in his face. She saw regret, doubt, even pain. She wanted to smile and assure him she was fine but that she missed him dreadfully. She wanted to ask how he was doing and about that picture in the paper. Ten other flighty, meaningless thoughts came to her all at once, but she didn't have the opportunity to voice even one. A car horn blared impatiently behind her, and Dori realized the traffic light was green and she was holding up a long line of commuters.

"That *was* Mr. Parker, wasn't it?" Danny said as she stepped on the gas and rushed forward.

"Yes." Her throat felt dry and although earlier there'd been laughter, Dori now felt the compelling need to cry. Swallowing the urge, she took the next right-hand turn for Danny's school. A quick glimpse in her rearview mirror revealed Gavin traveling forward. No wave, no backward look. Perhaps he regretted their relationship, perhaps she'd read him wrong from the start and it hadn't meant a thing. But Dori couldn't allow herself to believe that. She had to trust her instincts. Otherwise it hurt too much.

Saturday and Sunday passed in a blur of vague anticipation. After seeing Gavin on Friday morning, Dori had half expected that he'd call her during the weekend. She should have known better than to second-guess Gavin Parker. He did things his own way. When and if he ever admitted to loving her, she'd never need to doubt again. That was how Gavin was. She knew with absolute certainty that when he truly fell in love, it would be a complete and enduring love, a love to last a lifetime.

The only bright spot in her disappointing weekend was a phone call from Melissa, who wanted to confirm that Dori would attend the Mother-Daughter Fashion Show as she'd promised. During the conversation, the girl casually mentioned that Gavin was in L.A. to broadcast a football game.

Monday evening, Dori dressed in her best professional suit, a charcoal gray two-piece with a white silk shirt. Danny had agreed to submit to the humiliation of having Jody from across the street come to babysit. He was vociferous in letting Dori know that this was a sacrifice on his part and he wanted her to tell Melissa all about his unselfishness.

A light drizzle had begun to fall when Dori pulled into the school parking lot. She was surprised by the large number of cars. Dori had assumed Melissa was exaggerating when she'd declared that she'd be the only girl there without a mother or some other woman as stand-in—a sister, a stepmom, an aunt.

Melissa stood just inside the doorway of the large auditorium, waiting for Dori. A smile brightened her face the moment she caught Dori's eye. Rushing to her side, Melissa gave Dori an excited hug and handed her a program.

"Is this the world-famous creation, designed by the renowned Melissa Parker?" Dori inquired with a proud smile. The corduroy dress was a vivid shade of dark blue.

"Do you like it?" Melissa whirled around, holding out the sides of the skirt in Hollywood fashion. Sheer delight created large dimples in her round cheeks. "I think it turned out so pretty."

"It's wonderful."

Taking her by the arm, Melissa escorted Dori down the middle aisle of folding chairs. "I'm supposed to seat you right here."

"Where are you going?" Dori glanced around her curiously. Only a few women were sitting near the front and it looked as though these seats were reserved.

"Everything's almost ready, so I have to go backstage, but I'll see you later." She started to move away but abruptly changed her mind. "The choral group is singing first. They really aren't very good, but please applaud."

"I will," Dori promised, doing her utmost to maintain a serious expression. "I take it you're not singing."

"Only if I want to offend Ms. Curran."

In spite of herself, Dori chuckled. "Well, break a leg, kid."

Another woman, a day student's mother, was seated next to Dori a few minutes later and they struck up a pleasant conversation. It would've been very easy to pretend Melissa was her daughter, but Dori was careful to explain that she was there as a friend of the Parker family. Even at that, Dori felt she was stretching the truth.

The show began with the introduction of the school staff. Then Dori applauded politely at the end of the first series of songs presented by the choral ensemble. Melissa might not have had a finely tuned musical ear, but her assessment of the group wasn't far off. Nonetheless, the applause was enthusiastic.

Following the musical presentation came the fashion show. Dori straightened in her chair as the announcer, a girl about Melissa's age, stepped toward to the microphone. Obviously nervous, the girl fumbled with her papers and her voice shook as she started to speak.

Melissa in her blue dress was the fourth model. With natural grace, she walked across the stage, then turned once, holding out the skirt with one hand, and paused in front of Dori to display the even stitches of her hem. The mothers loved it and laughed outright.

At the end of the fashion show, the principal, Ms. Curran, approached the front of the room to announce the names of the students who'd made the honor roll for the semester.

"Ladies," the soft voice instructed, "when the name of your daughter—or honorary daughter—is read, would you please come forward to stand with her."

When Melissa's name was called out, the girl came to the front of the auditorium and cast a pleading glance at Dori. Heart pounding, Dori rose from her seat to stand behind Melissa. She noticed that all the women with honor-roll girls came from the first few rows; this was the reason Melissa had escorted Dori to the front. She wished Melissa had said something earlier. But then, it wouldn't have made any difference.

Dori's smile was proud as she placed her hands on Melissa's shoulders and leaned forward to whisper in her ear. "Daughter or not, I'm extremely proud of you."

Twisting her head, Melissa looked up at Dori, her expression somber. "I wish you were my mother."

"I know," Dori murmured quietly, the emotion building until her throat felt swollen with the effort not to cry. Still, she had to brush a stray tear from her cheek and bite her lip to keep from sobbing out loud.

The final names were read and there was a round of applause. "What now?" Dori whispered.

"I'm supposed to seat you and bring you a cup of tea and some cookies." She led Dori to her seat. "I'll be right back."

"Okay." Dori crossed her legs and, with nothing to do, scanned the program for the fifth time. Her gaze rested on Melissa's name. This child could easily take the place Dori had reserved in her heart for the daughter she'd never had—and never would.

"You enjoyed that little charade, didn't you?" Gavin's voice taunted. Dori turned in shock as he sat down in the vacant chair beside her.

The words ripped through her with the pain of a blunt knife. Her program slipped to the floor and she bent to retrieve it. Fixing a stiff smile on her lips, she straightened, forcing herself to be calm.

"Hello, Gavin," she said with a breathlessness she couldn't control. "What brings you here?"

"My daughter." His emphasis on *my* was obviously intended as a not-so-subtle reminder that she was an intruder.

"Melissa invited me," Dori said in an attempt to explain her presence. "It's a Mother-Daughter Fashion Show." The minute the words were out, Dori knew she'd said the wrong thing.

"You're not her mother," he replied in a remote, impersonal tone.

"No, and I haven't pretended to be."

"That's not how I saw it. Melissa's name was called and you hurried to the front like every other proud mother."

"What was I supposed to do?" she whispered angrily, her hands clenched in her lap. "Sit there with Melissa giving me pleading looks?"

"Yes," he bit back in a low controlled voice. "Did you think that if you maintained a friendship with my daughter we'd eventually resume our relationship? That's not the way it's going to happen. I asked for some time and you're not giving it to me." He paused and raked a hand through his hair. "Your coming here tonight makes things impossible."

A weary sigh came from deep within Dori. Gavin assumed the worst possible explanation for what she'd done. Perhaps he was looking for a reason to hate her and now he had all the excuse he needed.

"I've fended off a lot of women bent on ending my independence," he said harshly, "but you're the best. You know I love my daughter. She's my weakest link."

Unable to bear any more of his sarcasm, Dori stood. "You've got it all wrong, Gavin. Melissa is your strongest point. You're arrogant, egotistical and so stubborn you can't see what's right in front of your face."

"Dori, what's wrong?" Melissa approached her from behind, carefully holding a cup of hot tea in one hand and a small paper plate of cookies in the other.

Dori took the delicate cup and saucer out of Melissa's shaking fingers and handed them to Gavin. If he wanted to play mother, then he could drink the weak tea and eat the stale cookies.

"Daddy…" Melissa choked with surprise and turned stricken eyes to Dori. "I didn't tell him, honest."

"I know," Dori assured her.

"What are you doing here? I didn't tell you about… the tea…. This is supposed to be for mothers and—" The words stumbled over her tongue.

"Sit down," Gavin ordered. "Both of you."

As they seated themselves, he dragged his chair around so that he was facing them. Dori felt like a disobedient child but refused to give in to the sensation. She'd done nothing wrong. Her only motive in attending the fashion show had been kindness; she'd responded to the pleas of a young girl. Dori had come for Melissa's sake alone, and the fact that Gavin was the girl's father had almost deterred her from coming at all—despite what he chose to believe.

"I think you'd better tell me what's going on." His eyes challenged Dori in that chilling way she hated.

"I've already explained the circumstances," she inserted dryly. "However, it seems to me that you've added two and two and come up with five."

"Dad," Melissa demanded with open defiance, clearly taking note of Dori's unapologetic tone, "what are you doing here? This isn't for fathers. You're the only man here."

"The notice came from the school about the fashion show," he explained haltingly, glancing around him. "I have every right to come to my daughter's school any time I please."

"But it doesn't give you the right to say those kinds of things to me," Dori said calmly, and drew together the front of her suit jacket. People sitting nearby were beginning to give them unwanted attention.

Gavin's features hardened and one brow was raised derisively. Without looking at his daughter, he said, "Melissa, get Dori another cup of tea."

"But, Dad—"

"You heard me."

Reluctantly, Melissa rose to her feet. "I'll be back in a couple of minutes." She took a few steps toward the rear of the auditorium, then turned to Dori again. "They have coffee, if you'd prefer that."

"Either one is fine," Dori answered with a smile and a reassuring wink. She probably wouldn't be around to drink it, anyway.

Gavin waited until his daughter was out of earshot. "This whole situation between us has gotten out of hand."

Dori crossed her arms and leaned back in the hard folding chair, suddenly weary.

"We had a nice thing going, but it's over. You broke the rules," he said accusingly. "If you attempt to drag it out, you'll only make it painful for the kids." His voice was harsh with impatience. "I'm seeing someone else now," he explained. "Melissa hasn't met her yet, but she will soon."

Dori drew in a ragged breath and found she couldn't release it. It burned in her lungs until she regained her composure enough to slowly exhale. "I'm sure she will."

She didn't know how she could remain so calm when every breath was a struggle and every heartbeat caused her pain. Deep down, Dori had suspected that Gavin would do something like this. "I'm only surprised you waited so long. I scare you to death, Gavin, and you're running as fast as you can in the opposite direction. No doubt you've seen any number of women in the past week—all of them young, blond and gorgeous."

"You think you know me so well." He eyed her coolly. "But you're wrong. I saw what was happening with us and came to my senses in the nick of time."

Dori marveled at her self-control. Even though the whole world felt as if it were dissolving around her, she sat serenely, an expression of apparent indifference on her face. Whatever Gavin might say, she still tried to believe that eventually he'd recognize that he loved her. All she had were her hopes. He was stubborn enough to deny his feelings for her all his life. Dori didn't know what made her think she could succeed where so many others had failed.

"If you expected to shock me with your sudden interest in all these women, you haven't. And despite what you say, I *do* know you."

"You don't know me at all," he said with an angry frown.

"From the beginning, I've found you very easy to read, Gavin Parker." Inside, Dori was convulsed with pain, but she refused to allow him even a glimpse of her private agony. "You love me. You may not have recognized it yet, but someday you will. Date anyone you like, but when you kiss them, it'll be my lips you taste and when they're in your arms, it's *me* you'll long to hold."

"If anyone loves someone around here, it's you." He spoke as though the words were an accusation.

Dori's smile was infinitely sad. "Yes, I'll admit that. I love you and Melissa."

"I told you not to fall in love with me," he said bitterly. "I warned you from the beginning not to smell orange blossoms, but that's all you women seem to think about."

Dori couldn't deny his words. "Yes, you did, and believe me, I was just as shocked as you when I realized I could fall in love with someone so pigheaded, irrational and emotionally scarred." She paused to swallow the ache in her throat. "I don't know and I don't even want to know what Deirdre did to you. That's in the past, but you're still wearing all that emotional pain like...like a shroud."

"I've heard enough." A muscle flexed in his jaw.

Letting her gaze fall, Dori tried to blink back the burning tears. "If you've found someone else who can make you happy, then I wish you the very best. I mean it sincerely, but I doubt you'll ever find that elusive contentment. Goodbye, Gavin. I apologize, I truly do, for ruining a promising agreement. With someone less vulnerable than me, it might have worked."

His gaze refused to meet hers. For all the emotion revealed in his eyes, she could have been talking to a man carved from stone. Without a word he was going to let her go. She'd persisted in hoping that somehow she'd reach him and he'd stop her—but he hadn't.

"You're not leaving, are you?" Melissa spoke from behind them, setting a cup on the seat of the beige metal chair. "I brought your tea."

"I can't stay." Impulsively she hugged the girl and brushed back the thick bangs that hung across Melissa's furrowed brow. "Goodbye." Dori's voice quavered with emotion. She wouldn't see Melissa again. Coming here this evening had been a terrible mistake.

Melissa clung to her, obviously understanding what had happened. "Dori," she begged, "please…don't leave. I promise…"

"Let her go," Gavin barked, causing several heads to turn.

Instantly, Melissa dropped her hands and took a step in retreat. Dori couldn't stand another minute of this. With a forced smile on her face, she hurried out of the auditorium. Once outside, she broke into a half trot, grateful for the cover of darkness. She desperately needed to be alone.

By the time Dori pulled into her garage, the tears were making wet tracks down her face. She turned off the engine and sat with her hands clenching the steering wheel as she fought to control her breathing and stem the flow of emotion.

A glance at her watch assured her that Danny would be in bed and, she hoped, asleep.

The babysitter eyed Dori's red face curiously but didn't ask any questions. "There's a phone message for you on the table," the girl said on her way out the front door.

Dori switched on the kitchen light and smiled absently at the name and number written neatly on the message pad. She reached for the phone and punched out the number, swallowing the painful lump that filled her throat.

He answered on the third ring. "Hi, Tom, it's Dori Robertson, returning your call."

"Hi, Dori," he began awkwardly. "I hope I'm not bothering you."

"No bother." She looked up at the ceiling and rubbed her burning eyes with one hand. "I had a school function to attend for a friend, but I'm home now."

"How are you?"

Dying, her heart answered. "Splendid," she murmured. "Getting ready to do some Christmas shopping. Danny's managed to limit his Christmas list to a mere three hundred items."

"Would you like some company? I mean, I understand if you'd rather not, feeling the way I do about Paula."

"I take it you two haven't managed to patch things up?"

"Not yet," he said with an expressive sigh. "About the shopping—I'd appreciate some advice on gifts and such."

"I'd be happy to go with you, Tom."

"I know you've been seeing a lot of that ex-football player."

"I won't be seeing him anymore." She choked down a sob and quickly covered her mouth.

"How about one night this week?"

"Fine," she said, replacing the receiver after a mumbled goodbye. Leaning against the kitchen wall, Dori made an attempt to regain her composure. She'd known what she was letting herself in for from the beginning. It wouldn't do any good to cry about it now.

She wiped her eyes and looked up to find Danny standing in the doorway, watching her.

"Oh, Mom," he said softly.

Ten

Danny sat at the kitchen table spreading colored frosting on gingerbread men. His look was thoughtful as he added raisin eyes and three raisin buttons to each.

The timer on the stove went off and Dori automatically reached for the padded oven mitt.

"You know, Mom, I don't like Mr. Parker anymore. Melissa either. I thought she was all right for a girl, but I was wrong."

"The problem is, Danny, we both love them very much and telling ourselves anything else would be lying." For several days Danny had been brooding and thoughtful. They'd had a long talk after the Mother-Daughter Fashion Show, and Dori had explained that they wouldn't be seeing Gavin or Melissa again. Surprisingly, her son had accepted that without argument.

"I don't love anyone who makes my mom sad," he insisted.

"I'm not sad now," she assured him, and it was true, she wasn't. There were regrets, but no tears.

Licking the frosting from his fingers, Danny examined the "new father" requirement list posted on the refrigerator door. "How long do you think it'll be before we start looking again?"

Dori lifted the cut-out cookies from the sheet with a spatula and tilted her head pensively to one side. "Not long." Gradually, her pain-dulled senses were returning to normal. Dating again would probably be the best thing for her, but there was a problem. She wanted only Gavin. Loved only Gavin.

When she finished sliding the cookies from the sheet, Dori noticed that Danny had removed the requirement list, strawberry magnet and all, and taken a pencil from the drawer. Then he'd carried everything to the table. Dusting her floury hands, she read over his shoulder as his pencil worked furiously across the bottom of the page. "I'm adding something else," he explained needlessly. "I want a new father who won't make my mom cry."

"That's thoughtful, but, Danny, tears can mean different things. There are tears of happiness and tears of frustration, even angry tears. Sometimes crying is good and necessary." She didn't want to explain that the tears were a measure of her love for Gavin. If she hadn't loved him, it wouldn't have hurt so much when they'd stopped seeing each other.

"Mr. Parker wasn't a very good football player, either," Danny complained.

"He was terrific," Dori countered.

"I threw away all the football cards I had of him. And his autograph."

He said it with a brash air of unconcern as though throwing away the cards had been a trivial thing. But Dori knew better. She'd found the whole collection of treasures—the cards, the autograph and the program from the Seahawks football game he and Gavin had attended—in the bottom of his garbage can and rescued them. Later, he'd regret discarding those items. He was hurt and angry now, but he'd recover. Next autumn, he'd be pleased when she returned the memorabilia so he could brag to his new junior-high friends that he had Gavin Parker's autograph.

"While the cookies are cooling, why don't you bring in the mail."

"Sure, Mom."

Usually Dori could count on Danny's good behavior during the month of December, but lately he'd been even more thoughtful, loving and considerate. She was almost beginning to worry about him. Not once had he nagged her about Christmas or his presents. Nor had he continued to pursue the new father business. Until today, he'd said nothing.

The phone rang as Danny barged into the kitchen, tossing the mail on the counter. He grabbed the receiver and answered breathlessly.

A couple of minutes later he turned to Dori. "Mom, guess what? It's Jon. He wants to know if I can come over. He's real excited because his dad's moving back in and they're going to be a real family again."

"That's wonderful. Tell Jon I'm very happy for him." Dori wasn't surprised. From the care with which Tom had gone about choosing Christmas presents for his wife and family, Dori realized how deeply he loved them. He'd never told her why he and his wife had separated, but Dori was genuinely happy to hear they'd settled their problems. Did she dare hope that Gavin would recognize all the love waiting for him and return to her? No man could kiss her and hold her the way he had and then cast her aside without regrets. Paula had her Christmas present and Dori wondered if she'd ever have hers.

"Can I go over? I'll finish decorating the cookies later."

"Don't worry about it. There are only a few from the last batch and I can do those. Go and have a good time."

"Thanks, Mom." He yanked his coat from the closet and blew her a kiss, something he'd taken to doing lately instead of giving her a real kiss.

"You're welcome," she called lightly. "And be home in an hour." The last words were cut off as the back door slammed.

Dori watched Danny's eager escape and sighed. Her son was growing up. She used to look at him and think of Brad, but now she saw that Danny was becoming himself, a unique and separate person.

She reached for the stack of mail, which appeared to consist of bills and a few Christmas cards. She carried everything into the living room, slouched onto the sofa and propped her slippered feet on the coffee table. The first envelope had a return address she didn't immediately recognize and curiously she ripped it open. Instead of a card, there was a personal letter written on notebook paper. Unfolding the page, Dori's gaze slid to the bottom, where she discovered Melissa's signature.

Dori's feet dropped to the floor as she straightened. After the first line, she bit her lip and blinked rapidly.

Dear Dori,
I wanted to write and thank you for coming to the

mother-daughter thing. Dad showing up was a real surprise and I hope you believe me when I tell you I didn't say anything to him. Really, I didn't.

Dad explained that I shouldn't bother you anymore and I won't. That's the hardest part because I really like you. I know Deirdre is my real mother, but I don't think of her as a mother. She's pretty, but I don't think she's really very happy about being a mother. When I think of a mother, I think of someone like you who buys groceries in the Albertsons' store. Someone who lets me try on her makeup and perfume even if I use too much. Mothers are special people, and for the first time in my life I got to see one up close. Thank you for showing me how I want to love my kids.

I feel bad that things didn't work out with you and my dad. I feel even worse that Dad says I shouldn't ever bother you again. I don't think I'm even supposed to be writing this letter, but it's only polite to thank you properly. Anyway, Dad refuses to let me talk about you or Danny. He doesn't seem to have time for me right now, but that's okay because I'm pretty mad at him anyhow.

I'd like to think of you as my mother, Dori, but I can't because every time I do, I start to cry. You told me once how much you wanted a daughter. I sure wish I could have been yours.
Your almost daughter,
Melissa

Tears filled Dori's eyes as she refolded the letter and placed it back in the envelope. This was one lesson she hadn't ever counted on learning. This helpless, desolate feeling of grieving for a man incapable of commitment. Yet there was no one to blame but herself. He'd warned her not to fall in love with him. The problem was, he hadn't said anything about loving his daughter and Dori did love Melissa. And now, instead of two people facing Christmas with heavy hearts, there were four.

Gavin Parker could take a flying leap into a cow pasture and the next time she saw him—if she ever saw him again—she'd tell him exactly that. How long would it take him to realize how much she loved him? Let him be angry; she was going to answer Melissa's letter. And maybe in a few months, when it wasn't so painful, she'd visit Melissa at the school and they'd spend the day together.

Dori's gaze rested on the gaily trimmed Christmas tree and the few presents gathered about the base. This was supposed to be the happiest time of the year. Only it wasn't. Not for Danny or Dori. Not this year. The stuffed lion Gavin had won for her sat beside the television, and Dori couldn't resist the impulse to go over and pick it up. Hugging it fiercely, she let the soft fur comfort her.

When the surge of emotion subsided, Dori took out some stationery and wrote a reply to Melissa. Afterward she felt calmer and even a little cheered. Later that night, when Danny was in bed, she reread it to be sure she'd said everything she wanted to say and decided no letter could ever convey all the love in her heart.

Dearest Melissa,
Thank you for your sweet letter. I felt much better after reading it. I know you didn't tell your fa-

ther about the fashion show, so please don't think
I blame you for that.

I'm going to ask you to do something you may
not understand right now. It's important that you
not be angry with your father; he needs you more
than ever. He loves you, Melissa, very much, and
you must never doubt that. I care about him, too,
but you'll have to love him for both of us. Be patient with him.

Later, after the holidays, if it's all right, I'll come
and spend a day with you. Until then, do well in
your studies and keep sewing. You show a definite
talent for it—especially for stitching hems!

You will always hold a special place in my heart,
Melissa, and since I can't be your mother, let me
be your friend.
Love,
Dori

Dori was grateful that December was such a busy
month. If it had been any other time, she might've fallen
prey to even greater doubt and bitterness. Every night of
the following week there was an activity she and Danny
were expected to attend. But although she was with family and friends, she'd never felt more alone. She felt as if
she'd lost a vital part of herself and she had—her heart.
She'd given it to Gavin. And now she was caught in this
limbo of apathy and indifference. After he'd panicked
and run from her love, Dori had thought she could just
take up where she'd left off and resume the even pace of
her life. Now she was painfully learning that it would be

far longer before she found her balance again. But she would, and that was the most important thing.

At the dinner table two days before Christmas, Danny stirred his mashed potatoes with his spoon and cleared his throat, apparently planning to make a weighty pronouncement. "Mom, did you know this is Christmas Eve's eve?"

Dori set her fork aside. "You're right," she said, nodding.

"And since it's so close to Christmas and all, I thought maybe it'd be okay to open one of my presents."

Dori didn't hesitate for an instant. "Not until Christmas morning. Waiting is half the fun."

"Aw, Mom, I hate it. Just one gift. Please."

A stern look silenced him, and he concentrated on slicing his roast beef into bite-size pieces. "Are we going to Grandma and Grandpa's again this year?"

They did every year. Dori wondered why Danny asked when he knew the answer.

"Yes, just like we did last year and the year before that and the year before that and—"

"I get the picture," he mumbled, reaching for his glass of milk. He lifted it to his mouth, then paused, an intense, almost painful look edging its way across his face. "Do you suppose we'll ever see Mr. Parker and Melissa again?"

"I don't know." A sadness invaded her heart, but she managed a strained smile. She hoped. Every minute of every hour she hoped, but she couldn't say that to Danny. "Why do you ask?"

"I don't know." He raised one shoulder in a shrug. "It just doesn't seem right not seeing them."

"I know." Her throat worked convulsively. "It doesn't seem right for me, either."

Danny pushed his plate aside, his meal only half-eaten. "Can I be excused, Mom? I'm not hungry anymore."

Neither was Dori, for that matter. "Sure," she murmured, laying her knife across her own plate.

Danny carried his dishes to the sink and turned back to Dori. "Do you *have* to work tomorrow?"

Dori wasn't too thrilled at the prospect, either. "Just in the morning. If you like, you can stay home by yourself." Danny was old enough to be left alone for a few hours during the day. Usually he preferred company, but on Christmas Eve he'd sleep late and then he could watch television until she got home around eleven-thirty.

"Could I really?" He smiled eagerly. "I'll be good and not have anyone over."

"I know."

The following morning Dori had more than one doubt. Twice she phoned Danny from the office. He assured her he was fine, except that he had to keep answering the phone because Grandma had called three times, too. Dori didn't call after that, but when the office closed, she made it to the employee parking lot and out again in record time. On the drive home, she had to restrain herself from speeding. Waiting at a red light, Dori was convinced she'd done the wrong thing in leaving Danny on his own. He wasn't prepared for this kind of responsibility. True, he was by himself for an hour after school, but this was different. He'd been alone in the house for three and a half hours.

The garage door was open, and with a sigh of relief she drove inside and parked.

"Danny!" she called out, slightly breathless as she walked in the back door. "I'm home. How did everything go?" Hanging her purse in the hall closet, she walked into the living room—and stopped dead. Her heart fell to her knees, rebounded and rocketed into her throat. Gavin was there. In her living room. Dressed casually in slacks and a sweater, he was staring at her with dark, brooding eyes. She looked over at Danny, perched on the ottoman facing Melissa, who sat in the nearby chair.

"Hi, Mom." Danny looked as confused as Dori felt. "I told them it was okay if they came inside. That was the right thing to do, wasn't it?"

"Yes, yes, of course." Her fingers refused to cooperate as she fiddled with her coat buttons. She was so happy—and so afraid—that her knees gave way and she sank weakly onto the sofa across from Gavin. "This is a…" Her mind went blank.

"Surprise," Melissa finished for her.

A wonderful surprise, her mind threw back. "Yes."

"They brought us Christmas gifts," Danny explained, pointing to the large stack of gaily wrapped presents under the tree.

"Oh." Dori felt as if this wasn't really happening, that somehow she'd wake and find it only a vivid dream. "Thank you. I have yours in the other room."

A hint of a smile touched Gavin's mouth, but his dark eyes studied her like a hawk about to swoop down from the skies to capture its prey. "Were you so sure of me?"

"No, I wasn't sure, but I was hoping."

Their eyes met as he spoke. "Danny and Melissa, why don't you go play a game while I talk to Dori."

"I'm not leaving my mom," Danny declared in a forceful voice. He sprang to his feet defensively and crossed the small room to sit beside his mother.

Shocked by his behavior, Dori stared at him, feeling an odd mixture of pride and disbelief.

A muscle moved in Gavin's rigid jaw when Melissa folded her arms and looked boldly at her father. "I agree with Danny. We should all hear this."

Dori dropped her eyes to keep Gavin from seeing the laughter sparkling there. The kids were obviously going to stay to the end of this, whether they were welcome or not.

Gavin slid to the edge of his seat and raked his hand through his hair in an uncharacteristic gesture of uncertainty.

"I've been doing a lot of thinking about our agreement," he began on a note of challenge. "Things didn't exactly work out the way I planned, but—"

"I'm not interested in any more agreements," Dori said honestly and immediately regretted interrupting him. Not for anything would she admit that it hadn't worked because she'd done exactly what he'd warned her not to do. She'd fallen in love with him.

Another long pause followed as he continued to watch her steadily. "I was hoping, Dori, that you'd hear me out before jumping to conclusions." Speaking in front of the children was clearly making him uneasy.

Dori made a limp, apologetic motion with her hand. The living room had never seemed so small, nor Gavin so big. Every nerve in her body was conscious of him and she ached for the feel of his comforting arms. "I'm sorry. I won't interrupt you again."

Gavin ignored her and turned his attention to Danny instead. "Didn't you once tell me that you wrote a requirement list for a new father?"

"Yes." Danny nodded.

"Would you get it for me?"

Danny catapulted from the sofa and into the kitchen. Within seconds he was back, thrusting the list at Gavin. "Here, but I'm not sure why you want to read it. You already know what it says."

"I think Dad might want to apply for the position," Melissa said, her eyes glowing brightly. "Dad and I had a really long talk and he feels bad about what happened and decided—"

"Melissa," he said flatly, "I'd prefer to do my own talking."

"Okay, Dad." She leaned back against the chair with an impatient sigh.

Dori's head was spinning like a satellite gone off its orbit. Her hands felt both clammy and cold and she clasped them in her lap.

Gavin appeared to be studying the list Danny had given him. "I don't know that I've done such a terrific job in the father department, but—"

"Yes, you have, Dad," Melissa inserted. "You've been really good."

Despite herself, Dori found she had to smile at Melissa and her *reallys*.

"Melissa, please," Gavin barked and paused to smooth the hair he'd rumpled a few minutes earlier. The muscle in his jaw twitched again. "Dori." He said her name with such emotion that her heart throbbed painfully. "I know I don't deserve someone as wonderful as you, but I'd consider it a great honor if you'd consent to marry me."

The words washed over her like warm, soothing water and she closed her eyes at the sudden rush of feeling. "Are…are you saying you love me?" she whispered, unable to make her voice any stronger.

"Yes," he answered curtly.

"This is for *us*—not because of the kids?" She knew that Melissa held a powerful influence on her father. From the beginning, both Melissa and Danny had tried to manipulate them.

"I want to marry you because I've learned that I don't want to live without you." His response was honest and direct.

"Then yes, I'll be your wife." Dori's was just as straightforward.

"Okay, let's set the date. The sooner the better."

If he didn't move to take her in his arms soon, she'd embarrass them both by leaping across the room.

"I'm sorry, Mr. Parker, but you can't marry my mom," Danny announced with all the authority of a Supreme Court judge.

"What?" Dori, Melissa and Gavin shouted simultaneously.

Danny eyed all three sternly. "If you read my requirement list for a new father, you'll see there's another requirement down there now."

Gavin's gaze dropped to the paper clenched in his hand.

"You made my mom cry, Mr. Parker, and you might do it again."

A look of pain flashed across Gavin's face. "I realize that, Danny, and I deeply regret any hurt I've caused your mother. If both of you will give me another chance, I promise to make it up to you."

Danny appeared to weigh his words carefully. "So you'll never make her cry again?"

Frowning thoughtfully, Gavin studied the boy in silence. As she watched them, Dori felt a stirring of love and tenderness for her son and for the man who would soon become her husband.

"I hope never to cause your mother any more pain," Gavin muttered, "but I can't promise she won't cry."

"Mom." Danny transferred his attention to Dori. "What do you think?"

"Danny, come on," Melissa said with high-pitched urgency. "Good grief, this is what we all want! Don't blow it now."

Danny fixed his eyes on his mother, unswayed by Melissa's plea. "Well, Mom?"

Dori's gaze met Gavin's and her heart leaped wildly at the tenderness she saw. "Yes, it's what I want." They both stood at the same moment and reached for each other in a spontaneous burst of love and emotion. Gavin caught her in his arms and crushed her against his chest as his hungry mouth came down on hers. With a sigh of longing, Dori received his kiss, glorying in the feel of his arms around her. She knew that coming to her and admitting his love and his need had been difficult, and she thanked him with all the love in her own heart.

Twining her arms around his neck, she held him fiercely. She was vaguely aware of Danny murmuring to Melissa—something about leaving so he didn't have to watch the mushy stuff.

Gavin's arms tightened around her possessively, holding her closer while his hand slid along her spine. "I've missed you so much," he whispered hoarsely against her lips, then kissed her again, harder and longer as if he couldn't possibly get enough of her.

The sensation was so exquisite that Dori felt tears of happiness spring to her eyes and roll unheeded down her cheeks. "Oh, Gavin, what took you so long?"

Drawing back slightly, Gavin inhaled a shuddering breath. "I don't know. I thought it would be so easy to forget you. There's never been a woman in my life who's haunted me the way you have."

Her eyes shone with joyful tears as she smiled mischievously up at him. "Good." What she didn't tell him was that she'd felt the same things.

"Once I'd been in the sunlight, I couldn't go back to the shadows," Gavin said. He buried his face in her hair and breathed in deeply. "I tried," he acknowledged with an ironic laugh. "After Deirdre I didn't want any woman to have this kind of power over me."

"I know."

He shook his head. "How is it you know me so well?"

Smiling happily, she told him, "I guess it comes from loving you so much."

"Everything happened just the way you predicted," he said. "No matter who I kissed, it was your lips I tasted. When I held another woman, I sensed that something was wrong, and I wanted only you."

"Oh, Gavin." She spread tiny kisses over his face. Her lips met his eyes, nose, jaw and finally his eager mouth.

She didn't need to be told that these lessons had been difficult ones for Gavin. Surrendering his freedom to a woman had been an arduous battle between his will and his heart. But now he'd find a new freedom in their love for each other. He'd finally come to understand that, and she knew he'd love her with all his strength.

Gently his thumb wiped a tear from the arch of her cheek. "The worst part was seeing you in the car that morning with Danny." Dori heard the remembered pain that made his voice husky. "You were laughing as if you hadn't a care in the world. I saw you and felt something so painful I can't even describe it. You had me so tied up in knots, I was worthless to anyone—and there you were, laughing with Danny as if I meant nothing."

"That's not true," she said. "I was dying inside from wanting you."

"You've got me," he said humbly. "For as long as you want."

"I love you," Dori whispered fervently, laying her trembling hand on his smoothly shaved cheek. "And I can guarantee you that one lifetime won't be enough."

Cradling her face between both his hands, Gavin gazed into her eyes and kissed her with a gentleness that bordered on worship.

"I told you it'd work," Danny whispered in the kitchen.

"I knew it all along," Melissa agreed with a romantic sigh. "It was obvious from the day we went to the fair. They're perfect together."

"Yeah, your plan worked," Danny agreed.

"We're not through yet." Her voice dropped slightly as if she were divulging a secret.

"But they're getting married," Danny said in low tones. "What more could we want?"

Melissa groaned. "Honestly, Danny, think about it. Four is such a boring number. By next year there should be five."

"Five what?"

"People in our family. Now we've got to convince them to have a baby."

"Hey, good idea," Danny said eagerly. "That'd be great. I'd like a baby brother."

"They'll have a girl first. The second baby will be a boy for you. Okay?"

"I'd rather have the boy first."

"Maybe," Melissa said, obviously feeling generous.

* * * * *

Get 4 FREE REWARDS!

We'll send you 2 FREE Books plus 2 FREE Mystery Gifts.

Both the **Romance** and **Suspense** collections feature compelling novels written by many of today's bestselling authors.